A Turning Wind

A Turning Wind

J.G. Harlond

A Turning Wind by J.G. Harlond

ISBN-13: 978-1-946409-40-9(Paperback)
ISBN —--978-1-946409-41-6 (e-book)

BISAC Subject Headings:
FIC002000 FICTION / Action & Adventure
FIC014000 FICTION / Historical
FIC027050 FICTION / Romance / Historical

Cover Illustration by Christine Horner

Address all correspondence to:

Michael James
Penmore Press LLC
920 N Javelina Pl
Tucson AZ 85748

For Tim and Guy.

"The wind goeth toward the south, and turneth about unto the north; it whirleth about continually, and the wind returneth again according to his circuits."
—Ecclesiastes 1:6, King James Bible

Old Arab proverb

Do not tell all you know,
Do not do all you can,
Do not believe all you see,
Do not spend all you have.

Because
He who says too much,
He who does all he may,
He who believes all he sees,
He who spends all he has,

Very often
Says what is not wise,
Does what he ought not do,
Judges without thinking,
Spends more than his purse allows.

Characters—In Order of Appearance

Names marked with an * are recorded in history.

Ludo da Portovenere—Genoese rich-trade (silk and spice) merchant

Leonora Gasca Figaroa—widow and owner of spice business in Goa, India

Armando Cabrera Mendes—Leonora's brother-in-law, Portuguese official of the Casa da Índia in Lisbon

Simón Gomes Solis—Portuguese official in Goa

Armando Duarte Solis y Solis—cousin to Simón Gomes

Toxo (Tosho)—Galician mariner, captain of the carrack *La Magdalena*

Javi—Galician mariner and brother-in-law of Toxo

Captain George Guthrie—captain of the galleon *Tulip*

José—cabin boy to Ludo on the *Tulip*

Marcos Alonso Almendro—Spanish owner of wine and spice business in Plymouth, England, one-time servant to Ludo

Joanna Almond—Marcos's English wife

Edward Beale—Joanna's father

Sophie Beale—Joanna's mother

Queen Henrietta Maria*—Catholic wife of King Charles 1st of England

King Charles*—British king, currently in dispute with Parliament and the Scots

Rogelio—Roman cleric and Vatican agent belonging to the secret Black Order

Lord Dungetty—Lord Steward at the Palace of Whitehall

Alina—María de los Ángeles Santoña Gómez de Fulford, Baroness Metherall

Fanny—Alina's English servant

Thomas Fulford, Baron of the County of Cornwall in England

Tomás—son of Alina and Thomas Fulford living at Crimphele, Cornwall

John Hawthorne—one-time English priest, now tutor to Tomás at Crimphele

Sir Arthur Hopton*—British Ambassador to the court of King Philip IV of Spain

Christopher (Kit) Windebank*—English secretary to Sir Arthur Hopton in Spain

King Philip IV of Spain*—Habsburg monarch and ruler of the Spanish Empire

Queen Isabel*—formerly Elisabeth Bourbon of France, daughter of Marie de Medici* and the late King Henry IV of France*, sister of Queen Henrietta Maria*

Conde de Pamanes—Alina's father, an impoverished Spanish grandee

Diego Rodríguez da Silva Velázquez*—Spanish artist at the court of Philip IV

Luis Méndez de Haro y Guzmán, Marqués de Carpio*—nephew of Count-Duke de Olivares and future chief minister of Spain

Inés de Zúñiga y Velasco, Countess-Duchess de Olivares*—wife of Count-Duke de Olivares and governess to Spanish royal children

Paco—farrier and Kit Windebank's father-in-law

María de los Milagros García González—a Spanish woman, bodyguard to Alina

Brother Caritas— a Spanish Franciscan Grey Friar living in voluntary exile on the isle of Ibiza

Doña Juana—Brother Caritas's landlady

Paulo Pannini—childhood friend of Ludo in Portovenere—deceased

Rabbi Rafael—elderly Chueta rabbi living in Ibiza

Duke of Braganza*– pretender to the Portuguese throne

Luisa de Guzmán—Duchess of Braganza*

Murat Reis*—born Jan Janszoon, a Dutchman who 'turned Turk' and became a legendary pirate captain

Lysbeth*—daughter of Jan Janszoon (otherwise known as Murat Reis)

Padre Bernabé—Spanish missionary priest

Part One
Crossing Oceans

Chapter 1

Goa, India, September 1639

It was a ramshackle affair for such valuable goods. A makeshift marketplace created out of crimson and brightly striped awnings. Lengths of scarlet, orange, turquoise, purple and blue formed curtains between trees, sheltering the splendid commodities from the late summer sun. Vendors were still laying out their wares when Ludo arrived: gems and trinkets in copper and gold, ivory combs and bangles, shimmering sari silk and embroidered fringed shawls, all transported from one coast of India to the other on heads and shoulders. The costly cargo had passed through the famous alluvial diamond valleys of Golconda, the human caravan collecting ever more precious gems along the way—a cargo now watched over by guards with arm muscles that rippled 'beware' and vicious knives tucked in wide belts.

Curious, colourful, magnificent... everything Ludo had hoped for. He was delighted. Yet, wandering among the displays, he began to wonder why he had come—what, apart from uncut diamonds, he was actually seeking.

As he finished his first circuit, a white bullock ambled in pulling a cart laden with clay flagons. Happily over-paying an urchin for a drink of water then returning the cup, Ludo strolled back among the folding tables, trestles and floor mats, this time stopping to examine a miniature chest of drawers decorated with inlaid mother-of-pearl for women's trinkets. It was pretty, but no, not special enough to add to his ship's cargo. Moving on, he encountered an awkward Englishman dabbing at his forehead with a sodden handkerchief. The pink-faced *sahib* was struggling to keep up with an Indian agent's heavily accented sales patter without losing his cherished dignity.

"Let me tell you how they are found," the Goan agent was saying as he ran a hand seductively through a wide lacquered bowl of uncut diamonds. "When it rains, water rushes down the mountains, taking these precious stones with it and leaving them trapped at the bottom of gorges and in caverns. When the dry season comes and there is not one drop of water to be had, when the heat is enough to kill an Englishman as he walks from his door, brave men risk their lives to collect the stones. But they must go where wild serpents thrive. Venomous serpents and vast—serpents that crush and swallow men whole..."

Ludo shuddered along with the Englishman: snakes were another of the reasons he had made no attempt to travel inland during his stay in Goa.

". . .but these diamonds are precious not only for the means by which they are obtained, not only for their special rarity, but for their quality. Look, *sahib*, see how fine they are, how they bring light into our lives. Each one is perfect, flawless..."

The Englishman put a forefinger in the bowl and peered at a stone the size of a sparrow's egg, then at another in the shape and form of a woman's fingernail. The Goan agent took his hand and placed an uncut stone in the sweating palm then exchanged it for a cushion-cut diamond ring magicked from among his robes saying quietly, "This is not for everyone to know, *sahib*, but I should tell you, there may not be many more of these diamonds. Each year there are fewer. It is said the serpents now eat them to preserve their heritage."

Ludo swallowed a grin and gestured with a hand to attract the agent's attention. Half-convinced, half-enthralled, and knowingly walking into an enticement worthy of his own invention, Ludo stepped forward and cocked his head to one side enquiringly. The agent retrieved the ring from the Englishman and put it in Ludo's open palm then whisked a heart-shaped ruby from thin air and put it next to the ring.

Ludo's hand was broad but there was barely room for the two wonderful gemstones. The agent picked the ring from Ludo's hand, leaving only the ruby to burn through his palm in the warm light of the coloured awnings.

"A gem worthy of a queen, *sahib*," the agent murmured.

"Worthy of a queen... it is indeed," Ludo murmured. This was what he wanted: this ruby. "But it is too much for a humble merchant such as me."

"No, *sahib*, this ruby *is* for you. This is what you seek."

Ludo shot him a surprised glance. The agent's expression was open, generous, but two black-bead eyes under a startlingly white turban bore into Ludo, hypnotising him, holding his gaze.

"You must know, *sahib*, a ruby of this quality has such virtues from the sun that a man living in ignorance or consumed by sin, or pursued by mortal enemies, is saved by its wearing. When stones such as this are found they are named: this is 'Rani Saahasi'. There is no perfect translation that I know in Portuguese. In English you could call it 'Queen of Courage'."

Ludo forced himself to look away, shook his head to clear his vision and pulled himself back to the multi-coloured market place. But his fingers clenched the ruby of their own accord: the stone, as red as pomegranate seeds, as cool as the waters of Kashmir, sang in his palm. He had to have it.

"No," he said. "No, I cannot risk my small income on a bauble such as this."

The Englishman's jaw dropped. Ludo willed him to move away, not wanting to risk haggling against the flushed-faced mister as well. The Englishman stayed exactly where he was.

Reluctantly, Ludo held out the ruby saying, "I seek smaller, uncut gems..." As he spoke a set of long-nailed, hairy fingers plucked the stone from his palm and the thief escaped round the trunk of the nearest tree.

A troop of other practised thieves appeared above, peering with the faces of buffoons between the different coloured awnings, then scrambling helter-skelter from branches or shimmying like circus performers down supporting wooden props. The Goan agent screeched, not unlike the unwanted visitors, and grabbed the corners of his open cloth on the low table behind him, hugging the rapid sack to his bony chest so no more of his valuable goods could be taken. Suddenly there was a commotion around the bullock cart carrying water; a thief had upturned the clay cups and made off with a jug, carrying it awkwardly on three legs for she had a baby on her back. Her sister, meanwhile, discovered a display of brass incense holders and bells. Seizing as many as she could, she began to juggle, the bells ringing into the air then clanging to the soft mud beneath her feet. Then up went a candlestick, and then another and another, caught by one cousin and tossed to an uncle who, brandishing it as trophy, bared his teeth at the buyers and headed for home.

But as he went, more of his clan arrived, targeting push-carts, floor mats and head-rolls, some stealing arm bangles and pushing them up their thin, hairy arms before running back up the tree trunks into the branches and awnings, or jumping on tables, scattering wares that had crossed perilous oceans and scorching plains to be brought undamaged across mountains and marshes down to Goa.

Ludo started to laugh at the shock and surprise of the invasion, then stopped as if the scene were frozen in time when the ruby he so coveted dropped to his feet from above.

"Choke on it, choke on it!" the monkey cursed, for it was inedible and he did not want it.

Slowly, slowly, hardly believing his luck, Ludo bent to pick up the gem. His right hand closed over it and it was his.

But it was not.

He started to walk out of the covered square, but his legs would not move. The ruby held him to the spot, telling him perhaps *that a man living in ignorance or consumed by sin, or worse—pursued by a mortal enemy—is saved by its wearing.* Ludo did not believe he was consumed by sin or that he lived in a state of ignorance. He *was* pursued by enemies—one, possibly two, or even three if you counted the ridiculous Count Hawk— but he was no thief. No common thief, anyway.

Stretching out an arm like a conductor bringing a concerto to a close, Ludo patted the Goan agent on the shoulder. "Your ruby, master," he said.

The merchant smiled a black-toothed grin. "You see, *sahib,* it *is* for you, for has it not returned to your hand already?" Grasping his precious sack with one hand, he folded Ludo's fingers around the stone with the other, saying, "It is my belief that though you may give this gem as a gift or sell it to another, it will come back to you again and again—and one day stay forever."

Again, Ludo felt himself drawn into the Goan trader's words, and again he pulled himself away. "If that is so, I would own it first by honest means. Tell me your price."

And so the haggling began, fortunately without the Englishman, who had hastened away in fear of the mischievous monkeys—who themselves had disappeared as quickly as they had arrived.

Less than an hour after he had entered the annual marketplace, Ludo had been relieved of what remained of his carefully accrued Dutch gold and Spanish silver. Leaving in something of a daze, he returned to Dona Leonora's house carrying two special *bizalho* boxes designed for the carriage of jewels from Goa and various chamois pouches rattling gently with all manner of uncut stones. A cushion-cut diamond ring was tucked deep into one of his breeches pockets—perhaps for the lovely, very wealthy Portuguese widow, Leonora. In another he had a heart-shaped ruby named 'Rani Saahasi': Queen of Courage.

Chapter 2

Gently dropping a cotton sack of mixed feathers, mostly peacock, on the floor of the godown, Ludo cast around the open space. Various men and women were sifting and sorting dried ginger, peppercorns, and a dozen other spices to be shovelled into sacks and transported by his ships across the oceans to Lisbon. The air was full and heavy with aromas; it was also stiflingly hot. Keeping a watchful eye open for the twelve-foot python Leonora encouraged as a rat-catcher, he moved a tall ladder under a ventilation window then climbed up carefully, for the ladder was none too new. As the shutter swung open hot, damp air rolled in. Ludo took a deep breath, studying the crowded view of verdant treetops, then remembered what the treetops were likely harbouring and descended hastily to the floor.

Picking up his featherweight sack he wandered through the warehouse, stopping at different open barrels, wicker baskets and crates to enjoy the sharp tang of cloves, the unmistakable combination of mace and nutmeg, to run his hands through a sack of red and green peppercorns, enjoying how single hard grains could form liquid silk as they ran through fingers. Somewhat lost in the moment, he became aware of voices,

Portuguese voices, and moved back to the wall to stand in the shadow, still mindful of the dreaded python.

Two men, overdressed for the oppressive humidity, were conversing in low voices as they moved at their ease between the spices. One pushed his hand into an open sack of peppercorns as Ludo had done and made a comment. The other man, shorter, younger perhaps, consulted a list, laughed and pointed at a pyramid of cinnamon bales. The two men stopped speaking and bent over the mound of stitched sacks, each containing roll upon roll of delicate cinnamon bark. Ludo tried to identify what they were saying, Portuguese being a language he had not fully mastered despite spending an entire year sailing in and out of Goa.

The owner of the Gasca Figaroa spice business, the lovely widow Leonora who had hired him to transport her cargo, appeared at the entrance to the godown, hands clasped before her in an unmistakable gesture of distress. The smaller of the two men, the one holding the list, looked at her and said something. His tone was disrespectful. His compatriot took a folding knife from a pocket and slit open a bale of cinnamon. Sniffing the contents, he then pulled a short, tightly tied bundle from the bale.

"This isn't cassia," he said. "How did you get it?"

"It is from our plantation in Ceylon. It is dried there and packed ready for sailing. It all belongs to us—that is, to my late father's business."

"My question remains: how did you get it? Portuguese ships have been turned away from Colombo for months by the Dutch, how did *you* get in?" He added something else that Ludo didn't catch and stared accusingly at the young widow.

Setting down the sack of feathers again then removing the straw coolie hat he'd taken to wearing, Ludo stepped forward and said in Spanish, for Spain held dominium over Portugal, "*Buenos días, caballeros*, may I be of assistance?"

The two men stared at him in surprise then exchanged glances. The one with the list said, "We are officials of the Casa da Índia in Lisbon."

"I'm pleased to hear it. And you are inspecting our next cargo because...?"

The 'our' threw his interlocutor, as Ludo hoped it might. The taller man came to his assistance. "Simón Gomes Solis," he said, removing his elegant hat. "My colleague, Armando Duarte Solis y Solis," he waggled the plumed headgear at his companion. "We are authorised to assess and control all cargo destined for Lisbon in order that it may be accounted for accurately on arrival."

"That is not what you told me!" Leonora's face flushed. "You said you were confiscating it."

"And why might they do that, *cariño*?" Ludo asked, turning to Leonora, whose face now flared red with embarrassment. Ludo looked her in the eye, willing her to play along.

She lowered her lashes and said, "My brother-in-law, my late husband's brother, that is, sent them."

"Asked us to visit," Gomes corrected her. "Which we would have done anyway."

"To assess what is here," added Solis y Solis, "this being such a..." He searched for words.

"Large—successful—competent business?" Ludo suggested.

The man made a moue with his black-moustachioed mouth then turned to Gomes for help. None came.

"May I ask what authority you have sirs, to... er... 'assess' the commodities here?" Ludo asked, his face open, ingenuous.

Gomes' eyes narrowed like a theatre villain, making Ludo bite his inner lip.

"We are factors for the *carreira da Índia* trade," Gomes stated self-importantly. "A correct list of the entire cargo must be drawn up before the goods are loaded for Lisbon. It is normal practice."

"It is what I always do, have never failed to do," Leonora said quietly.

Gomes ignored her. "All cargoes out of Goa belong to Portugal."

"And Portugal belongs to Spain," Ludo added. "Meaning there is no reason to *confiscate* Doña Leonora's goods for they will eventually reach Lisbon, God willing, and be taxed there accordingly—to the benefit of the Spanish crown, am I not right?" Ludo cocked his head to one side.

"*Meaning* we can and will requisition the lady's goods *because* she is a subject of the Spanish crown, as you so rightly say, added to which, this firm no longer has a licensed owner," Gomes replied. "By precedent established in the reign of the late Philip the Second we are entitled to requisition the entire business, the owner being deceased."

"The firm of Gasca Figaroa is mine now. I inherited the company from my father," Leonora said. The two men gave her pitying smiles. She turned to Ludo. "It is a matter of religion. My father was a New-Christian."

"And that means...?" Ludo asked, although he knew very well what it meant, for Leonora had told him how she was harassed for her religion, obliged to worship at the Catholic church as often and as openly as she was able to dispel the persistent rumours about her family being "*Judiasers*", Christian converts who still practised their Jewish faith. From what he had seen in the past year, he believed Leonora was no *Judiaser*, but truth carried little weight in gossip about a wealthy, good looking, young widow, who also ran a business with numerous male employees—and hired him to fetch and carry her goods.

It was Leonora who answered his question. "It means they can take what they wish or I will be denounced to the Inquisition—simply because I am a New-Christian—in their eyes.

"And how can that apply if you are wed to a Genoese merchant, who has been licensed, indeed contracted by the King of Spain's Chief Minister, the Count-Duke of Olivares, to bring the royal cargo safely into a home port, *cariño*? I do not follow."

Leonora's dark eyes opened in a combination of surprise and something else Ludo didn't want to acknowledge. He glared at her, willing her to continue with his ruse, then turned to the men and said, "The lady here is, as she says, of a New-Christian family—three generations, was it not, *cariño*? But who bothers with this anymore? Of course, confiscating a successful business can provide funds needed to pay for wars and also, let us not forget, finance the Inquisition. As I mentioned, I am Genoese and a member of a banking family operating in Madrid and Seville, so naturally I have insight into these matters. Perhaps being Portuguese and living so very far from Spain you were not aware of how your taxes and *confiscations* are employed, gentlemen."

Gomes stared at Ludo, challenging him with his eyes, but Ludo won the game and he was obliged to say, "Of course we know it."

"Then perhaps you should also know that this business is soon to be mine in accordance with a marriage contract, and, as I said and must repeat, being a citizen of the State of Genoa, and your good king beholden to bankers of that very state for his finance, I am also working towards the same goal: we do need the King of Spain to repay his loans, after all." Ludo took a quick glance at the two men, calculating how far they were falling behind his quick reasoning. Satisfied that they were getting lost, he continued a little more hastily, "After all, and as I said earlier, the tax on these goods will help provide for the Catholic armies fighting heretics in the Low Countries. Naturally I can see that you, being Portuguese, may not approve of the arrangement, indeed, you may not like the King of Spain or his chief minister, not an easy man to deal with I know from personal experience, although, speaking such thoughts aloud is tantamount to treason and I'd hate to put *you* in that situation..." Gomes opened his mouth to speak and Ludo raised an eyebrow, saying, "Better we change the subject, hmm?"

The shorter one holding the list stepped forward. "This is outrageous! How dare you accuse us of..." But he was unable to finish, having not comprehended what Ludo was suggesting.

Ludo gave a warm smile. "Shall we proceed with your inspection, then? So you can finish your report and we can load our cargo. By the way, how long do these reports, lists, manifests—hah, a tripling!—take no notice, I have a friend, who happens to be an English priest, would you believe, who likes to speak in trinities—where was I? Oh yes, how long do your missives normally take to reach Lisbon?"

Neither of the men wished to reply, but Gomes said reluctantly, "By ship, five or six months."

"Obviously by ship—how else?—although one could cross overland to Aleppo, I believe. But that is in the hands of the infidel, so best we say little about Aleppo, or Constantinople. Ever been there? Fascinating place. And there is always the risk the ship will not reach port, is there not? It is a perilous voyage. I trust you have completed a round voyage yourselves. Oh, the horrors of the Cape—pirates off Zanzibar, pirates off Pemba—

confronted them myself—and then if you even get to the Canaries there are the Salé Rovers to contend with. Less of a voyage, it is more a game of chance, is it not?"

Ludo's rapid patter left the two men reeling but they managed to nod their heads. Before they could think of anything to say, however, Ludo was off again. "Six months each way, of course your report only has to go one way, but then will it even be delivered to—who is it you're reporting to?"

"Ah... erm..." Gomes and Solis responded in unison.

Ludo gave his lopsided grin. "Six months, eh? Dona Leonora and I will be married well before that—is that not so, *cariño*?" Leonora glared at him again, eyes glowing with controlled anger. "Yes, well," Ludo added rapidly, "I digress. What do you gentlemen have left to review, by the way? The spices? Indigo? Lacquers? There are fabrics in the other godown ready for loading, *pronto, pronto*, in my ships once the rain ceases. I do hate having to worry about damp cargoes before one even sets sail."

Leonora moved to Ludo's side to say something, but he flashed her a warning glance.

Gomes, choking back a spluttering rage, placed his hat on his head. "We shall say good day to you then, sir. Forgive me, you said you were?"

"I said I was and I am—Ludovico da Portovenere, silk and spice merchant to Spain, Genoa, Tuscany, England and parts of the Levant, and very soon to be the lucky recipient of this delightful lady's hand in marriage." He took Leonora's hand— for the very first time—and brushed his lips above her knuckles.

The two men stared at him with undisguised loathing. Gomes said, "Ah, da Portovenere... yes."

They had evidently heard his name from somewhere and not in a positive light. Ludo sighed: he should have sailed on to

Manila and Cathay as he had planned two years before, but the widow Leonora had needed him, and she was so lovely... He looked at her, then at the thin-faced, mean-spirited Portuguese standing before them. Lifting Leonora's cool hand, he said, "Are you happier now, *cariño*?" Then he turned equably to the Portuguese cousins. "Was there anything else? Feel free to look —I can accompany you myself, if you wish."

Finally catching up with what was really going on, Armando Duarte Solis said, "We must have your assurance that this cargo will go to Lisbon, not to Genoa or anywhere else. As officials of the Casa da Índia here in Goa, we require you to present us with your ship's manifest prior to sailing."

"Yes, so you say," Ludo replied.

Gomes gave him a withering look. "It would not do, sir, to cross us," he said. "We are not without powerful connections ourselves."

"*Religious* connections," Solis y Solis added.

Ludo bowed wordlessly in response.

Irritated, perhaps thoroughly annoyed, the taller of the two hissed, "Come, cousin, we have finished here—for now."

Ludo watched them go, his face a picture of equanimity, his mind racing through a plan to create two ships' manifests and pack two-thirds of the widow's cargo into the hold of a creaky old carrack named *La Magdalena* instead of his galleon, *Tulip*. He could then sell her goods, untaxed, where he chose, for he was damned if he was going to let the Solis cousins get a single maravedí to finance their comforts. All the fuss about receiving an itemised manifest before Leonora's goods were even loaded suggested they were fiddling the books somewhere along the line—replacing Leonora's list with one of their own, most likely, so they could arrange disposal of unspecified goods in a manner to obtain profits on what was *not* on the list that actually arrived in Lisbon. The Portuguese in Goa were a tricky lot, but Ludo was, as he had so proudly claimed, a Genoese, and therefore at least one step ahead of any financial jiggery-pokery.

Ludo's rapid plan also circumvented another difficult issue. He had been greatly concerned about sailing into Lisbon, where he had stolen the *Tulip* from under the harbour master's nose—now he wouldn't have to. The *Magdalena* could disembark the listed Gasca Figaroa goods and he could sail straight on for Plymouth with all the rest.

Giving way to a smug grin, Ludo looked around to speak to Leonora but she was walking back towards her late father's house. She had left without a word. For a few moments he studied the retreating figure then picked up the feathers in their loose cotton bag and followed, a slight swagger of satisfaction in his step.

It was short-lived. The lady was furious.

As soon as he was shown into her office and the door closed behind him, Leonora turned on him angrily. "That was completely unnecessary and impertinent in the extreme. You have no right to say we are to be married, not without discussing the ruse with me. And as a ruse it will not work. Indeed it will make my situation worse—if that is possible."

Ludo bowed his head, which perhaps was not the reaction Leonora had been expecting, so she continued, "Furthermore, *my* cargo *is* destined for Lisbon because *my* agent will be there waiting to unload it and take payment for the sales. He is officially licensed and has a long-standing agreement with our firm. There will be no changes, no deliveries elsewhere. As a New Christian I cannot risk any form of scrutiny or suspicion. This is how the Portuguese spice trade works—this is how my late father's business works. All that nonsense about the chief minister of Spain and marrying me... Really! Do you expect any of us to believe it?"

"It's not entirely untrue: I am acquainted with Olivares. I was at one time what you might call his 'chosen man'. Unfortunately"—Ludo's thoughts drifted back to a disagreeable reality—"our agreement did not go quite according to plan." *His* plan, that was. "But yes, I see, *madonna*. I spoke without thinking, forgive me."

To Ludo's surprise, Leonora's face fell. She clasped her hands together once more and said very quietly, "You haven't been wooing me, then, for... for matrimony?"

Caught between hurting the lady's feelings and a moment of truth, Ludo grasped words from the air. "How could I dare aspire, *madonna*?" He dropped the bundle of feathers onto a chair and raised his hands in a typically Latin gesture. "You with so much and I a mere.... What could I offer you?

"Rather a lot, from what you have just been telling my countrymen." Leonora sat down heavily.

The houseboy appeared at the door with a laden tray. Waiting while he set it down on a low brass-topped table then left, Leonora picked up an exquisite black silk fan and gently moved it to and fro. Eventually she said, "I should ask you to leave, cancel our verbal agreements. You have made my situation here... impossible. These men will speak to my priest to verify what you said, they will alert people, who will inform them when no ceremony takes place, not to mention all the trouble that will come if our spices are not registered in Lisbon. We have a standing agreement with an agent there. He will be suspicious."

"Ships sink, *madonna*. The cargo might not reach Lisbon because of a cyclone or a dozen other hazards I mentioned earlier. I wasn't joking—the voyage is perilous."

"I know that—we lost a ship last year. Or at least that's what they had me believe. A fortune went down with it. The year before, our payment in silver failed to arrive... I do know about the hazards of the deep."

Ludo lowered himself into a low bamboo chair, rattling the arms a little to ensure it could take his weight.

Leonora flicked her fan pensively and continued, "Truly, I do not understand why you have caused so many problems for me after all the trouble you and your crew went to running the blockade to bring our cinnamon out of Ceylon."

Ludo gave a crooked grin. "An adventure, *madonna*: I love outwitting the Dutch. And you have to admit, dyeing the carrack's sails with your own indigo and bringing your cinnamon out under the Dutchies' very bows at night was a stroke of genius. My Spanish friends Toxo and Javi deserve the praise, of course. They sailed the ship, I merely provide the strategy."

"And that is what you think you are doing now, is it?—providing a strategy that will impoverish if not imprison me?"

"*Allora, madonna!* Have I not saved you from having your cargo confiscated? Would they have taken all of it, by the way? What gives them the right?"

"Because, according to them, the business has no owner. My father has died, my husband has died, the business therefore has no valid owner and, according to them, they can requisition it."

"Not now, they can't."

"I wish I could believe you, but honestly you have set them against me with an even stronger desire to acquire my father's firm. They hate us New Christians—especially when we do well."

"But the frenzy about pure blood has died off, Leonora, largely thanks to that old fox Olivares. He's even using Portuguese Jews as bankers to limit the hold we Genoese have over the Spanish Crown. Frankly, I can't see why the Inquisition needs to be active here at all."

"Well, they are. Very active. My family on both sides have been Christians for more than three generations but we still suffer appalling threats. They use any excuse to extract money and benefits—and succeed. Cargoes from Goa—our cargoes— can more than triple in value once unloaded in Portugal. Men like the Solis cousins will do anything they can to get hold of even some of our spices." Leonora sighed. "I suppose I should thank you for trying to help me, but the fact is these officials will always have the upper hand, legitimate or not."

Ludo scowled. "There has to be a way round it. We can't alter your religious situation—albeit the logic of punishing a person who actually chooses to be a Christian defeats me—but we can remedy your situation regarding the business."

"How? I can't marry just anyone and lose all my father and husband worked for that way."

Ludo flinched at the slight. Getting to his feet, he said, "Give me a few hours. I'll see you for the evening meal, if I may, and we can speak again then. In the meantime, please do me a favour. Make two lists: one with as much as can be loaded into the carrack *Magdalena* for Lisbon; another that will include pepper and spices, fabrics and the like to go into the *Tulip*'s hold to sell in England. I will load that in with the goods I have purchased myself and find a secure way to compensate you once your pepper and spices are sold."

"But—"

"Please." Ludo gave her one of his most winning looks. "I must get back to the *Tulip* and talk to the captain now or I would stay to help, but the sooner we sail, the better—don't you think?"

Leonora flicked her fan this way and that, then sighed and placed it, folded, on her lap. "I suppose so," she said.

"Good." Picking up the bundle of feathers, Ludo started to leave then stopped. "Here's a thought: why not sell *all* the cargo *before* it leaves Goa? Offer it to those two rogues at a knock-down price and take what you can for peace of mind."

"Ludo, I shall lose a fortune! You know how much pepper fetches in Europe. It's worth thousands of cruzados alone."

"Yes, I know," Ludo huffed. "I have been selling silks and spices myself for many years, remember. But would you not prefer to receive less money and live more peacefully in comfort here in Goa?"

Leonora looked at him, genuinely surprised. "What is the point of that?"

"Well, you could live as a respectable widow here and—"

"Die of boredom."

"Quite. I see your point. Not to worry, we'll sail within a week. After that there's nothing you can do but organise the next cargo."

"The same thing will happen once you have gone. They won't tolerate a woman running a business, not when I am doing better than anyone in the colony." Leonora tapped her left hand with her fan. "They will destroy me sooner or later, Ludo. The Solis cousins were sent by my late husband's younger brother. He will do anything to get his hands on 'Gasca Figaroa'."

"Why would he do that to his late brother's wife?"

"Because she is childless. When I refused his *kind offer* to care for me, he made an official claim to the business, saying it is *his* inheritance because I have no son. It is not his inheritance because Pedro, my husband, was my father's employee. The firm was my father's: he made it prosperous from nothing when he left Portugal."

"But is that not a solution to your problems? Marry the brother-in-law and let him take over."

"I do not like him. Besides, he is already married. Please be aware, he will probably interfere more now, as a result of what you said earlier to his friends."

Ludo sighed. He was getting angry. His voice dry and serious, he said, "I have travelled more than half way round the world to this harbour, survived all the torments of the seas, run Dutch blockades at night, and here I am caught up in a blasted inheritance drama with another woman!" His tone rose as he realised the vague but not entirely dissimilar situation with the Spanish girl he'd saved from corsairs in Santander and tried to help thereafter. Pulling himself back to the present, he said, "What's his name, by the way, this nose-out-of-joint brother-in-law? I like to know whom I should avoid."

"He is another Armando: Armando Cabrera Mendes."

"Cabrera—goatherd—I must remember," Ludo said, picking up his cotton sack and adjusting it under his arm. The drawstring top fell open, revealing the tip of a bright tail feather.

Leonora gasped in horror and jumped to her feet. "Peacock feathers!"

"Yes, dozens. Look, they'll fetch a pretty price in London and Amsterdam. Feathers on hats are all the rage—they were when I left, anyway."

"Take them away! Burn them! Get them out of my house!" Leonora screamed.

"You surely don't believe that old superstition, *madonna*? Belief in the evil eye is positively—"

Dropping her fan, Leonora pulled the bag from his arms, ran to the balcony and tossed it over the railing. She then set her shoulders straight, smoothed her blue cotton gown and turned back to him. "Until this evening," she said coolly, in control of her emotions once more, but, Ludo perceived, not her future, nor, perhaps, his.

Chapter 3

As Ludo strolled along the beach, silver-buckled shoes in hand, thunder rumbled overhead. With luck it would be the last downpour of the day. Captains and crews of the various carracks sitting out in the bay—licensed Portuguese traders in the main but also a few intrepid individuals like him—were all anxious to load up in the dry. Most of them were planning to sail as soon as they could so as to get back within the year on the monsoon trade winds.

Ludo whistled to the boy José waiting by his skiff pulled up on the strand. Before moving into rooms in the harbour, Ludo had lived aboard the *Tulip* moored out in the bay and kept José, an efficient cabin boy and a small but skilled oarsman, on a permanent basis. The boy did his best to prevent anyone pinching the boat; he also kept him up to date with local gossip.

Pushing the skiff out into the water with Ludo's help, José asked, "*Tulip* or *Magdalena*, sir?"

"*Magdalena*, José, and smartly about it, if you please."

As José jumped aboard then pulled out beyond the gentle surf, Ludo studied the *Magdalena*, moored just beyond the fort's cannon range. She was an ageing carrack that he had acquired to bring Leonora Gasca Figaroa's goods out of Ceylon. Knowing the run into Colombo was going to demand a lot of the vessel, he had made numerous repairs, but left her rickety-looking on purpose. Despite this, however, she was sturdy and sound, and had proved relatively nippy for a carrack, which was just as well, because he was sending her through pirate waters off Zanzibar then round the infamous Cape of Good Hope with a cargo worth—as Leonora emphasised earlier—thousands and thousands of cruzados.

Toxo, *Magdalena*'s captain, was at the gunwale as Ludo climbed aboard. His brother-in-law Javi joined him within seconds, wordless as ever.

"In your cabin, Toxo," Ludo said, addressing the small, wiry Galician as *Tosh-o* in his Genoese accented Spanish. "Get your maps and charts; we have a lot to plan."

The stern cabin Toxo shared with his brother-in-law was neat and clean, their galley table covered by a bolt of fine white cotton.

"What's all this, taken up dress-making?" Ludo laughed.

"Javi makes our clothes—always has," Toxo explained, his voice devoid of humour.

Ludo lifted a half-made linen waistcoat from the table and examined the stitching. Nodding in approval, he then noticed what the two men were wearing: a colourful version of Indian pyjamas tied at ankle and wrist for movement aboard ship, light and airy for the intense day-time heat and humidity. "What an excellent idea," he said. "Have you got time to make something for me—for when we sail?—which will be in about four days if I can get the remaining cargo shifted tomorrow. Ah, and while I think about it, mount a twenty-four-hour guard."

"Someone wants to harm you, or is it the cargo? Don't tell me they'll be firing on us again from a fort?" Toxo's voice was toneless but Ludo knew he was referring to the time he had sent them to test a colander of a round-ship in the Tagus estuary, nearly getting them killed by cannon fire in the process. The small ship had sunk, but they'd had the longboat ready just in case.

Ludo deliberately misunderstood him. "I was telling the lady about it again this very morning—how you slipped into Colombo and out again with her cinnamon, right under the up-turned snouts of the Dutch navy blockade: artists, the pair of you."

Toxo grunted, unimpressed. Javi resumed stitching what looked like a long pocket. Ludo watched him for a moment then said, "Are you going to sew that inside the garment?"

"Outside—on the waistcoat."

Ludo leaned forward for a better look. "Better than wearing the dratted things under your breeches," he muttered. Pockets were normally worn separately inside clothing, tied around the waist with a drawer string. "I hate having those little sacks flopping around my own not so little sacks. Will the waistcoat be lined?"

"Not for on board, not for this climate," Javi replied without lifting his gaze from the needle.

"Stop a minute," Ludo said. "Listen, what about if you make a few pockets that can be closed with a button and sew them *inside* our shirts? That way the contents won't fall out on board, and they can't be snipped away by a cut-purse when we're ashore, either."

"For gold coins?" Javi asked, without taking his eyes from his needle.

"For you, yes. For me, no. I'm talking about a safe place to put gemstones. But they're rough, uncut, so the pockets need to be thick and strong."

"I could wax the cotton on the inside and use double or triple layers."

"Yes, excellent—do it! Test some small stones off the beach and see what happens. Remember we're at sea, as well. I could get a dunking at any time and I wouldn't want to lose them in the water."

"What's this all about?" Toxo asked.

"I've got a few valuable gems, that's all. I don't want to lose them on the way home—or for them to be seen by coolies and customs officials. Which reminds me—I'm giving you one of those *bizalho* boxes with diamonds and the like in it. It'll be your sign-off pay—sell them wisely."

Toxo's beady eyes narrowed and his mouth twisted into something like a smile. "Make plenty of pockets, Javi," Toxo said, "we're going to be worth our weight in *jodido* diamonds. Your wife can have a tiara for the next babe's christening." Not expecting any response, he began pulling a set of charts from a high cupboard. "Can we do this on the deck?" he asked, looking at Ludo. "Or is this another secret?"

"This is another very *secret* secret, my friend, so we'll do it in here, and just to be on the safe side set a hand to watch your door. Someone without Spanish: I don't want this plan made known until you get to the Zanzibar islands. Understood?"

Toxo grunted and called to someone on deck. After a few words in some mutually comprehensible argot, he then closed the cabin door. It was stifling but Ludo had good reason to ignore the discomfort.

"Before we start," Toxo said, looking his *patrón* straight in the eye, "this will be our last trip for you. Javi and me are going home. We've had enough of all the heat; and that jungle out there gives me the willies. We've decided it's been worthwhile ferrying stuff here and there, we've made a good bit on the side thanks to you, but we've been away for over two years now and I've a fancy to see my wife while I've still got me faculties. So, assuming we get round the Cape without this wooden bucket sinking, we're going home. Right," he added, not giving Ludo a moment to speak, "what are you up to?"

Ludo nodded his unspoken acceptance; he too hankered for cooler waters and familiar places. Keeping his thoughts to himself, however, he said, "You'll be taking *la Magdalena* into the Tagus. Everything on board will be unloaded and registered there because Dona Leonora has a license to trade only through the Casa da Índia. Once her agent takes charge and you're empty, you can take *Magdalena* round to Pontevedra or Vigo, wherever you prefer—she's yours until I need to reclaim her." The brothers-in-law exchanged glances. Ludo smiled. "I'll never part with *Tulip*, but *la Magdalena* is yours for the time being— once you get back."

Javi muttered something in Galician from the table and Toxo responded, but as neither of them addressed him directly, Ludo continued with their itinerary. Placing a plump forefinger over Goa on the map, he then crossed the Indian Ocean in a south-westerly direction to a set of small islands off the coast of East Africa. Tapping a thumb nail on a specific island, he said, "We leave port together and you stay with me for the first week until I signal to separate. *Tulip* will then head north-west for the Gulf of Oman; you aim for the islands off Zanzibar. It'll take about a month, I think. Hopefully, if there is anyone following, they'll pursue me, not you. But make sure you aren't boarded, whatever the excuse. If the Portuguese do come for you, even if they say they've got official documents or permission, manoeuvre so they can't actually get aboard, or, better still, run up a fever flag. Get away from them as fast as you can and put in here." Ludo tapped a small island south of the much bigger island of Pemba. "Whether you're followed or not, tuck into a cove around about here and wait for *Tulip* to catch up. I'll be calling at Hormuz. That could take five days, maybe a week, plus the time it takes to get into the Gulf and out again. Don't anchor anywhere too obvious, and stay well out of Zanzibar." Ludo tapped his nail again on the tiny oval representing an island. "Find somewhere deep enough but small enough for you to defend the ship if necessary. It probably will be."

"Necessary?" Toxo asked.

"Yes."

Toxo grunted in reply but made no comment, so Ludo continued. "Once you're in, run up a fever flag or put out that there are lepers aboard, whatever will keep bumboat traders off your decks. Take on fresh water and fresh food, of course, but don't encourage anything else. There'll be pirates, and they use any excuse, so arm your crew. You'll have to deal with them as best you can. Get your second mate to organise plenty of gun practice. Don't waste ammunition, but make sure you've got gunners who can load and reload fast. If pirates have a go at you there'll be hand-to-hand fighting so make sure the crew can use your pistols as well to prevent it, if you can. This part of the coast is at the mercy of cut-throats—you've been warned. Whatever happens, nobody gets to take a stick of cinnamon until Lisbon, understood?"

Across the cabin, Javi said something. This time, Toxo translated it aloud. "If we're anchored too long those dhow-boys off Zanzibar will take the lot, you know they will. They're relentless, clever devils. They'll try to board us for sure."

"Not if you're full of the *peste*."

"So why can't we anchor off a port, somewhere safer?" Toxo asked.

"Look, I want the Portuguese here thinking what's supposed to be going into Lisbon is in *Tulip's* cargo, but you'll be taking most of the Gasca Figaroa goods, not me. Most of what I'll be carrying is the stuff we've been collecting over the past year from along the coast here. You're right about the Zanzibar dhows, though. After the Oman and collecting *Magdalena*, I'm going to try and get down to the Cape without putting in anywhere for more than a day or two. *Tulip*'s crew won't be happy, which is another reason we're discussing this in private, understand?"

"They *won't* be happy. Men need shore leave and fresh food. We're having enough trouble getting hens and rabbits, looks like we'll be living on rice and that lentil dhal stuff for months on end as it is."

Ludo sighed. "I know, and the sooner I can get to you the better. That way we'll sail for Portugal together and I should get you past the Barbary Coast unhindered."

Toxo sniffed at the reference to Barbary corsairs but refrained from comment. Instead, he pushed Ludo's hand off the map and after dipping a pen into a small pot of ink, circled the tiny island they had been discussing. As he did so, he asked, "Are you expecting more cargo to come in for *Magdalena*, or do we sail with what's already loaded?"

"There's a good load still waiting to be ferried out to you; some chests of tea have arrived as well, and more bales of cotton. I'll take the silk from Cathay, and the Sumatra nutmeg. It's all packed and sealed, but we can't do anything until Dona Leonora has given me her new cargo lists and decided what she wants us to do."

"And you'll do what she says, will you?" Toxo gave Ludo a sideways look.

Ludo responded with a tilt of the head and one of his one-dimpled grins then turned to look at the silent man stitching at the table. "Javi, anything you want to know?" Ludo waited a few beats, "No—silly question. Right, I'd better be getting back."

Toxo opened the cabin door and dismissed the sentry with a nod of the head. Ludo ducked under the lintel and descended to the scrubbed deck below. In the short time he'd been in the stuffy cabin there had been a change in the air. There was a distinct odour of rich, damp earth swelling off the land. Peering up at a threatening, purple-hued sky, he said, "Clearing up shower, do you think?"

"Worst *jodido* climate I ever been in," Toxo grunted then changed his tone and said. "You've told us where we'll be going and why, but what about you? Where are you going, and more to the point, what happens if we don't meet up—if you don't find us? Do we really get to keep *Magdalena* and what's in that box you're giving us?"

"Yes, you do." Ludo cast an eye around the vessel for eavesdroppers. "If we lose each other I'll find you in Galicia, sooner or later."

"You're not sailing into the Tagus at all, then? Just us?"

"Yes. I should have explained that better. If Dona Leonora agrees, and makes up the lists I suggested, only *Magdalena* will sail for Lisbon, not me. Obviously I'm trusting your silence one hundred per cent on this."

"Obviously," Toxo huffed. "What'll you be doing, though, or is that not for our ears either?"

Ludo put a hand to the darkening stubble on his chin. The heat had been too much for a full beard, whatever the fashion. "In principle, I'm buying pearls and sailing for England. Some of my cargo is for a young man I know there, but I'm putting in to Hormuz to buy pearls before we meet up. I expect to be hindered, as I said, and I'm laying a false trail so if the Portuguese want to try and claim Dona Leonora's goods at sea, hopefully they'll follow me and not you."

"But we will have all her cargo for Lisbon."

"Yes—more or less."

"Ah, like that is it?"

Ludo gave a curt nod in response.

"What I don't understand," continued Toxo, "is what the Portuguese have against us? If we're Spanish—well, *Magdalena* is with us on her—and you fly a Genoese flag, what reason have they got to intercept our cargo?"

"Mm, I have rather put my foot in it and stirred the muck with the mud. They may, of course—and this is a possibility that's not altogether terrible—insist you sail *alongside* them. If they do, accept the offer, but keep the lady's cargo uncounted and intact at all costs, all right?"

Toxo nodded. "Understood."

"Where do I find you in Spain if things go awry?" Ludo asked.

"Vigo. Ask for Paco de Tui at the tavern Gaviota on the quayside, he'll send for us." Toxo paused, looked down at his feet. "But, *patrón*, you understand we've had enough long-distance seafaring; most we'll be doing after this will be coastal trade—Portugal, France, maybe across to England."

"Excellent. That may serve me very well."

"You've got *more* plans in the north, then?" Toxo's tone was still soft. "Not coming straight back? We were actually wondering if you were going to stay here forever."

"No, not here: I shall return—if I survive the voyage—if the trade proves as lucrative as I believe—but it will not be 'forever'."

"So you're going back for good? You're going back for something special?" Seeing Ludo's reaction to his questions, the wiry mariner sniffed and looked away, then said, "Tell me, or don't tell me, won't make no difference to old Toxo."

Ludo stared at him, seeing the Galician in a different light to the crafty, impoverished mariner who'd lost his livelihood and been hired in Lisbon—when Ludo had been trying to outwit an agent of the Count-Duke of Olivares, and a far, far more dangerous man from the Vatican named Rogelio.

Ludo stared across the gunwale at the sand and trees along the shoreline. He had stayed here, as far away as possible and as long as possible, to evade those two adversaries, specifically the latter, but he had had enough of Goa and its climate; he was ready to go back, despite the dangers. Ludo nodded his head again and smiled at Toxo. "Yes, it's by way of 'something special'—not exactly, but it's a perceptive question. What *am I* going back for?" Ludo paused, took a deep breath and in a low voice, as if speaking to himself, he said, "My aim for many years was to make myself rich. Now I'm not so sure."

"You are rich. By our standards."

"By yours, perhaps, but not by my..." he paused then added hastily, "by mine. I was aiming to be... No, *I intend to be...* richer, wealthier in every way, than the richest family in Genoa."

"So that's why you had us risking our lives off Ceylon for the bark of a *jodido* tree—to make you richer?"

"No." Ludo laughed, surprised. "That was for Dona Leonora."

"But you want to get rich—richer than whoever they are— because..."

Ludo caught a glimpse of José waiting in the skiff alongside the carrack. The boy's mop of black hair and ability in a boat reminded him of another youth, nearly thirty years ago in Portovenere. "Because I want to get my revenge," he said firmly.

Toxo's bushy eyebrows shot up. "Revenge, is it? Well now, revenge is sweet, they say, but it can also take over your life and ruin it. Only warning you: nothing personal."

"You do not approve."

"Fff! Not for me to approve or not approve, not for me to ask why or who, neither."

"But you'd like to know all the same," Ludo managed a grin.

Toxo shrugged.

"We're assuming we get home in one piece," Ludo said, changing the subject.

"Have to—we'd never leave harbour if we didn't believe that, *patrón*."

"True." Ludo turned his gaze back at the shore, towards the irregular rooftops of new colonial homes and newly planted trees that lined rough-made avenues. "Speak to George Guthrie, *Tulip*'s captain; he's an expert on the Africa coast. He's made the round trip from Plymouth twice now."

"Three times lucky. He knows your plans? You trust him?"

"I don't trust anyone, Toxo, you know that, not even myself half the time."

When Ludo returned to the elaborately decorated Figaroa mansion that evening, Leonora was sitting at her work table in the first floor office. She held out two neatly written lists labelled 'A' and 'B'.

Avoiding Ludo's eye, Leonora said, "Have you heard? The Golconda caravan has left. The weather will break soon. The winds are turning. You can sail as soon as you like now. Did you get what you want, by the way? From the Golconda agents, at their market? The uncut stones you were looking for."

Ludo studied her face; she was nervous, it was not like Dona Leonora to prattle. Her wide brow, white and smooth despite the merciless Indian sun, was furrowed. There were tension lines around her generous mouth. "Do you want to ask me something, *madonna*? Or tell me something?"

Leonora looked away, saying, "Both."

"Well, ask first and let us go from there."

Leonora turned her full gaze on him and said bluntly, "Who are you—really? Who is Ludo da Portovenere?"

"A merchant from the state of Genoa, ma'am. That you already know. If you want more personal details, I can only tell you my mother belongs to the great banking and sea-faring house of Doria. But I remain a merchant—out of choice. It brings me adventures in distant lands, where I meet charming..." Ludo checked his words; Leonora didn't deserve this. "There is more to my sad tale, but for now suffice it to say I have a very sound business, and two vessels at your disposal in your harbour. Is that what you wanted to know?"

"I know this already—as you say. But *who* is Ludo da Portovenere. *What* is he—other than a merchant?"

Before Ludo could reply, Leonora took a deep breath and confounded him by saying, "No matter. I have decided that I will marry you, Ludo, on the understanding that you sell what is on list 'A' to the Spanish Crown via my Portuguese agent, Armando Cabrera. List 'A' *must* be declared in Lisbon or I will lose our licence to trade goods from Goa. List 'B' is available for you to purchase as you requested—if you don't—if we don't..." Leonora paused, failing to complete what she had evidently been practising. Edging back her chair then standing with her fine, blue-veined hands pressing down on the ebony table top, she said, "You will also undertake never to return to Goa."

Ludo stared at her. "You don't want me to return—ever?" Leonora shook her head. Trying to read her face and failing, he said, "This isn't quite what I had in mind. In fact it is very far from what I have only just been preparing—for my future business concerns, that is." He sighed and looked at the two lists. "Still, I see you understand the need for two ships, two sets of cargo. And my other intentions."

"Your *other* intentions? That I need to be *seen to be married*? Yes. I don't believe it will halt my problems entirely, but it will help—thank you. We shall be married tomorrow evening in the chapel of Santa Catarina. I have spoken with the priest."

Ludo looked at Leonora with a cloudy sense of admiration: for a woman of her upbringing and nature, what she was saying took courage.

As if reading his thoughts, Leonora said hastily, "It is a marriage of convenience only, a document—that is all. I shall retain the right to divorce you due to non-consummation— should you ever return."

"I think your reasoning may be flawed here, *madonna*, but I shall do as you wish." Ludo bowed low, sweeping his coolie hat to the tiled floor like a courtier and gathering his thoughts. When he raised his head his eyes were twinkling with mischief: a wife in a port as distant as Goa was no wife, and the lovely Leonora had just released him from having to explain why his stolen galleon *Tulip* would not be sailing into Lisbon, where he was a wanted man—not that he had ever intended going there.

Apart from all that, he had also acquired a significant business in his long-term plan to rival and eventually undermine his unknown Genoese cousins.

Chapter 4

The wedding was celebrated by a small man lost among filthy ecclesiastical vestments, his neck grimed yellow with sweat and dirt. Ludo himself was wearing a figured silk jacket dyed in midnight indigo and a plain shirt with a soft loose collar of the lightest bleached cotton. Leonora had dressed in a Hindustani widow's white with a Portuguese mantilla of exquisite black lace. Their witnesses were the godown foreman, Pereira, and his dowdy wife. Various local men and their wives, and a few personal acquaintances of Leonora attended the supper hastily arranged in her father's old house. Ludo was charming, amusing and kept the Oporto wine flowing after all the cool *verdejo*—which had not travelled well—had been consumed. They were entertained by a pretty boy singing what sounded like one the saddest songs ever penned. Apart from that it proved quite a jolly affair under the circumstances.

As the last guest left, Ludo joined his new wife on the balcony above the street door to wave farewell. Once everyone was safely on their way, and unlikely to turn back for yet another meaningful look and cheery wave, he took Leonora's hand in his and led her away from prying eyes.

Without speaking a word, he raised the hand and kissed her knuckles then taking both hands he pulled her into an embrace.

Gradually Leonora relaxed and set her head against his shoulder.

"Come, *madonna*," Ludo whispered. "We make a handsome couple and this marriage should not be assigned to a cold bed. I have been wooing you for many months, though you chose to ignore my intentions, rightly perhaps, as you identified—they were not so honourable then. But give me this one night, I beg of you."

"But..."

Ludo placed a finger on his new wife's lips and nuzzled her neck, drawing in the scent of her skin, cinnamon, vanilla and cloves, and subtle odours he could not name but that always told him when she was near without a word being spoken. "Your reasoning was flawed," he whispered. "I did warn you."

"Why? Ah, because I was a widow when I married and therefore not *virgo intacta*."

"Something like that."

"But I do not want to trap you, Ludo. I have done a terrible thing forcing you into this situation, I was trying to leave you a way out... I am so sorry."

"Sorry? That is a foolish thing to say. Hush, *carina*..." Lapsing into Genoese and using endearments without guile for once, he whispered, "Which way?"

No translation was needed. Flushed with wine, Leonora led her husband to her chamber.

Waking during the night, Ludo pulled the rumpled upper sheet over Leonora's smooth shoulders then lay back on his pillows and tried not to think about what he had let happen. Leonora was beautiful in a dark and soft and gentle way, yet intelligent and not without courage. She was his ideal woman in many ways. So why did he have misgivings, and why was he anxious to leave?

Why not stay and enjoy this matrimony? Because there is unfinished business in Genoa, because I am not ready to settle down yet, because I need to be free of the past before I can start anew.

Next morning Leonora sat up in bed and pulled on a shift of the flimsiest natural cotton Ludo had ever touched. He stroked her arm, kissed her lips, then got out of the high, un-curtained bed and pulled on his breeches and shirt. Sitting on a chair across the room, he said, "Leonora," then paused, for he was feeling light-headed, and not entirely because of the wine they had drunk, "I may regret this, but you ought to know one or two things before I leave."

"Are you going to tell me why you came to India with your wine-red sails? I have often wondered."

"I came with the intention of sailing on to Cathay, as far as I could get from Christendom, a certain powerful Spaniard, and a particularly nasty Catholic churchman."

Leonora's eyes opened wide then shut completely. "You do not have to tell me more. You have committed a crime. You are an escaped convict. I do not want to hear more." She started to get of bed.

"No, wait—it's not like that." Ludo raised a palm in the air. "I am certainly not a convicted man, far from it, although I was pursued and in fear of my life. I have committed no illegal act that I know of, although I do circumnavigate legality quite often. I only took a ship that was owed to me according to a royal agreement sanctioned—nay, promised—by the Conde-Duque de Olivares—"

Leonora turned to him, her eyes wide open again. "Olivares! So it is true, you are acquainted with him. Then tell me, is it true he is protecting New Christians, Marranos, from the Inquisition now? Tell me about him. How did you come to his notice?"

"Oh, it's a long story, too messy and trivial to relate. I completed a tricky task in Holland at his behest but afterwards, when I should have collected my reward, he tried to cheat me into less than was agreed. A lot less than was agreed."

"What was promised?"

"A fine ship. I was given a leaky tub—so I took a new galleon, the *Tulip*, instead. You perhaps should also know that I fell foul of a certain Vatican agent, who would like to be sure I can no longer..." for once Ludo struggled for words.

"Well, whoever he is and whatever his intention, he is unlikely to find you here, although I'd be wary of the Solis cousins; you have made enemies there. They'll be delighted to inform on you."

"Which is why, should any representative of the Vatican come seeking me here you can tell him—truthfully—I have left on travels unknown."

Leonora put her hands to her cheeks. "I wish now it were otherwise. What will you do when you return to Europe? You can't spend the rest of your life trying to avoid capture."

Ludo shrugged. "I have close friends along the Barbary Coast; they will shield me if necessary, for a short time. They are not entirely reliable, of course."

"But this is no way to view your future, Ludo." Leonora bit her lip, then said, "You must take positive action. Attack is the best form of defence, is it not? My late husband was interested in the old form of bull-fighting, where young men leaped over the backs of the bulls. The art was to take the bull by the horns and flip right over him... Pedro said it was a good metaphor for dealing with the difficulties in life, and so I believe. Take your bull by the horns and set yourself free."

Ludo looked at her in surprise: her advice was so apposite to what he had been struggling with during his wakeful hours it was uncanny. "Wise counsel," he said and began tying his cuffs at the wrist. "I must go, *madonna*. I need to review what is in the holds of two ships against the lists you gave me, and we still need to ferry out the last of your cargo."

Leonora watched him in silence as he prepared to go, then said quietly, "Ludo, what is it you really want?"

"To sell my cargo and the precious gems I have acquired. The New World, as far as I know, has no diamonds or rubies. They send silver, gold and emeralds across the Atlantic Ocean, but not diamonds."

"No, I mean, what do you want to do or complete in your life?"

"You're the second person to ask me that in twenty-four hours." Ludo stared around him as if seeking an answer written on a wall. "I used to want a ship, now I have one. I used to want to be richer than—a certain family in Genoa—but I think I may have found another way to rival them... Having my own vessel was always a priority. Now I have two. Within a year, I may have three."

"You wanted a ship, not a home?"

"No, well... if I were to settle down, find a home, it wouldn't be here in Goa, *madonna*—I'm sorry."

"Where would it be?" There was a catch in Leonora's voice.

Noting how her fingers clutched the white sheet, Ludo put on his shoes and keeping his head down, said, "On the coast of Genoa. I once thought of having a house with a terraced garden overlooking the Ligurian Sea. It was only a passing thought. I must go." He got to his feet, walked to the bed and kissed Leonora's brow beneath her natural widow's peak of raven black hair.

"But you don't have a home anywhere," she said.

"I'm known throughout the Middle Sea as Ludo da Portovenere, which is where I grew up. Portovenere is as good as anywhere. Shall I see you later this day, *madonna*?"

Leonora smiled. "My home is your home until the day you leave. Come back this evening... please."

Ludo grinned his boyish, dimpled grin. "Promise," he said. "In the meantime," he continued, "*adieu*," and blew a kiss from the door.

Returning to his bachelor lodgings, Ludo changed his clothes and with mixed feelings arranged for his personal belongings to be sent temporarily to the Figaroa mansion. Then he set off with a sprightly step to the beach to store his *bizalho* boxes and various chamois leather pouches of gems in his cabin on the *Tulip*. The *bizalhos* were covered in stitched, waxed cotton and would remain sealed until he reached England—if they got round the Cape. The pouches were small enough to go in pockets and stay on his person for safekeeping. The priceless ruby, which he was tempted to give Leonora, would go into one of the inside pockets Javi was sewing into his shirts.

On the way, he crossed paths with the boy with the white bullock pulling the water cart. The beast was as far as one could get from the black bulls of Iberia, but it brought to mind Leonora's advice.

He wanted to return to the Middle Sea; he wanted to pick up his old life without the fear of the Rogelio's chosen assassin appearing behind him with a dagger or lacing his next meal with poison. To do that, he had to become a valuable person again, and to do *that* he needed to be very useful to someone that mattered, someone with access to the royal Spanish court or the royal English court: someone who could make him untouchable. To be really safe, and to eliminate the immediate risk to his person from Rome, the ideal solution was to make himself indispensable to Spain again, or the Vatican itself, or, better still, both. And that meant finding a way back to the Count-Duke of Olivares, with whom he had dealt in the foolish business of the tulip bubble.

And now, thanks to the Solis cousins there was a way to kill two if not three birds with one stone. One precious gemstone. All he had to do was create a new persona for himself based on his previous silk and spice merchant role and offer Olivares sufficient advantages and enticement to enable him to keep the *Tulip*, and let it be known that Ludo da Portovenere had a new, very lucrative business in the East.

By the time he returned to his wife's home later that day, Ludo had fashioned a new, short-term life plan. To sail to Plymouth, then pursue certain goals in the Mediterranean before perhaps—maybe—God-willing—returning for another cargo of expensive, highly lucrative peppercorns.

He did not give Leonora the ruby, but she accepted the diamond ring gracefully. It was slightly too large for her finger but she said she could get it altered. Embarrassed and confused —which was not the reaction Ludo had been expecting—instead of cooing over the beautiful gift Leonora began fretting about how he was going to keep her goods safe from water-damage and theft during his voyage.

Ludo responded patiently, explaining how cargoes were distributed on a galleon, something Leonora already knew, confirming his suspicion that during the day she had become nervous about their second evening together and was trying to fill time with trivia. Regarding his private cargo, he said nothing until she asked, "What about your bizalho?"

Ludo looked at her sharply, surprised and a little dismayed that she appeared to know so much about his acquisitions. Laughing, he made light of her query, "You would be surprised, *madonna*, how easy it is to hide all manner of goods aboard a ship. I found an entire woman hidden among sheepskins on one occasion."

"A woman! What did you do with her?"

"Put her ashore at the next port of call and forgot all about her."

It wasn't strictly true—he had never quite managed to forget the Spanish girl, Alina, but it was not a complete lie. Ludo disliked barefaced lies, they were too easy to detect. A smidgen of truth, on the other hand, could conceal all manner of trickery. Not that in his heart he wanted to trick Leonora; she was too good for that.

Chapter 5

It was a leave-taking such as he had never enjoyed or suffered before. A lovely woman wearing a dress of bright apple green and a wide straw hat to cover her delicate face, standing, hands clasped around a rolled parchment, waiting for his carefully prepared parting words.

Leonora also had her farewell prepared. Moving out of the hearing of bystanders, she handed him a rolled document. "Ludo, take this for me—us. Should you actually meet the count-duke, or one of his scribes or staff—whoever works directly for him—please, ask him to amend this document. It states that my father and the firm of Gasca Figaroa are licensed by the Spanish Crown to send spices to Lisbon. As you are now my legal husband and therefore—technically—now the owner, you can ask to be released from this bond. You are not a subject of Spain or Portugal; find a way to free us from the royal monopoly that we may trade in the commodities of our choice, with whom we choose, from here on. . ." Leonora looked at him and smiled. "Do you understand what I am saying?"

"The words, yes—their entire and perhaps secondary meaning, I'm not so sure."

"I am saying that I am willing to share my father's business with you—*if* you can find a way to release us from obligations to the Spanish crown, and... any hints about my family's past. As your legal wife, I do feel safer, but this would free Gasca Figaroa from burdensome obligations and taxes... and," Leonora looked at him and smiled, "and if we are free to trade as we choose we could extend our business into timber—copper—minerals... and that way you would become richer!"

Ludo grinned. "But that will require me to return."

"Yes." Leonora lowered her head, tears suddenly welling in her eyes.

Ludo gathered her in his arms, crushing her legal document, and swung her off her feet. Around them a small group of colonial merchants clapped with approval. Beaming, Ludo looked at the small crowd and noted the Solis cousins, glowering. Bending as if to whisper sweet nothings to his wife, Ludo said, "Come, if I am to return there is something I must say well away from our audience." With a strong arm around her shoulders he walked Leonora down to the water's edge saying, "Your parents' parents' faith is carried by the woman in the family line, is it not?"

"Yes but, I can't—I don't—"

"I know, I know all about that, but listen, if—as the wife of a Genoese merchant who travels the world and has friends of many faiths in far and strange places—if you choose to continue the religion of your maternal line, you have my blessing. Only be careful—as you said, we have made enemies in the past few days."

Leonora turned to her him, her eyes brimming with tears. "But then you might—"

"No, we shall be all right. Let me at least see if I can find a way to make your life here safer and freer. I will take the document and speak to whomsoever necessary, but apart from this I have a plan of my own." He tapped his right hand over a recently stitched pocket in his voluminous shirt.

Leonora lifted her chin and kissed him softly. "Come back to me," she whispered. "Come back to me, please."

Ludo kissed her now, in part to conceal saying more, but also because Leonora was indeed a lovely, lovely woman. Then he walked her back to her compatriots and raised his hat in a final farewell.

"May God be with you," Leonora mumbled. "Stay safe."

"Safe and sound! Never fear, *carina*. I shall return safe and sound, although I regret it may not be for some time. But Ludo will return."

Assuming he even gets into the Indian Ocean, or across it murmured a warning voice in his ear, for even from this point on the beach Ludo could see the tall masts of Dutch naval vessels.

Paying them no great heed, however, Ludo was rowed out to the *Tulip* by his new cabin boy José, who had signed to stay with him until Plymouth. The crew, a mixed rabble of races and experience, came to attention as best they could as he was formally piped aboard. He cast an eye along the motley ranks lined beside the ship's railings: a few low-bellied, low-browed Portuguese; half a dozen swaggering Spaniards; various sunburnt English tars, who, like the Spaniards, had likely jumped ship before the Philippines and Cathay for fear of the China Seas; the rest were lascars, including the dark-skinned Ceylonese who had joined him at Colombo, and various Asiatics and Malays, whom he doubted would sail beyond Zanzibar. There were also a few too many untried galley hands and young cabin boys eager for adventure and green to their roots.

He turned to inspect his officers standing alongside Captain Guthrie... It wasn't a full complement and *Tulip* was a huge three-master galleon. The best he could hope for was to keep them as far as the Canaries. It was not an auspicious start, but if this was all Guthrie could muster, so be it.

Captain Guthrie and his Spanish pilot stepped forward to greet him. Ludo shook their hands, establishing what he wanted from his crew from the start. Then he addressed the crew in a mixture of ship-board argot and English in deference to the captain. "We have to be quick and canny, boys. Hollanders are still blockading the port so we won't slip out of Goa until dark. Then it's duck and dive between them, and keep the carrack *Magdalena* in your sights in case we have to go to her rescue— she's not as fast as us and loaded to the gunnels. We'll be separating before Hormuz, but, for now, we need to be the hare distracting the hounds. It'll be fast and furious, eh, and a very fine voyage!" Ludo raised his old black leather, fancy-plumed hat in the air. "For fine adventures, and finer rewards cry 'aye'!"

Every hat and head-rag rose in the air. "For fine adventures and finer rewards!" the rabble shouted in a satisfying unison.

And that, thought Ludo, *should alert the Dutch to the chase very nicely.*

Less than twenty nautical miles from shore, sailing within sight of the carrack *Magdalena*, Ludo was lamenting his bravura. He had climbed up to the main-mast crow's nest himself for the first time before it got too rough, and now he was back on deck, breathing hard and aching from head to foot. He was very unfit, but that would be remedied. Still unable to speak clearly, he silently passed his spyglass to the one-time British naval officer, George Guthrie.

"She's a Hollander, all right, and massive," Guthrie said, looking in the direction Ludo was pointing. "I can only make out one, though, and I don't think she's heading a convoy. If you're still planning to send the carrack on alone, now may be a good time."

"It's a lot sooner than I planned, and broad daylight. You're sure it's a Hollander, not Portuguese?"

"She's too big, sir. Too well armed, I would say. Word in the port before we left was that the Portuguese have applied to the Dutch for help against Spain."

Ludo stared at the captain. "The Dutch and the Portuguese? But they're enemies."

"Rumour has it Spain is their common enemy now, so they're joining forces. I'm surprised you haven't heard."

"No, well I've been a bit occupied in personal matters lately. A common enemy? Ah, of course, Portugal has applied to the Dutch to help them escape from under the Spanish yoke. Of course. That makes sense. But does it help us, Guthrie? Does it help us?"

"Well, we may not need to worry whether a flag is Dutch or Portuguese—or then again, maybe it doubles your worries." Guthrie looked at Ludo sharply. "Did I hear right, that you have been upsetting your colonial hosts in Goa?"

Ignoring the query, Ludo swore in three languages. "Not to worry, it's easier knowing *everyone* is the enemy. What will they try—to board us and sail *Tulip* back to Amsterdam with a Dutch captain, or simply blast us out of the ocean? By the look of her they could, and easily. The Dutch aren't too fond of me, either, to be honest." Ludo shaded his eyes and stared at the distant ship. "*Maldizione!* Still, I was expecting trouble. You know the *Magdalena* broke the Dutch blockade to get cinnamon for the Gasca Figaroa firm. They will have been waiting for us to sail and think we'll be easy picking out here. But if there's only one of them, will they go for *Magdalena* or us? Damn it! After all we did stuffing the carrack over-full, hoping to get away with it." Ludo paused, thinking rapidly, calculating, assessing the wind and weather, then said, "*Magdalena* has indigo sails so she'll be difficult to see as the sun goes down. Can you double back towards the Dutch and let *Tulip* knock them off course so they lose *Magdalena*?"

"I can try, but we're both hard enough to see, with our dark sails. It was a stroke of genius dying *Tulip*'s sails burgundy red, but it might mean they follow the wrong ship."

"It's a risk, but break off now and set us across their bows, then turn us north-west again. It's much earlier than I planned, but Toxo will understand what we're doing, we've discussed it long enough."

"You said you were expecting trouble."

"I'm always expecting trouble. Not quite this soon, and not quite like this, but it's more or less what we prepared for. If it's just the Dutch after revenge and booty, it's not all that bad. Not that I want any personal confrontations with Dutchmen." Ludo didn't give George Guthrie time to ask why. "Come on, turn us across their bows and make sure you keep their attention long enough for *Magdalena* to slip away."

"Should we be gun-ready, sir?"

"Yes, but for God's sake stay out of *their* range as long as possible. I don't want us sinking before we've even reached the African coast."

Guthrie touched the telescope to his forelock, handed it back to its owner and quickly made his way forward to speak to his officers.

Tulip soon began to veer out of the wind and struggle back and across her own wake. It was slow going but it gave the Dutch cause for thought. Ludo set off round the galleon, warning the crew not to light night lamps until given the all-clear, and clearing cabin boys and galley hands off deck.

The Dutchman, confused at first by their tactics, then turned for them, coming hard and fast within firing range. *Tulip*'s First Mate appeared at Ludo's side. "Cap'n's respects sir, and what do you want us to do?"

"Hold *Tulip* on this course for as long as you can without getting rammed, then pull round north-west and head for the Gulf of Oman. Tell him to stay out of firing range as far as possible. Send an experienced hand up to the crow's nest. There's still some light, and a full moon later: I want to know if this is a Dutch trader or one of their navy vessels. We especially need to know if she's part of a fleet." The First Mate turned to go but Ludo put out a hand to stop him. "Tell Captain Guthrie to be sure the carrack *Magdalena* is out of sight before setting us on course for Hormuz."

Darkness fell before any other ships were sighted or the guns on either ship spiked. Nevertheless, *Tulip* remained on alert throughout the night and Ludo awoke, slumped on the poop deck, to a dry, red dawn. Rubbing sleep from his eyes— although he doubted he'd slept more than half an hour at any one stretch throughout the night—he scanned the horizon then went to the base of the main mast and called up to the crow's nest. The answer was "Not a ship in sight". Sighing with relief, he made his way to his stateroom to wash and change his salt- and sweat-sodden clothing.

Two more Dutch ships picked them up a week later, before *Tulip* reached the Gulf. Their size suggested they were part of the Dutch East India Company: the VOC. Ludo mused on flags, wondering if they saw him as a pirate because he flew no national flag, and would attack, or would see him as an enemy Spaniard—for *Tulip* was obviously Spanish in design—and attack? Either way, *Tulip* was in trouble, and running up a

Portuguese flag might bring them even more, for if what Guthrie had reported about the Dutch and Portuguese now being allies, the Hollanders would use it as an excuse to come aboard.

Riding the dip and roll of heightening waves at the stern, Ludo wondered what to do for the best and decided another bit of evasion was probably the only answer. He trained his spyglass on the nearer ship again and cursed in picturesque Genoese harbour slang: her gun ports were open. *Tulip's* new crew had only practised an emergency drill twice so far and the Dutch were very skilled sailors. Slamming the spyglass shut, he raced forward to speak to Guthrie.

This time, in less calm waters, they managed to lose the huge VOC *retourschepen* and Ludo relaxed. But too soon. Three more Dutch ships were waiting for them as they sailed into the Gulf—navy vessels, and intent on preventing foreign rivals getting into the Straits off Dubai. Ludo slammed his hand down on the gunwale, furious beyond cursing, and set off to find Guthrie again. They needed to get into Hormuz so he could buy pearls for his new enterprise in Spain. He was planning to buy his way into the count-duke's forgiveness using his Genoese family name and what every woman and most men at the court in Madrid craved: diamonds and pearls. Diamonds he had, but he still needed the fabled Arabian Gulf pearls.

"It's a trap, sir," George Guthrie explained, turning the chart for Ludo to see better. "If we get in close enough to the island for you to disembark they can board us. If we slip between them it's because they want us to, and I fear we'll never get back out again if we put in anywhere round Hormuz. They'll take *Tulip*, cargo and complement. We can put up a fight, but then we risk being so badly damaged we'll either sink or have to throw cargo overboard."

Ludo sniffed and examined the chart, tracing his forefinger around the bell-shaped island of Hormuz. "You're right. It's not worth the risk. I can get pearls in Zanzibar. Triple, quadruple the price I expect, but I can get them there. Take us back out. I don't want *Tulip* damaged. Can we stay close enough to the coast that we can slip into a harbour somewhere unseen?"

Guthrie was appalled. "That makes us a sitting duck, sir."

"I know, I know. But if we're at anchor there's less chance of being blown to pieces. They'll board us and we might lose our cargo, but the crew won't lose their skins."

Guthrie gave him a sideways look. "Aye, well, there is that. But it's a mighty risk, sir."

"A risk worth taking, Captain. If you're determined to have some fun, though, could you put us across a harbour mouth so we can fire first and ferry the spice cargo to land if need be?"

"Coastline down here,"—Guthrie's forefinger traced the Omani coast—"is all rocks, sir. I was in Muscat a few years back —we'll have to take care."

"That's what I pay you for, Captain Guthrie," Ludo said sharply. "Keep my ship safe and I'll reward you well. Damage her and I'll strangle you with my own bare hands."

Ludo stormed back on deck in a torment of conflicting emotions: he hated other people getting the upper hand, but he loved his galleon more than any woman and feared for her safety even more.

Chapter 6

After barely a month at sea, Ludo decided to take the advice he had given Toxo: creep into a deep-water cove and wait for the hounds to lose the scent. George Guthrie sailed closer into the Omani coast and the pilot eased them into Salalah, a safe harbour unfrequented by regular trading ships. The shoreline looked as if it had nothing to offer but dates and searing sunlight, but Guthrie insisted there was underground water to be had, so barrels were loaded onto pinnaces and men rowed ashore, delighted with the early break in their long voyage. Ludo, dressed in the cotton pyjamas Javi had made him, for the heat was infernal, joined them in the famed land of the Ichthyophagi.

Turbaned fishermen were attending their boats on a paradisiacal beach. Using his Middle Sea Arabic, Ludo bid them good day and stopped to chat. Within a matter of minutes he'd been given the name of a pearl dealer. Laughing at his success, he followed a skinny boy across the beach to a white, box-like house, where he shared a water-pipe with an ancient pearl dealer and examined a pretty casket of pink, black and ivory-white pearls. They then spent a convivial hour agreeing a price and Ludo set out for the *Tulip* to collect the money.

Crossing back onto the beach, he stopped in his tracks and stared in disbelief. Two young men draped in billowing cotton were leading two small horses on long ropes along the sand. Two foals skipped and bucked behind them, stopping to rear in play-fight, then galloping to catch up with their dams. One of the mares was silver-white with a greyish mane; the other was a bright chestnut: her foal was the darker of the two, but one day he, too, would be the colour of gold. A sudden breeze lifted off the sea, setting palm leaves aquiver. The chestnut dam raised her head and her tail formed a perfect ark. Whickering insistently, she pranced nervously until her foal, floating through the air on tiny hooves, arrived at her side.

Ludo, who had no great love or knowledge of horseflesh, was awestruck. Here were the original Arab horses that his acquaintances in Constantinople used as bloodstock for their larger cavalry beasts. He couldn't take his eyes off the dark foal, for it was the most perfect, charismatic creature he had ever seen.

Dragging himself away, he made for the pinnace and was rowed back to the galleon. Within the hour he was on the beach once again, with double the gold he had offered, in case the pearl dealer found it necessary to renegotiate—or offered him a special extra. The beautiful horses had gone, their hoof prints erased by the wind as if they had never existed.

The pearl dealer accepted the agreed price for the pearls. He also accepted two sapphires in exchange for a box of frankincense. Pleased with the transactions and agreeing to further their impromptu business by bringing pots and pans and good merino wool from England and Spain when he returned from Christendom, Ludo made his farewell. The pearl trader showed him to the doorway in his high patio wall.

"There were horses on the beach, mares and foals," Ludo said.

"Ah, they will be our sheik's favourites, my friend, taking their morning exercise. The stallions are brought out at night when it is cooler, but the mares catch the untainted morning breeze. In the horse world it is the mother who is of greater value."

"One of them was the colour of spun gold."

"Indeed," the pearl dealer smiled knowingly, his irregular jagged teeth marring Ludo's memory of exquisite beauty, "and you wish to make her famous."

"Famous? How can a horse be famous?"

"Pure Arab horses are born of the wind, this is known. They float on the wind as ordinary beasts and humble man must walk on the earth. They are strong, beautiful and brave, for they must live and prosper here in as harsh a place as Allah could create. Come, I will take you to the stables."

"No, thank you, I have no need for horses. I was only curious. Besides, I shall be at sea for months and months."

"As you wish, my friend, but I believe your meeting with these wondrous animals happened for a reason."

Ludo frowned. "A reason? How might that be?"

"Ah—you ask me?" The pearl dealer lifted his hands in the air. "How must I know what brought you here and what you will take from us?"

The next day Ludo was rowed ashore as dawn lit the sky. He loitered among the leaning date palms, chatting with dhow fishermen preparing their nets and boys bringing empty kreels from shuttered, silent houses.

This time the foals came first, galloping, racing each other, heads tossing, tufted soft manes rippling in the breeze. At an invisible signal they skidded to a halt in the fine sand and ambled back to the security of their dams. Ludo leaned back against a tree to study them as they passed. The darker of the two foals paused and gazed at him with huge round eyes. He cocked his head to one side, exactly the way Ludo did himself, then tottered up to him and stretched his muzzle forward, sniffing with low, barely audible snuffles. Ludo held his breath. The colt's muzzle touched his shirt, then his cheek. It was as if he had been chosen by a messenger from Allah himself.

Instinctively, Ludo blew softly on the colt's nose. But then, suddenly aware it was on its own with a stranger, the colt backed away and returned to its mother's side. Ludo followed. He followed the grooms and mares all the way to the stables and begged entry when his way was barred. A surly, weather-wizened man came to the gate. "You want to buy a horse," he said. It was a statement, not a question.

"Yes," Ludo replied without thinking.

"Come this way."

The gate was opened and he entered a sanded patio. Water trickled from a fountain, reminding him of a *cortijo* in southern Spain. The buildings were whitewashed and bleached by the sun —exactly as they were in Andalusia. The ground plan was the same, too: airy stables set around a fountain, a substantial house set between them. Stallions stamped and snorted in open boxes along one wall. Mares dozed or suckled their young bedded on clean sand along another.

A younger man came out of a door and the two grooms discussed his presence as if he were not there.

"I'd like to buy the chestnut mare and foal you exercise on the beach," Ludo said when they paused.

The two men looked at each other and laughed. "Forget it," said the older of the two. "Our master will never part with them."

"Take me to him," Ludo replied.

The sheik was seated on cushions in a high-ceilinged room. There were no intricate tiles such as those of the Arab homes Ludo knew in North Africa, only brightly coloured wall-hangings and mats, and on a low oblong table a large patchwork cloth.

Ludo was led up to the sheik, who peered at him through unsmiling eyes then said, "You wish to take my joy from me and transport it across the world."

"That is so, Excellency," Ludo replied, wondering how he had divined where he wanted to take the mares, having not thought it through himself.

The sheik stared at him until Ludo was forced to look away. Across the unfurnished room an eagle owl blinked, surprised, perhaps, to see a stranger. A small hawk chained to another perch shook its jesses. The owl had the same amber eyes as its master. Ludo shifted from one foot to the other, not unlike the smaller bird; then, aware of what he had done and how it might be interpreted, he stood straight, folding his arms across his chest.

The sheik, an elderly man, similar in appearance to the pearl trader in a flowing white robe and square-set head cloth, tapped his beak-like nose. It was flattened at the tip. As Ludo's vision became more accustomed to the low indoor light, he tried to decide if the flattening were natural or the result of an accident or fight, then chastised himself for becoming distracted and wondered how the sheik might be reading his features: the newly-grown beard that still itched, his Indian cotton pyjamas, his swollen hands, reddened from helping on deck after a long period of living in comfort.

Breaking the tension, the sheik snapped his fingers and a servant brought in a tray of sherbet and sugary date and almond morsels. He then indicated a cushion and invited Ludo to sit at the low table covered in a cloth with yellow and gold, white and red squares. Appliquéd onto the squares were fat, winding snakes and unstable ladders that tilted up and across the cloth. Words and phrases had been embroidered into certain squares in black but Ludo couldn't read them.

"It was brought to my father's father, or perhaps his father's father, many years ago, from India," the sheik said. "It is called *moksha patam*." He placed two ebony, white-spotted dice on the middle of the cloth.

"Ah, it is a game, like *parchis*."

"Yes and no. *Parchis* requires a certain skill; *moksha patam* depends to a greater degree on the fall of the dice—and an individual's luck."

"A game of chance."

"More than mere chance, my friend: truly it is a study in *karma* and *kama*, destiny and desire. We shall play together."

"For the horses? If I win, I may take them?"

"No."

"Then forgive my bad manners, Excellency, but I have no time for games."

The sheik handed Ludo the dice. "As a guest you may throw first."

Ludo delayed his response, taking a sip of sherbet to hide his annoyance. He was not in the mood for mystical games of chance; time wasted here could put his ship in jeopardy. If *Tulip*'s pursuers found their hiding place and he was not aboard... Ludo closed his eyes, not wanting to complete the thought, and rattled the dice in his accommodating palm out of sheer habit.

The sheik pointed to a ladder. "The ladders take you up to the end of the cloth and finally, if you win, bring you to 'salvation'. The snakes take you down through your earthly vices. Look." He pointed at the words stitched into the cloth. "Your first chance to rise is through 'faith', then 'reliability', 'generosity', 'knowledge' and 'asceticism'. But you can be brought back down again by 'disobedience', 'vanity', 'vulgarity', 'drunkenness' and 'debt'. The longest and therefore the worst of these snakes are these which bring you back or near to the beginning, meaning you must start your climb all over again: watch out for 'rage' and 'greed', 'pride', 'murder' and 'lust'. This one fat serpent here crossing the entire cloth is 'lying'—telling that which is not true."

"There are fewer ladders than snakes," Ludo said.

"Such is life."

Ludo jiggled the dice. "And there is no one ladder that can take you straight to the top, but this snake up here can take me right back to the beginning."

"No one single virtue is sufficient for salvation. What good is generosity if you are unreliable and guilty of greed and self-love?"

Trapped, Ludo tried to relax and indicated he was ready to begin. It was, after all, only a game—although as the sheik had pointed out, not exactly a game, for once he had begun he couldn't help but wish for more virtues and lament his vices. In *parchis*, with a bit of cunning and friendly dice you could win within an hour. Not so here.

Ludo lost, devoured by the serpent of 'disobedience' twice, then by 'greed' when he was close to finishing. He wanted to blame the sheik, who had maintained his scrutiny of his guest throughout, unnerving Ludo each time he threw.

Glad that it was over, Ludo tried to pull on his old mask of bonhomie and said cheerily, "Is there a prize for you, Excellency?"

"Is salvation not a prize?"

"I doubt I will ever find out, Excellency. Where I come from there's no point even trying. And as I am no Hindustani I do not have to worry about the Wheel of Re-incarnation."

Across the room, the eagle owl glowered.

"Neither am I of Hind, my friend, but I do believe a better life is attainable while we are on God's earth. Only a complete fool dismisses the possibility of returning—being condemned on the Wheel." The sheik drank from his cup of sherbet and ate a sweetmeat, taking his time.

Ludo forced himself not to squirm, pondering whether the actions related to 'whim' should be classified as a vice. Then his blood ran cold: on a whim he had walked into a trap. He had made himself a prisoner while the sheik's men were unloading his ship. Rapidly he cast about for a guard, but saw only the owl and the hawk, wisdom and aggression.

"You are nervous, my friend. You fear I shall not let you go. You fear we shall take your cargo. It is within our power, but I would have hoped this past hour had shown you we are aware of the penalty of greed. Not that we have no need of your cargo. Spices from India, silks and tea from Cathay? You have tasted our sweetmeats: cinnamon from Ceylon would be most welcome here. Perhaps on your next voyage you will allow *me* to purchase from *you*?"

"Gladly, Excellency." Ludo endeavoured to keep relief from his voice.

"As an example of my trust and good faith, let me offer you a gift." The sheik reached beneath the low table and brought out a curved dagger in a decorated leather sheath. "It is a *khanjar* from my personal collection."

Ludo accepted the short weapon, whose only possible purpose could be for decoration. Inclining his head, he said, "Thank you, Excellency. I shall wear it at my side with pride."

"That is good. Now you will return. But first, let me tell you, Ludo da Portovenere, a man whom I see is accustomed to getting his way, why you are leaving without my beautiful horses. Listen carefully to our proverb about the Arab horse: *God spoke to the south wind, saying: 'I will create from you a being which will be happiness to the good and misfortune to the bad. Happiness shall be on its forehead, bounty on its back and joy in the possessor'.*"

Ludo stared at him, trying to gather the full meaning behind the spoken words. The sheik smiled for the first time and said, "*Joy in the possessor...*"

"That is the whole point of my being here," Ludo replied. "I would find much joy in being the possessor."

"No, my friend, you would sell them to a stranger and forget them in a week."

Ludo left without the beautiful horses.

Before *Tulip* sailed, however, before he had even counted and classified his new pearls and stowed them for safety, he had a barrel of cinnamon and a bolt of green Chinese silk sent to the sheik, and a small case of tea sent to the pearl trader. If he did return it would ensure a welcome; and he was not ungrateful.

Standing at the prow that evening as *Tulip* slowly gathered wind into her sails on a pink and orange-hued, molten sea, Ludo was joined by the wiry Scottish sea captain.

"It's too quiet, too still," the Scotsman said. "Too quiet below as well. You'd think they hadn't had a jolly at all."

"Well they have, and that's it for a good month at the least," Ludo replied. Then, turning from the gathering night, he said, "Join me for a night cap," and led the way to his cabin.

They settled around Ludo's galley table and José served them warm, sweet Oporto. Ludo pulled a face. "I'll be glad to be drinking proper wine again," he said. "This stuff is too thick and sickly for nights like this."

Guthrie wiped his brow with a none too clean kerchief. "A good pint of ale, warm or not—that'd do me right now."

"You'll be pleased to be back on home territory? Or do you get fidgety on dry land? I do."

Guthrie put down his glass and looked at Ludo. "Oh, I do as well. A week is fine, but once I've got my land-legs back—well, I'm anxious for the water again. Shall you be sailing again directly after Plymouth, sir?"

"I'm not sure yet. Not sure about anything, if the truth be known. I've just tried to make a foolish and unforeseen deal with an Omani sheik, and been saved by his wisdom. Prior to that, I made another unexpected arrangement with a woman. Charming as she is, I regret she was definitely not part of any original plan." He scratched his chin pensively. "Ask me again once we're in Atlantic waters."

"As you wish sir, but I'll not be making plans for the Atlantic, let alone being at home, until Zanzibar is behind us. I have a dread of those cutthroats in the dhows. Crafty little buggers."

"They are, but you should be all right with me aboard. We managed on the voyage out, remember. I can deal with Barbary corsairs, anyway. Mind you, we're a long way from Morocco, so maybe not in these waters." Guthrie opened his mouth to say something then closed it. Ludo grinned. "Don't tell me you didn't know about my Salé Rover connections, Captain."

Guthrie lowered his head. "I was told by more than one when you took me on, sir. And again on the voyage out. 'Warned' might be a better word."

Ludo grinned. "I bet you were."

"Is that how you got your sailing experience, sir?"

"It is—that and half a dozen visits to the Levant and Constantinople for my rich-trade—buying and selling silks and spices."

"It gives you an edge over the lads below decks; they've a respect for your sea-faring knowledge, which is unusual for men such as them. I've no complaints, sir."

"Me, neither." Ludo poured them each another measure. "Do you believe in luck, Guthrie?"

"Hard to be a mariner and not believe in luck, sir, but if you're meaning luck as in destiny—no. We make our own future. I'm a Calvinist in this; a good Protestant believes the good things you do in life build your credit for entry into heaven."

"I thought that was the Catholics and their *opus dei*."

"Happen it's similar; the Protestant of course is thinking of financial credit."

"Aren't we all," Ludo sighed.

For a while the two men sat companionably and listened to the sound of their ship creaking gently, then the crack of canvas as her sails caught a stronger wind.

"That is a wonderful sound," Guthrie said. "It'll speed the month to Zanzibar."

Ludo nodded and relaxed in mind and body for the first time in many weeks.

After a further few minutes, and after his cabin boy José had presented them with a plate of soft, fresh dates, Guthrie spoke again. "Going back to making unexpected decisions and planning ahead and about what is said about, erm, you, sir..."

"The one-time pirate Ludovico da Portovenere—yes, continue."

"Well, if you'll forgive my impertinence, I'm curious to know, sir, why it is—if you are happy at sea and have had such, erm, a colourful career up to now—how is it you are so subdued, sir?"

"Am I? Yes, I suppose I am." Ludo's face shut down. He blanked his expression and sipped at the last of his drink. After a long pause he said, "I don't have to answer this, but as you are my captain and we have at least another quarter of a year together through difficult waters I'll speak honestly with you. I am suffering from a disease."

Guthrie tried not to appear shocked or appalled and to Ludo's amusement failed in both. Ludo laughed. "No, not the clap nor a pox nor anything remotely contagious, but it is wearing me down, as you have noticed. The disease I speak of is uncertainty, also known as indecision. You are perceptive, like the captain of the carrack *Magdalena*, although he was less diplomatic with his questioning."

"About what, sir? What do you doubt? Is it a matter of religion? Have you been called?"

"God forbid, no! And I mean that precisely. I leave religion to people with nothing better to do with their lives—misery-mongers in the main, excepting yourself of course, if you're biblically inclined."

"We favour the new plain church over the old ways in my family, and the new King James Bible. I'm all for reading the Word of Our Lord in my own tongue but my cousins still favour the Latin Mass; they're strongly papist. It makes for an awkward Christmastide."

"I'll bet. But I never understand why one person's preference of worship does so upset another. You see it among the Arabs as well. Ah, well... On a different note, did you see the horses I nearly bought? Now that was a foolish wish, based on what I fear might have been love at first sight. Although, now I come to think of it, if that's the case it must mean I'm capable of self-knowledge if not knowledge itself—whatever that is—so there is hope for me, Guthrie."

"Knowledge balances luck nicely, I'd say."

"That is probably true. Does it mean that *knowing* we may succumb to the Fever Coast, or we may not make it round the aptly named Cape of Good Hope, lessens or strengthens the element of luck involved?"

Guthrie shook his head. "Too deep for me, sir—that is, far too deep."

"For both of us. Tell me, where do you call home? I'm hearing something of Scotland in your voice, but I thought you were an Englishman."

"I was born near Edinburgh. Never lost the accent, it seems, though I rarely return to my mother's old home, I regret. I married a southern lass, you see."

Ludo gradually led the conversation in another direction and sent the captain on his way with a rosy face and the remaining dates for his morning repast.

Turning into his bunk, sweat slick across his broad naked chest, for it was still extremely hot, Ludo mused over the captain's questions. *Why am I so low in spirits when I am in the one place I have always loved, on board a ship? My own ship. Because when I land, I am a wanted man? Because I fear word will find its way to an evil-minded, murdering, Vatican priest and his team of assassins? Because I acted on a whim and cheated the Spanish chief minister and must return cap in hand to keep my ship* Tulip *safe? Or because I should not have left Goa?*

For a while he slept, only to be woken by a noise the entire ship was complaining about, like the raucous mewing of a cat being skinned alive: the peacocks. He sat up, hair on end, with an appalling sense of superstitious fear. Leonora had warned him. The evil eye on peacock feathers brought bad luck. Having the feathers in a house brought death. Did that apply to a ship? He had laughed at her, put a long, bright tail feather in his straw coolie hat for fun. *Could the bad luck they'd had so far be for that?*

Well, whether they were bad luck or whether they weren't, the crates containing the birds were going ashore at Zanzibar, to be exchanged for the rabbits and chickens they'd been unable to acquire in India. He hoped Africans didn't hold the same stupid superstition. He hoped the Solis cousins hadn't recognised his name and passed the information in a letter to Lisbon that could be forwarded to Madrid or Rome. *Could such a letter even be aboard—or on the* Magdalena—*carried secretly by a mariner or more likely an officer, for a price?*

Doubts swirled around Ludo's head until he was just drifting back to sleep and sat bolt upright. His Goan coolie hat with a peacock feather was on a chair across the cabin. He rolled off the bed, opened the window and threw the hat out into the ocean in one movement. The north-easterly wind picked it up and whisked it away—and sharp spray slapped him the face. He laughed, leaned out as far as he could and let it do it again for good measure and lessons learned. Then he sniffed the air: the wind had quickened; they'd be with the *Magdalena* within the month.

Chapter 7

The carrack *Magdalena* was low in the water, so untouched. Toxo had used their time wisely and she looked brand spanking new, with fresh paint on her bows and her name picked out in red and gold. She was also surrounded by at least half a dozen dhows, some with sails up and bobbing gently on the tide. The single, tilted sails reminded Ludo of shark fins circling prey.

He trained his spyglass on *Magdalena*'s decks: men were stationed everywhere with fire arms and the gun ports were open. *Magdalena* was under siege. He sent José for Captain Guthrie.

"Drift into the bay and get as near to the carrack as possible," Ludo said. "Crush or ram as many dhows as you can in the process. And make us gun-ready."

Guthrie turned to leave, but Ludo held his arm. "Do all the damage you can, but don't for God's sake damage the carrack!"

While Guthrie and his mates set the ship on her new course and sails were brought down, Ludo stood at the quarter-deck rail wondering what to do: attack the dhows or merely shove them out of the way. And for all the *Magdalena* looked good it was possible she'd not been able to take on fresh water or supplies; she might be in grave need of provisions. The voyage was turning into a nightmare. If they stopped for *Magdalena* to re-victual along the East African coast, that was another week at risk.

Coming to a decision, he shouted at the nearest hand, "Send me the Master of the Foredeck and tell him to bring arms, then get me a gunnery mate. I want powder monkeys working like the blazes and flints ready."

Ludo should have spoken to *Tulip*'s captain first, but there was no time for niceties. Three of the dhows had already guessed his intentions and were pulling out from under the carrack's bows, intending to either get out of *Tulip*'s way or—preposterous as it seemed, for they were so small compared to the galleon—preparing to attack. If that was the case, he was taking charge.

There was a scream of alarm and an angry outburst of shouting as *Tulip* bore down on her first victim. The dhow tried to go about but all was confusion. A boy went overboard. The single sail fell with a crash and the dhow keeled through mishandling. Men were in the water, screaming for help. One of *Tulip*'s deck hands arrived breathless at Ludo's side: "Cap'n's compliments, sir—do we go to their aid?"

"No!" Ludo shouted, looking at the Master of the Foredeck who was back at his side. "It's a ruse, a stunt. Arm your men and shoot anyone within firing range." He turned back to the deck hand. "Tell the captain to signal *Magdalena* to follow into open waters as fast as possible."

As he was speaking there was a commotion behind him. Other local pirates had been following right under the *Tulip's* high stern. Grappling irons were being thrown over the gunwales on both sides of the quarterdeck; they were swarming aboard *Tulip* exactly as Toxo had foreseen.

Ludo laughed at the cheek of it and yelled a warning in a tongue he hoped they understood. Whether they did or not, five members of Guthrie's new crew, backed up by older European hands carrying muskets and wheel-lock pistols, lurched at them with short swords and vicious fish-gutting knives. Another boy in an unravelling turban screamed in pain and fell back into the sea. His place was taken by a much older man, whose hand gripped the gunwale a second too long. A Lascar sliced down with his blade chopping off first the right hand at the wrist, then the left. There was an obscene howl of agony as the torso arched back into the sea below. The left hand slithered off the rail and plopped to the deck. One of the English hands kicked it to another, who picked it up and hurled it into a dhow below. It was a timely warning. One of the crew still in the dhow gave a piercing shriek and threw it into the water; another man hollered at his compatriots, calling a halt. The next round of would-be boarders ceased climbing and dived into the sea.

Then came a heart-ripping scream. It was from the handless old man attempting to swim back to his boat, then another from a pirate at the prow of the nearest dhow. Pointing, he screeched again and again. The pirates in the water swam frantically for their vessels. For the handless man it was too late. Then another disappeared below. The water turned pink, then a bubbling, heaving, thrashing scarlet.

Ludo stood back from the rail, a freezing shiver running down his spine: he had seen shark fins after all.

As the local pirates tried to drag their fellows out of danger, *Magdalena* weighed anchor and hoisted her sails. The captain of the *Tulip* commanded a change of course without consulting his ship's owner and the two heavily loaded vessels returned to the open sea.

The two ships put into Zanzibar, but to the crews' annoyance and disappointment it was in and out as fast as transactions could be made. Ludo acquired gold with the last of his surplus finance and the victuallers acquired the hens and chickens they needed, and that was that.

Hampered by the carrack's slow progress, the voyage towards the Cape thereafter became more and more tedious. After escaping the tail of a cyclone off Madagascar, getting round the Cape proved a damaging, terrifying experience. Guthrie signalled to the *Magdalena* to follow *Tulip* into a safe haven he knew, over-looked by a table-topped mountain. They would remain there for repairs, and to regain their strength.

Repairs and refurbishment took far longer than Ludo liked and he became more and more short-tempered. There were pleasures to be had ashore in a scruffy bivouac settlement for deckhands with beer bellies and no fear of the clap, but it was not remotely to his taste and he spent his time checking and re-arranging their cargoes, and talking with Toxo and Javi about what to expect in Lisbon, avoiding as best he could why he would not be going into the Tagus estuary with *Tulip*.

Eventually they put back to sea and crossed the Equator then entered dark, brooding, lake-like waters that mirrored the black-clouded sky above. After what seemed weeks in the Doldrums, the weather in the Gulf of Guinea turned stormy. Mile-high waves crashed down mercilessly on the two struggling ships. With everything battened down, they fought on, battling the elements to reach home, with both Toxo and Ludo in constant fear that their precious cargoes would be damaged, turn mouldy with damp or, worse, be lost altogether.

Gradually the wind calmed and the waves crept back into the sea. Gentle rain showers brought everyone up on deck, running and jumping and sliding across the slick surfaces, revelling in fresh air and sweet rainwater. Ridding themselves of lice and weeks of crusted salt under armpits and between the thighs, cabin boys and old hands ran naked around the ship. Ludo folded his arms and watched from the poop deck rail like a benevolent father.

Heading up for the Cape Verde Islands, the ship's surgeon came to report to Ludo in his cabin. The surgeon, a young, fresh-faced Scot with not an ounce of humour about him said, "I've the record of sickness and sea scurvy aboard thus far, sir. Will you take a look at it?"

"And how will that help them recover? Do they think I have the divine gift of healing like the King of England? Shall you be asking me to rub their heads and cure them of lice as well, Mr McIntyre?" Ludo was only half joking.

The Scot looked at him dourly. "It was Captain Guthrie who told me to report to you, sir."

"Very well." There was silence. "And...?" Ludo asked.

"Is it true, sir? I have heard that the King of England, who I must point out is also the King of Scotland, in fact the Stuarts provided England with their monarchs... I digress: I was asking if it were true about the king curing ailments by a touch of the hand."

Ludo raised his eyebrows and shrugged. "So I have heard. Pity you and I can't do it, too, eh? We'd be free of boils and bleeding gums and rotting flesh by now."

"No unguent for boils and blisters, remains, sir. But the problem declined after the Cape shore leave, sir. As did the bleeding gums. In fact, that ailment and the fatigue that accompanies it died away."

"Which leads one to wonder if it's a disease borne of sea ennui." Ludo stood at his open stern window, then turned and fixed the ship's doctor with a sharp glare. "By your silence I fear you think I am harsh, Mr Surgeon."

The Scotsman shuffled his feet under the scrutiny. "There's been little chance of boredom on this voyage, sir, except in the Doldrums."

"True. Perhaps I am ascribing to others what I feel myself."

The doctor clearly didn't know how to respond, but he said, "I believe this ship is healthier than my previous voyage. In fact I'd say we are relatively free from illness, sir. Nevertheless, if I may, I'd advise putting into the Cape Verde Islands for fruit and vegetables—but no meat because you can't be sure what it is. The natives eat all manner of disagreeable creatures from the bush: rats the size of terrier dogs, and monkeys..." The young man shuddered. "They resemble babies when they're spitted over a fire—I've seen it done."

Ludo grimaced. "A good reason to stay out, then. I'll speak to Captain Guthrie."

Guthrie waited until the carrack *Magdalena* came into sight a day later then signalled and the two vessels put into a broad cove, staying well off the beach—close enough for a sailing pinnace to put in for fruit as the doctor requested, but far enough out to make a hasty exit if pirates arrived on the scene. Toxo was ferried across and spent three hours with Ludo, discussing final arrangements for Dona Leonora's spices and how much sugar *Magdalena* could squeeze in her hold from the Canaries, which he and Javi could trade in Vigo as they had done in the past.

They sailed again that evening, Ludo having explained to Captain Guthrie that both he and the captain of the *Magdalena* wanted to put in to Gran Canaria for a brief refit before facing the dangers of the Atlantic off the coast of Portugal—and give the crew shore leave before the long, last lap.

As they sailed out of the Canary Islands a week later, the entire crew cheered like schoolboys. This was indeed the last lap for many of them, who'd be seeing their loved ones within a month. All of them, Lascars from the East and Plymouth-born Jack Tars alike, would be spending their pay on drink and floozies as fast as they disembarked. The mood dropped like a lead on a line, however, when Ludo told Guthrie to open all gun ports. Powder monkeys working in threes filled and tied silk powder pouches as fast as they could. Teams of gunners shoved the *Tulip's* thirty guns into place and manoeuvred the iron balls ready for loading and firing. Galley hands were relieved of their normal duties to act as runners; more experienced mariners were issued with pistols and dispatched along yardarms. The entire ship was on alert until further notice. Word soon got round that the *patrón* was planning to sail *Tulip* straight for the Barbary stronghold of Salé. Which was true.

As the carrack *Magdalena* passed and saluted them on a course set for Lisbon, George Guthrie did his best to hide his nervousness and failed.

"There's no need to fear for me," Ludo said, when he gave the captain a list of the goods he wanted transported into the harbour from the ship. "They may ignore orders, but that rarely happens. Jan Janszoon van Haarlem, who you probably know as Murat Reis, keeps his cut-throats under better control than many navy captains can. We do know each other, believe me, so do not fear for my personal safety."

"Janszoon was captured by the Knights of Malta," Guthrie said. "Did you not know? That means they'll have a new leader who *does not* know you, sir, and this ship is a very fine prize. Or the *Magdalena*..."

"The *Magdalena* has sailed on as we agreed. As to the risk, yes, *Magdalena* is at risk, and going into Salé is always a risk—and that's why you'll have every fuse ready to light at the first sign of trouble. But I doubt it will happen—we have raised a Moorish flag after all, and I do know my way about here."

"And that's another thing, sir. I really can't countenance this changing of flags; it's not correct. If you wish to avoid trouble with... whoever it is you wish to avoid trouble with... Well, I see nothing ill in using the Union flag as we are bound for Plymouth, and it would save a deal of trouble with the Dutch."

"But not with the Spanish or Portuguese—which despite rumours are still one and the same."

Guthrie scowled. "The Union flag should be respected everywhere, sir, even in Spanish ports. The nations have been at peace for a good many years now."

"On this I cannot comment, but speaking of 'respect', and as you yourself said earlier in this voyage, I do have 'an edge' when it comes to matters such as this. The strategic use of flags is a trick I learned off Murat Reis no less, so stop fretting. You northerners are far too rule-bound."

Guthrie swallowed his discomforts and cast a glance at the goods on Ludo's list. Reading aloud, he said, "One bale of raw silk marked with an 'S'; two bales of Canary sugar cane; one barrel of mixed nutmeg and mace, one of cinnamon; box of mixed *drogas* marked with the number '1'. May I ask who all this is for, sir?"

"My father, if the old devil has escaped and he's still alive. For his current wife or wives, if not."

Guthrie blinked rapidly then said, "Ah, right, yes. Erm... Yes, I'll arrange for the pinnace to be loaded," and hastened down the companionway towards the hold.

Whether the father of the owner of the galleon named *Tulip* was still alive and living in the self-proclaimed pirate stronghold of Salé, Ludo never informed his captain. But he did return to his vessel after twenty-four hours with an interesting, light cargo, including a box of enigmatically named 'seeds of paradise' and a case of Italian wines and grappa. Packets of dried grapes and dates were passed among the crew and they sailed on up the Atlantic coast with the *Tulip*'s hold untouched and her crew unharmed.

Then their real troubles began. Ludo sat at the polished table in his cabin, drinking grappa. He had before him a section of a map outlining the North African coast as far as the Straits of Gibraltar and the Spanish coast as far north as the Bay of Biscay. Absently, he marked details with a reed pen and blue-black Indian ink. Then he let his mind wander back over the next decision to be made: whether or not to put in to Cadiz. It would enable him to sell his silk and cotton fabrics to merchants with whom he had been trading for many years, and buy in fresh water, milk and meat. But it also meant he'd lose a good few of his crew, notably the eastern Lascars, whose skills with sails and ropes he had come to admire.

Something else was nagging him to stay out of Cadiz, though. He was anxious to put the dangers of the Portuguese and Galician Costa da Morte behind him and cross the Narrow Sea to Plymouth as fast as he could. Not least, because Marcos, his one-time servant, now a man of business on the Barbican at Plymouth, was waiting for him there. Marcos needed the mace and cinnamon, and the special seeds he'd acquired in Salé for his new enterprise.

Having got this far safely, it was absurd to be in a quandary, but underpinning the decision to put into Cadiz or not lay two other factors: the not insignificant personal risk to his safety in mainland Spain, should anyone of note become aware of his presence, and the emotional pull of returning to England—

which he did not want to acknowledge. Still undecided, he tossed back his grappa and stone cold sober went to bed.

In the early hours, Ludo was woken by a tremendous storm with thunder and lightning. His mother had told him he'd been born in a thunderstorm at sea and he had always belittled the superstitious beliefs of landlubbers and many mariners that the sound and fury were conjured by the devil. Having spent a very short night in a turmoil of options and indecisions, Ludo now watched the sky crash down upon his vulnerable ship and let the weather decide matters for him.

Having reached Christendom with a dry cargo, he wasn't going to risk unloading bolts of bright silk, whose colours could be ruined by water-damage, nor his precious Chinese *cha* and Malaka and Indian spices for a few Spanish reales. Sending word to Captain Guthrie, Ludo took position on the prow, and soaked in spray from the churning sea they sailed on, passed by Cape St Vincent and then on and on during sleepless nights in roiling waters, until, exhausted but intact, they passed the mouth of the Tagus and faced the final onslaught of the Costa da Morte—the Coast of Death—off Galicia.

As the weather quietened, Guthrie joined Ludo for a night cap. The man's tendency to whine and fear the worst irritated Ludo, but he had proved an excellent captain. Holding *Tulip* to the slower *Magdalena*'s speed to maintain the two-ship convoy all the way round the African coast was no mean feat. But when Guthrie now began to lament the foul weather Ludo was sharp with him. "Three weeks and you're home and dry, Guthrie; spare me your moaning for a while longer, please do."

Guthrie was put out. He drank the last of his wine and got up to leave, saying, "We'll stay well off the coast; it's lethal in a storm."

"I do know that," Ludo retorted impatiently. "I've sailed round here more often than I can count on two hands. Do as you see fit, I'll not interfere. Just get us to Plymouth in one piece. I'll be damned if we get this near and have a mishap."

"It happens, sir."

"*I know*! Good night, Guthrie."

The next day the skies cleared and Ludo strolled out on deck, chatting with the exhausted crew, who had made the most of the cold rain to clear salt from their scalps, if not all the lice. It was too chilly to be on the open deck for long, though, so he wandered back to his cabin and pulled out the ship's manifest. There were another two lists to be made: the goods going to Marcos in Plymouth and those he would sell himself. Sitting down to divide the quintals of cinnamon and nutmeg, pepper and mace, sorting what item of cargo would go where and at what suggested price, he was reminded of Leonora's lists, her cautious smiles and warm embraces. He hadn't thought of her like this for weeks—months.

Then *Tulip* sailed into another almighty storm. Gusting westerlies pushed her nearer and nearer the murderous, jagged coast. Angry waves lashed the decks and they lost a boy overboard. A deck hand slipped and fell, knocking himself unconscious. Men struggling to prevent cargo from shifting were injured in the hold. Torn rigging fell from the main mast. By the end of three consecutive days on alert, five men had been severely injured, and still the crew fought on hour by hour to hold the ship off the rocks.

"Can we put in to Vigo?" Ludo asked, dripping water over the pilot's charts.

"Best thing if we can. It won't be easy, though," the Spanish pilot responded.

"What's the alternative?"

"*Yo que sé, Patrón.* I'll try for Vigo if you like. It's home for me, so I know the worst of it."

With immense skill *Tulip*'s pilot navigated the narrow entrance to Vigo and Captain Guthrie gave the order to drop anchor in the most sheltered spot they could find. The storm raged for another twelve hours then the sun came out as it only can in Spain, and the crew woke to another world. Ludo sent word to Guthrie that he was to arrange work parties to repair the damage, but all men were to take turns in six-hour shore leaves, not a minute longer on pain of a flogging and being turned off without pay. The crew cheered and set to their tasks as the first pinnace set out for the quay with Ludo aboard.

Chapter 8

Vigo, Spain, March, 1640

The street was filthy, ankle deep in mud, muck and manure. Ludo, wearing leather boots cracked by storage in the heat of Goa then on board ship, slipped on the cobbles a third time and cursed the climate in particular and humanity in general. Before he had had time to locate a decent eating-house rain was once more lashing down, his cloak was soaked and his mood fouler than the weather. Opening a heavy door, he ducked under a low lintel and surveyed the interior of a gloomy but warm *mesón*. Enticed in by the delicious aromas of bean stew and fried chorizo, he searched for signs of a servant. When it became evident that no one was going to attend him, he removed his cape, spread it over an empty bench and swung himself onto the other side of the table beside the only small window. Tugging at his plain black waistcoat, which had become rather mildewed in the course of the voyage, he pulled out a large handkerchief and dried his neck, congratulating himself on opting for the more sober attire of a burger and not an expensive doublet, which would have been ruined.

Unasked, an unseen hand pushed a cup of wine onto his table with a wooden platter of salami and green peppers. A small girl—or perhaps a boy still in petticoats—scampered away out of sight. The wine was acid, but the peppers had been fried in good oil and tasted delicious. Ludo licked his fingers and looked around to order more. A young man, too well dressed to be a servant, entered the *mesón* at that moment and rushed to his table. "You're here, sir—thank goodness. I feared I'd missed you. The lady is waiting."

"Already!" Ludo laughed. "I've only just got here." Evidently surprised at the response, the young man stepped backwards. "Thank you, but I'd rather eat first," Ludo explained. The boy appeared confused, unsure what to say. Ludo tilted his head to one side and closed an eyelid. "Will she wait?"

"She has been waiting, *señor*, for over a week, I think. She is very anxious; she feared you would not come." The boy's voice was in the process of breaking but he spoke like an educated Castilian; he was certainly no Galician pot-boy or pimp.

Intrigued, and partly convinced he wasn't going to get a proper full meal for another hour at least, Ludo got to his feet. "Show me to her, boy, and I'll make my own arrangements."

Instead of taking the narrow staircase leading off the eating room as Ludo was expecting, the boy helped him into his cape then waited at the open door to the street. Ludo followed, loosening the small curved dagger he had acquired in Salalah from its ornate sheath at his waist. He never carried a sword, but small daggers, even fancy ones, were advisable in any port.

The boy stopped at the end of the street and peered around, apparently checking to see if they were being followed, then continued to the end of the next street and repeated the action.

Soaked again, Ludo put out a hand. "I don't know where you're leading me, boy, but I'm in no mood to be robbed in back alleys." He turned and strode back the way they had come.

"No!" the well-dressed young man called. "You must come. We've been waiting."

"It's 'we' now, is it?" Ludo muttered. "And who are 'we'?"

The boy peered round Ludo yet again. "My mistress's mistress couldn't come this time. She's in Santiago with..." He nodded his head frantically, "you know. So I came with my mistress. Please sir, there'll be hell to pay if you go back and they think I haven't done what I should... and my mistress will be in such trouble." The boy was in an agony of secrets and unspoken explanations.

Ludo motioned him on. "Oh, very well, just get me out of this rain."

They stopped at a pair of imposing iron gates. A gatekeeper draped in a waxed cloak cranked open the side gate, keeping his head down so the deluge dripped off the brim of his hat, and they entered the spacious courtyard of a three-storey mansion. Two men in dark green livery were on guard in the shallow porch over the main door but the messenger was given access without a word spoken. Ludo handed his cape to a bobbing, pink-cheeked maid and followed another up a wide staircase. The young man remained in the lower hall, watching him ascend, then he disappeared through a ground-floor doorway.

Ludo was shown into a large room that appeared far smaller for being entirely curtained in tapestries. The door was closed behind him, and when he turned he could not find it. As his eyes adjusted to the gloom, though, he detected an L-shaped cut among apple trees and a winding blue river crowded with swans and herons and fish. He'd been in a room like this before. Where? Then he remembered the family room at Crimphele in England and banished the memory.

As he walked towards the window, believing the room vacant, a woman's voice hailed him. She spoke in French. Ludo, surprised and disconcerted because he could see no one, replied without thinking in his native tongue. The woman responded in Tuscan Italian.

"*Dove sei?*" Ludo asked, swinging round to locate a rotund matron lifting herself from a seat camouflaged by a group of flaxen-haired maidens, fawns and a spotted-rump doe in a sunlit patch of forest. The doe's eyes were beguiling. Something about the sylvan glade in which she stood held Ludo entranced after so many months at sea.

"*Bene, bene, proseguiamo nella mia lingua,*" the woman said. "You are quite right; if we are overheard they will be less likely to follow our conversation, and a lot less suspicious. I told them I was expecting my nephew! *Allora*, I'm getting old and foolish, speaking French in Spain. Forgive me."

"*Madonna*, there is nothing to forgive."

"I haven't spoken to anyone except that stupid boy for days, and he hasn't a word of Tuscan, can barely manage French. It is many years now since I spoke with anyone other than—you know—in my own tongue. You're not from Tuscany, though..."

"Genoa, *madonna.*"

"Genoa? *Boh, fa niente.*" She gave a Latin shrug that shook her entire vast cleavage under its laced casing, then paused as if considering whether his origin being the State of Genoa and not Tuscany was indeed relevant. "Well, where you are from makes no matter where you are going; at least you are here now," she gushed. "My lady feared the storms might prevent you from arriving altogether. *Her mistress,*" the words were spoken with a knowing incline of the head, "suffers from a most dreadful *grippe* in Santiago. They were making a private pilgrimage to pray for another son. It's so sad—they die before they even cry... so very sad, and she's no longer young and there's only the one boy to... *My* lady's the third lady-in-waiting of the Royal Chamber, you understand, so I'm there to do the light sewing most days and we see it all. They think they are private but no one's private in Madrid, not even in that great palace." The woman stopped, panting a little for breath, then started again in a quieter manner, "Well, that's of no interest to you, but the fact is she is also unwell and that's why I am here to speak with you."

"My condolences and I hope your and *her mistress* recover soon," Ludo paced his words, trying to gauge what was going on.

The woman, who was indeed getting old, for she was wrinkled like a bed sheet beneath her old-fashioned headdress, dabbed a minute handkerchief at her dark eyes and moved towards Ludo. After examining him at closer quarters, she gave a short "Hah," of satisfaction—or perhaps resignation. Ludo could not tell.

"I was afraid you'd be English," she said.

Eyes sparkling with curiosity, Ludo turned on his most charming smile. "I'm on my way to England now, *madonna*."

"Of course you are. Why else are you here?" The dame held out a plump, be-ringed hand. "Do you have anything for Her...?" she opened both hands now in another purely Italian gesture and dropped her dainty handkerchief.

Ludo bent to retrieve it, then whispered, "I have some exquisite pearls."

"Pearls!" The dame's eyes flashed acquisitively. "Here?"

Ludo pulled a small pouch from an inner pocket. He had been carrying them on the off-chance of meeting a jeweller in the town—one never knew when an opportunity might present itself. Opening the pouch, he poured a few pearls onto the palm of his left hand. The old woman clapped her hands to her florid cheeks. Ludo smiled into her eyes and said, "Direct to you from the far distant Arabian Sea, from the land of the Icthyophagi."

"The Ichy-fagi! Imagine. *Allora!* Arabia! Let me have them!"

"These? Or the better ones?"

"Whatever you've got here—now."

"All of them?"

The woman narrowed her eyes. "You do know *who* they are for, don't you?"

Ludo transferred his pearls into the plump waiting hand. The matron stuffed them directly into a deep pocket among her ample skirts then from another, extracted a small package. "To be delivered as before," she whispered dramatically.

Now Ludo was a in a greater quandary. He turned to look out of the window, as if to see who might be outside, gathering his thoughts and trying to decide whether or not to tell the old woman she was making a mistake—possibly a very great mistake. Surreptitiously, he peeked at the package. It was wrapped in fine linen and tied with gold ribbon; he could see writing beneath the fabric but no name.

The old woman eased his dilemma by giving him no more time to think. She left the room, taking his pearls with her.

"*Maledizione! Idiota!*" Furious with himself, Ludo spat the words at a gentle maiden dipping her hand in an embroidered blue stream.

Staring around himself this way and that, seeking the hidden doorway, willing the old dame to reappear from among the flora and fauna crowding the walls, Ludo waited for her to return with his payment. She did not. He paced to the window and back to the centre of the room and stood looking at the empty chamois pouch hanging like a dead mouse in his left hand. After an angry moment or two he transferred his gaze to the curious package in his other hand. Then he began to laugh. When he stopped his stomach rumbled so loudly and insistently that he gave up waiting and finally exited the strange room between the third apple tree and the river.

Strolling back to the same eating house in a leisurely fashion despite the continuing rain—giving the boy time to catch up and rectify the case of mistaken identity—Ludo realised that nobody he'd spoken to actually had any idea who they were really expecting, and the real messenger, if he hadn't sunk, drowned or been captured as a foreign spy, was unlikely to find the house by himself when he did arrive anyway. The incident had cost him a considerable sum in pearls so he wasn't about to throw the package away. Whatever it contained, and he wasn't going to risk opening it until he was safely back aboard the *Tulip,* was going to have to work for him one way or another as recompense.

An hour later, slightly fuddled on local wine and content after a spicy stew, he began to socialise among the diners at his long trestle table then joined the drinkers at the bar in the now packed *mesón.* The city itself was heaving with men, he learned: reluctant recruits to the Spanish Flanders *tercios* and mariners of every age, colour and creed.

"What's going on?" Ludo asked a mean-looking soldier who'd survived some close combat, judging by the scars on his face.

"We're on our way to get killed in the Narrow Sea or in the *mierda de* Flanders again. Didn't you know? Not content with trying to drown the entire *jodido* army last year, that bastard Olivares—"

"The Count-Duke? The king's chief minister?"

"Keep your voice down—that's him, and he's got ears from here to the Vatican and back."

And don't I know it, Ludo thought. "What's he got to do with your being here?"

"What's he got to do with anything and every *maldita cosa* in this country? He's sending more *tercios* to the Low Countries —to shore up the walls with dead bodies because the French are at us again—and because the Portuguese over there..." he pointed a shaky finger in the rough direction of Oporto, "are fed up with him and want their own king back. And frankly, when you look at the whole fucking mess Felipe and fucking great House of Habsburg have made of Spain, can you blame them? Naturally it's another 'great big secret', like the fuck-up in the Narrow Sea last year, so everybody's talking about it. Those idiots in Madrid don't know when they're beat. I mean, what sort of king or minister or whoever is supposed to be in charge of this fucking dump of a country lets thousands of men drown then has another go to see if he can drown the rest? I heard it was fourteen thousand what went down because of the Frenchies' ships, but I says, 'No, there aren't that many of us left with two arms and two legs in the whole of Castile'—and that was last year. *Cretinos!* You'd honestly think he'd give up with the Dutch once and for all after that, but no, we poor devils are off to fight more losing battles—if we can dodge the fucking French along the way. Somebody should shoot him, I tell you! Get me to Madrid and I'll do it meself." The soldier stopped, looked around, then sniffed and started again in a lower voice, "Some do say we're going to invade France on the way. Wouldn't surprise me; only thing that surprises me these days is that my belly hasn't got holes in it like a colander."

"Another drink, then, my friend, to test for leaks?" Ludo said affably, then slipped away to get back to the *Tulip* as soon as possible. Guthrie needed to round up their crew and get her out of Vigo on the first tide: Spanish troop ships always needed seamen, and they weren't fastidious about how they got them. If

Tulip didn't sail fast, her crew's shore leave would terminate in a damp lock-up, then a long, unpaid one-way trip to Flanders.

Back on board, safe and warm in his freshly cleaned cabin, Ludo placed the curious package he'd been given by the Tuscan *nonna* on his galley table. Breaking the seal took a matter of seconds with a sharp razor over a stub of candle.

The package contained one wide sheet of carefully folded, thick paper. It was a letter. In French. In a cramped but elegant and faultless hand—suggesting the writer was accustomed to penning secret missives—the letter said:

> *My dearest Sister,*
>
> *I wish you greetings and hope you continue to enjoy robust health. I am making a pilgrimage to Santiago to pray again for safe delivery of a healthy son. May God grant this boon, for I cannot bear the loss of another dear baby. Balthasar continues to thrive, thanks be to God, but my Husband grows more anxious because he has but one boy.*
>
> *Forgive me, sister, I should not dwell on my tragedies for I have other important news that I beg you to act upon, if only for the sake of your loving Sister. That I must suffer the loss of my children is a sad matter, but I can honestly say what grieves me more is the enmity of our brother. Did we not celebrate two matrimonies between our houses to bring peace for Spain and France? My heart goes out to dear Ana in Paris, how she must suffer. I blame the C-D entirely and as F will not stand up to him, I must. It is the C-D's policy—and all to gain but one small portion of French soil. He <u>must</u> be stopped before in the process of*

pursuing this foolish war Balthasar loses his <u>entire inheritance</u>. Furthermore, my Husband's land is being impoverished on this aging man's whim. You and I both know that if Louis wins against F, there will be nothing left for my Prince! So I have come to an important decision, but for this I need your help.

Please, Marietta, I beg of you, act on my <u>previous</u> request. Send me someone trustworthy. I speak of an agent upon whom we can rely for total discretion. I will arrange his entry into the Alcazar and the means of his leaving thereafter. I have no one here I can rely on so it must be an outsider to this place. Please, Sister, help me. I have no one to turn to. The C-D's odious wife watches my every move (I believe she would remain awake during the night to report on my dreams if she could) so I cannot instigate any action here, but if <u>you</u> could send me a foreigner who is already primed to be utterly vigilant and report <u>only to me</u> then I believe I can oust my enemy and save my son's future.

It is no small enterprise, but I have begged and begged F to <u>be rid of</u> the C-D. He says I do not understand matters of state and we cannot be without his 'wise counsel'. This is nonsense! F will see this when the hated being is gone forever. Only in this manner will my dear Husband start to listen to me and take action himself to bring peace. He has been so misguided.

Remember how your life improved with Buckingham gone. Once my hated Enemy is gone from our midst, I promise, as I have before, we will do all in our power to bring <u>your</u> husband's country back to Rome (as Maman demanded of you, did she not?). We *have access to the wealth of the New World; we can send you financial support. But first, we must be rid of this bloated madman F relies on so greatly.*

On other matters, I hear from Maman she has quit Holland and resides with you. Beware, Marietta, she can cause trouble in so many ways. I assume she is also out of funds (again). It is the greatest pity Maman could not prevent Luis from renewing the war. But for that she could be in Madrid with us. I do not say 'living in peace', for dearest Maman creates battles of her own wherever she be. Persuade her if you can to return to Tuscany—for your own tranquillity.

Marietta, send me someone soon for both our sakes. I see our brother of France taking my Son's throne from beneath him! Helped by my Enemy here. Please give each of your children a kiss from the aunt they have never met.

Oh that we could be together again.

As ever your loving sister, E

Ludo gulped a tot of rough Spanish brandy in one swig, gasping when it hit his throat. Then, with a slightly shaking hand, for the content of the crowded paper had unnerved him, he lifted the letter to his candle flame—and snatched it away again. He knew he should burn it—immediately. If it got into the wrong hands—and it was already in the wrong hands... The F—the Husband—could only be King Felipe of Spain. And the C-D could only be the Count-Duke de Olivares, who wouldn't waste a snap of the fingers on breaking his neck if he got wind of it.

Although... Ludo leaned back in his chair, taking his time with his reasoning, there could be untold benefits... not that he was going to provide the Queen of Spain with a paid assassin, if that was what '*débarrasser*' signified in the context. To 'be rid of him'—rid of Olivares, though, could also be both interpreted *and* instigated in various ways.

But did he want to be involved, tempting as it was? And if he were to go to the Queen's aid, would it be worth it? What might he demand as his reward? Musing on possibilities, Ludo suddenly remembered the loud-mouthed soldier in the eating house and laughed at the irony: the queen and the common man in perfect accord.

Slowly, he read through the letter a third time, translating the French into his mother tongue and deciphering its true meaning in his head. The writer could only be the sad but reportedly competent and intelligent Queen Isabel of Spain, known previously as Elisabeth of France. The recipient had to be Henrietta Maria, otherwise known as Queen Mary of England, loyal wife to King Charles Stuart, and a loyal Catholic in a Protestant nation. Their mother was the famously ill-tempered Marie de Medici; daughter of a Tuscan banker and a Palatine Habsburg princess—mother also to the King of France. The Ana mentioned was the King of Spain's sister.

Four queens! A winning hand—if he knew the game.

Except the game was clear enough—to defeat the noxious, conniving but nonetheless astute Conde-Duque de Olivares. It did not surprise him, and not only because of what the soldier had been spouting. Had he not had first-hand experience of Olivares' conspiracies himself in expediting the nasty financial scandal that had ruined good men and caused more suffering that he cared to remember in Holland? All managed at a distance by the infamous Count-Duke in cahoots with a Vatican cardinal, and overseen on the ground by an evil-minded priest from Rome named Rogelio.

He had not seen Queen Isabel when he'd been in Madrid at Olivares' request, but he knew all about the king's reliance on his *valido* and chief minister: the over-insistence in the letter was probably justified. And he wasn't unsympathetic to the queen's reasoning; the prince, the king's only son, Balthasar, could very likely lose his inheritance if war with France was prolonged—and France won. Not that he, Ludo da Portovenere, Genoese merchant with a lucrative new business in the East, cared one way or the other, really.

... But then again, the Genoese played an important role in Spanish financial matters... and if he laid claim to his mother's name...

The seed of an idea that had been sown by the foolish Solis cousins in an Indian spice warehouse started to germinate.

Taking advantage of the letter was a means of improving his social status. And if he were to become valued by Queen Isabel... or by King Felipe himself—which could be managed—that would make him untouchable by the Vatican agent Rogelio, *and* enable him to keep the *Tulip* forever. Indeed, it was almost worth playing this hand of queens to improve his social position alone. Not that he wanted a title or even lands, for the obligation that came with them were not at all to his liking—but obtaining the respect of monarchs and the right to pass through palaces would annoy his mother's family beyond measure.

Gazing at the flames of hell in the humble candlestick on his table, Ludo's calculating mind began fashioning a plan. *There is a way here to make myself necessary to not one but two royal houses via the daughters of Marie de Medici...* The thought led him back to the unspoken name-dropping of the buxom Tuscan servant. She was old enough to have been in Marie de Medici's Florentine household, had probably travelled to France with her 'mistress', then transferred to the French princess's retinue when Elisabeth of France became Queen Isabel of Spain. Ludo drew on what he knew from his visits to Florence and what he knew about the Medici family, pulling in random bits of gossip he'd picked up over the years. The Tuscan heiress, Marie de Medici, had become Queen of France, then very soon the dowager queen, acting as regent for her infant son Luis and in constant argument with the French Chief Minister, Richelieu. Marie de Medici's own mother had been a Habsburg Catholic, so the cause of tension was almost certainly the French anti-Habsburg campaigns. Marie de Medici was said to be a harridan of the first order. What a royal rigmarole.

José, his cabin boy, came in to turn down his bed and made to re-fill his glass but was waved away. Then Ludo called him back. "José, where are you from?"

The boy brushed his mop of black hair off his face. Brown from his months in the sun and a competent young seaman, he often reminded Ludo of someone, but he was never quite certain who.

"My family live near Oporto, sir," José replied. "It's a small village, but the captain took me on in Goa, sir."

"How old were you when you went out to Goa?"

"Eleven, sir. I'm fourteen now."

"Do you not want to go back to your village? You should have said. I could have made arrangements for you to sail on *la Magdalena*. You could have asked to sign off in Vigo and got a ship round the coast."

The boy wrinkled his nose and brow. "I'm not sure as I'd be welcome, *patrón*. My mother married again, after my father went to sea—he was an officer of the quarter-deck on a ship for New Spain, only he didn't come back—and she's got little ones now and—"

"You'll be another mouth to feed, and maybe an awkward reminder to the new husband." Ludo reached out and patted the boy's thin arm.

"That's the way of it, sir. We'll never go hungry, my mother being a de Souza, but after my father died—he was much older than her—she married again and my new father arranged for me to go to sea in the *carreira da Índia* trade."

"I know the story. I know a young man called Marcos with a similar tale, too, and he's done very well for himself. Let's see if I can do the same for you. We'd better start feeding you up, though, or you'll slip through the scuppers. Do you not eat the leftovers from here on top of your rations?"

"Can I?"

"Of course you can. What have you been doing all these months?"

"Feeding the baby goats and cats, sir," José's voice was a whisper.

"Well stop feeding them and remind me to arrange for you to receive better rations. Did you get a chance to buy anything on your shore leave?"

"I couldn't go, sir. There wasn't time and I had to clean your cabin, and then we sailed again before..."

Ludo pulled a face, feeling guilty. "No, that is a pity, but it was for the greater good, as they say." The boy blinked, uncomprehending. "Never mind. Listen, if you're not anxious to go home, would you stay with me? I'll be needing a servant I can trust when we get to Plymouth."

The boy's eyes lit up. "Thank you, sir. I'll do it gladly. Can you tell me where we'll be going after Plymouth? Will it be straight back to Goa?"

"I haven't made up my mind yet. We'll be in Plymouth a few weeks, months maybe. *Tulip* needs to go into dry dock for a thorough refit. Once I've sold my cargo I may go upriver to a house I know... Actually, no, I'll be travelling on to London. I'm not entirely decided, but stay with me for another quarter and I'll see you right if you sign off, and even if you don't." Ludo smiled and the boy blushed like a girl. "Off you go, then. I shan't need you again tonight."

The boy, who also needed new clothes, scampered out of the door.

"History repeats itself," Ludo muttered to himself. Except his own home background had been nowhere near as straightforward as he suspected José's was. Pouring another measure of brandy, Ludo tried to banish unwanted memories of another boy who had gone to sea because of a new step-father, but seeing it now from a different perspective he wondered if his mother hadn't been trying to do her best for him—sending him off to live the life of a pirate instead of a having to survive in a hostile home as a child of shame.

Another idea flickered round the edges of his mind. *If I claim my mother's Doria name and do business using that name...* The idea flickered out. A decision regarding the paper on his table had to be made first: his vendetta could wait.

Ludo stared at the queen's words again. If—when—she discovered her letter had not gone with the regular courier, and she found where it had gone, he was as good as dead. If he divulged any of the contents there would be a monumental scandal, or worse. If he revealed how Spain would help Britain become a Catholic kingdom once more, it could even lead to a full-scale war. In each scenario lay his demise. Dare he risk delivering it in person to Henrietta Maria, Queen of England?

Yes! Because, treated carefully, this letter is worth far, far more than the pearls it cost me... Thinking of the pearls reminded him of a large ruby. Reaching into his secret shirt pocket with his forefinger and thumb, Ludo da Portovenere pulled out a perfect red plum.

"*Rani Saahasi*," he said to himself. "Queen of Courage—there has to be a connection here."

Part Two
England

Chapter 9

Plymouth, England, April 1640

By coincidence, for he had no way of knowing the *Tulip* had sailed into Plymouth Sound, Marcos was on the Barbican speaking with other importers when Ludo's pinnace moored alongside the merchants' quay. Marcos gaped in surprise and a good deal of relief. The odds against surviving the voyage to India and back to English waters were reckoned one in three.

The two men stood and looked at each other for a second, then joined in a bear hug.

"You made it!" Marcos said, clapping Ludo on the back in the Spanish style and trying to disguise the catch in his throat. "You old devil, you made it!"

Ludo stood back and gave his lopsided grin. "Take more than Neptune to sink old Ludo. You've grown—no, sorry..." Ludo tried to retract his words.

"Sorry? For what? Ah, because young Marcos is no longer a boy to be teased." Marcos laughed. "No, indeed, no more teasing. I've a servant of my own now, although he's more of a clerk. He's in my office as we speak."

"In *your* office? Doing your accounts, is he?" Ludo cocked his head.

Marcos smiled bashfully, knowing it was a deliberate reference to the uneasy relationship he'd had with Ludo in Holland. To divert the conversation he said, "Did you manage to find the spices I told you about?"

"Yes, and far more. Take me to the Old Ship Inn and I'll tell you what I've got on board for you. Oh, and I've got these—there's more in the hold." Ludo handed Marcos a brightly coloured drawstring bag. "Careful, don't open it here—it's your seeds of paradise."

"They exist, then! I must try them immediately."

"Well, use them sparingly! They're not easy to acquire, believe me. I got them in Salé, in the end. This is something we need to discuss—if the Dutch continue the way they are going in the East you might be better off buying your goods in the Canaries and Morocco, and dealing with merchants there yourself."

"The Dutch—in the East? Oh, the VOC, I remember. Have they been giving you problems? What for now?"

"The VOC and their blasted navy—the Dutch are everywhere. Must be because there's no room left on their godforsaken lump of mud. We had to sail right under their noses and steal the cinnamon in Ceylon for you—although it was the owner's by rights. Then we had to avoid them to get out of Goa. They nearly caught us—far too close for my liking. Then the devils were sitting in the Gulf of Hormuz and we had to change course altogether."

Marcos grabbed Ludo's arm. "I never asked you to put yourself in danger. What happened?"

"Ah, adventures, adventures! I nearly ended up buying horses."

"Horses? You?"

"I know, but they were very pretty. It's a long story. Come on, I need to book a room."

There was no possibility of conversing more as they walked, the quayside and alleys of the Barbican being crowded with merchants' runners, costermongers' barrows, women gutting fish, women selling pies, women selling themselves, brick-makers' kilns and carpenters' saw-horses, and bevies of apprentices of all trades shirking round braziers. Once inside the higgledy-piggledy inn, Ludo pushed through the crowded dining room and got them seated in a relatively quiet booth. Marcos immediately began to quiz him about his 'adventures' and what he had seen on the other side of the world. Ludo told him of the sights, the sounds, and the amazing amalgam of odours in a spice godown, of strange upside down trees with roots in the air, of hairy monkeys and hooded snakes, and rainbow-coloured colonial houses, and, finally, the way Portuguese merchants were tied to the Spanish monarch through crippling licences.

Eventually Ludo leaned back and cast around him. "Some things don't change, though. This place is always crowded. It must be worth a fortune. Now, where was I? Ah yes, I've brought you the bark called cassia you wanted to try as well. They tell me it is cruder in flavour as compared to the cinnamon, but it's cheaper, in Goa at least—while you can get it. You can tell the difference between cassia and cinnamon by the way the bark rolls: if it looks like a scroll rolled into itself then it's cinnamon; if it is rolled like a document it is cassia. As I said, the Dutch have as good as taken over Ceylon and are strangling Goa so you might want to explore getting cassia elsewhere, too, unless you can buy it off the English East-Indiamen coming into Plymouth."

"I've been buying in some goods from the East India Company. They've got a monopoly licence from the Crown, but we can get some goods direct from them—with the right contacts. A group of us were discussing it last week, in fact. Some of my acquaintances want to invest in a voyage to the East, but I haven't got the funds for that." Marcos paused and looked at Ludo, "You're talking as if you are not going back?"

Ludo gave a light shrug. "We'll see. How's your juniper berry drink coming along? With the spices I've brought you can start bulk production. Assuming you've found the perfect recipe."

"A good recipe, but not perfect, not yet. I've been experimenting with different proportions of coriander and liquorice, which I can get here without much trouble. It's still not much like the Dutch drink, but that might be because of the water here, or the distilled grain I've been using."

"You haven't started selling it yet?"

"Some, yes. Finding the right bottles at a sensible price wasn't easy, but that's rectified now. In fact, if you go up to the bar here and ask for a tot of Almond gin you can try it."

"Almond?"

"My surname is Alonso Almendro—an *almendro* is an almond tree. Trying to do business in England with a Spanish name is not very wise. Especially in the Plymouth area: home to that great hero and murdering pirate, Francis Drake."

"Bit misleading for the drink, though. Do you put almonds in the mix?"

"No! But people here call me Marcus Almond or Mark Almond so—" Marcos put a hand to his mouth and closed his eyes then whispered, "We'd better speak English or keep our voices down. You warned us about speaking Spanish here once, remember? Nothing much has changed in that, either. There's still a good deal of suspicion and ill feeling about Catholics. It's come to the fore of late because of the king's Catholic French wife. People say the king's spending all our taxes building new churches in London so she can attend a papist Mass wherever the fancy takes her. And she's an almighty spendthrift herself—apparently has galas and masques everyday at the palace and twenty-five meat servings at every meal. Ordinary working people get taxed extra for farting these days, *and* we're fined if we don't go to a Protestant church on a Sunday. Whether it's all true or not, I don't know—I doubt it—but there's a lot of ill feeling and tension right now, that's for sure. I do sometimes wonder if I did right staying here, perhaps I should have come with you."

"You don't see her then?"

Marcos immediately knew who—and why Ludo had asked an apparently irrelevant question: he wasn't referring to a queen in a palace a week's coach journey away but to another Catholic foreign wife much closer at hand. The original reason Marcos had stayed in Plymouth.

"No. I haven't seen her since I left Crimphele and came here," Marcos said, looking away.

"Ah, well, that's women for you. She was married anyway. Not that he looked like he'd last long. Mind you that type—the pale, weedy ones—are a tenacious lot. What about that tiresome priest, Hawthorne?"

"I did see him, last year. He's become the little boy's tutor and thrilled about it. Thomas returned to the court and left him in charge of the boy at Crimphele."

The unspoken name of Alina, otherwise known as Maria de los Angeles Santoña Gómez and various other noble *apellidos*, or Lady Fulford, wife of the sickly Sir Thomas Fulford of Crimphele in Cornwall, hung in the air between them.

Marcos briefly revisited a moment when her presence and vibrant personality had marked him for life, but he had no wish to discuss her. A flustered serving girl conveniently interrupted his unwanted thoughts, plonking a jug of warm ale and two mugs on their table. She had gone before he could order any food.

Ludo smacked the table with annoyance. "Get her back before I faint," he said, lifting his nose like a hound to follow the scent of a tureen being carried to a nearby booth. Then he turned back to Marcos, "What did you say about the meals in the palace?"

"Some of the wine merchants I supply have contacts in London. They were telling me about how deals are made to sell the food and wine that goes back *untouched* to the royal kitchens. Whole sides of ham, entire roast suckling pigs, complete jelly desserts, not to mention all the cakes and puddings. According to some it's a disgrace, but there are others who've created a nice bit of business selling the leftovers through shops and alehouses."

Ludo beamed and tapped the table with a forefinger.

"What?" demanded Marcos. "I've seen that look before, and always before some mischief."

"*Allora*, Marcos, what are you saying? Don't you respect my business ventures?"

"No."

"Well you should, because otherwise you'd not be sitting at this table wearing silver buckles and telling me what goes on in a palace in London, England. Who suggested setting up a wine import business with your home town in Spain, hmm, hmm?"

"Me, actually. I started planning it before we *disembarked* in Flushing, if you want to know. See, I've learned the lingo as well."

Another serving girl passed tantalisingly near their table with trenchers of crisp bacon then disappeared. "Six months at sea and I die of starvation in an English eating house," Ludo moaned. Then he leaned in closer. "Your wine business is doing all right, is it?"

"It was slow going at first. I went back to Sanlúcar and arranged for dry sherry and *oloroso* and good brandy to be shipped directly to my warehouse. The dry sherry didn't travel well and it was really hard to sell to start with—cost me a lot of my savings, but I'm doing pretty well now. I don't get much trouble from competition, even those who know I'm Spanish." Marcos grinned. "I've made out I'm Dutch a couple of times to get out of a sticky situation; helps not having black hair and being able to speak with Amsterdam traders in their own tongue. Not that I'm interested in buying, selling or dying wool."

"There, you see. I did you a favour taking you to Holland."

"Yes, and I thank you for that. Not for nearly getting me killed by drowning or cannon fire, nor for nearly getting me lynched, but, yes, for the rest I am grateful." Marcos cast Ludo a quick glance. "Have they given up trying to find you?"

Ludo pulled a face. "Why do you think I sailed east?" He drummed his fingers on the table then added, "I thought getting to Cathay would solve my problem, but I only got as far as Goa, and that, as you know, is a Portuguese trading post—and guess who's there? The Inquisition. So, no, I doubt they have given up, and I wouldn't be at all surprised if they haven't followed me all the way there and back again. I'd have to go to the moon to lose Fra Rogelio... In fact, now I think about it, this is probably part of his sinister little game: keeping me looking over my shoulder, never being sure if or when he'll get close enough to have me assassinated for knowing too much, even when nobody cares about *what* I know. His sort are sick in the head. Never cross a man who finds pleasure in…"

Another serving girl passed within reach and Marcos grabbed her arm. "Bring us two plates of pie, any pie—just bring it."

Once she was gone, Ludo leaned against the high backed seat and said in English, "Changing the subject back to more pleasant matters, how do you plan to extend your wine business?"

"I need to make it pay better before I can even think about that. Why? Any suggestions?"

"Yes. Royal patronage."

Marcos laughed, "Where do you get your ideas from?"

Ludo winked and leaned forward with a conspiratorial air. Slipping back into Spanish, he said, "You import good wine from Andalucía, why not sell it where people will appreciate it? This ale…" He flicked a hand towards the jug on their table in a gesture of dismissal. "Men who drink this don't know the difference between *fino*, sack and grappa—you're wasted down here in a provincial port. Why not move to London and trade with the palaces, where people will appreciate you?"

"I am trying to perfect the Dutch drink, remember?" Marcos said. "What you're talking about is called a 'royal warrant', and you have to pay for the privilege of selling to royal households. Apart from finding the money for the fee, I personally don't have those contacts."

"You just said you did."

"I was repeating hearsay. What's really behind this idea, anyway?"

Ludo once again closed a black-lashed, sea-green eye and cocked his head to one side.

"Oh, no," Marcos sighed. "Why need I be involved?"

"Because it will make your fortune and you can live like a lord on the money we make. Better than a lord, if that *patetico* Sir Thomas at Crimphele is anything to go by. You can be a lord yourself and win a fair milady if you fancy it."

"No. In that respect you are wrong. We can get rich; we can have big houses and servants for every room, but in England as in Spain being rich doesn't make you a lord. A tradesman is a tradesman, be he rich or poor. And tradesmen do not win the hearts of fair 'miladies'—ever."

"Shame."

Two plates of steaming chicken and rabbit pie finally arrived. As they ate, Marcos said, "Tell me more about your cargo. We need to get to work on unloading, I can't be sitting here all day."

"Understood; me neither. Do they still have the salon upstairs for transactions?" Marcos nodded.

"Good, it'll be quieter up there. You need to tell me exactly what you want and—"

"At what prices."

Ludo's thick black eyebrows shot up. "You did learn well in Holland."

"I had a good tutor. Please continue."

"We'll start on your goods first, then what's only for me to sell. I've got most of that in special boxes, what the Portuguese in Goa call *bizalho*."

"Like that little sea-chest you carried around with you in Holland?"

"Similar—the contents are no less precious."

Marcos eyed him suspiciously. "What, for example?"

"Pearls and diamonds, some sapphires and rubies," Ludo whispered. "I've got musk for perfume in one."

"That's worth a fortune."

"I know." Ludo grinned.

"I'll arrange to get the unloading done as soon as I get back to our yard—that's if you still want me to act as your agent?" Marcos said more slowly, "Which I will gladly do, *patrón*, on a ten per cent basis and a negotiable portion in whatever future transactions you're hatching in these *bizalho* boxes."

"Hmm," grunted Ludo, "I was expecting something like that when I saw your silver buckles. That hasn't changed; you're still a fancy dresser, which is all to the good. You do have the look of a 'Supplier of Exotic Spices to their Royal Majesties'."

"Why are you so intent on a royal warrant? Where's all this coming from?" Marcos asked.

Ludo shrugged. "Let's say I have a fancy to meet a monarch. I'll let you think up your own title if we can get a warrant. You can make a pennant to go with it. Five."

Ignoring the jibe about his invented heraldry and the make-do pennant he'd created when he was an ambitious boy in Spain, Marcos cocked his head to one side, mimicking Ludo so perfectly the wily Genoese merchant burst out laughing. "Eight."

They settled at seven per cent.

Later, sitting in the salon above, Marcos said, "These plans to supply the royal palace—I'm not saying it's impossible, but there are two big questions we need to address before—*if*—we do anything."

"Go on."

"One relates to actually getting paid for the goods we supply, and the second relates to how we get those goods, if you're thinking of sticking with tea and spices. Firstly, the aristocracy never pay anybody if they can help it, so it's wiser to sell from a warehouse to a retailer, in my opinion. If *he* defaults you can cause him all manner of problems, but not the aristocrat on the receiving end. Secondly, you've been telling me that trade with the East is being taken over by the Dutch so we might as well buy from the VOC in Amsterdam or off the ships that put in here, *or* off the English traders that put in. You don't need to risk going back to sea. You don't seem too keen on it anyway. If you want to make it more exciting, invest in the English East India Company, that's already got a royal monopoly for the rich-trades. That's if they'll let you, of course."

"Hmm..." Ludo made a face. "I don't much like working for or with other people."

"It has its advantages. I've benefited a lot from working with Mr Beale here. I've learned a lot about how things are done and he's put business my way and I've even..." Marcos trailed off, feeling this was not the moment to tell Ludo about all the changes in his private life.

"Mr Beale? You already have a partner?" Ludo queried.

"No, he's more of a... I don't work with him as a partner, but I do work for him, if you see what I mean? Like I have done and will do with you. More or less. About the royal warrant," Marcos added quickly, changing the subject, "it's a good idea, I suppose, if you can afford the fees, but I don't think in the long run it's within my reach."

"There's a small issue I haven't quite explained," Ludo said quietly.

"I thought there might be."

"Getting a warrant to bring goods from the East into England—getting a royal licence or warrant or charter or whatever they call it would help my... someone I know. It would solve her problems."

"Her?"

"Yes: her."

Surprised at Ludo's defensive tone, Marcos waited a few moments, then said, "Let's go to my warehouse. You can tell me how you think your goods should be stored. Then come home with me and meet my wife Joanna."

Ludo stopped eating and stared at Marcos. "Now you have surprised me!"

Chapter 10

After leaving the inn, Marcos led Ludo through a labyrinth of narrow lanes to a newer residential area and the gate of an impressive three-storey house, notable for a vast quantity of decorated woodwork around tall glass windows. Instead of entering through the front door, however, they passed into a large cobbled back yard.

"Well done," Ludo said, appreciatively, "stables as well."

"Not mine, unfortunately," Marcos replied. "My father-in-law deals in wool, and other goods from Holland, depending what he can buy low and sell high. I help him with transactions sometimes as I speak Dutch. He also runs a haulage business—hence the stables. There's another yard down the road where he keeps the carts and wagons and more horses."

"Does he send goods to London?"

"Yes, but they go by sea."

"And this is all Mr Beale's house and business?"

"The business is Beale's and Son, but the son died last year; that may be why he allowed Joanna to marry me."

"Ah, so you're the son-in-law. I see." Ludo's eyes twinkled.

"No, it's not like that. Joanna is lovely. I mean, I married her because of her, not the business."

"No, of course, not."

Refusing to be drawn into Ludo's teasing, Marcos said, "I'll introduce you to Mr Beale. He's always looking for opportunities—like you."

Ludo nodded thoughtfully then, putting an arm around Marcos's shoulders, he directed him back out of the yard onto the street, saying in a low voice, "If I make over part of my cargo to you, with further cargoes to come, could you keep it entirely in the family?"

"Depends what goods we're talking about and *how* we sell them. If you mean can I find the buyers and do the selling, and leave Mr Beale to arrange distribution, I'd be very interested, especially if it's an annual import of—what?—spices, silk, tea?"

Ludo squeezed his shoulder. "Done! That gets us out of Portuguese obligations very nicely." Marcos gave him an enquiring look, but all Ludo said was, "I'll explain later."

They wandered back into the courtyard and through a side entrance, into Edward Beale's fine new house. As they stepped across the threshold a very pretty young woman with fair hair and big blue eyes emerged from a door, laughing at something someone had said or done.

"Oh!" she squeaked with surprise, then composed herself and waited for Marcos to introduce her.

Grabbing her delicate hand, he pulled her towards him, saying in English, "Here is an old friend, my dear, come to meet you."

The girl bobbed a curtsey. "Joanna Almond," she said. "Pleased to meet you, sir."

"Ludovico di Doria da Portovenere," Ludo replied, sweeping his old leather hat with its long plumes to the tiled floor.

Watching Ludo play his charm over his little wife, Marcos opened a door behind her. "This is the family hall; Mrs Beale will join us soon, no doubt."

Ludo followed Joanna into the room and cast an appreciative eye over the furniture and fittings. The entire room was panelled in fine wood and there was a marble fireplace.

Looking at a substantial sideboard then the shelves of a matching dresser, Ludo asked, "Is this Dutch Delft-ware?"

"Yes, they love it here," Marcos replied, watching his wife's pink face as she in turn studied Ludo. Stepping between them, he said, "I was going to tell you about how I met Joanna—I came into the kitchen one day and she was trying to catch a kitten under a table full of jams and chutneys and bumped her head..."

"A kitten," Ludo turned back to Joanna with the full focus of his charm. "Of course, little kittens, what else!"

Standing on the quayside next day with his wife, as laden skiffs brought the exotic East from the *Tulip* anchored out in Plymouth Sound to his humble warehouse, Marcos wondered how Ludo and Edward Beale were going to get along. Or, more to the point, who was going to get the upper hand. He had sketched out Ludo's proposal regarding royal warrants to his father-in-law over supper, and to his surprise Beale had looked favourably on the enterprise. But Marcos had his doubts, although he couldn't name why.

Ludo, dressed in his sober burger's outfit of black arrived in a pinnace and Marcos took him directly to Edward Beale's office, newly built in his stable block. The office was lined with shelves bearing ledgers, and a clerk sitting on a high stool at a lectern was in the process of recording invoice payments into a weighty ledger. Edward Beale himself was writing out bills in a florid hand that matched his florid cheeks, the face of a jovial tippler, given the lie by bulging leg muscles showing through plain stockings, and the span of his workman's hands, which would give a lesser man pause. Marcos knew him to be an astute man of business, and sat back to watch as Ludo was introduced.

Beale opened the meeting with a surprising tactic, by showing willing yet putting Ludo on the spot immediately. "This proposal, sir, to supply luxury goods to royal houses—it's an interesting proposition. What commodities specifically do you have in mind, taking into consideration that once we have obtained said warrant or warrants, we are then obliged thereafter to supply said goods on an annual or six-monthly or even a monthly basis? Be honest, sir, for I do know cargoes from the East are subject to loss and therefore impossible to guarantee."

Ludo nodded, taking Beale's measure, and said, "They are, for which I may have to obtain partners in my venture, who will of course obtain a relevant percentage in the proceeds. This will ensure my galleon is always in prime condition for her voyages with an experienced and willing crew. That in itself does not come cheap. If the venture proves worthwhile, after two years I will invest in a third ship."

"Third?" Beale queried, "I thought you'd only got the one."

"Ah, no, I have a fine carrack in dry dock in Vigo. My lady wife also has connections to shipmasters with vessels in Goa. Her late father's business is extremely sound, importing goods from Cathay and Malaka, and producing their own spice crops for export. The firm Gasca Figaroa can supply all manner of exotic goods from cinnamon and pepper to musk-oil and dyestuffs. I personally oversee the valuing and purchase of the precious gems, pearls and the like. In fact I was able to close a significant deal for the future supply of exquisite pearls on this very voyage."

Somewhat to Marcos's disappointment, Beale soon fell prey to the Genoese merchant's charm and enthusiasm. The new plan was that they—the three of them—should supply King Charles and his queen with whatever they could: spices, gem stones, pearls... whatever the office that issued these warrants deemed necessary.

Before closing the matter, Beale turned to Marcos and said, "How will all this square with the English East India Company, eh? Will we be in competition with them? They have a royal monopoly dating back to the last days of Good Queen Bess."

"I don't know," Marcos replied, "and that's the truth. I can find out."

Ludo raised a hand. "This matters not, Mr Beale. I am a merchant of Genoa. An established and successful merchant of Genoa, I have traded with the Low Countries in competition with the great VOC. I have my ways of getting round monopolies. Being an individual helps, and being of the State of Genoa, bankers to many good companies, not to mention the crown of Spain, helps."

"But you won't be *an individual,* sir," Beale remonstrated, "you must count us in—or me, at least, if young Marcos decides he can't risk his income on such a grand scheme."

Marcos grasped his forehead as if his head hurt: the old devil had done it again, wrapping him into a potentially highly lucrative business, but full of all manner of financial dangers and inconveniences.

Oblivious to his fears, Ludo leaned back in his chair and, taking his time, said, "Please, don't worry, Mr Beale. I will find a way and we shall all three enjoy the rewards."

And Marcos's heart sank with the weight of his new dilemma: to take the risk with Ludo and very probably become wealthy—very wealthy—in the process, or hold what he had in his hand, covet his wife and security and stay exactly as he was now. The young Marcos, the lad with the pennant made from a girl's petticoat, had grown up.

After Ludo had returned to the quay, this time accompanied by Mr Beale, Joanna squeezed Marcos's arm. "He's very charming, your friend," she said.

"Mm," Marcos replied, "but he's making too much of an effort. He's lost a lot of his bounce."

"Bounce? How can a grown man have bounce?"

"I know what I mean."

"But does it matter, if you're going to be doing business with royalty? Oh, Markie, it's all so grand!"

"It is, and that's what worries me. What does he want to go to London for when he can do as much business as he likes here in Plymouth or up in Bristol? Why this sudden interest in trading with *palaces*?"

"What's wrong with that? I think it's wonderful."

Marcos blew through his cheeks. "It'll tie us to your precious 'royalty', that's why. We've got enough problems here, Jo-jo, hiding our religion. It might not end well for us."

"But his family provide loans for the Spanish king—he said so. Where's the problem?"

"He said that, didn't he?" Marcos remembered Ludo introducing himself—for the first time in his hearing—as Ludovico *di Doria* da Portovenere, then the mentioning in his off-hand-but-remember-this manner that the Doria were bankers to the Spanish crown. "Who knows, it could even be true." Marcos stared momentarily at the cornucopia carved into the mantelpiece across the room then he said, "I'd better find out exactly who and what *the Doria* are. And if they really exist."

Chapter 11

Palace of Whitehall, London, May 1640

Ludo asked the wherryman to stop rowing, and the small Thames boat bobbed on the choppy water. Sitting very still, he examined the vast walls of Whitehall and its many roofs and chimneys, then said in an unusually dour voice, "I was not expecting so large a—what would you call it? It's more than a palace, more of a town."

Marcos nodded but said nothing: it wasn't what he had been expecting either.

"We may have more trouble finding who we need to speak to than I anticipated. It'll certainly be more difficult to get near the royal chambers... I may have to play the ace up my sleeve faster than I intended. Actually, I'm not too sure how to play this yet. Your business is a good start, though. But will it get me to the royals faster than naming mine?"

"*My* business—*your* business? What you proposed to Beale was going to be 'ours'." Marcos then realised something else that didn't fit with why he thought they were visiting the Palace of Whitehall. "Why do you want to get into the royal chambers—if you can, which I very, very much doubt? What's that got to do with your spices and my juniper-gin? You can't imagine the queen writes her own shopping lists, surely?"

"No, but I might tempt her with some special merchandise from my little box."

Marcos gave a dramatic sigh. "I knew you were up to something."

Ludo extended a calming hand but Marcos had smelled a big water rat and wasn't about to be appeased. "Why did you convince me to come with you if you're going straight for the royal chambers for your own business? We only need to speak with a victualler or steward or whoever issues warrants here. Then he'll go to some sort of secretary. The king might—eventually—sign our warrant, but I wouldn't be too sure of that —*if* we get it." Marcos was angry. "You don't need me here at all, do you? All that palaver with Beale about trade ventures and being a somebody in Genoa is a cover, an excuse. *Madre mía*, you can't go messing Joanna's father about like that—he'll go mad. He'll cause you all sorts of problems in Plymouth if you cheat him. He might even..." Diverted from his tirade, Marcos stopped speaking to point at a row of cannon facing onto the river then laughed, "Looks like they're expecting you."

"Ha-ha. You always were a feeble joker. Look over there as well. Those are marksmen with muskets or whatever the English call those long guns. They're stationed all along the wall. You haven't omitted to tell me England's at war as well, have you?"

Marcos studied the way the Palace of Whitehall had become a fortress. "I thought they were exaggerating. All that business about Parliament and the king being at loggerheads, it must be true."

"Ask the wherryman if there's something we ought to know," Ludo said.

Marcos looked at the wherryman, who didn't look like he'd give a starving nun a crust of bread let alone useful information to well-dressed foreigners, but he switched to English nonetheless and addressing the rat-faced river-man directly he said, "Has there been trouble in the Palace, wherryman? Why all the marksmen and cannon? Or is this normal?"

"Ain't normal, ain't good and bodes ill, if you asks me," the man replied.

"And it's because...?"

The wherryman sniffed and rubbed the fingers of his right hand against his thumb. Ludo presented him with a shiny coin.

"Started when the king went to war with the Scots and now he's come back and started getting rid of anyone as opposes him, or so they say. He's likely expecting trouble, and like to get it, if you asks me."

Ludo cocked his head to one side and winked. "Nothing for us to worry about, then."

The wherryman muttered something about foreigners that Marcos didn't fully catch and Ludo returned to their previous topic in the annoying way he had of jumping from one subject to another in the least appropriate locations.

"I suppose we can trust your father-in-law to sell our wares while we're away—the goods *will* be handled properly? I can't risk a barrel of pepper getting damp, for instance, after all the trouble getting it here in good condition. I'd prefer it if he used a formal banking arrangement as well, not leave the silver in his office coffers for clerks and servants to steal."

"Why are you worrying about all this now, in the middle of the River Thames? I'll be there to arrange all the storage and sales anyway?" Marcos huffed.

"Not necessarily. That is, you won't be next year, if all goes to plan."

Marcos was about to ask what 'plan', but decided to fight it out later when they got back to their lodgings in Lambeth.

"Edward Beale won't cheat you, if that's what you mean? But you'll have to be careful on another score. He said before I came away that there's talk of trouble and much as he fancies being a supplier to the royal household he doesn't want to suffer because of us coming here. Meaning, if it looks dodgy, which it already does, if there's trouble afoot, I'm to back out on his behalf and go straight home to Devon." This was not strictly true, but taking another look at the armaments along the riverside wall of Whitehall Marcos was preparing a way out. "Seeing these cannon and soldiers, I'm coming to think Mr Beale actually knows something you don't. That'll be a first, won't it?"

Ignoring Marcos's sarcasm Ludo said, "What sort of trouble is he anticipating?"

Marcos gave a light shrug. "Not sure, but he says we're to 'stay neutral'."

"Neutral?" Ludo echoed then turned to Marcos, deadly serious. "Tell me what that means, now." Before Marcos could say anything, though, Ludo switched languages and said to the wherryman, "Give us a moment more, will you."

"Not easy staying out here in this current, sir. Tide's on the turn. It'll cost you."

"And I shall pay," Ludo replied. Then, keeping his eyes on Marcos, making him even more nervous, he said, "*Explícame*."

"Some time ago, King Charles issued a special maritime ship tax as an emergency measure to supposedly help arm the navy to fight your blasted pirates but was probably a ruse to raise money for himself. Those of us living by the sea and knowing about pirates," he looked meaningfully at Ludo, "paid it. But then it was issued again and again, and to people living inland who had to pay as well. Now, according to Beale, there are many people saying England would be better off it was run by an elected government from Parliament and not by a king on his own or with his fancy favourites. They say Charles Stuart invents taxes to line his pockets and live like a—well, like a king, I suppose. And that isn't right when ordinary folk are going hungry to pay the taxes. For all Mr Beale is in favour of having a royal warrant to supply palaces, he says merchants like him need profit to re-invest in their businesses not to put rings on royal fingers."

"Tch, that's a pity—the rings on royal fingers, I mean." The dimple in Ludo's left cheek appeared and disappeared in a twisted grimace.

Marcos laughed, "Is that what's in your box there?"

"Maybe. Keep your voice down, what you're saying smacks of treason."

Marcos looked at the wherryman then at his river tyke in the prow to see if they were listening then remembered they were speaking Spanish and that in itself was a source of trouble. Becoming angry again he said, "If you're really here just to sell pretty baubles I can't see why you need me. You could have left me back in Plymouth to get your goods moving there if you're so worried about Mr Beale not being up to your demanding standards! You say one thing then you say another... I don't know where I am—and I've got my own business to worry about as well?"

"You're here because your English is better than mine," Ludo hissed. "*You will* benefit from the venture—sooner or later. I'm trying to kill two birds with a few 'pretty baubles' that's all." Ludo reverted to English, "Wherryman, take us into the stairs." Turning back to Marcos he winked. "Faint heart never won a fair lady. Isn't that what they say? Only she's dark, her being part Tuscan Medici."

"Tuscan Medici? What are you on about?" Then Marcos twigged, "Oh, no, *Dios mío*, the Queen!" His surprise and fears were instantly interrupted by the wherryman swinging the boat round to get out of the way of a beribboned barge full of fine gentlemen. Marcos gripped the gunwale as it rocked in their wake.

Amused, Ludo looked at the wherryman, saying, "Very neatly done, sir."

"Only doing my trade, milord."

"You must take many different people into Whitehall stairs," Ludo continued.

"Different they are sir, many and different like you and like you say."

"Tradesmen and lords, eh?"

"Both and more."

"And what do these people tell you when they return? What else can you tell me, a foreigner going into your English palace?"

"That you'll be more welcome in Whitehall than in the city, sir, beggin' your pardon for speaking honest."

"No, be as honest as you like sir," responded Ludo, unconcerned, "I come here as an envoy from the East, and do not intend to stay. Tell me what you like and what you can."

Marcos gazed blindly at the departing barge, wondering why he had let himself be unnerved by Ludo's serious tone and wherryman's references to honesty when for sure what was about to transpire would be 'neatly done' by the silver-tongued Genoese, who could talk himself into a cage of lions and back out again without a scratch. Then he turned his attention back to what the wherryman was saying.

". . . You can't get near the king nor the queen, as you have to stay ten yards from their feet at all times and no one eats at their end of the table for fear of poisonin' them. But they act in theatricals like common comedians."

"They eat a lot, I've been told."

"Couldn't say to that, sir, but there's a good trade in leftovers. My belly's proof of that."

"Rumour is not wrong, then," Ludo said. "Good."

"You want the palace stairs or the privy stairs, sir?" the wherryman asked.

"Take us to the Scotland stairs: that is the tradesmen's entrance, isn't it?" Marcos intervened rapidly, hoping to prevent Ludo sending them straight into the pikes of the yeomen-of-the-guard on the narrow landing stages. This way, with luck, they could do their business with the chief steward, the victualler and sommelier, or whomsoever they managed to speak to and get away again as fast as possible.

"Scotland dock for the kitchens and buttery and coal yards, or the opposite end for the bowling green gardens?" queried the wherryman. "Envoys and ambassadors always go into the palace stairs."

"We'll take the palace stairs, wherryman," Ludo said, brooking no further dispute.

Before they could leave the short stone quay to enter the grounds of Whitehall, however, two yeomen crossed pikes and Ludo put a warning hand against Marcos's chest, signalling he would do the talking. In his brightest and best English, but emphasising his Genoese accent, Ludo said, "I am here on private and personal business for Her Majesty Queen Henrietta Maria."

"Credentials," said one of the men, proffering a hand for their official papers or a letter of introduction. To Marcos's astonishment, Ludo produced such a letter.

"You're from the Duchy of Tuscany?"

Ludo inclined his head. "I am Ludovico di Doria—as it states here. I carry a personal message for the Queen from Her Majesty's royal mother's family."

The two men looked at each other. One said gruffly, "There is someone who can verify this?"

"I fear that may only be the queen herself, for I have never been in this particular palace before and my mission is personal. However, I am sure that if you say the name of Doria doors will, um—open. My secretary here is from Madrid, if that helps in any way?"

"Madrid?"

"Her Majesty's sister is the Queen of Spain, sir, residing in Madrid."

The pikes were quickly uncrossed and they were led off the landing stage.

A gentleman usher was sent for. A yeoman remained at their side until he arrived and then Ludo repeated his rigmarole. After the briefest of interrogations and the most cursory inspection of Marcos's spice samples and Ludo's Portuguese *bizalho* jewel box, the usher, accompanied by another armed yeoman, led them into the palace. Following the scarlet-liveried yeoman with some difficulty—for the corridors they traversed were in a chaos of movement, crowded with men and women of differing levels and liveries hurrying hither and thither—it occurred to Marcos that Ludo might actually be intending to get into the royal apartments unaccompanied. Horrified, he was immensely grateful to the silent yeoman in his old-fashioned outfit.

"Is there to be a banquet or royal occasion today?" Ludo asked as they entered a spartan anteroom.

"Not today, no, sir. Her Majesty is removing to the palace of Oatlands in Surrey for the birth of her child," the usher replied.

"Ah, we come just in the minute of time then, is that not so? *Un bambino, come è dolce. . .*" Ludo deliberately slipped into poor grammar and Latin sentiment, making Marcos close his eyes with embarrassment.

Another gentleman usher arrived and gave a polite bow. Addressing Ludo, he said, "You wish to speak to Her Majesty, I understand, Excellency. I regret that may not be possible under the circumstance. Please wait here while I locate her secretary."

As soon as they were alone, Marcos exploded. "*Excellency*!"

"My introductory document—by implication. But their interpretation, not my assertion: have I actually said I'm an ambassador?"

"No, but—"

"Quite. As you see, my English is not all it could be. That's why I need you here."

Marcos gave Ludo a very sideways look, only to be clapped on the back by a strong, sea-reddened hand. "Smile," Ludo laughed, "we're in. Now, follow my lead, try to keep up with my Genoese, and avoid using any Spanish until we are actually with the queen."

"And you really think she's going to see you, just like that?" Marcos snapped his fingers. Ludo ignored him so he said, "I've heard the name Doria before somewhere."

"I should think you have. As I told your father-in-law, they act as bankers to monarchs and nobles across Christendom and beyond, not to mention being famous admirals and seafarers."

"And that will get—"

"Tsst!" Ludo raised his free hand and grabbed Marcos's arm. Pulling him closer, he hissed, "You are my secretary. I'm carrying a personal letter from the queen's sister and I intend to persuade her into buying the pearls I've brought, and a few other items. We'll leave your spices and gin drink for tomorrow, or later today if we're lucky."

Marcos stared at him in disbelief. "Why didn't you tell me this before?"

"Would you have come if I had?" Ludo raised his black eyebrows. "Hmm?"

The lady-in-waiting sent to meet them was an elderly woman with a soft grey moustache. First she quizzed Ludo about his mission then, to Marcos's great surprise, she led them to the chapel where the queen and her attendants were at prayer.

Leaving them just inside the entrance to the ornate nave, the lady-in-waiting hastened back to her queen. A gust of wind pushed at the open door behind them and a weak ray of sunlight spread across the flagstones. Soundlessly, a tall, very thin man in clerical black emerged from a side chapel. Marcos reached out to touch Ludo's arm.

"I know," Ludo responded. "What's *he* doing here?"

Father Rogelio, a Vatican agent working directly for a cardinal nephew of the Pope, registered their presence but said nothing and continued on his way down the left-hand aisle towards the congregation of titled women.

Marcos shuddered. Ludo didn't move a muscle. They remained at the main door until the service ended then stood back as the royal group, accompanied by two elderly Catholic priests, reached the porch. Of the Roman cleric, whom a humble grey friar had once named '*la bicha*'—the serpent— there was no sign. Outside, a group of ladies in cream silks and summer-flowered cottons left in one direction, the queen and a few more in another.

A second lady-in-waiting came to their side. Addressing the noble envoy, she said, "You wish to speak with Her Majesty?"

Ludo bowed and bade her good day. "I carry an important package from Her Majesty's royal sister Queen Isabel of Spain, ma'am."

The lady put out her hand. "I shall be happy to convey it to her, Excellency."

Ludo smiled warmly but shook his head. "I also carry a spoken message: a *personal* message."

Looking somewhat flustered, the lady-in-waiting said, "I regret I am required to inform you, Excellency, that Her Majesty thanks you for your journey, but she has a great many concerns to attend to. She bids me ask you to visit her in Oatlands Palace one month hence."

Ludo inclined his head. "Forgive me, *madonna*, I bring tidings of Her Majesty's family from Tuscany and Spain. I have no wish to inconvenience Her Majesty, and naturally I shall be most pleased to attend her whenever, wherever she requests, but my mission is not without urgency. I *must* speak with her this day."

"Oh dear," the lady-in-waiting said anxiously, turning this way and that, then hastening away in a rustle of russet silks to catch up with the royal party, now disappearing down a colonnaded walk way.

Marcos gazed questioningly at Ludo, who said not a word, and in silence they remained where they were until the woman returned and bid them follow her to what Marcos feared might be the queen's apartments. In this he was wrong. They proceeded to a room used as an art gallery displaying paintings of various epochs and subjects, some in frames lying face outward against the wall on the stone floor. Four male servants were nailing masterpieces into protective wooden casings for transportation. The queen was discussing something with a gentleman sporting an elaborate collar and slashed sleeves of yellow over olive green; she then spoke to a plainly dressed young man wrapping a small wooden triptych. Ludo and Marcos waited while she pointed at paintings on the opposite wall and another young man took notes at her side.

The lady-in-waiting in russet coughed politely to gain attention. "Your Majesty, the Tuscan—erm, the Spanish Emissary is here."

Without turning her head, the queen lifted a delicate white hand vaguely in the air. Ludo stepped forward. Marcos stayed where he was to observe the troublesome Queen Henrietta Maria, or Queen Mary as she was known in England, knowing Joanna and her mother would want an inch by inch description once he was home. Hearsay had it she was a frivolous little harridan and no beauty. She was indeed small of stature, but the mass of uncovered black curls framing her features distracted the eye from her narrow face and protruding teeth. She was evidently in the final stages of a pregnancy.

Without a word, the queen continued her scrutiny of three paintings of horses. In one there was a mare and foal inside some sort of red tent. The grey mare's face was dished and attractive with huge eyes. The foal lay across her forelegs.

Speaking quietly in Tuscan, the language of the Queen's mother, Ludo said, "An Arab mare, Your Majesty. A delightful study. If you will forgive my rudeness, may I say I own such a mare as this. Two, in fact. Are they not beautiful? Born of the south wind, according to legend—they appear not of this earth. This study is indeed divine, and so apt, if I may add?"

The Queen of England took a sharp breath and stared at her interlocutor. The clerk at her side, unaware of what had been said, noted the change in atmosphere and looked from one to the other, then for some form of explanation to Marcos, who stared straight ahead of him, having nearly fainted with the effrontery. Surely the queen would send them flying from her presence now. They would achieve nothing for his spices or juniper drink this day or ever. Worse, he would have to return to Plymouth and tell his father-in-law he'd been right; the long journey had been what the English called 'a fool's errand'.

Ludo gazed guilelessly at the painting of the mare and foal, giving the simultaneous appearance of rapture and innocence, although Marcos was sure this was not the case. Ludo never said or did anything by accident.

The queen placed a hand on her lower back and replying in the Tuscan Italian of the Medici said, "Tell me more. But first, tell me who you are, Excellency. I am informed you are an emissary of my lady mother's retinue of Tuscany, yet she is here in London with us."

Marcos closed his eyes and muttered a rapid prayer. Undeterred, Ludo replied, "Yes, indeed, Your Majesty: a slight misunderstanding. I come, in fact—by way of many distant travels—from the East and, as it happens, via Spain—and am in turn, only distantly connected to the house of Medici, being Genoese by birth, and your royal sister of Spain—who treats with me, my being a Doria and Genoese, you see, hence the Spanish connection. But I have come, as I say, from the East, by way of Spain and bring you something of import both valuable and personal. One item in particular that may enchant you from the distant East..."

Marcos studied his new shoes and stopped listening. When he looked up again Ludo, having succeeded in confusing the queen, was giving her his most charming smile. Without blinking or giving the slightest appearance of being confused, however, Henrietta Maria said, "And that is?"

Marcos bit back a smile, for now Ludo had lost his tangled thread.

"Oh, er, well, this, Your Majesty." He proffered the box from under his left arm. "And I bring you a letter, ma'am. Would you like to hear about the horses, the content of this most special of caskets, or receive your package first?"

"Tell me of these wonderful creatures first, then we will go to my apartments. I take chocolate at this time each day."

Astounded, Marcos waited while Ludo recited some verses about the wind and Arab horses, waxing lyrical about their airs, their colours, even their eyelashes. Despite his cynicism, Marcos became caught up in the discourse and was surprised when Ludo said, "For this alone, you should take this painting with you ma'am. But if you permit, I can arrange for you to see these beautiful creatures in real life. A colt would make a most excellent gift for the Prince of Wales, would it not?"

"His Majesty my husband and His Royal Highness both adore horses," the queen replied, her face lighting up with a genuine smile. "Come," she said, and led her ladies and visitors out of the picture gallery, back into the half-enclosed, cloistered walkway, past the privy garden and on and on until they reached her apartments near the city gates. As they entered her sumptuous sitting room two women jumped to their feet, each dropping a circular embroidery frame to her side as she sank in a regulatory curtsey. The taller of the two, with a pile of golden ringlets falling loosely over a perfectly oval face, was Maria de los Ángeles Santoña Gómez de Fulford: Lady Alina. Her face flushed pink when she looked up from her obeisance and saw Ludo.

Marcos raised his free arm in delight, then remembered where he was. The queen, ignoring the women, took a seat at a small table bearing a silver jug and a china cup with a saucer.

She spoke to an attendant lingering behind the table, who disappeared to fetch another cup and saucer. Marcos waited at the door as Ludo da Portovenere, merchant and sometime pirate, was invited to sit with the Queen of England.

The chocolate was served. Keeping one hand on his precious casket, Ludo took delicate sips from an exquisite dainty cup and conversed with the queen like an old acquaintance.

Despite his curiosity to see how the interview was going to proceed, Marcos could not prevent his gaze wandering across the other side of the salon to Alina. Catching his eye, she patted an upholstered chair at her side and he carefully manoeuvred himself so he could stand beside her, not daring to sit in the queen's presence.

"Marcos," Alina whispered getting to her feet and speaking in Spanish, "whatever are you doing here?"

"*Lo mismo te pregunto yo,*" Marcos replied, his face alight with joy. "How do you come to be here?"

"Thomas has been elevated from baronet to baron," Alina whispered. "He had to pay dearly for the privilege, and, as if that were not enough, he's been sent back to Oxford to create a sort of library for the royal children and tutor the princes. As a baroness I am required to serve a number of months each year as a lady-in-waiting. When Her Majesty discovered I was Spanish and a Roman Catholic she asked me to attend her in these apartments during the day."

"You have achieved your greatest wish, then. Do you find it to your liking?"

Alina beamed. "It is a fine beginning."

"Beginning?" Marcos repeated, then instantly remembered how ambitious Alina had been. How she had sworn she was the daughter of a Spanish grandee, despite having work-a-day hands and knowing how to make bread. It had been her ambition that had forced him away in the end, forced him to accept she would never lower herself to love a humble being such as Marcos Alonso. All the same, he was delighted to be at her side once again. "You are well, I see."

"I am better now, but we had a sad misfortune earlier this year. A baby daughter—she died within the week."

"Oh, Alina, I am so sorry. But your son, Tomás, he is all right?"

"Healthy and as strong as an English ox. I do miss him, but when Her Majesty removes to Oatlands, today or tomorrow, I am released to return to Cornwall."

"Excellent. I shall accompany you."

"But what about...?" Alina inclined her head towards Ludo, whose own head was still bent in earnest conversation with the queen.

Marcos smiled. "He's up to something, so what he'll be doing tomorrow or even later today is anybody's guess."

"Nothing has changed there, then?"

"Actually," Marcos measured his words pensively, "I think something has changed. Outwardly he's his old self. But he's also—how can I say?—a bit aggressive: sharp at the edges and less dynamic at the same time. He's more speculative, as well. More secretive. I think something has happened to him."

"And that something brings him to Whitehall Palace to speak to the queen?"

Marcos shook his head. "I have no idea, to be honest, what has brought him here. It might be to sell the pearls and other jewels he's got in that box, it might be more. It isn't only to help me, that's for certain."

"Ah, another Ludo box: how he loved that miniature sea chest. If he's brought pearls he'll be in the queen's favour. Look how she wears them."

Marcos studied a very long strand of massive pearls looped around the royal shoulders. "Maybe it is for his pearls," he said.

"What's in *your* little casket?" Alina indicated the cedar wood box at Marcos's side.

He lifted it in front of him and opened it just enough for the aromas of nutmeg and mace, cinnamon and cloves to escape.

Alina's eyes opened in surprise. "Spices—how wonderful. May I have some to take home?"

Before Marcos could reply, his attention was diverted by Ludo taking a small package from up his sleeve.

Together, he and Alina watched the queen examine the package, undo the ribbon and linen around it, then examine the seal on the letter contained within. She then placed it inside *her* sleeve.

Marcos tried not to laugh. Alina shot him a look and it was as if they were back at Crimphele together, sharing their thoughts, both silently attempting to understand the Genoese merchant they knew only as Ludo da Portovenere, wondering what he was about to do next. As yet, neither of them had ever been right and they had each suffered because of it. But the mere fact that they were together in this room told Marcos something: Ludo was right in saying he would benefit from the adventure.

Queen Henrietta Maria beckoned Alina with a movement of her fingers. Alina went to her side, helped her to her feet and they moved to a writing bureau, where Alina made preparations to act as an amanuensis. Marcos looked questioningly at Ludo, who studiously ignored him.

After a few minutes Alina sanded what she had written, folded the thick paper into a square and sealed it. She then handed it to the queen, who held it out for Ludo to collect. He did so with a low bow.

"Return in the morning before ten," Queen Henrietta Maria commanded. "I shall speak with His Majesty. If you wish to extend your business arrangement in India, you must speak with him. Your secretary may go to the Lord Steward later—I will send a note." The queen then touched Ludo's elbow and they moved to the window where they spoke in whispers for a few more minutes until Alina was asked to accompany them to the palace jetty or city gates.

Marcos followed Ludo and Alina back along sunless corridors until they reached the stairs for the visitors' wherries and barges. Two men in clothes that suggested they should have been at the Scotland Dock entrance, not the palace stairs, were already there waiting. The men exchanged glances as Ludo and Alina sparred in Spanish on the narrow jetty. Marcos, only half-listening and entirely left out of the conversation, watched a big riverboat arrive empty at the stairs. The wherryman's tyke jumped out and held it for them.

The men stood back for Ludo to get in first, but he said, "Please, gentlemen, it is a large enough boat and you were here first."

"After you, sir," one grunted, it being obvious Alina was not crossing the river.

Ludo kissed Alina lightly on both cheeks in the Latin manner and said something that made her blush. Marcos looked at her and said, "I have much to tell you. But it can wait until we travel down to Plymouth together. Tell me when you can leave tomorrow and I'll make the necessary arrangements."

Once in the boat, Ludo settled himself on a bench with his precious box on his knees and took an over-sized silk handkerchief from a pocket like a magician. Marcos sat beside him and watched, fascinated as Ludo twirled the handkerchief into a rope then tied one end to a button hole in his jacket and the other to the handle on the top of his box. The workingmen got into the stern.

"Tuck your box inside your jacket," Ludo said quietly.

"It's too big," Marcos replied.

The river tyke pushed off and jumped in, and Alina waved farewell but remained standing on the jetty. A breeze lifted her hair and Marcos felt a tug of the old pain across his chest; she was more beautiful than ever.

Half way across the heaving, brown, beer-frothed river, the boy in the stern began to shout. One of the men had jumped to his feet and grabbed him by the ear. Then both men were standing and the boy was squirming about, swearing he had taken nothing; the boat was rocking wildly. Marcos tucked his box firmly under his arm and grabbed for the wooden seat beneath him, but too late. The men were moving between him and Ludo, and then he was in the foul water of the Thames, going down, down and down, swallowing enough scum to ruin his gut forever. Closing his arm around the box, which had miraculously stayed with him, he surfaced and began to swim one-handed towards the boat. A paddle crashed down into the thick, swirling water, pushing him out and away. The other paddle came down on his head. He gulped and surfaced again, kicking water to get further away from the boat and nearer to the landing stage. Ludo's black hat surfaced.

Marcos, for all that he was in a perilous situation, suddenly had a clear remembrance of being chastised by Ludo for joking about his black hat floating on water. "Help him! Save Ludo!" Marcos yelled in English to the men in the boat, which was now pulling out across the rising tide, heading for the south bank. "Hey!" Marcos screamed. "Hey!"

A skiff appeared from nowhere with an elderly gnome-like creature at the oars. Marcos pushed his box over the gunwale, praying it wasn't a river gipsy who'd steal it and leave him to drown, then pulled himself up as best he could for his coat, breeches and new shoes were heavy with water.

Another small skiff joined them. Ludo was in it, minus his hat. Their rowers were indeed river gipsies, the last men on earth to trust in any country. Ludo was breathing heavily, foul with stinking water and in a fouler humour. He said something to the creature rowing his boat and the two skiffs turned for the palace stairs.

Alina, hands to her mouth with the horror of what she had witnessed and her inability to do anything, was waiting. Other people had joined her. No doubt she'd been calling for help.

The river gipsies pulled alongside the palace stairs and Ludo miraculously managed to find some coins in his sodden breeches' pockets to reward his saviour. He then climbed the steps and stood before Alina. Speaking in English for all to hear he said, "So, milady, once more you try to send me to my death on a river. Remind me never to be on the same quayside as you ever again."

"Oh, dear," Alina replied drily, "your clothes have suffered: I do hope you won't be obliged to wear the same outfit for a whole month like someone I know."

Marcos gaped at them, speechless.

The only good thing that had happened that day in Marcos's opinion, apart from meeting Alina again and being allocated a tiny room in Whitehall after their ducking, was the fact that they had achieved direct access to the Lord Steward of the Whitehall Palace on the Queen's personal recommendation. For this alone Ludo was to be thanked.

Placing the samples from his cedar wood box—nutmeg, mace and pepper, scrolls of cinnamon and rolls of cassia—in a row on a chest, he sniffed for dampness and was agreeably relieved. The casket had proved surprisingly watertight. Satisfied there was no significant damage, he climbed into the high tester bed, exhausted after a day of tension, excitement, upsets and near drowning. Revelling in the soft comfort, he wondered where Ludo was sleeping then closed his eyes; he really didn't want to know.

Chapter 12

Wearing borrowed robes, Ludo and Marcos swept hats not their own to the floor of the picture gallery. King Charles Stuart, reigning monarch by Divine Right of Scotland, England, Wales and Ireland, and various colonies in the New World, stroked the head of a doleful wolfhound at his knee with one hand and flicked the wrist of his other for them to approach.

"Ludovico di Doria, Her Majesty the Queen tells us you wish to speak with us," said the king in a voice that held a hint of stammer and a demand that they not tire him.

Ludo stepped forward, but before he could say anything the king got to his feet and went to stand before the painting of the Arab mare and foal. The king, whose slight figure, fresh face and fine beard made him look younger than his years, indicated the painting and beckoned Ludo closer.

Fearing an error in protocol, Marcos stayed where he was and strained his ears. Alina rustled to his side in a far more elegant gown than she had worn the previous day. "I am to accompany you to the Lord Steward's office," she whispered.

"Now? I can't leave without permission and I can't speak to him without Ludo."

"You are going to have to. Ludo arranged it last night—they are waiting for you."

Marcos shook his head and whispered, "I can't leave that rogue here with the king—he could promise anything. You know he's telling everyone he's from a banking house?"

Alina shrugged. "If he is, he's come at the right time. The king is desperate to raise money for another war against the Scots. Her Majesty may have proposed this audience now as a means of getting foreign silver. If Ludo is up to anything he has met his match in the queen, believe me."

"But what is he up to?" Marcos hissed.

Alina cocked her head to one side and mimicked a wicked grin. "It's out of our hands, whatever it is," she said. "Come."

Marcos followed her out of a concealed side door. As they walked down the draughty Stone Gallery, Alina said, "The queen sent a message to Lord Dungetty yesterday evening—at Ludo's request, I expect—and he must see you now or not at all because they are finally leaving for Oatlands this afternoon."

"I can't believe I need to see a lord about supplying the royal household with spices and fine wines, and eventually my juniper drink. That's hardly a lord's job."

"It is in the Palace of Whitehall." Alina stopped and turned. "You've changed your mind."

"Yes." Marcos watched flakes of cherry blossom flutter down upon the manicured hedge of the privy garden. "I see trouble coming out of this and I've other things in my life now."

"Such as a pretty wife?" Alina raised her eyebrows, smiling.

"Such as a very pretty wife and my own business. Well, nearly my own—I run part of it: wine imports and now the spices."

"In that case you certainly do need to see Lord Dungetty. Come on, if nothing else you have to go through with it or displease the queen. Besides,"—Alina put a hand on Marcos's arm and whispered urgently in Spanish—"you ought to know she's anxious to develop any link she can with Spain—for the royal household and some personal matters. After what went on last night, after you got back from your dunking, it looks to me as if the scoundrel you travel with is her chosen man."

"Oh, no," Marcos's shoulders slumped in despair. "What has he been telling her?"

"We'll have to find out, shan't we?"

"Actually, I'd really rather not. Is there any way out of this?"

Alina twiddled her skirts with her right hand pensively, taking him seriously, for which Marcos was grateful. After a moment she asked, "Do you think what Ludo is up to is connected to what happened in that boat? It wasn't an accident, was it?"

"No, but I think it might be to do with what happened in Holland. Ludo made a very powerful enemy there, and that enemy is here, possibly with the queen herself."

Alina's hand flew to her mouth. "Is she in danger?"

"No, *she* isn't, but I think Ludo is; and I'm in the same boat by the looks of it—literally. I did try to tell you this last night before we retired. You weren't listening."

"I was distracted, trying to get you clean clothes and beds to sleep in. Let's talk about it later." Alina wrested the cedar wood box from under Marcos's arm. "We'd better get a move on or Lord Dungetty will have left." Then she stopped. "What you said about Ludo having an enemy—you ought to consider how having the queen's patronage will protect him, and you. Don't do anything to cross her if you can help it."

"You mean if Ludo acts on her behalf in some way? Whatever could he do for a queen? He's a merchant trying to sell his pearls and jewels and..."

"And a member of the banking house of Doria, or so he says."

Marcos looked at Alina and shook his head. "I knew there'd be trouble. Nothing is ever simple when Ludo's around."

"No, it isn't." Alina's voice was quiet.

Marcos gave her a searching look. She responded with a shy smile and said, "Come on—you have work to do, and it is to your benefit as well."

They were shown into a spacious office by a weary-eyed secretary with rolls of parchment under each arm and candlesticks poking out of his pockets. The Lord Steward bade them welcome tetchily, getting to his feet with the aid of a stick then grimacing with pain and sitting down again behind his laden desk. Alina gave him a brief summary of why they were there and reminded him courteously but firmly that it was the queen's personal wish that this gentleman representing 'Marcus Almond and Partners' be included as a supplier to the royal household, and that the Genoese merchant Ludovico di Doria da Portovenere be provided with a licence to transport spices, silks, precious gems and pearls from the East.

"And where is the second man?"

Marcos shot a glance at Alina, who, quick-witted as ever, said, "The Genoese merchant, Ludovico da Portovenere, is with His Majesty as we speak. It is he who brings goods from the East. Mr Almond, here, has an importation firm in Plymouth."

"I have some samples here, milord," Marcos said, opening his cedar wood box.

"Yes, yes." The nobleman dismissed him with a wave of the hand. "Excellent, I'm sure. Plymouth, you say? That is a long way away."

"We arrange haulage, milord," Marcos said.

The suffering nobleman stared at them in turn for a few seconds then said, "Spices and *exotic* goods from the East, as I call them, have been requested expressly therefore by Her Majesty the Queen?"

"That is correct, Lord Steward," Alina said gracefully. "Naturally Her Majesty was concerned that the gentlemen go through the proper channels. Hence our visit to you this day."

The Lord Steward huffed, mollified, but only to a certain extent. "We'd better get on with it then. I need to conclude these transactions and get back to my apartments if the household is to move before midnight. Randolph!" he called to a secretary, who hastened to his desk. "Write three standard letters of appointment forthwith. What was it for?"

"Wine and spirits from the firm of Marcus Almond and Partners in Plymouth, Devonshire, and spices from the East," replied Alina promptly.

"And the third—remind me."

"Er—sundry 'exotic goods', including silks and pearls, Lord Dungetty."

"Put 'miscellaneous luxury items'," the Lord Steward instructed.

Marcos watched the scribe with a mixture of fear and excitement, hardly believing it was actually happening. After the warrants were sanded, the Lord Steward signed them, sanded them again and handed the first two to Marcos, naming his firm as 'suppliers to the King of fine wines', and 'suppliers to the King of pepper and spices' respectively. The 'miscellaneous' warrant for Ludo was left on his desk.

"A question," he said, tapping his desk top impatiently, "Tell me, Mr Almond, do you purchase your spices from the English East India Company imports, or are you, as I fear, going to be importing them directly through this Ludovico da Portovenere, wherever that is?"

"Mm, both," Marcos stated, for he could make it true.

"And can I assume you are not intending to undercut other suppliers?"

"No," Marcos said, frowning. "Do you mean there are fixed prices?"

"That I will leave you to discover. Suffice it to say, we—the royal household, that is—do not wish to raise any form of animosity among importers or even tradesmen at present."

Marcos's heart sank; the Lord Steward was intimating royal suppliers were disgruntled, if not angry—for lack of payment, no doubt. "I understand," he said, trying not to show his disappointment.

"And this Genoese merchant, he is not resident in England? I can't go upsetting the East India Company—we owe them too much already."

The comment confirmed Marcos's suspicions, but he managed to say, "The merchant is of the State of Genoa, but he will trade from the East, from India, I believe."

"You believe? Hmm..." Lord Dungetty huffed, handing him Ludo's licence to trade from India. "Well, the risk is his, not mine. How do you wish to pay? We would prefer specie at your earliest convenience. Now would be ideal."

"I can bring the silver to you later this day, if that suits, milord? How much will it be?" Marcos had come prepared with a chest of silver—now under lock and key in Lambeth, where they were supposed to be lodging.

The Lord Steward muttered to his secretary, who scrawled three sums on a piece of paper and handed it to Marcos.

Marcos gulped. The fees for his goods alone came to more than a year's income. He looked at Alina, unsure what to say, wondering if he could back out now.

Lord Dungetty sighed heavily. "Are you trying to tell me you cannot afford the warrants? Please don't waste my time."

"No, no," Marcos said hastily, "I was merely concerned about bringing you payment this afternoon."

"Before four of the clock, if you please. We have much to do this day."

"Certainly, Lord Steward." Marcos bowed his head.

It was done, then—he was committed to pay. *Thank heavens for Edward Beale*, Marcos thought, for without his silver he would be in serious difficulties, unless of course Ludo had sufficient funds for both of them—being a member of a banking house...

Lord Dungetty interrupted his speculation. "My secretary will inform the kitchen stewards accordingly. Is there anything else?"

"Thank you, Lord Dungetty—no," Marcos said.

Leaving the gout-ridden Comptroller of the Royal Domestic Household seated in his carved chair, Marcos and Alina hastened back the way they had come. A gentleman usher stepped back as they re-entered the concealed door in the long room. Ludo and the king were now seated together by a window. Laughing, and evidently in a good humour, the king turned to them enquiringly. Alina dropped to a low curtsey and Marcos flourished the hat off his head with such haste he almost dropped his box of samples.

"Has the queen sent you, my dear?" asked the king, obviously addressing Alina. "Is she ready to leave?"

"The queen has sent me, Your Majesty: she regrets she will not be ready for another two hours at least."

"And that is why you slipped away before speaking to me?"

Alina flushed scarlet. "No, Your Majesty, it is that, I was required also to..." Alina broke off and Marcos wondered why. The monarch didn't appear to be a tyrant or anything like it. She started again, "Her Majesty required me to attend with this gentleman here... to go..."

"Tell us slowly," demanded the king gently. "We cannot bear to see a pretty face so discomposed." He was addressing Alina as if she was the only person in the room and she blushed scarlet again.

"Lord Dungetty has acted on Her Majesty's request for the royal household to be supplied by these gentlemen."

"Ah, that. Yes, we know all about it. Her Majesty wants these two gentlemen to bring us pearls and goodness knows what from the East. Yes, yes." Charles Stuart turned his attention to the beautiful hound at his knees, stroking her nose as if she were now the only being present in the room.

Nobody moved. After a while he said, "There *is* a small dilemma, but we think we have a solution. To our knowledge, our East India Company is bringing in textiles from India and goods from China. What you have suggested, sir," he said, addressing Ludo, "goes beyond those imports, but let us stipulate quite clearly: you may *not* bring in tea from Cathay or Indian cotton fabrics. So what other special treats can you bring us?"

Ludo's eyes sparkled. "Grey and pink pearls from the Oman, diamonds and rubies from India, and, as we spoke of earlier, Your Majesty, the Arab horses."

Marcus felt his throat go dry. Being a tradesman dealing with imported goods in Plymouth he knew all about the East India Company. It was one thing for the king to buy goods by private arrangement from a private merchant-venturer, quite another for Ludo to set up against a crown monopoly.

An usher entered and whispered in the monarch's ear.

"Very well," the king replied. Turning to Ludo, he said, "We wish we could discuss your travels further, however we are called away."

Charles Stuart rose and Ludo jumped up so fast his lightweight chair toppled backwards. A deft usher rescued it before it hit the floor. Ignoring the embarrassment, the king continued, "We could talk of travels for hours, but the queen must repair to Oatlands. Good day to you, *signor*." Then in a lower voice he said, "My personal aide will supply you with the communication for Madrid. You may wait here until he brings it. Are there any further matters regarding Spain that you think we may have overlooked?"

"No, sire. I understand." Ludo's voice was serious. "As Your Majesty says, we have discussed the matter sufficiently, I believe."

"Good." Then the king added something Marcos couldn't catch except ". . . how soon can you expedite this arrangement in Castile?" He bent his head slightly and fondled one of his dog's ears, perhaps avoiding Ludo's eyes.

"I will leave at the earliest opportunity, sire. My own ship will be ready within the month."

The king suddenly smiled. "Of course, you voyage greatly abroad—that solves our domestic issue regarding the East India Company. Excellent—you cannot be in competition with British merchants if you are not British—hah! All settled then, eh? The letter of introduction and my special communication will be brought to you forthwith. Good day to you then, sirs."

Ludo and Marcos made their bows, Alina dropped in a curtsey. The king exited the picture gallery with the wolfhound at his waist. Marcos glanced at Ludo, whose sculpted black beard was twitching with suppressed amusement or satisfaction, or both.

"What?" Marcos demanded. "What have you got yourself into?"

"Diplomacy, my young friend: I am now a veritable, respectable emissary for the King of England. You may call me 'Excellency' from now on."

Marcos opened and closed his mouth then finally said, "We have to bring the silver to pay for our warrants by four of the clock. We'd better get back to Lambeth, and hope to God we haven't been robbed."

"You had better go, then. As you have just heard, I am to remain here until I receive various letters."

"For Madrid?" Marcos said. "Why?"

"Nothing I may discuss. Off you go to fetch your silver; I can manage perfectly well here on my own." Ludo surveyed the room. "Perhaps the Lady Alina would care to wait with me." He cocked his head to one side and to Marcos's disappointment Alina smiled and seated herself in the nearest chair.

Alone, Marcos traversed the length of the Stone Gallery once more, but this time bearing the warrants for which they had travelled to London. As he walked he tried to keep his mind off the rash promises he feared had been made: to supply precious gems, giant pearls and Arabian horses to the Queen of England. What Ludo was also doing for King Charles, he had yet to discover.

Chapter 13

Next morning, as they waited in a Whitehall Palace anteroom for Alina, who was saying farewell to her fellow ladies-in-waiting, Marcos leaned against the hard back of his chair and in a forced relaxed tone said to Ludo, "Alina thinks what happened in the wherry wasn't an accident."

"She's right."

Marcos waited for Ludo to explain. When he didn't, he said, "You mean the boat incident was arranged? Those two men were trying to steal from us?"

"No, they weren't thieves, they were under orders to try and drown us—or me, anyway. Think analytically, Marcos—why didn't they take our purses or our caskets?" He tapped his now empty Portuguese *bizalho*. "Bit of a disappointment discovering we could swim—but what did he expect?—me from Portovenere, you from the beachfront of Sanlúcar. Another of his miscalculations, and he's making a big one now if he thinks he can get rid of me and stay cosy with the English monarchy, which is partly why I have just invested two entire days making myself indispensable to both king and queen for the foreseeable future."

"He, who? That Vatican agent?"

Ignoring him, Ludo continued, "A few thousand Dutchmen are bankrupted by their own greed: it wasn't as great a financial collapse as his masters had hoped; it didn't even touch the new Dutch banks the way the Spanish wanted, so I ask you, what is left to cover up? *Dio mio...*" Ludo muttered. He was silent for a few moments then said quietly, "What truly bothers me is that it's personal. He wants me gone because he thinks I got the better of him and hates me for being me, simple as that."

"Personal—*personal*,—it's the word of the week, isn't it? *Personal* for the king, *personal* for the queen..." Marcos stopped. Ludo was right—he wasn't thinking analytically. "You *are* talking about that priest from Rome who chased us out of Holland—Rogelio."

"*Santa María!* Don't tell me I have to watch my back for anyone else. It's enough having to watch out for Portuguese colonial trade factors and certain men associated with a missing ship belonging to the Spanish Armada, not to mention the Dutch navy I upset getting in and out of Ceylon and Goa. And now we are going to be at odds with the British East India Company as well. Believe me, I do not want to add anyone else to this gang of admirers. I might have to start carrying a proper weapon at this rate."

"You don't, do you? I've always wondered why."

"I've never had any stomach for physical violence, Marcos, never. I saw enough of it as a small child to last me a lifetime. If I'd had a stronger stomach I'd have 'turned Turk' as they say and would be on a pirate vessel or nestled in the lap of luxury with a North African harem right now, not prancing around a draughty palace in England creating a demand for my goods. If you must know, I am of the opinion that bearing a sword invites trouble. I upset enough people without the risk of being called out to be cut to pieces in a stupid duel. I do wear this pretty little dagger, though." Ludo opened his black damask jacket to reveal a curious curved dagger tucked into his waistcoat. "An Omani sheik gave me this little beauty. It's called a *khanjar*."

Marcos touched the half-moon sheath decorated with an intricate geometric design and Arabic lettering. "It's curved," he said. "Doesn't that make it awkward to use?"

"No idea. I'd show it to you, but this might not be a good place to be flashing a weapon about, useless as I suspect it is."

"Alina used to carry a knife in her skirts."

"I remember only too well." Ludo closed the conversation by getting up and pacing the room. After he resumed his seat Marcos waited for the right moment to ask a burning question, then, because he could wait no longer, said, "So what's in the letter they gave you yesterday?"

"Letter? I've got a list, if that's what you mean. Although I believe Alina has been given a missive to carry to Spain."

"Alina? I thought the king was sending you—"

Ludo raised a finger to his lips; then, handing Marcos a folded paper from his breeches' pocket he murmured, "Would you like to see the queen's list?"

Marcos looked at exactly what Ludo had described: a list. "It looks like one of my wife's shopping expeditions—er, no, it's not like one of Joanna's lists at all—*¡demonios, qué pedido!*"

"A shopping list to take me back around the world, eh? If I choose to go."

"For pearls and Arab horses, rubies and diamonds, and whatever 'special treats' you encounter. That was the expression the king used as well."

"Exactly: a good wife can get her husband to buy her anything—take warning."

"Except we are paying for the pleasure of doing all the work," Marcos added.

"True, for now, but next year—next year we should both be getting very rich. Not that I won't be risking my life at sea as part of the bargain."

Marcos smiled then remembered how Ludo was involving him and his father-in-law's savings for the Goa venture and gulped. In a less jocular tone, and keeping his eyes on his feet, he said, "There's more to it, though, isn't there?"

Ludo cocked his head. "*Forse si, forse no,*" he muttered in Tuscan Italian.

"But what does the king want? What's happening in Spain?"

"Ah, that. His Majesty was easier to manage than I'd expected. Unfortunately I am not at liberty to discuss it, and certainly not where walls have ears." He indicated the usher standing at the door, not unlike a prison guard.

"He won't speak Spanish or Tuscan," Marcos hissed. "Please, be serious and tell me why you really came to London."

"To deliver a message, and if possible get an English licence to trade in the East."

"Ludo, why do you need an *English* licence for anything?"

"It solves a problem in Goa."

"In Goa—what has happened in Goa? Ludo, stop, please. Tell me what is going on: why have you come to London, really, and where are you going next?"

Ludo smoothed back his black hair, tied neatly at the nape of his neck with a discrete black ribbon, and looked away. "I acquired a Portuguese business and a few new Portuguese enemies in Goa. I also need to keep my galleon, *Tulip*. I can't risk the Spanish trying to steal her back, and I need... another document signed by the Spanish chief minister. To these ends, I need to treat with the Count-Duke of Olivares in person. I have, somewhat by accident, found a means of direct access to him under the protection of the English monarchy—meaning he can't fling me in a dungeon or worse without causing a diplomatic upset. Of course, he can pretend I never arrived in Madrid, but you will be with me as a witness."

"Me? I'm not going to Madrid."

"Oh, I think you will."

"Not if it puts me in danger, I won't. I have a wife to think about."

"That scenario is unlikely—don't worry."

"Don't worry!" Marcos rested his head on the back of his chair and closed his eyes, then he said, "So what's next?"

"First, we return to Plymouth. I need to check on *Tulip* in the dry dock and make some arrangements with Captain Guthrie. I also need to arrange for silver to be delivered to King Charles directly, and send some goods from my current stock to the Palace of Oatlands. Once all that is done, we're going to Spain, to the court of King Felipe, fourth of that name, ostensibly on the King of England's business, but, as I have just explained, also on mine. I also need to get a message to Vigo. I don't suppose I could persuade you to do that for me?"

"Er, no, definitely not. I had no intention of leaving Plymouth before you arrived, and after what you have just said I shall most definitely be staying in England, thank you very much. I've got a wife at home expecting a baby."

"You've just invented that."

"Indeed I have not! Joanna will have our baby in the autumn."

"And you will be pacing outside her chamber with perspiring brow? I think not."

"I will."

"Marcos," Ludo turned, his eyes piercing through Marcos's thin shell of self-respect. "I rescued you from ignominy when you were a beardless loon with ideas far, far above your station.

I have taught you all you know. Is this how you plan to repay me? What happened to the eager young man who *insisted* I take him to Flanders?"

Marcos looked back at his feet, saying, "He grew up and got married and settled down."

"Hah! We'll see about that!" Ludo laughed, then changed his tone and, speaking barely above a whisper, continued, "Listen, I am instructed by the reigning monarch of the British Isles to treat with the king and chief minister of Spain on a very pressing *personal* matter, *in person*. Your Spanish naturally being better than mine and you being the secretary who was present at my royal interview, I obviously cannot do without you."

Marcos didn't know whether to laugh or cry.

When Alina finally arrived, rosy-cheeked and flustered, she announced that the queen had arranged a barge to take her to Oxford before she travelled down to Plymouth, so she would not be joining them on their return trip to Plymouth. Ludo announced he would be departing by ship as planned: Marcos could travel with Alina if he preferred.

Marcos looked from one to the other. The atmosphere crackled between them, and once again he wondered where Ludo had spent the last two nights. On the night of the dunking he had had a room in the palace—but he had not returned to their lodgings in Lambeth on the previous night, either. Angry that he was allowing himself to get hurt again, Marcos said, "I shall travel with Alina, obviously. One of us must escort her."

"She'll have a maid," retorted Ludo. "The Lady Alina would not be expected to travel alone."

"Even so..." Marcos said, looking at Alina, who smiled back gratefully.

"I do have a maid, of sorts," Alina responded. "She is from the Crimphele estate, though, so I'm expecting her to run back to her mother the minute we cross the Tamar. Heaven knows how she'll manage in Spain."

"Spain?" Marcos said. "I thought you were coming back to Plymouth with me."

"I am. Then I'm going to Spain—with Ludo."

Marcos looked suspiciously at Ludo, who shrugged his shoulders.

"Actually, I'm not sure I want her to travel to Spain," Alina gushed, "especially knowing what sort of journey we have ahead of us once we land."

"Her? Who?" In his suspicion and nervousness about what was really happening Marcos was becoming confused.

"Fanny, my silly maid," Alina explained. "I fear she will not be up to the journey across Castile."

"Precisely why I am sailing back to Plymouth," Ludo said. "We'll be seeing enough of equine arses in the next few weeks without adding to the quota in England. I can never decide which is worse: haemorrhoids from sitting in a coach for days on end or from sitting on a saddle." He paused. "I don't suppose Mr Beale could supply us with a modern coach with those new-fangled springs for decent overland transport?"

"No," Marcos grunted.

"Pity. Never mind—we can stop at Alina's family home on the way to Madrid if we cross to Santander instead of La Coruña."

"Ah, you must be referring to my *late* father," Alina said adopting a tragic tone. "I regret he passed away before I arrived in England. You must have forgotten. It was you who brought me the sad news yourself, remember?"

Ludo gave her a charming grin in response and put his old leather hat on without another word.

"You found it?" Marcos said, noticing the hat for the first time.

"I certainly did. I sent someone out to fish for it. Can't lose this hat, best friend I've got—next to you and *madonna* here," Ludo replied, then, tucking his *bizalho* box beneath his arm, he walked to the door of the anteroom. "I'll see you in Plymouth, my dears, so *hasta luego y fate buon viaggio e arrivederci a presto!*"

As he left, Marcos suddenly realised what Alina had been saying about the barge. "What do you mean Oxford before Plymouth or before Spain? Why *are you* going to Spain anyway?" He peered at her and met a haughty gaze he remembered well.

"What?" she responded narrowing her eyes. "Why shouldn't I go back to Spain? It's my country same as yours."

"You are very defensive all of a sudden. Do you want to tell me why, or is this not the right time?" Marcos watched Alina grab a handful of skirt. "Go on, tell me."

"Later," she whispered. "Not here."

Later, travelling in the considerable comfort of red velvet cushioned seats on the royal barge making its way into the upper reaches of the River Thames, Marcos said, "Do you think Thomas will mind you going to Spain—with me? If I go, that is."

Alina looked out at the opposite bank and gave a slight shrug. "It is to his benefit in the long run, although I confess I'm not happy about being away from him or my little boy again for so long."

"I can understand that."

"Ludo doesn't."

"Ludo has never had a wife to think about. But why *are you* going to Spain?" Marcos insisted quietly.

"To deliver a personal message from the queen to her sister, and... erm, follow the outcome of something I cannot discuss."

"You as well. 'Personal'—Ludo used almost identical words."

"Did he? Perhaps they are using both of us for the same end."

"You are speaking in riddles—the same as him."

Before saying anything more, Alina lifted the curtain behind their seat, studying who was within earshot then peered forward to check that her maid was still in place in the bows. Continuing in Spanish, she said, "The queen is in a difficult situation with her sister of Spain. Did you know King Charles created a tremendous scandal in Madrid some twenty years ago?" Marcos shook his head. "He went there to woo King Felipe's younger sister Marianna, then left after something like two years of Spanish hospitality and cancelled the betrothal using the excuse that it was because he was not at liberty to marry a Catholic. Then he married Henrietta Maria, who's an ardent Catholic. Felipe took this as a personal insult to Spain and the Habsburgs, naturally. Added to which, after what happened in the battle last year off the coast of Kent between the Dutch and the Spanish, Charles and Henrietta Maria fear King Felipe thinks England may be actively working against Spanish interests again."

"And are they?"

"I don't think so." Alina lowered her voice. "Charles can't afford poor relations with Spain now."

"Why not?"

"The queen... because of what may happen if these Parliamentarians do what they are threatening to do. Not that I can believe they will ever have troops or enough power to carry it through. But there is a risk."

"Oh, so Charles and Henrietta want support from Spain that way."

"It works both ways. There is a secret treaty being written up right now, as I understand, giving Spain access to English waters and English ports in their fight against Flanders. Henrietta Maria has been pushing Charles to help the Catholic cause against the Dutch Protestants. England helps Felipe and Felipe helps England."

"Logical. Why is it secret, though, if there are going to be Spaniards in the country?" Marcos paused then answered his own question, "My God, the English will go mad—they hate Spaniards in Plymouth. Francis Drake is a saint in their eyes for preventing a Spanish invasion. Took Mr and Mrs Beale months to accept me into the family, and then only because I'd already got my own little business."

"Exactly. There's also the added complication of Henrietta Maria being French, and France always being at war with Spain... You can see why Charles and Felipe are trying to keep matters private until it's all concluded."

Marcos tried to think analytically as Ludo had instructed. "Hence the *personal* messages—so the respective ambassadors are not seen to be conferring together."

Alina adjusted her skirts. "There is that, too."

"So you and Ludo are being used to avoid normal diplomatic channels. Sounds a bit unreliable—whatever can they be thinking of, trusting Ludo? Still it makes a certain sense. But supposing the Parliamentarians' threats are merely hot air? What can Spain give England apart from oranges and wine in return for using her harbours?"

Alina touched a gold crucifix at her throat.

"*Jesús Cristo*, not the Holy Mass?" Marcos, his eyes like saucers looked at Alina and said, "I hope the queen isn't putting you in danger with this feminine diplomacy."

"It may prove quite an adventure, and, as you suggest, the rewards are great."

"But you surely aren't being asked to influence or even get involved in a treaty—on this scale?"

"No! No, my task is quite other. Related, but quite, quite other. It's, as I said, personal."

Marcos sighed, unsure if this was better or worse.

After a while Alina whispered, "Marcos, don't repeat any of this anywhere, will you?"

"Of course not. Although I think you might be wrong. I can't see Ludo allowing himself to be caught up in matters of religion —again."

"Neither can I; not really. He hasn't told you precisely why he's going to Madrid, I suppose."

"No, I am instructed to accompany him, but I am not deemed worthy of a reason. Apparently the Genoese are very close to the Spanish court, being their bankers. I *suspect* King Charles wants Ludo to... Actually, I've really no idea, and why Charles should trust anything to Ludo, given that they've only met the once—that defeats me."

"Does it? He wouldn't be the first to fall under Ludo's spell."

"No, well..." Marcos examined the lace on the cuff of his right sleeve. "I was much younger then."

"So was I."

Marcos looked at Alina. "Have you ever told Thomas?"

"No."

"Good: don't."

After a tranquil pause, neither Marcos nor Alina wishing to examine the past, Alina ran her fingers through the bright tassels hanging from the velvet awning above and said lightly, "Apart from what we were just discussing, Ludo was looking very pleased with himself."

"He's achieved what he came for, apparently."

"Which was?"

"A licence to bring goods to Britain from the East Indies: he's going back to India."

"But... but he can buy his goods in the Mediterranean and sell on and save himself all manner of dangers. Oh, look—how pretty!" Alina pointed to a flotilla of stately swans paddling slowly downriver. Marcos waited. Eventually she said, "Her Majesty wants me to keep an eye on Ludo in Spain."

Marcos roared with laughter, then sobered. As if watching the female swan and her fluffy-feathered brood, he said, "Why? What has she asked him to do—apart from sail the world and collect exotic luxuries?"

Alina shook her head in genuine despair and whispered, "She has asked him to go to Spain to get rid of someone."

"*Get rid of*—Ludo? No, you've got it wrong."

"That is what she told me. He is going to 'get rid of someone for Queen Isabel'—her words."

"And who is this 'someone', or are you not at liberty to reveal that? Heavens, she doesn't want you to make sure he does it and report back to her? Or help him!" Marcos was joking, but Alina's face told him he'd hit the mark. "*Madre mía de mi vida*, what is all this?"

"I'm not supposed to mention it to anyone."

"I'm not 'anyone'. Tell me—maybe I can help."

"The queen had a private meeting with Ludo last night, after you returned to your lodging. The letter he brought—it was something to do with helping Queen Isabel—she's Henrietta Maria's sister—in Spain. I haven't seen what's in the letter, but it's related to helping Isabel get rid of her worst enemy, who's acting against her husband's interests by not making peace in Flanders or with the French. Ludo brought the letter from Spain and the queen, Henrietta Maria, is sending him back to... do the job."

"I can't believe it. Ludo is many things, but he's not an assassin. That's awful." Marcos paused, then said, "It has to be for a massive reward. Ludo doesn't do anything for free."

"Perhaps it was the hidden extra of your trading licences."

Marcos went cold. Would Ludo do that for him? It was possible. But surely—an assassination... Ludo played for high stakes but he was no murderer. He suddenly went cold again remembering how Alina had evaded his question about her involvement. "What's your role, Alina?" he asked.

"To give the queen in Spain the letter from her sister in secret, and to report what Ludo does."

Now it was Marcos's turn to look out at the river. Then quietly, slowly, he said, "And what is *your* reward for all this?"

Alina looked at him, a smile creeping into her features, her eyes beginning to twinkle. "Her Majesty says I shall become her chief lady-of-the-bedchamber when I return, but Thomas is only a baron, you see. A lady-of-the-bedchamber has to be the wife of at least a viscount."

"And King Charles will elevate Thomas to a viscount on her bidding. So you are to be a great lady after all."

"Yes, I am. And this is only the start, because Thomas is a Catholic as well, and that means he may have an important role in... the future." Alina's happy face then darkened. "Although I fear the queen's good graces depend more on Ludo than on what I might achieve."

"He doesn't give a tinker's cuss about religion."

"That's what worries me."

Chapter 14

Oxford

Alina did not tell her husband Thomas even half of what she had been asked to do in Spain, but he was more upset than she'd feared he might be none the less.

Standing at the window of his Oxford college study, tapping the sill nervously, he said, "This is too much. Her Majesty has no right to ask this of you."

"What can I do?"

"Develop a sickness. Go home to recuperate and stay there. Wait until I can join you then discover you are once more with child—for example."

Alina smoothed a forefinger over a deep scratch in the heavy oak table at which she was seated. The scratch had been filled with lavender scented beeswax, but it was still visible. This was how it was with them—for her at least. Lifting her head and pushing away a loosened curl from her forehead, she said, "I cannot do that. And think, Thomas, you will be named a viscount."

"Which will cost me another fortune the estate of Crimphele cannot afford." Thomas turned from the window, his face dark with suppressed anger. "The price of titles rises by the month. How do you think Charles is paying for his wife's masques and masses? You've seen the Queen's Chapel at St James's, and that was just the beginning. Who do you think pays for their banquets and balls, Alina? Royal estates don't provide for half of it."

"I never thought about it. But Crimphele, Home Farm and your lands—their yield is good, isn't it? You could pay—if need be?"

"Our income is good enough to keep us while we're there, but it won't stretch to royal revels or what'll be expected of me as a viscount. Supposing I'm told to provide a trained band—do you think our Crimphele labourers are even up to it?"

"You're angry, and I thought you would be so pleased," Alina's voice trailed off. She fixed her gaze on a point above her husband's head. "We will find a way to pay, and the labourers as well, if that is required. This is too good an opportunity to lose."

With a meaningful intake of breath Thomas returned to the table, where he turned a page of a tome and pretended to read.

Alina got up and wandered around the small, oak-panelled room, running her fingers along a shelf of ancient books, pausing to look at a display of butterflies and moths in a glass case. "You still find time for your hobby; that is good. What is this pretty one with purple on its wings?"

Ignoring her attempt to distract him, Thomas said, "I suppose we have no choice. We cannot refuse the queen. If you could delay a month I could get permission to accompany you."

Alina moved to his side and leaned her head on his bony shoulder. "That increases the risk too greatly. We must think of our little Tomás at Crimphele."

"Oh, my love, would that I could go in your place."

Alina gave an embarrassed smile and there was an awkward silence. Eventually she said quietly, "Thomas, if anything does happen to me, on the crossing, on the journey there or coming back, or in Madrid…"

"Why should anything happen to you in Madrid? You are going to be in the royal palace, aren't you?"

"Yes, yes of course. I only meant if—for any reason—I do not return…" Thomas hugged her to him, muffling her words, but Alina pulled away. "No, listen to me, please. Ask the king if you may go back to Crimphele, and stay there with John so you are near our child. Then promise me you will marry again—"

"No!" Thomas's voice caught with emotion. Dropping his arms, he turned back to stare sightlessly out of the mullioned window. For a while they were silent again, then he said, "My dear, could you bear to go directly to Madrid, as the queen requested, as fast as possible. Don't go back to Crimphele first. It will only upset our little one more if he sees you and then you disappear again. I'll get down there as soon as I can."

Alina put her hands to her face, trying to control her tears. She knew her husband was right and it broke her heart, because every day for months she had been torn by the dilemma of revelling in court life and its prospects and longing to be back at Crimphele. She had achieved an important goal in her life, but at the price of not seeing her small son for many more months to come.

"Did you think to visit your brothers?" Thomas asked as Alina was leaving.

"I would like to call in at my old home on my return." Alina wondered if this was the moment to explain why her supposed dowry had never arrived, and that her father was probably alive and well and gambling the last of their silver spoons at a game of cards in the Alcázar of Madrid, or wherever the court was currently residing. But all she said was, "I hadn't better delay on the journey there."

Having given it much consideration, she had decided it would be better if her father discovered she was alive and well, married to an English nobleman—and not in a Barbary harem—*after* she had fulfilled her duties to her queen. If he learned beforehand, that she now had the ear of one queen and was about to discuss highly secret matters with another, he would take advantage of the situation for sure, and it was delicate enough without his bonhomie and fancy laces muddling matters. Preventing her father, a penniless grandee, from parading her at court was paramount for the success of her venture as a silent courier and reluctant witness.

As he followed Alina down the stairs leading to the green quad Thomas said, "Marcos will be with you at all times, won't he?" There had been an unspoken suspicion since the moment he had learned that she and Marcos had arrived together at the Christ Church landing stage.

"He'll take care of me, but he will be visiting his family in the south so, no, he won't be with me *all* the time."

"Alina,"—Thomas put a hand on her shoulder, bringing her to a halt before the outside door—"I did know about you and Marcos."

Alina frowned, "About Marcos? What is there to know? There has never been anything—he didn't ever... No, you are wrong. Marcos is like a brother or cousin to me."

"Habsburg royals marry their first cousins and nieces. Cousins marry in Spain."

"Not these cousins." Alina smiled and kissed her husband's cheek.

"So the emerald wasn't from him?"

"What emerald?"

"The one I found in your chamber when I returned from Oxford the first time, when I was ill with the pleurisy."

Alina's stomach did a dip and a dive as she remembered an emerald the size of a blackbird's egg on her pillow the morning Ludo had left without a word. She recalled hurling it across her bedchamber and watching it fall safely out of sight behind a tall chest. Her face flushed from cold to hot, but her words were calm and measured. "I don't think Marcos has ever been in a position to buy precious jewels, Thomas. Besides, he's married now to a plump little Plymouth dumpling, so you have nothing to worry about in that direction."

Gathering her shawl about her shoulders, shaking slightly—for in the five years of their marriage this had been the closest Thomas had ever come to discovering her relationship with Ludo—Alina forced herself to say, "If you suspected Marcos of being—actually, no! Do you know how much I suffered while you were away on royal matters after Tomás was born? How dare you accuse me of..." the stress of the moment stripped her mind of correct English phrases; she was thinking in Spanish and groped for words.

Thomas said quietly, "You might try seeing the months Marcos was with us at Crimphele—when I kept him on as steward—as my punishment. It was a test, I admit. But perhaps I was testing myself more than you or he."

Alina swivelled round, her skirts shifting motes of dust that danced around the chilly hallway like her husband's doubts. "Have you been thinking all this time that Marcos was my lover?"

"I was never sure. When he left to set up his own business I was more at ease."

Alina's shoulders slumped; she suddenly wanted to fall to the floor and let life ride on by. It was a very close call and she was not without guilt, but in this Thomas was wrong: she had only ever thought of Marcos as a friend, or like one of her annoying younger brothers. "You were wrong," she hissed. And before her husband could say anything more she stepped outdoors and called to Marcos, who was sitting on a bench waiting for her.

Chapter 15

Plymouth

In Plymouth, Marcos's wife Joanna sobbed and sobbed against her husband's chest, soaking one of his better waistcoats. He dabbed her eyes and promised he wouldn't go. Then he spoke to his father-in-law.

"You *must* go, boy!" said Edward Beale. "It could do us a power of good for the future, this could. Listen..." He beckoned Marcos to sit with him on a blue padded window seat. "And this is to go no further. Not a word outside this room, understand?—not to Joanna or her mother—least of all to her mother."

Marcos sat beside him, intrigued. "What?"

"There's a move among the business people here that's—how shall I put it?—treasonable. They're saying Pym in London, together with most of Parliament, will challenge the king and take over the country. They say they're going to *execute* the king's adviser Strafford if they can, and it doesn't take much imagination, boy, to work out where all this might end."

"*Madre mía!* So it's really happening," Marcos gasped, but then he was angry, "After what I've just paid in London, all the effort we've just gone through to get a warrant to supply goods to the royal palaces, not to mention what happened on the Thames, *que fastidia!* How will it affect us?"

"Ah, well, now, we got to play careful and play wise. Carve with two knives and both hands, so to speak. Think on it, boy: you and your Ludovico have found favour with the king, but what if the king isn't with us much longer?"

"Exactly!"

"Or, what if he *defeats his opposers and rules without Parliament* again? We need to butter our bread on both sides, see?" Edward Beale continued, mixing his metaphors but making his meaning clear. "You go along with the royal party supporters—keep in with the court people best you can—and do a bit of negotiating on your own to make sure your supply of Spanish wine and sugar is safe; find a way to increase the salt we get, as well. And I'll play along with the Parliament men here. I do that, anyway, so they won't notice much change."

"But you are a Catholic. Won't that make a difference?"

"And how many people know that, eh? It might make a difference one day, yes, but for now Mrs Beale and me go on like we already do. Buggered if I'm going to pay a fine for not going to church of a Sunday and rousing suspicions into the bargain."

"But Mrs Beale has a rosary. There's a crucifix in her chamber—I've seen it."

"Not after today there isn't."

Marcos nodded and his father-in-law slapped him on the back. "You'm a smart boy, Mark. I knew it soon as I met you. You go to Spain and visit your suppliers and get better deals where you can, and leave me to worry about what's happening here. One thing, though, don't you be tempted to stay there, will you?" His tone carried a warning. "That would break my little girl's heart."

"No, Father, I shan't be tempted to stay. I've got all I want right here: my own business, with your help, of course, and a new family, and a little one on the way. I'll go if I have to, and with your permission I would like to visit my parents in Sanlúcar as well. I'll visit my suppliers like you say, but I'll be coming back as soon as I can."

"That's it, boy." Edward Beale slapped Marcos on the back again, a mark of affection with an extra buffet as a reminder that his daughter's happiness and a thriving business arrangement was at stake.

As Marcos opened the door to leave, though, his father-in-law raised a hand. "One thing, before you go. This merchant from Genoa—who is he, really?"

"Ludo? I've told you. You've met him. I thought you liked him."

Edward Beale scrunched up his beefy face in a grimace. "Liking's neither here nor there in business, boy. What I'm asking is: who is he, really? I know where he's from and that he's nimble with a deal, but is he to be relied upon?"

"No!" Marcos laughed. "But I'll be careful. I *am* careful—he taught me that the hard way. I shan't go spending money we haven't got for goods we don't need, if that's what worries you, Father."

"It doesn't. Well, it does, but I trust you in that."

"So?"

"Curious, that's all. I was wondering why a merchant with his background in Genoa, who can get you into a royal palace and come out with all manner of ventures and advantages—if all that's true?—is bothering with us."

Marcos looked across the room, seeing images of Ludo in conversation with a king and queen. His father-in-law was right to ask: it was all a bit odd. Did Ludo really only want to make himself rich—or was there something else going on?

Part Three
Spain

$$Chapter\ 16$$

Northern Spain, Summer 1640

Alina had never seen so many shades of brown. After leaving the green rolling hills of Santander, very like the gentle countryside of Devonshire, then climbing and climbing until the poor horses could take not another step, they had arrived at a *posada* on the edge of a windswept plain. The wind scorched all it touched, driving sharp grit into soft crevices of her neck and around her eyes. Once indoors and safe from the elements, conditions were not much better; the atmosphere was stale and suffocating, and despite their modest travel wear Alina and her small maid Fanny attracted too much attention.

After eating as fast as she could, Alina left the *posada* and walked up and down the hard-baked horse road, fanning herself and staring out at this new, unknown Spain. "I had never been anywhere until that day Ludo saved me from the corsairs," she said, half to herself. "Fanny, untie your bodice—you'll faint again if you don't."

"That boy will look at my chest, milady."

Fanny was referring to Ludo's cheerful and very competent servant, José. Alina narrowed her eyes. "Do as you are told. 'That boy' hasn't got a beard yet and you haven't got anything to look at yet, either. You'd do better to make friends with him and get his help when you need it, not ignore him the way you do."

"But he's foreign."

"I'm foreign, everyone is foreign, you stupid girl. In fact now we are in Spain *you* are the foreigner!" Alina lost her patience then immediately regretted it: Fanny was still very young and felt alone and different in a strange country; she knew what that was like. "Have you drunk enough small ale? You mustn't become thirsty in hot weather," she said in a softer tone.

Fanny nodded. "Will it always be hot like this, milady?"

"For the next two or three months, yes; on the coast we had the sea wind, but the wind here is coming from the south across miles and miles of hot land so it seems worse."

Ludo breezed out of the *posada* with a length of white muslin in his hand. Dunking it in the horse trough, he then swung it around in the air like a windmill and examined it closely for flora and fauna. Finally giving it another swing, he wrapped it around his head like a Mohammedan's turban. Alina and Fanny stared at him.

"*Qué pasa?*" he demanded in Spanish.

Alina shook her head. "*Nothing, nada, niente.*"

"Oh ho, three words in three languages, a tripling trinity worthy of our priestly acquaintance Father John Hawthorne, bless his boring soul."

Alina shook her head in mild despair at Ludo's good spirits. He beamed at her and came to stand very close. Brushing her ear with his lips he whispered, "I do believe coming home has knocked a full five years off your troubled brow, *carina*. You remind me utterly of the naughty young woman I saved in Santander all those years ago."

Alina pulled away. "But I'm not—and don't you forget it."

"Not what, a delightful young woman?"

Alina's eyes narrowed. Backing away further, she bent down and picked up a stone and weighted in her hand ready to throw.

Ludo raised his hands in alarm. "No, please no! You never miss!"

"And well you should remember it," Alina shouted, but as she took aim at the none-too-white turban she caught the expression on her maid's face and dropped the stone into her other hand, then held it to her face as if examining its markings.

The maid continued to stand with mouth agape and Ludo roared with laughter. Marcos appeared at the doorway with Ludo's servant José, whose arms were loaded with provisions for the next stage of the journey.

Catching a buffet of heat coming off the land, Marcos said, "*Rayos y truenos*, it's hot. I'm going to take a siesta round the back in the shade. Better for the horses as well if we delay leaving for an hour or two."

As he spoke a traveller wearing a peasant's straw hat—but astride a rangy bay nag few peasants could ever afford—arrived at the *posada*. Ludo and Marcos simultaneously gave him a '*buenos días*'. The man kept his moustachioed face low and grunted something over his beast then rode to the rail, barely acknowledging them.

Ludo and Marcos exchanged glances. "Are you being followed?" Marcos asked out of the corner of his mouth.

Ludo shook his head. "No, I can't believe he's followed me here. Not across the Channel. Not all the way up here, not very likely."

"You hope." Marcos turned to Alina, "You can take a siesta in the *salón*. The landlady says it's cooler in there and she doesn't mind if we stay until later. This heat can't get worse."

It did get worse. The coach, the best Ludo could acquire in Santander—and it had taken over a week to make the purchase and find a suitable coachman prepared to make the long journey with no return date—became filled with choking dust. The seats were hard and unforgiving, the road nothing more than a wide, rutted track. Alina pulled back a leather curtain, hoping against hope that the exterior air would be cooling down. It was not. The evenings were as hot as the blistering days; sweat ran between her breasts and soaked her undergarments between her legs. The men, who had stripped down to their wide-sleeved shirts with her permission, mopped their brows and were just as uncomfortable. Staring at the endless expanse of brown and ochre, at miles and miles of stubble and stones, she wished herself anywhere but here.

When they finally reached Burgos, Alina begged that they stay two nights, to rest the horses she said. Marcos, who was stroking the white blaze of one of the four-in-hand agreed. "We should. These poor beasts need a break—look at them."

Ludo pulled on his waistcoat and huffed, "I didn't know you were so fond of horses, Marcos. You've been fussing round them since I got them."

"I used to look after travellers' horses before my father went to Flanders, when we still had people coming to the *hostal* who needed their beasts cared for."

"I didn't know that."

"No reason why you should." Marcos's voice was sharp. They were all out of temper with the journey and each other. "What difference does it make?"

"None whatsoever. José, arrange for our luggage to be brought in. And don't forget to help the ladies if they need it. I'll check the rooms for fleas and cause another scandal by asking for a bath. What is wrong with these people—why don't they wash, or approve of those who wish to?"

"It's because they're afraid of being called out and accused of *judaizar*. People say washing shows you're a Jew—or a Mohammedan," Alina explained. "My father used to drone on and on about our Christian pedigree and untainted blood, our *limpieza de sangre*: what the English call being blue-blooded."

"*Dio mio*! Who in this world has blue blood?"

"I have, stupid, look!" Alina held out her white wrists to show her blue veins. "Blue, see!"

"All right, all right, if it makes you happy and get's me a bath, I'll wear my turban for the rest of the week and you can tell the lady of the house you're my other Hebrew heiress."

"I can what!" Alina retorted. "How dare you!"

Ludo waved a hand. "Calm down, no insult intended—on the contrary. I only want a tub of water—is that so much to ask?" Keeping his arms raised in surrender, Ludo walked back to stand at Alina's side. "Why have you become so aggressive, *carina*?" he asked quietly. "You were not like this in London."

"What do you mean 'aggressive'? I'm not aggressive! It's you. You've bullied your way back into a relationship I should never have let happen in the first place, you've—"

Ludo took her elbow and led her away from the others. "I have not *bullied* you into anything. Far from it, if I remember correctly—who was the girl who tried to seduce me on the ship crossing from France, mm?"

"That was years ago!"

"Perhaps it was, so let's get one thing straight between us now: you have no quarrel with me. If you are harping back to what happened in Cornwall, it is I who was the injured party, remember, physically as it happens. I still bear the scar."

Alina grabbed a fistful of skirt. Kneading the dry cotton in tension, she whispered, "I know, and in one way I am sorry. I didn't plan what happened to you—how could I? I always dreamed you'd come back for me, but when you did... things had changed. I have changed. Please, forget what happened in Whitehall. I cannot let that start again—not now. I was being very foolish. What happened in Whitehall—it was a mistake. It *must not* continue. Please, forget it."

Ludo took one of her hands and brushed a knuckle with his lips. "As you wish, milady. Although I fear I shall not be able to forget, *carina*. But if it will keep you sweet, I shall never mention it again. Truce?"

"Truce."

"Good. Now let us see if we can find a way to get clean without causing a religious scandal." He cocked his head on one side and gave Alina his boyish grin, "Coming?"

"In a moment. Let me organise Fanny first—I think she's crying again."

Ludo strolled away and Alina started towards Fanny, who was, as she suspected, crying again. "What is it this time?" she demanded, sending the girl into a howl of despair. "What is it? What ails you?"

"Everybody's talking and angry and I don't understand what they're saying," she sobbed.

Alina touched the girl's shoulder. "I do know what this is like, Fanny. And I can also promise that if you stay alert and calm you will learn much more quickly. Can you do that for me? Try to learn my language?" The girl nodded. "There we are, then. Now, go up to our room and prepare my clothes for tomorrow."

Leaving the girl gulping sobs, Alina walked to the door of the busy cathedral city *hostal*, trying to calm her increasing sense of an unnamed panic. She had foreseen that the journey would be tiresome—tedious, even—but not that she would be looking after grown men and moaning servants again, just as she had in her father's house, and she deeply resented it.

Sometime later, while she was enjoying a cool tub of cleansing water, Alina remembered what Ludo had said after she'd explained why people were reluctant to admit to taking a bath. Flushing at the appalling implications, she turned the word 'other' this way and that, wondering who she was, and where the 'other Hebrew heiress' might be.

The next day was equally trying, but when they stopped for the night in Lerma there was good news. The court was in El Escorial for the summer, meaning they would not have to travel all the way to Madrid.

Tired of the company of men, Alina ate her evening meal and went up to her room. On the landing she passed a vaguely familiar figure: an ill-dressed man with drooping shoulders and a drooping moustache. "*Buenas noches,*" she said automatically.

The man lifted his straw hat respectfully, but avoided her eyes and went to a room further down the corridor.

Fanny had made some effort with their clothes, and two clean shifts were hanging to dry on the windowsill. The maid herself was fast asleep in a cot across the other side of the room. Too alert to sleep, Alina went back downstairs to take a turn in the patio below. It was a cloudless night, a full moon lighting the buildings all around. She ambled towards the stables. Horses in stalls were resting, one hind leg tipped up at the toe, bones locked in equine slumber. The *hostal* had provided their beasts with fresh barley straw, a luxury in this epoch of the year. She inhaled the warm, sweet scent and was taken back to a time when her father still had more than one poor broken mule and his own fine gelding in their stable—when he was home. Across the aisle, a large, rangy bay lowered itself to the floor with a groan. Its flanks were still white with dried sweat. She had seen this horse before. And its taciturn rider—the man they had met at the previous *posada*: someone else taking the road to Madrid despite the heat of summer.

Alina was awoken by a dull thud. At first she thought it was Fanny falling from her cot. It was not. There was another thud, the sound of feet on floorboards, a muffled yell. She sat bolt upright, hearing Marcos call for help.

Ludo is ill. Ignoring her dishabille, Alina sprang from her bed, out of her room, and flung herself into the men's chamber, seeing nothing in the dark but a bulk of intermingled black shapes. There was a scuffle and a crack, then a clay pitcher crashed to her bare feet, spilling tepid water over her toes.

"What's the matter?" she called. "What's happening?" Before her words were finished she was spun against the door frame as a male figure rushed out of the room.

Marcos staggered towards her, bent double. "It's all right, he's gone. Get a candle; I want to see what he's taken."

Alina dashed back to her room for a candle and tinderbox, stubbing her toes on uneven floorboards. Fanny slept on. Grabbing what she needed, Alina returned to the men's chamber, where Marcos was leaning out of the open window.

"Take my place here and tell me if you hear a horse leave," he commanded. Alina did as she was bid, handing him candle and tinderbox.

Marcos was still half doubled over. "What's wrong?" she asked.

"I got punched," he groaned, clutching his stomach and visibly shaking even in the gloom.

Once the candle had flared to life, though, Marcos rushed to the bed. "Ludo," he hissed. Ludo didn't answer. Marcos lifted the lighted candle above the bed. Ludo was slumped half in half out, barely conscious. "*Por Dios*," Marcos muttered, trying to lift him back into the bed.

"What?" Alina ran to the bed then dropped to her knees beside Ludo. Stroking his face, she whispered, "Ludo, Ludo, wake up, what's wrong?"

"This," Marcos said, holding the candle nearer to the sheets so Alina could see the blood.

"Oh, my God! Oh, my God!" Alina ripped back the single greyish sheet to reveal Ludo's bare chest spurting blood. "What must we do?" she screamed. "Ludo! Don't die! Help, somebody, help!"

Roused from other rooms, men gathered at the doorway. "Someone fetch a surgeon," Marcos shouted.

"Here, let me look." An older man, wearing a floor-length nightgown despite the heat, stepped into the room. "I've been in Flanders and done a bit of physicking in my time."

Marcos gently pulled Alina from Ludo's side. The man took the candle then told Alina to get more, as many as she could find. Pulling up the top sheet, he stuffed it over Ludo's chest to absorb the fresh blood, then gradually inched it back little by little. Probing Ludo's wound with a forefinger, he said, "Dagger blade, by the looks of it. Doesn't normally knock them unconscious, though."

"It hasn't," Ludo croaked. "Can I move?"

"Not yet. Stay as still as possible." The Flanders physician turned to Marcos. "Get me brandy and something clean for bandages. My sheets will do."

Alina watched, frozen to the spot, until Marcos shouted at her, "Get José! He's sleeping above the stables—tell him to find more candles!"

"See if you can get clean water, *señora*. But it must be clean," the old soldier said.

Forgetting all about Ludo's servant, Alina raced off, grabbed the jug from her room, and returned in such haste that she lost her footing and lurched forward, but was saved by one of the onlookers. Another took her jug and carried it like an offering to the old soldier, who tore a length off the hem of his nightgown and began cleaning around the wound.

Marcos arrived with the brandy and a rough cotton sheet, and the soldier set to work, dabbing strips of sheet in alcohol.

Ludo, eyes wide open, was studying the soldier's hands. "How bad?" he asked.

"You could do with stitching, which I can't do here without a proper needle, but if you stay still long enough the bleeding should stop, all right. The cut looks twisted but it's not too deep. Must have tried to get you through the sheet. Lucky you had it over you. The important thing is to stay quiet and let the skin knit together, understand? Keep as still as possible, for as long as possible." The soldier began dabbing around the cut with brandy, making Ludo heave with shock. "Tsss, quiet now," he said. "Stay still or it'll bleed more."

"I know," Ludo grunted.

Satisfied Ludo was in no immediate danger of dying, Marcos returned to registering their bags for signs of theft. "He didn't get anything, I don't think," he said.

"Check my shirt," Ludo whispered. "The pocket inside..."

"Don't talk," the soldier said. "Don't move, don't talk."

"I know," Ludo hissed. "I know."

"You mean this?" Marcos held something in the air but in the poor light Alina couldn't see what it was, a ring perhaps. Marcos took it to the window to examine it but was distracted by the sound of hooves. "Sounds as if he must have been staying here, unless it's a coincidence."

Alina rushed back to the window. "The bay gelding and the man with the moustache, the one we saw before Burgos," she said. "I saw him this evening before I came to bed."

Marcos nodded. "Why am I not surprised?" Then he turned his attention to whatever it was in his hands and after a moment or two replaced it where he had found it. "You're bauble is safe," he said, looking across at Ludo, "but you're not."

"Never have been," Ludo grunted. "What about my *bizalho*?"

Alina said, "Your what?"

"He means his samples," Marcos explained. "What he's taking to show them at the court, I think."

"But he's not going there for that..." Alina started to say then stopped. If that was Ludo's cover it was wise not to draw attention to it.

Chapter 17

Real Sitio de San Lorenzo El Escorial

The small mountainside town of San Lorenzo El Escorial smelled of freshly sawn wood and the sharp odour of pine trees. The air of the Sierra de Guadarrama, despite the season, was so refreshing after the dust of the plains that Alina made no bones about trudging up the steep streets with her male companions in search of lodgings on foot. José tagged along behind them, his mop of basin-cut, black hair wet with sweat as he struggled with one of Alina's smaller portmanteaux on his shoulders. Fanny, giving a short run now and again to keep up, maintained her miserable expression and pulled such a face of disgust when offered a cool, milky-looking drink made from beans, according to Marcos—or roots, according to Ludo—that Alina raised her hand to slap her, and Ludo caught it just in time to prevent an incident in the street.

The court being in residence, lodging was scarce and they were forced to accept a suite of rooms on the second floor of a new building high above the Habsburg palace-monastery complex. Unfortunately it was also near the market place, and the buckets of fly-ridden, steaming offal and decomposing onions did nothing to cheer the maid who was going to have to shop there for food. The rooms themselves, however, were spacious and newly whitewashed.

"Will this do, milady?" Ludo asked.

Alina looked around then fixed him with a challenging gaze. "It will raise questions as to my respectability."

"In that case, perhaps you could ask the landlady if she has alternative accommodation—for you alone," he said drily. "This suits me very well."

"You'll be safer with us, you know," Marcos intervened. "And you've got Fanny to think of, remember."

Alina vacillated, then gave a dramatic sigh, "I expect I shall just have to make the best of the situation." She turned back to Ludo. "Please tell the proprietor I would like a strong lock placed on my door at her earliest convenience."

"Would that be on the inside or outside, milady?" Ludo queried, cocking his head to one side.

"Inside, stupid!"

The next morning, Marcos accompanied Ludo back into the town. Ludo was stronger now, after two weeks in Lerma recuperating from the stab wound in his shoulder, but Marcos was anxious he didn't overdo it. Taking a leisurely stroll through the town they studied the appropriate male attire for the court, learning that pastel silks and satins with abundant ribbons at the knee were much in vogue. In one outfitter's shop they learned that the king himself, however, favoured black with either black or white stockings, and that he had invented a new type of collar to replace the ruff.

Pausing to look in a second window, Ludo huffed with relief. "Looks like the ruff is finally out of fashion, thanks be to God. Ah, but no—what is that?" He pointed at a wired, brilliantly white gauze collar with wings projecting out from under the cheeks to lie at right angles from what would be a human neck.

"More like a square dish than a collar," Marcos said, studying it with his head tilted. "Is this what that tailor said the king has invented?"

"Whatever it is, I shan't be wearing it," Ludo grunted. "All I need is to have my head ready on a plate for them."

Laughing, Marcos said, "Expecting to get it chopped off, are you?" Then he caught Ludo's expression and remembered, firstly, that Ludo didn't like jokes about death, and, secondly, that he had recently survived a stabbing, which was no laughing matter at all.

Ignoring the comment, Ludo opened the door of the shop. "Come on, let's see what they have ready made—you might look pretty in pink."

Appropriately attired the following day, Ludo in expensive black silk that had travelled all the way from the Orient, and Marcos in far less expensive brown cotton, they walked down the busy streets to the palace named *el Real Sitio* in search, Ludo informed his new secretary, of Sir Arthur Hopton, British Ambassador to the Court of Felipe IV.

The ambassador had been allotted a small, north-facing office above the palace courtyard. It was as bare as a monk's cell and entirely appropriate for the man seated there. Sir Arthur Hopton was lean, with a long face and an even longer nose that terminated in a bulge the size of a carbuncle; his fine white web of hair gave him the look of an Old Father Time. Despite his apparent age, however, he also looked remarkably fit, and very sharp. His secretary, by contrast, was dark and round, red-faced and corpulent from over-indulgence. They made an odd pair, Marcos thought.

"So you are not here in any *official* capacity?" Hopton inquired drily, resuming his chair after Ludo had introduced himself.

"Not an official capacity, no," Ludo responded genially. "I'm a merchant of the State of Genoa, so naturally I am always open to possibilities."

"Of a commercial nature?"

"Indeed: of a commercial nature," Ludo repeated with his open-faced smile that Marcos knew to his cost bode ill.

Sir Arthur Hopton gave a brief sigh. "I do not concern myself with mercantile affairs while here in the sierra. Arrange another meeting when we are returned to Madrid."

As if failing to hear him, Ludo continued, "Of course being a member of the house of Doria... perhaps you should read my letter of introduction," and handed the taciturn ambassador a letter written by King Charles's secretary but signed by the royal hand.

The ambassador's bushy white eyebrows shot up the moment he saw the seal. They rose higher when the seal was broken and he saw the signature. He read the letter twice then placed it on his desk.

Without asking permission, Ludo picked it up, re-folded it, and, keeping it in his hand, he said, "I am also acquainted with the Conde-Duque de Olivares, whom I should like very much to see on a personal matter not unrelated to my commission from King Charles. I understand the count-duke is a personal friend of yours, Sir Arthur."

Hopton eyed Ludo suspiciously from behind the laden table serving as his desk. It was covered with scarlet felt, neat piles of folded correspondence and parchment documents tied with red ribbon. Turning to the secretary standing behind him, Hopton said, "Kit, show this gentleman's secretary the palace gardens."

Looking first at Ludo then at Marcos, he continued, "Kit is renowned for knowing all there is to know about the court and its customs. Your secretary will benefit greatly from his knowledge. He has a reputation as 'a perfect Spaniard', is that not so, Kit?" The words carried a barbed reference to something, but the secretary inclined his head impassively.

Taking this as a cue, Ludo turned his beaming smile on the young Englishman. "Ah, you are Christopher Windebank—delighted. We were informed that you act as a guide to visitors, and that you have a great fund of knowledge about this country and its customs. Marcos, of course, is a true Spaniard, albeit from the south and unfamiliar with your court protocol here. Please do not hesitate to instruct him." Ludo indicated Marcos standing behind him. "Allow me to introduce Don Marcos Alonso Almendro, *hidalgo de* Sanlúcar de Barrameda."

Marcos blinked twice, but caught Ludo's warning glare and said nothing. Kit Windebank offered Marcos his hand in the English manner.

"Perhaps," Ludo continued, "after the gardens you could show him something of the new palace; it is a remarkable feat of architecture."

Kit Windebank and Hopton exchanged glances, Hopton giving the briefest nod of assent. And in this manner Ludo neatly disposed of anyone who might testify as to what he was up to—in his unofficial, mercantile capacity. Marcos gave a polite nod and followed the ambassador's plump secretary out of the door.

To Marcos's relief, Kit Windebank proved an agreeable companion. They walked around the sculptured laurel bushes and clipped box hedges of the royal gardens, rubbing their white-stockinged legs against low spreads of sharp scented rosemary and lavender. Looking up at the imposing, austere yet elegant stone edifice that comprised the *Real Sitio* and the monastery of El Escorial, Marcos said, "It's not like a normal castle or palace at all, is it?"

"Forbidding in its simplicity and entirely in keeping with the granite sierra soaring above, wouldn't you say?" Kit Windebank rattled off part of what was evidently his tour guide patter.

For all the young Englishman was dismissive, the place was forbidding. This was a Spain about which Marcos knew nothing and Kit Windebank knew everything, and Marcos was grateful for the education. He was also aware there was more to the tour than admiring the sights.

Kit led him back to the pillared courtyards, saying, "The monastery was started by Philip the Second. He who married Mary Tudor, the queen they call 'Bloody Mary'."

"She tried to return England to Rome."

Kit stopped and gave him a knowing smile. "It's built on a grid design to represent the griddle upon which San Lorenzo was tortured."

Marcos had no idea how to respond, so he merely nodded his head.

Kit gave him another knowing look. "Power and religious piety—the legacy of Carlo Magno... I'm boring you, sorry. Come, let's go back in."

Wandering through high-ceilinged public rooms, Kit changed his topic of conversation and tried to engage Marcos in conversation about Ludo. Marcos skilfully ducked questions with vague responses, pausing to admire portraits, asking about the sitters—anything to shift the conversation elsewhere. Not that he could supply the information Kit had evidently been tasked to glean. Despite what Alina had revealed to him in the Thames barge, he had no certain idea what Ludo was up to apart from the glib reasons he'd been fed in London about acquiring documents from the Count-Duke of Olivares for someone in Goa—which he only partly believed, for it sounded far too selfless and lacking in a profit motive for anything Ludo might do. That Ludo was after another warrant to supply luxuries from the East was far more likely.

As to what Alina had hinted—well, he really had no idea whatsoever what that was about. What Alina had told him did not smack of an enterprise Ludo might associate himself with. Marcos halted, wondering what Ludo was really doing while he and Kit were sightseeing.

Joining him, Kit Windebank said, "Are you well? Not feeling the heat, I hope."

"Er, yes, actually. I have been living in the Low Countries and England for a number of years. I'm rather out of touch with hot summers."

"The Low Countries—Flanders, Holland? Were you with the *tercios*, fighting to regain Spanish territory?"

"Yes, in a manner of speaking," Marcos fibbed, cursing himself for dropping that little gem of information where the Count-Duke's spies could find it. "I was looking for my father, to be honest..."

Gradually turning the conversation to the portraits of the current inmates of the palace and, by continuation, the gossip, Marcos learned various bits of information about which he was certain to be quizzed by both Ludo and Alina later that day. By the time Kit suggested they adjourn to a nearby tavern, he was quite pleased with himself: he hadn't lost the cheeky-sneaky touch that had helped make him a wealthy young man during the tulip scandal in Holland. In fact, he was feeling rather a lot like his old self. Perhaps he had the makings of a diplomatic secretary after all.

Chapter 18

Once the younger men had left, the elderly British ambassador filled two fine goblets with minted water from a thick ceramic jug and invited Ludo to sit.

Ludo waited, his features calm and open, as if expecting the Englishman to begin the conversation. He did not. He sat down behind his table once more, spine erect, arthritic hands steepled, clearly waiting for Ludo to explain his presence. Which, after an awkward silence, he was forced to do.

"Can I assume, Sir Arthur, that the correspondence regarding my visit has not arrived? We were delayed in Santander, then again by an accident in Lerma, so I thought I had arrived well after you had been informed."

"Informed? About an unofficial or commercial matter?"

Ludo rubbed the silk of his breeches; it was somewhat itchy and the material by no means as cool as the tailor had promised. "As I mentioned when we were introduced, I am Ludovico di Doria da Portovenere, and naturally with the Doria name..."

"You are involved in financing the Spanish monarchy."

"In a manner of speaking. In this visit, however, I am instructed to act for His Majesty King Charles as, shall we say, a special emissary. Which is why, as a matter of courtesy, I have come straight to you, and why I assumed you would have received notification of my arrival."

"But your business, if it is a matter of business and not diplomacy, is extra-official?"

Ludo swallowed a small sigh of annoyance. The old man was a pedant. He cocked his head to one side and gave a rueful grin. "My *understanding* is that you, sir, have an *understanding* with the His Majesty King Felipe's chief minister."

"The Count-Duke of Olivares and I are old acquaintances."

"Excellent." Ludo paused as if seeking words. "In that case, may I invite you to be present in my conversations with him?"

"You want a diplomat as witness; this is not entirely personal, delicate or secret, then."

Ludo vacillated, fearing he had made a mistake. He needed Hopton with him as a witness to ensure Olivares didn't throw him into the nearest dungeon. If he carried out Leonora's request before he passed on the message Charles had asked him to convey there was a greater chance of staying at liberty. Hopton would have to intervene on his monarch's behalf. He briefly scrutinised the old man sitting at his desk. For all his asperity he was clearly very astute. Trying to pull the wool over his eyes would be foolish, and very likely self-defeating.

Choosing his words carefully, Ludo said, "To be honest, Sir Arthur, I would have you with me for two reasons: the King in England has asked me to give the king here in Spain a personal message, but the King of Spain's Chief Minister may not be happy about it. That is, the content of the message—if he learns of it—may not be to the Count-Duke's liking. He might even prevent me from conveying it. In this respect, I would like to have an interview with King Felipe at the earliest instance. But there is another matter, related to my business in India, that I should also like to expedite with a witness on hand—a witness whose neutrality can be relied upon, and who might keep an account of what transpires."

Sir Arthur Hopton went puce in the face and jumped to his feet. "Am I to understand you wish *me* to act as your *secretary*, sir!"

"No, indeed, no! Although, it being such a tricky matter, your experience as my second would be..." Ludo held up a hand, still slightly rough about the knuckles from so many months at sea.

Sir Arthur Hopton exploded. "Your second, sir! What is this matter? Money, I expect, if you're a Doria."

"Money, of course, at the root of it. And a much more delicate issue of a king's right to choose how he governs his country—and how that country worships on a Sunday, if you follow?"

"Well, of course I do! What do you think I've been doing here all these years, playing card games?"

"Please don't misunderstand: I am not here to undermine your role in the slightest manner—far from it."

The Englishman's face twitched with annoyance. He was silent for a few moments, then tapped his table decisively. "Return at this hour tomorrow. I will speak to Olivares and ascertain whether he will see you."

Ludo suppressed a smile. "Thank you, Sir Arthur."

"You won't get near the king without Olivares intervening, you know. You'll have to be very sharp to speak with him alone." Hopton paused then said more quietly, "You should be aware, *Signor* Ludovico, the Count-Duke is by no means well. He still runs the day to day business of the empire, however, and, as I say, I doubt very much if you will be able to speak unaccompanied with the king without his permission." Sir

Arthur tried to choke back the last word. "*Authorisation*, I should have said."

"Quite. That was my understanding. Another reason why I'd like to talk to the Count-Duke beforehand and—see what transpires thereon. If you follow?"

"No sir, I cannot say I do." The ambassador made a move towards the door. "Olivares is unwell. The heat is not agreeable to him, and we are neither of us as young as we would like to be."

Ludo picked up his new lightweight hat and followed him, saying, "In what way, Sir Arthur, is the Count-Duke not well?"

Keeping a bony hand on the closed door latch, Hopton studied him coldly then said, "The Count-Duke is prone to agues and other ailments; his doctors, in my opinion, bleed him far too much, far too often. It leaves him weak, light-headed and... er... *fanciful*."

"By 'fanciful', you mean he has *fancies*? Imagines things?"

"There are times when one may query the logic or wisdom of his orders, or indeed actions. It gives his enemies ammunition against him, which is..." Hopton evidently regretted the trajectory of the discussion and changed direction. "I advise you to present your petition in a timely fashion early of a morning, while he still has energy. I will go now to enquire if this will be agreeable to him. I shall also enquire of my administrators as to whether any letter has reached the palace regarding your visit." He looked knowingly at Ludo, who met his gaze.

Walking down the wide stone steps to the public courtyard, Ludo ran a finger under the soft, lace-edged *Valona* collar around his neck and eased his wounded shoulder, hoping the scar hadn't opened, for he had risked leaving off the bandage because it rubbed in the heat.

The interview had been trying but he had succeeded in provoking Hopton into watching him, albeit for the wrong reasons. Knowing he was on a mission from King Charles, he would be obliged to intervene if matters went awry with Olivares and he disappeared from the palace. The Doria name would only provide so much protection. He was as good as walking into the lion's cage.

Descending the final steps, Ludo squared his shoulders and regretted it as the scar pulled uncomfortably. For a while he wandered around the courtyard, peeking in doors as if he were lost, then he left the palace by the north gate and set off up the hill, relatively content with his morning's work. Perhaps Alina would join him for a private supper that evening, while—hopefully—Marcos let himself be entertained by the sly-looking Kit Windebank.

Alina declined Ludo's suggestion of private supper, preferring to eat alone at her table by the window overlooking the palace.

Marcos finally arrived, bouncing noisily from one wall to the other of the narrow staircase leading up to their rooms, around midnight.

Ludo, who was still awake and waiting for him to arrive, followed his one-time servant into his room and opened the window, then sat down in a low chair.

"This Kit Windebank," Marcos said, divesting himself of a wine-stained jacket, "knows all the best taverns and whorehouses in town—in Spain, I wouldn't wonder."

"That's where you left him, did you, in a stew?"

"I did. Wasn't easy, either—getting away, that is. I'm not interested in that sort of thing any more."

"Any more?"

"I saw enough of it in Flanders and Dunkirk. Make me queasy, those dirty tarts do. He says there's a good class of girls that travel with the court, but even so..."

Ludo, lounging back in open-necked Indian pyjamas over his re-bandaged shoulder, waited until Marcos had been sick—twice—in the chamber pot before asking what he wanted to know.

"So, what did this 'perfect Spaniard' tell you about Spain?"

"Can this wait till tomorrow?" Marcos was green.

"No. Drink some of that boiled water and wine and stay by the open window. You stink of—what is it? Tobacco?"

"I think it was the pipe that did for me."

"Very likely. Come on, so far all I know is that young Kit is Hopton's eyes and ears, and a wide boy."

"Wide and wider. He knows everyone, knows every bar, knows every *jodido* cat, if you ask me."

"I am. Continue. Start with the palace and work your way round to the town."

"All right." Marcos gulped at the wine and water. "*Vale, pues el rey.* . . he's bossed about by his wife and Olivares makes all the decisions. The queen and Olivares can't stand each other."

"That bit I already know."

"Felipe only likes hunting and having portraits painted. Bit like Charlie in England about his paintings—got hundreds of them."

"And?"

"Sorry." Marcos put a hand to his mouth and counted to ten.

"So nothing terribly life-changing: no impending peace treaties with the Dutch or the French I need to know about?"

Marcos tried to shake his head and thought better of it. "Portuguese are making trouble. Some duke called Braganza, I think, is challenging Felipe to get the crown of Portugal back into Portuguese hands—or on his head, anyway."

"Is he?" Ludo sat up. "So it was true and it's actually happening. Now that is a useful bit of information." Ludo's eyes glinted. "Oh, yes, that is very interesting. What else? What does your Kit think about it?"

"Thinks he'll probably succeed because Spain's bankrupt from fighting in Flanders and protecting itself from the French, and Hopton thinks Olivares is over-stretched and too ill to manage another campaign on our borders. Actually, basically, from what Kit says, I think Felipe can't be bothered—and Olivares really is too sick to..."

The word sent Marcos over the pot again.

"All right," Ludo said. "Take your basin and go to bed."

Ludo wandered back to his room then sat by his own open window, wondering how he was going to proceed, and where the titbit about Portugal fitted in, because that made all the difference. He could take advantage very nicely of Spain losing the port of Lisbon and all that the Portuguese brought into it from the East. It could also make Felipe and Olivares positively inclined to invest in the *Tulip* and the other ships he acquired— for, now he thought about it, he could one day own an entire fleet—because they would need extra income from taxation and duties to regain Portugal, and maintain troops in Catalonia and on both the French and Portuguese fronts. He got up and started pacing the room, pondering the best strategies.

Then he stopped. He had done what he could to avoid Lisbon, but if what Marcos had just told him was true, it might be worthwhile going there after all. If he made an ally out of the pretender Braganza, maybe he wouldn't need to rely so heavily on a Spanish deal. If he was useful to Portugal—and Portugal regained a monarchy—it would lessen threats to his new business in Goa because the Portuguese might actively protect his business. *If* he could prove himself valuable to them, of course.

Would that finally keep Leonora safe? Knowing how her countrymen treated her now, he doubted it. *So forget about Leonora... No, you have an obligation; if you can't love her, you can at least protect her. And, by extension, your new spice business.*

Ludo pushed his thick hair off his face then shook his head, so it fell back across his perspiring brow again. The trouble was that a pretender to a throne was a bad bet; it would be safer to stay with a legitimate king, who was also a Habsburg...

... and there was Marcos and his blasted father-in-law, Mr Beale, to consider. He had made an agreement with them on the understanding it would improve their businesses substantially.

So, no, he had to deal with Olivares and King Felipe, regardless, because if the pretender to the Portuguese throne failed, he'd be back at square one, down the snake of what—greed, debt, pride? *"Male ne abbia!"* he cursed. "Why am I responsible for all these people?"

Later that night, turning possibilities this way and that in a sleepless bed, Ludo realised there were no real options: he would have to make himself useful to all players and continue the game as he'd begun it in Whitehall—as it had been begun for him by Olivares and an un-named Vatican cardinal—except the outcome this time would be entirely to his own benefit.

Chapter 19

The Conde-Duque de Olivares, a once large man shrunk into premature old age, with sallow, emptied wine-skin features, adjusted his leg on the gout-stool and beckoned Ludo closer. Sir Arthur Hopton positioned himself slightly to their rear, spine straight, arms folded across his chest like an ill-tempered school master.

Olivares studied Ludo before speaking then said, "Take a seat here, beside me. We have met."

"We have, sir, a few years ago in Madrid." Ludo took a chair, somewhat lower than that of the Chief Minister's and deliberately made no mention of the tulip scandal, waiting to see if Olivares connected his face with what he had been asked to do in Holland. He evidently did, suggesting he was either satisfied at the outcome or, more likely, remembered that Ludo had taken a new Spanish galleon from under the very nose of the Lisbon harbour master as his reward.

The Count-Duke's eyes, tucked into folds of old flesh, continued their study then after a brief silence, he said, "You did not tell me, on that occasion, that you were a member of the Doria family."

"Did I not? I apologise. I assumed you knew—me being a merchant from the State of Genoa. Was that not why I was chosen for your enterprise?"

Olivares ignored the question and continued, "But this matter today is not Doria business—or is it? Do the English not have enough bankers of their own to finance their passive foreign policy? I find that hard to believe. This matter is related to England, is it not?"

"It is, sir, in part. I am instructed to convey a message as a personal favour, and to make," Ludo turned to Hopton in appeasement, "an entirely *personal* request from one monarch to another..."

"That's a bit rich coming from Charles Stuart after the manner in which he insulted His Majesty King Felipe—not to mention the unnecessary deaths he caused in the sea battle last year. He could have come to our aid—*should* have come to our aid—and did nothing. And why? Because his *Catholic* queen is French. Please, Don Ludovico, do not expect us to look kindly on any request from England."

"I understand, but this matter comes from King Charles himself, not, shall we say, from England. King Charles is most aware of the discord he caused, which he would have you know was entirely due to pressure from his parliament and subjects— something he is eager now to rectify, if you follow me?"

Olivares looked at Hopton. "Do you follow him?"

Hopton nodded. "I believe so."

Ludo waited for Olivares to continue. When he did not, Ludo said, "This, in part, Excellency, is why I am here, and why this is a strictly personal and private affair, and must not under any circumstances be discussed in open court."

Olivares and Hopton exchanged glances, both suspicious if not angry.

"Well, get on with it." Olivares winced as he shifted position in his chair, which Ludo noted was as large and ornate as a throne. "What is this request?"

"I'm sorry, Excellency, as I have said, it is entirely personal for King Felipe, I'm afraid. Undoubtedly he will appraise you of the matter forthwith, but I may only speak with him in the first instance."

Olivares' bushy grey eyebrows drew together in annoyance.

"I told you," Hopton said, going to the Chief Minister's side.

"And you want me to act as your secretary and make an appointment with His Majesty for you, I suppose," Olivares hissed.

"Exactly what I said," muttered Hopton.

"Yes," replied Ludo. "However, I do also have some business with you of my own. But I'd prefer to see the outcome of my interview with His Majesty before going into that, if you don't mind."

Olivares' mouth dropped open and Hopton moved forward to wave away a bluebottle flying perilously near the human abyss. "You want *me* to make an appointment for you with His Majesty the King of Spain without knowing any details of the matter, and then afterwards you want to discuss something else with me—and you expect me to look favourably on both? You sir, are an *embustero, un sinvergüenza*: a cad."

"Let me add," Ludo smiled, ignoring the insults, "that the matters I'd like to discuss with both you and your monarch are greatly to your financial favour."

"Hmm," Olivares grunted, but then indicated for Ludo to continue.

"It relates to my galleon and Spain's trade with the East."

"Ah, yes, our ship. I wondered when we'd get to that." Olivares made a grimace that could have been a wry smile but was more likely a wince of pain.

"My *ships*, Excellency—I have more than one. It also relates to the fortune that arrives in Lisbon on Portuguese East Indiamen, and the taxes paid on those goods. If Spain were by any chance deprived of this source of income... Well, let us say, I have an interesting proposition to make. By the way, are you aware that certain Portuguese factors and agents both in India and in Lisbon are, shall I say, taking greater advantage of the profits to be made from pepper and spices than perhaps they ought?"

"Avoiding duties, failing to send the appropriate percentages here or selling direct? Names? Do you have names?"

"Solis and Cabrera, I believe. Two cousins—and their other relations as well, I expect."

"Hmm," Olivares grunted.

There was silence. Ludo waited.

"I'll speak to His Majesty," Olivares said.

King Felipe, in contrast, was charming. Ludo was shown into a pleasant room decorated in pale green silks and was offered a chair decorated in gold-leaf. Felipe, an exceptionally tall man of middle age, invited him to take a sugared lemon refreshment, or, if he preferred, an alcoholic sugar drink from the Caribbean. Once served by one of the many frilled flunkeys lining the walls, the king waved his attendants away. "Leave us, gentlemen; we would speak with our Genoese guest alone."

The preamble consisted of Ludo reciting the many countries he had visited, expanding on the delights and wealth of the Goan coast in India, and—speaking very diplomatically—on why Spain ought to make more effort to govern her East Indies colonies more closely, because she was surely losing a very great deal through the trade monopoly system in Lisbon, which was being run by Portuguese with only self-interest at heart.

A dark look came across the king's fair face. He scratched his long chin beneath its wispy blondish beard then said tartly, "We do not wish to hear of Portuguese colonies. If this is why you are here, inform the Count-Duke."

Ludo took the warning and sipped his lemon drink before saying, "I come directly from the Palace of Whitehall, Your Majesty."

Felipe frowned again. "We are displeased by England and the English, sir." Then a thought occurred to him. "Ah, but you are here directly from England, not India. Are you saying the English are backing the Duke of Braganza's claim to the Portuguese throne? That would not surprise me. The English have never done us one single favour. One only has to remember Catalina of Aragón."

Ludo started again on a double front. "The Portuguese in Goa are in distress, Your Majesty. The Dutch are taking their lands and controlling access to harbours. I fear Portuguese cargoes are at great risk. Indeed, it may only be a matter of months before the *Carreira de Lisboa* import trade is damaged irretrievably."

"Really? Well that is of mixed cheer, given what is afoot. Are you here to ask us to give them protection?"

"No, Your Majesty, I am here to offer you an *independent* means of developing trade with the East, which as you must know can bring in an absolute fortune."

"Probably it can, but we have the wealth of New Spain—the silver from Peru alone produces all our pieces of eight, I believe. This is a matter for my ministers." The yellowish beard on the Habsburg lantern jaw twitched with annoyance.

Kit Windebank had told Marcos the monarch was easy-going to the point of outright laziness, that he left daily management of his country and new-world empire entirely in Olivares' hands—but he was no fool.

"One can always do with extra funds—I speak personally, of course." Ludo opened his hands in a Latin gesture. "One simply never knows what little disaster is waiting around the corner, requiring one to delve into one's purse."

Felipe of Spain smiled back knowingly. "You are a Doria, you say."

"A merchant, sire, not a banker or an admiral, but I have some competence in, er... raising money, through trade, of course. I am of the Portovenere branch and being of Portovenere, naturally I have a special relationship with corsairs. So good that I have been asked to *supply them* with spices and special goods direct from the East: pearls and precious gems, cinnamon and nutmeg... If I am able to supply them at favourable rates on a regular basis, they may find less need to attack and plunder so many of your vessels returning from New Spain." Ludo glanced at the king: he'd got his undivided attention so he paused.

"Continue," the monarch said, evidently now interested.

"Obviously one has to tread with infinite care when dealing with Berbers—they are pirates, after all—but I have been led to believe by Murat Reis himself that they will look on my enterprise with favour because it relieves them from dealing with the Turks, you see, from whom they currently purchase all goods. They are also subject to religious tensions at present, which I won't go into, but the ordinary, native people of Salé, for example, are suffering at the cruel hands of co-religionists, who would have them all worship Allah in another manner. It is not dissimilar to the problems between Catholics and Protestants—"

"Heretics."

"—in Britain." Ludo edged warily towards Charles Stuart's business, having made sure his own enterprise benefited along the way. "But for any of this to succeed my vessels require a special licence from Portugal, or from Your Majesty's Chief Minister, to trade unhindered in the East—perhaps under a Spanish flag."

"Granted! If you can save but three of our ships coming from the Philippines each year you shall have any licence you care to name. It shall be concluded this very day. Speak to Olivares and he will supply you with the licence." The king's clear eyes then narrowed. "But what has this to do with England?"

"Ah, the heretics, as you mentioned. I have a personal request from King Charles."

"And that is?" asked Felipe cautiously, although a little better disposed to hear about England and the English.

"King Charles *begs* that Your Royal Majesty helps him in a great time of need, for he is seeking to return England to..."—Ludo looked around him to see if any gentlemen-in-waiting were within earshot—"the One True Faith."

"That is excellent news!"

"*But* for this he needs to be independent of his Parliament, and it is not impossible he may have to fight within his own kingdom to maintain his sovereignty; the Scots have already challenged him. He is, I believe, fighting to regain entry to Scotland right now. Or he was."

"Internal disputes are tiresome, and wasteful of resources. We have Catalonia, a thorn in our side. And now Portugal." Felipe picked at the upholstery on the arm of his chair then said, "So Charles looks to Spain for this support. Curious. His wife is French—why not go to them? Ah, because they are not all Catholics, of course. Why does everyone assume our silver wealth from New Spain is for giving away?"

"That, sire, is why I am suggesting you might consider investing in the East India trade—to increase your great wealth even further." Ludo took another sip of his lemon drink, watching Felipe fidget out of the corner of his eye. *He has no power over his finances,* he thought. *Olivares, the old dog, controls the purse strings.*

After a few moments Felipe said, "We continue greatly overstretched in our economy by the war in Flanders and the French campaigns. Nevertheless, we shall give this some thought. Be assured, we shall arrange to speak with you again on these matters. What, by the way—merely out of curiosity— could you or your ships bring us?"

Ludo reached into his jacket and two gentlemen-in-waiting who had been lurking near the door raced across the reception chamber, skidding to a halt as he flourished the huge ruby from his inner pocket.

King Felipe laughed, not a little relieved, and held out his hand. "A gift for us?"

It was not a question, and not what Ludo had in mind at all. Risking royal offence if not his neck, as Marcos had joked, he kept his thumb and forefinger on the ruby and said, "Fit for a queen, is it not, Your Majesty? It is from India. In your West Indies, I am told, emeralds dangle from trees; your mines spew silver... But look at this, the most beautiful and best of gems. Diamonds and rubies can only be found in the wonderful land of India in the east. The diamonds are to be found in dry riverbeds, although not without risks. Huge serpents called pythons swallow them—the stones—stones of this size and greater—but these serpents are themselves so great and so unimaginably dangerous they swallow the diamond and ruby hunters entire as well." Felipe blinked. Ludo, warming to his tale, continued. "But local diamond merchants have come up with an ingenious trick. They use eagles to swoop into the very maw of danger and return with the precious gems."

The King of Spain gazed at the Genoese merchant; then a smile played around his fleshy lips and he began to chuckle. "Into the very maw of danger, eh? Every enterprise has its risks."

"Yes, but one must judge them against the rewards, and the means by which rewards can be achieved, sire." The double meaning was not lost on the listener, who inclined his head. Ludo acknowledged the unspoken agreement and said, "I have a wide selection of other riches from India in my lodgings. You may be entertained by them."

Felipe schooled his face. "You are a gambler, Don Ludovico."

"Indeed, no, sire, although my voyages are perilous. I am merely a merchant, a Genoese merchant with contacts on the Barbary Coast, that is all, and a family name to back me." That last was a blatant lie, but if it helped it was worth it.

"A successful merchant, we see." Felipe rose to his feet and Ludo jumped out of his chair accordingly. There was a pause as the monarch beckoned an usher to his side, then said. "Return at this hour tomorrow. Bring your wares. We shall speak with the queen; she, too, might be interested in your enterprise. We will also speak with her on the English matter and decide what is to be done. You may not be aware, but Queen Isabel is sister to the Queen of England. She will be greatly pleased with the news you bring us, of that we are certain. As to aiding King Charles in his time of need—the matter has been in consultation for some little while, but we will speak with our Chief Minister and see where we can go."

Ludo inclined his head politely.

Felipe responded likewise then said, "We are giving a banquet tomorrow for… we cannot remember for what purpose, but we invite you and your party to attend."

Tickled ruby red with success and anticipating the next phase of his plan, Ludo followed the usher out of the royal apartments and left the *Real Sitio* in excellent spirits. First, he stopped at a tavern and drank a glass of cool white wine then set off to climb the steep street to their lodgings, deciding he would brook no refusal from Alina: she would have the midday meal with him to celebrate the satisfactory launch of his new Spanish venture. Had he not just also been invited to join the royal party on the morrow for their evening entertainments, where she could be presented as his… whatever came to mind—and from there, be introduced to the queen to fulfil her own mission?

Pondering how this might be managed, he traversed a covered archway leading to the town's *alameda* gardens: a shortcut he'd found the previous day, it involved climbing some steep steps before reaching a short, flat alley, then even more steps to the popular gardens. He put a hand to his left shoulder where the dagger wound pulled as he ascended, conjuring images of Alina with her glorious golden hair dressed in ringlets, her lovely fair skin tantalisingly visible in a low-cut evening gown.

The first lathe smacked across the back of his legs as he reached the alley. The second caught him across his spine so he fell. Rope-soled feet set about his ribs and stomach, but it was a heavy knobbed stick that did the harm. In the space of seconds Ludo was battered, bleeding, and entirely alone, and would have been in a worse state, if not dead, had not two monks coming down towards the monastery rushed to his aid.

Laboriously, he was lifted to his feet then helped up the narrow stairs by the two sweating monks, who eventually got him to his lodgings in a requisitioned handcart.

Ludo woke to Alina's touch. She was dabbing his brow and the side of his face, where blood had congealed, with a cool, damp cloth. He looked at her and tried to speak but she laid a finger over his lips. "Sssh," she whispered, "rest now."

The next time he awoke she was still there. Cautiously, he touched his swollen lips then pushed his hands across his bare chest to find out what, if anything, he was wearing. "Where's my jacket," he croaked painfully.

"What?"

"My jacket: did they take it?"

"Your jacket? No, why?"

"Get it for me."

Alina lifted the torn black silk coat from a chair.

"Inside," Ludo grunted. "Look inside."

Alina put her hand into an inner pocket and pulled out the ruby. Ludo tried not to smile—it hurt too much—but then realised what it meant, which was nothing to smile about: this assault hadn't been for robbery, either. *Could Rogelio be in Spain? Had he sent one—or more—of his lackeys to do his dirty work: the would-be assassin on the bay nag and now this? Had he been followed all the way from Whitehall? And, if so, why—why—why? Was royal patronage—Catholic patronage— in two nations insufficient? This wasn't about eliminating those involved in the Dutch scandal nearly five years ago: this was about something else.*

At some time during the evening Ludo tried to sit up: there were arrangements to be made for the next day; he had an invitation from a king. "Where's Marcos?" he asked.

"Here." Marcos was sitting at the window, open now to catch the fresher early-evening air, but with the wooden shutters unrolled over the balcony's iron railings to keep the light out.

Ludo beckoned him to the bed. "Listen, I need you to do things, and fast. We are invited to a palace banquet tomorrow evening, Alina included, and I want you with me at all times from now on. Tell José to make sure my clothes are right and ready..." Ludo struggled to sit up but it was excruciating.

"You aren't going to be fit enough to go anywhere tomorrow," Marcos said.

"That's probably what whoever arranged my broken ribs wants. This beating wasn't a robbery, either. Somebody is watching me very closely. Why do I suspect your friend Kit?"

"Kit Windebank?"

"I gave Hopton reason to have me watched, but I thought I was covering my back, not inviting him to attack it. Find out if your Kit is involved."

"I doubt it, but..." Marcos paused then said, "Actually, I wouldn't put it past him to arrange a bit of nasty business—he knows enough undesirables. Somebody's trying to put you out of action, that's for sure. But don't you think that that somebody has also followed you from Whitehall?—think of the wherry, and what happened in Lerma."

"I am. I do. That's why I need to be seen again tomorrow and why you need to find out who's watching me, and why." Ludo winced and eased himself back onto the pillow. "Alina has to go to this banquet, and I'm the only one who can get her in."

"Er, not so. If, as she says, she is carrying a message from Queen Henrietta for Queen Isabel all she has to do is go to the palace."

"Look at her, Marcos. She's a woman, remember, on her own. She can't walk in just like that. Think!"

Marcos looked at Alina again, but she turned away and started fiddling with the shutters.

Ludo closed his eyes. After a while he mumbled, "I need to find out who wants to stop what I'm doing."

"Yes, yes," Marcos said. "You've already told me, twice. Save your breath and energy for getting better."

"Snakes and ladders," Ludo hissed, not unlike the slithering creatures he so detested. "Leonora keeps a snake as a rat-catcher."

"Who's Leonora?"

"No one you know. Tell José I have a fancy for one of his sugared drinks."

Chapter 20

Marcos entered the vast, high-ceilinged hall behind Alina and Ludo, ever the dutiful page. Alina turned this way and that, staring at her surrounding so the lightweight silk of her gown swished around her despite the crush, until Ludo patted her hand and she came to an abrupt halt, no doubt remembering where she was.

"Is this what you have been waiting for?" Ludo muttered in her ear, giving Marcos a conspiratorial wink.

Alina took a deep breath. "All my life."

"Better than Whitehall?" Ludo asked.

"Oh, yes."

And Marcos knew why: because this was Spain. If Alina was who she said she was, one day she would have been presented at the Spanish royal court in Madrid—he assumed. His thoughts were interrupted by a man-at-arms pushing his way through the queue waiting to enter the banquet.

Marcos looked at Ludo, who shrugged. "They're everywhere," he said. "Anybody wanting to take a stab at Felipe tonight will have to be quick and nifty about it."

Marcos wanted to ask why there were so many royal bodyguards in evidence, but they had come within hearing of the courtier announcing guests' names. Seeing their turn was next, Alina laid her hand on Ludo's waiting wrist like a medieval queen in a tapestry. He patted her hand again and they shuffled forward.

As they reached the entrance to the hall Marcos gave a small inward gasp. He, too, had once dreamed of being presented at court—in *his* dreams, though, he had been a brave knight brought before his monarch to be presented with the 'Order of the… ' He was never quite sure what the order was named, but he knew they existed. Except that Marcos no longer did. That Marcos had been a boy with ideas well above his station… and yet, *look where I am.*

The moment of their introduction arrived and all eyes turned on Alina. With her fine, tall figure and mass of golden hair, shown to its best advantage by a dress of the deepest teal blue, Alina stepped forward, elegant, regal, on Ludo's arm.

"Baroness Metherall, María de los Ángeles Santoña Gómez de Fulford."

An English baroness with a Spanish name: heads came together. Then attention shifted to Don Ludovico di Doria da Portovenere, who, smiling his special wicked smile like an actor playing to a favourable audience, conducted his leading lady into the high-ceilinged hall of gilded mirrors and tall portraits. Marcos could see from Alina's posture that she was getting cross with him, but then she stopped and turned right round. Marcos had been introduced as *Hidalgo de Sanlúcar*. He tried to stifle a grin. *That will give milady something to think about.*

Slowly, keeping a watchful eye on how Alina behaved, and praying he wouldn't embarrass her or himself, Marcos entered the gala—the centre of attention for no one except perhaps the lesser, unmarried but slightly older noblewomen, who had noted he was unaccompanied.

As they were seated—not too distant from the royal end of the table—Alina smoothed her dress and sighed again. Ludo raised a questioning eyebrow.

"I was just thinking..."—Alina relaxed into a moment of truth—"I used to write stories about girls who had adventures and—"

"Now you are having your own," a man's voice supplied from behind.

Alina froze then turned slowly as if knowing exactly who would be there. Then, dropping her aristocratic poise, she cried, "*Papá!*" and jumped to her feet with delight.

"*Hija!*" Her father swung her off her feet as if she were a five-year-old.

Marcos cast a glance around their section of the table as royal guests gazed astonished and disapproving at such lack of decorum.

"I was told you were in a harem," Alina's father said, far too loudly, sending their audience into a collective gasp, "and now I find you are an English baroness."

"I have much to tell," Alina whispered, trying to regain her dignity. "I was going to visit you before leaving Spain again, but now you are here. Are the boys all right? Oh, I have dozens and dozens of questions!"

"All of which will be answered. For now, introduce me to your baron." The tall, very elegant Spanish aristocrat looked at Ludo.

Unseeing, Alina said, "Oh, I can't, he is in England, hopefully with our son. You have a fine grandson, *Papá.*" Suddenly remembering where they were conducting their intimate reunion, Alina dropped her voice and murmured, "*Padre*, allow me to introduce Ludovico da Portovenere. He is accompanying me this evening and..." she ran out of breath at her somewhat awkward situation.

Marcos stared at the man Alina called '*Papá*', realising everything she had said about being the daughter of a grandee was true. "*Idiota!*" he cursed himself. *You have never stood a chance with her, not before, not now, not ever. Be satisfied with what you've got.* And then he was. Content that he had a humble but pretty wife and a sound business back in England, he sat back to watch the spectacle: he was to play nothing more than a supporting role, and it was enough.

Ludo, who had already risen to his feet, bowed low and Alina introduced her father as the Conde de Pamanes. The count ran a practised eye over Ludo's appearance, calculating his worth, then responded with a smaller bow of his own.

Turning back to his daughter, the count said, "But why are you here?"

"To see—that is, I..." Alina leaned close to her father's ear and whispered urgently.

"Then it shall be arranged." The count gave Ludo a dubious look. "With or without your escort, *cariño*?"

"Er... with," Alina responded.

As the Conde de Pamanes made his way to the top of the table, Alina leaned toward Ludo and whispered in English, "Don't tell my father anything you don't want the world to know."

"Meaning he knows everyone and everything there is to know about the court?"

"Oh, yes, and what he doesn't know he invents. Be warned and be on your toes."

"I am already, my dear, tippy-toes, and I can't tell you how much it hurts," Ludo said, pouring wine into crystal goblets.

Within moments the Conde de Pamanes was back by their chairs with a lady-in-waiting, who summoned Alina to sit with the queen.

"That was quick," hissed Ludo.

"Tss," warned Alina, getting to her feet and arranging her voluminous skirts around her.

"Don Ludovico may accompany you, *cariño*," the count informed his daughter.

"Agh!" Ludo winced, not at the implied slight but from too sharp a movement.

"You have been in the wars, Don Ludovico?" the count asked, adding hopefully, "A duel?"

"In a manner of speaking." Ludo gave a wry smile. "Actually, I have been presented to His Majesty the King already, Conde, if that helps."

The count wriggled his nose, slightly embarrassed but clearly impressed. "So I have been told. Come."

Marcos watched Alina glide towards the royal table, then he turned and grinned as a plump young man in a spectacular arrangement of frills and buttercup yellow took her place.

Some time later, while Kit Windebank prattled on about who was and wasn't at the banquet, Marcos looked up and searched among the colours and bobbing heads to find Alina was deep in conversation with an attractive matron with a button mouth and dark Medici eyes—exactly the same dark, curly hair as her sister in England, for this could only be Isabel, *Reina de España*. Instead of the more open bodice with high-backed, butterfly-wing lace collars worn by many of her ladies, and despite the season, the queen was wearing an old-fashioned, high-necked gown of burgundy satin, giving her a far more severe appearance than that of her theatre-loving sister in England. This queen appeared to have little humour or kindness. Marcos drank deeply from his cup, muttering a silent prayer for Alina's safety.

Trying to see whether Ludo had drawn the condescending Conde de Pamanes into his web, Marcos noted that many curious eyes were on his lovely Alina, including those of the king, who, while feigning interest elsewhere, was watching her intently.

An hour later, Marcos was into his third course and umpteenth goblet of rich, dark red Rioja wine. Kit Windebank was a fine companion, but was making it almost impossible to stay alert for signals of intrigue, as Ludo had insisted. Kit had now reached the part of his tale where he was marrying the girl.

"You actually married her, before a priest?" Marcos spluttered.

"I certainly did. A good girl of very humble origins, raised according to the *catequesis*, a devout follower of the Virgin Mary with the sweetest little fanny in Christendom that kept me fantasising for months and months. Of course I married her—how else was I to pick her cherry?"

"But she's not here tonight?"

Kit's face darkened. "No, bless her; she was not raised for balls and banquets. That is—was—the problem. We were told we were too young; and I was told she was too humble and could never be raised up for polite society. Polite! Look at them. Did you ever see such a group of dissolute hypocrites in one room?" Kit swigged back the last of his wine and helped himself to more. "I think—no, I know—Hopton spoke to his devilish friends and Olivares' wife whisked her off to a convent before I could get back to our lodgings to warn her."

Marcos sobered, seeing genuine distress in his new friend's eyes. "And you haven't seen her since?"

Kit shook his head, then adopted a different attitude and swung his arm out across the laden board. "To all the pretty girls," he shouted in English, "who have taken her place."

"But you are still legally married?"

"Aye, and there's the rub—in more ways than one, I can tell you."

"Why don't you get the marriage annulled and return to England?"

"Because..." Kit drawled the word, "I have upset my father once too often, and this was the last straw—according to him. He prefers I make my way *here* rather than *there* now. The moral of this sad tale is—take heed—*never* underestimate how many people are watching you; and they'll mostly be doing it for Olivares."

"Funny you should say that. I was going to ask you if—"

"Sorry, got to go."

Marcos shifted round, trying to see where Kit was going and who had summoned him. The buttercup satin and excessive frills on collar and cuffs, made it relatively easy to follow him even in a crowded banqueting hall, but as Marcos watched he was distracted by a gentlewoman who had hastily taken Kit's place on the excuse that she had risen to request wine and *her* chair had been taken. Marcos smiled and let her think he believed her. He chatted with her politely for a few moments then excused himself to follow Kit Windebank up a wide stairway across the vast room. It was not entirely dissimilar to how he had once followed wealthy burgers playing high stakes for coveted tulip bulbs in crowded Dutch taverns. Marcos gave himself a mental pat on the back: he was getting back into the swing of things nicely, and thoroughly enjoying it. Ludo would be pleased.

It didn't take long to locate the yellow suit again. Kit was now with the lean, black-garbed Sir Arthur Hopton, conversing in whispers at the turn for another inner staircase. Keeping at a safe distance, but perfectly ready to admit to be following his new pal, Kit, if seen, Marcos followed them up. They entered an anteroom on the second floor.

Looking about him as if lost, Marcos watched a man-at-arms stroll casually from one long public room to another. The sound of voices suggested he had found someone to chat to. Staying in full view—for there was no excuse that would cover being furtive here—Marcos distinctly heard Sir Arthur Hopton say, "Wait here until I call you."

Marcos edged forward and heard Hopton entering an inner room, which Marcos thought might belong to the vast suite occupied by Olivares' staff. Then he looked up just in time see to a tall, very thin cleric, evidently not part of the banquet celebrations, entering the long salon from the opposite direction. Whether the cleric had seen him or not there was no way of knowing, but Marcos turned and walked purposefully back the way he had come, then slipped inside an open doorway from where he could keep watch. The cleric entered the same anteroom as Kit and Hopton.

Ruffling his hair in an attempt to look significantly the worse for wear, Marcos waited a few moments then once again entered the salon and sidled up towards the anteroom. Kit was sitting in a chair nearer the inner door studying his nails. Marcos shifted from one foot to the other, wondering how to play it. Before he had decided, though, Kit was called into the inner room. With a small sigh of relief, Marcos wandered into the anteroom and slumped down in a chair—obviously far gone in drink. He waited a while, accustoming his ear to the different tones behind the closed door then slunk over to the most strategic chair from which to eavesdrop.

Someone instructed Kit to serve chilled wine in a deep, gruff voice suggesting the speaker was in pain. Marcos's only acquaintance with the Count-Duke of Olivares was from what Ludo had told him, but he thought the voice fitted.

The second voice was clearly that of Hopton, speaking English-accented Spanish. He was easy to follow. The third man, the cleric, who Marcos thought might be the man from Rome that Ludo had good cause to fear, spoke in lilting, somewhat higher tones. It was possible, of course, that it wasn't Ludo's enemy; El Escorial was full of priests... But then Olivares confirmed his suspicion by addressing someone as Padre Rogelio. Slouched slovenly across a delicate chair, Marcos listened intently.

Olivares then began what appeared to be a meeting: "Let us start with that we know beside the contents of the letter she sent her sister in England. That was well intercepted, though I say it myself. I doubted the boy was up to it, but I was wrong for once. Innocent faces like his are a godsend at times. Pity I didn't tell him to steal the letter itself. That would have saved a deal of trouble now we know what was in it. You had something to tell me about the reply, Arthur."

"One of Henrietta Maria's ladies is with the Genoese merchant," responded Hopton. "It's almost certain she's carrying a letter for Isabel. She's Spanish, related to that idiot Pamanes, by the way. "

Olivares: "Interesting. I can use that—he's always after something and in debt well beyond what his estate can provide. Good. Has this rogue Portovenere been sent to do away with me?"

"I can't say, yet. It's not impossible, though," Hopton replied.

"No it isn't. Do we assume the younger man—the so-called secretary—is his accomplice?"

"I don't see either of them as paid assassins, to be honest. But I suppose that could be part of the ruse. I lack your expertise in such matters, but... That is. . ." Hopton paused.

"Spit it out, Arthur. No point sugar-coating poison, although our friend Rogelio here would disagree on that to my certain knowledge. Tell me what you think, plainly."

"I'd say that from what Kit has told me we can discount any serious *individual* threat from the young man posing as the secretary. And I'd say that if this Ludovico is the English queen's chosen man then what he's been chosen for will be more in the line of a political manoeuvre than a knife in the night, especially given what he's offering Felipe, which muddies the waters considerably. He's up to something more involved than passing you a poisoned chalice. He's undoubtedly a subtle operator, but to my mind he doesn't have the look of an assassin."

"*Boh!*" spluttered the Roman cleric but said no more.

"Hmm..." Olivares' voice was pensive. "Rogelio, tell us, how did *you* learn this Ludo character had been sent by Henrietta Maria?"

The Roman murmured something of which Marcos caught the word 'London' then added, "I've had him followed since. She is very unwise, like all her breed: she thinks she can influence events and make decisions and that they are for the good of her husband. She is stupid."

Olivares: "Like her blasted sister, then, eh? Except one cannot call Isabel stupid; bear that in mind if you have dealings with her. *She* is not to be underestimated, hence this little gathering tonight away from prying eyes and ears."

Marcos shifted in his chair, suddenly aware he was in considerable danger: Olivares was renowned for making people disappear. All manner of people. Ludo was no fool, making sure he'd been seen by the English ambassador and then having an audience with the king himself. Telling both that he carried a message from the King of England, whether it was true or fabricated, would help to ensure he did not disappear—too quickly, at any rate. Marcos started to leave but sat down again; Father Rogelio was speaking, his voice deeper and more strident now.

"... Henrietta thinks she's a blessing to Christendom, goes ahead with her own ideas without consulting us and *naturally* overlooks vital details. The question of England returning to Rome is a Vatican matter, not a fancy to be shared between sisters—God save us from their follies. Their mother, that Medici woman, is behind it. There is no end to the trouble she causes... When I think of all the diplomacy she has ruined—"

Hopton interrupted: "Yes, I am sure this is true, but for now we should focus on the more immediate risk to the Count-Duke's person. If this Ludovico *is* here at Henrietta and Isabel's request we should anticipate *how* he's going to act—if we are to successfully thwart him. I can't help wondering, though, why would a crude assassin go to all the trouble of involving me then making himself known and useful to Felipe?"

Olivares: "You said he mentioned he was a Doria as well. First I knew about that..." There was a pause. Olivares sipping his wine perhaps. Then he started again, "Although, no. It does make sense, and not impossible, given his affinity with the sea and mercantile role. Taking that galleon in Lisbon was quite a feat. But why try to make you think he is sanctioned by his blasted family, Arthur? The Doria don't meddle in this sort of nonsense—they don't need to—they're too busy controlling their own enemies, of whom, at this moment, I am fortunately not one."

Rogelio: "Ludovico da Portovenere is a Doria bastard and a degenerate fool." The Roman cleric's voice was iced with scorn.

Olivares: "Being a bastard son is not necessarily a handicap —they can be legitimised, as they are in France, or ennobled as they are in England and here. God knows, we've had famous generals from the wrong side of the blanket in this royal family alone—you only have to think of—"

Rogelio jumped in: "There is more to it in this case. This, in part, is my commission. Certain members of the Doria family want him out of the way."

Olivares: "Why?"

"Suffice it to say a distant, lesser, Doria uncle became his stepfather, and now a cousin is trying to claim the Genoa Doria mother's inheritance. Shall I go on?"

Olivares: "No. Families often contain the most treacherous of enemies, this I know. My own nephew has allied himself with Isabel. He covets my influence over Felipe..."

There was silence and Marcos feared the meeting had come to a halt, but to his surprise Olivares said loudly, "Well, whatever the family squabble is I can't afford to upset any of the Doria at present, nor for a long time in the future, as things stand. If they call in even half their debts we are in grave difficulties. And if this Ludo is one of them, legitimate or otherwise, I can't arrange for him to have an accident before ascertaining why he is actually here, especially considering what he is offering Felipe. So, Padre Rogelio, whatever your commission, you may *not* make any attempt on the Genoese merchant on Spanish territory, understood. He has a scheme to help Felipe that is too good to ignore."

Hopton, surprised: "But Count-Duke, your life could be at risk."

Olivares: "My life is always at risk, what's left of it. No. This is an order. Rogelio, you are not, I repeat, not to touch Ludovico da Portovenere, Doria or not, while he is in Spain." There was a mumbled reply and Olivares continued in a commanding tone, "I remember your animosity to him from 'thirty-seven. Do not let that encourage you, either."

"What's he offering, this Ludovico?" asked Hopton.

"Protection from Barbary pirates, safer sea lanes and spices from the East Indies."

Hopton's laugh was a bark of disbelief. "I bet he did, and did he offer all the riches of Araby with it? That's the most ridiculous attempt to please I have ever heard."

"Perhaps so, but I can use the offer against the Portuguese. If he can do this, he can also send corsairs into the Atlantic *and* let them prey on *carreira da India* vessels arriving from the East for Lisbon. If necessary—and if the Duke of Braganza succeeds in convincing the Portuguese to finally rebel against Spain—it means we can diminish imports feeding Portugal's finances."

"I suppose I should point out that da Portovenere also has the patronage and protection of His Royal Majesty King Charles Stuart—who may be a heretic in your eyes, Father Rogelio, but is a crowned head of state, nonetheless. I have eyes on him night and day for my own reasons," Hopton stated, as if giving a warning.

"As have I," Olivares added, then went on, "Good, so it is agreed: I use him to our benefit, but we naturally prevent him getting anywhere near Isabel..." *Too late*, thought Marcos, *he's dancing attendance as you speak.* "My wife is already advised regarding both the Genoese and the baroness. She has her own eyes and ears; they will keep us informed."

"It's a dangerous game." Hopton's voice was dry.

Marcos wanted to believe they had an ally in Hopton, and that his watchers were to their advantage, but the comfort was exceedingly brief, for Rogelio now spoke with ill-concealed hatred.

"It is not a game."

"You are letting this become personal again," Olivares intervened. "He's evaded you in the past and you want your revenge—three times, is it?"

"What about the woman?" Rogelio demanded, ignoring the question.

Hopton said, "If you are speaking of the Baroness Metherall, forget her. She is one of Queen Henrietta Maria's favourites and her husband is tutor to the Prince of Wales. She is not to be touched—*in any way.*"

Rogelio snorted. "Baroness or not, she'll be a whore if she's travelling with him. I've seen it before. A respectable woman reduced to whoring by him."

"She is most definitely *not* to be harmed," Hopton insisted.

Olivares spoke now, moving closer to the door, and Marcos was once more half way out of the damask chair but paused to listen. "You go too far, Rogelio. I shall say what needs to be done and when. Besides, this man completed a delicate assignment for us in Holland, *and* for the Vatican, do not forget that. I agree, we did not want him discussing it at the time. And at the time, I was happy to sanction his removal. But you failed. He outwitted you again and again. Which is another reason I want to try to turn him: he's a quick one to escape your nets. Tell your masters this, and urgently: we cannot let him disappear while we're drawing up a treaty with Charles Stuart—not while we need to use English recruits in Flanders, and have free access to English ports. It's all far too delicate."

Hopton laughed. "Keep your friends close and your enemies closer, eh?"

"I always have done, Arthur. Why else do you think you and Rogelio are here?"

Marcos wasn't sure if that was meant as a joke or not. Then Olivares was at the door, calling the cabal to a close by saying, "I will use him to Spain's advantage, making him beholden to me. Keep a close watch on the baroness, Arthur. Find out what message she's carrying, and what she takes back to England with her—if she goes."

Marcos sprinted across the anteroom, only to find two men-at-arms stationed either side of the door to the public salon, watching him. Feigning he hadn't noticed them, he slowly stretched his arms, eased his shoulders, and made an effort to straighten his hair and generally pull himself together, all the time his mind racing to find an adequate exit technique. His body gave him the answer as sheer panic brought on a loosening of the lower gut. Looking at the men he gasped out, "Where's the nearest close stool?"

One of them pointed vaguely in the direction of the stairway leading below. "Fourth door down," he said.

"*Gracias!*" Marcos ducked between them and stumbled towards the fourth door in genuine distress.

A few minutes later, adjusting his elegant new clothes, Marcos wondered how soon Olivares would be informed of his presence—for that was inevitable: 'eyes everywhere', was it not? Aware his difficulties were perhaps only just beginning, Marcos opened the door to exit the smelly retreat only to bump, chest to chest, into Kit Windebank. Summoning the last of his bravado, he cried, "There you are! I've been looking everywhere for you. Any chance we can get out of here and go back to that tavern we were in yesterday?"

"Yes, why not? But first we have to make our farewells. Let's go down."

Marcos paused on the wide marble staircase, looking at the scene below: a glorious swirl of colour as courtiers in pastel shades promenaded like dancers with their exotic, chosen partners, whirling together slowly then moving on in stately patterns through a vast unfurnished hall lit with hundreds of beeswax candles in a dozen sparkling chandeliers—exactly as he had always imagined. But away from the lights, beyond the glamour, there was also the whispering of secrets and speculations among more serious men in corners. And in that moment, Marcos knew for sure that this life, after all, was not what he wanted. Besides, he had never learned to dance.

Much later, as he emerged unscathed from a pitch-black alley, Marcos came to a decision. He wouldn't go back into *El Real Sitio* if he could possibly help it; he would wait to see whether Ludo really was going to do something to their benefit in Plymouth, and as soon as that was settled he'd go south to visit his parents then take ship again for England from Sanlúcar. For all Olivares' strictures to the contrary, both he and the priest had sound, albeit twisted, reasons for wanting Ludo out of the way, and Hopton would be just as glad to see the back of him. And even if they didn't try to eliminate the Genoese trickster immediately, no one in that room, he was certain, would have the least qualms about arranging an unfortunate accident for a so-called secretary who now knew more than he ought.

Chapter 21

Sitting in Queen Isabel's private apartment the next day, Alina was far more nervous than she had been at the banquet. Marcos's warning rang through her head: she—they—were being watched. Night and day. The reason for her being here was an open secret, her very presence a perceived threat to a very powerful man.

Taking Henrietta Maria's tightly folded letter from her pocket, she placed it gently in Queen Isabel's white hand then sat back, trying not to look at the queen as she read it. Alina desperately wanted to know and equally didn't want to know what had been written, both awed and appalled that Henrietta Maria could send Ludo to Spain as an assassin. In her heart she wanted to believe he would not, could not, even be part of an assassination, but she had her doubts. She herself had watched Ludo command a galley of cutthroat Berber corsairs: Ludo was capable of anything. Knowing this and living in such close proximity to him was wearing her out.

Doña Isabel lowered the thick paper and took a deep breath in annoyance—or disappointment. She then read the letter a second time, tracing a finger along certain lines. Eventually she folded it back into its square and turned to Alina. "You are aware of the content of this letter, Baroness?"

Alina shook her head, "No, ma'am."

"No? Truly?" the queen queried.

Alina turned away, staring across the room. An ill-made little woman wearing a diminutive outfit identical to the queen's own was sitting on the floor like a child, hugging a fluffy lap dog to her chest. The tiny woman looked up and met her gaze. *The things we must do to serve*, thought Alina. *I never guessed it would be like this.*

"Baroness," the queen said more sharply, "to what extent are you in my royal sister's confidence? You do have her confidence, I hope, or are you simply a messenger?"

Alina shifted in her chair, unsure how to respond or exactly what she was being asked. "I believe I am in the queen's confidence, Your Majesty. Queen Henrietta Maria has my complete respect and undivided loyalty."

"That goes without saying," responded Isabel. "Why else would you be here?"

Alina tried to smile politely. Across the room the tiny woman on the floor gave a slow wink. Unnerved and surprised, Alina spluttered, "How might I help you, ma'am?" She turned fully to the queen, anxious that her observer should not detect her doubts.

Isabel tapped the letter against the dark emerald of her skirts. "I understood this Genoese merchant Ludovico di Doria da Portovenere had come here... at my request. That my sister of England has sent him."

"I—I believe that is so, Your Majesty."

Isabel spread the letter on her skirts and read it again, re-tracing words with a ringed forefinger. "This is not what I had in mind. Not what I asked for." Angrily she folded the letter back into its small square and held it for a moment in the air as if about to drop it. "*Bien*," she suddenly stated, "*muy bien*. Let us see what he can do, and how quickly."

A sense of dread washed through Alina. Tension hung in the room like storm clouds, a threat over all their heads, until a young lady-in-waiting entered hastily, saying, "I beg your pardon, Your Majesty, but the Countess-Duchess asks if she may be received."

The queen's face flushed scarlet. Sitting bolt upright, she said, "Of course, tell her to join us—but not yet, no. We would speak of the baroness's journey first. Ask her to return later."

As the lady-in-waiting exited the long reception room, the queen placed her hand on Alina's as one fellow conspirator to another. "Not a word about this letter to *anyone*. Assure us we are the only people who know of its existence."

"Yes, Your Majesty, my queen was most insistent—"

Henrietta Maria had made no such stricture, but Alina had no time to concoct anything more, for the Countess-Duchess de Olivares sailed into the room: a tall, black-rigged galleon before the wind, and there was more than a squall in the offing.

Isabel shoved the folded letter into Alina's lap. It slipped off her silken skirt and slithered across the polished marble floor like a small serpent hastening to escape human feet. Alina rose to collect it, but the dwarf got there first. Scooting across the marble floor on a four-wheeled wooden platform, she scooped it into her plump little hands like a ball. Leaping from her lap, the dog began to yap excitedly, jumping up and down on all fours. The little woman screeched with laughter and tucked the letter down the front of her bodice, then leaned off her floor-level chariot to cuff the dog none too gently across the muzzle. It had been a matter of a moment, but the stifling atmosphere had been split by lightning.

The Countess-Duchess, a once beautiful woman disfigured by ill-temper, glowered down from her considerable height at the dwarf on the trolley and the dog slunk across the room, its tail between its legs. Alina hovered where she was, between chair and floor, uncertain about the etiquette of an English baroness appearing to be curtseying to a countess-duchess.

The dwarf solved the issue by clapping loudly and forcing another screeching laugh. "What fun, what fun—doggy didn't get it, doggy didn't get it!" she babbled, looking her mistress directly in the eye for instructions. Queen Isabel smiled vaguely and with the barest twist of a hand sent her diminutive attendant back to her place—with the secret letter.

In command once more, Isabel looked up at the Countess-Duchess. "Have you met Baroness Metherall, Inés? She is our Conde de Pamanes' daughter."

Inés de Zúñiga y Velasco raised her considerable eyebrows in exaggerated shock then, with a swing of the wooden frame tied about her hips, sent her voluminous skirts into a wide sweep, leaving in their wake balls of fluffy dust and dog's hair. Her glower now transferred to Alina, the Countess-Duchess said acidly, "If she is relating her *voyages*, Your Majesty, I hope the baroness has not told you *all* that occurred to her."

Queen Isabel looked surprised and somewhat confused. Alina on the other hand, knew exactly what was happening: she was to get no nearer the Spanish queen or her secrets would be revealed. The fact that she had been saved from a Berber harem —not sent into white slavery—was neither here nor there: the Countess-Duchess's version would be believed.

Alina's hands began kneading the soft material of her skirts on their far more modest *guardainfante* frame. Unaware of her agitated fingers, but consciously anxious to get away, Alina drew back her shoulders and forced herself to look the

Countess-Duchess in the eye, for the rules of the game had been drawn up and Alina's handicap established. She was damaged goods, exactly as Ludo had foretold on a crowded French quayside all those years ago.

Except in reality there was no contest, for Alina could never win. The Countess-Duchess was undermining whatever status or confidence Alina had so briefly established between herself and Queen Isabel. And if she stayed in the court any longer she risked jeopardising her good name—even further. Therefore, she must leave.

Maintaining her haughty posture as ice trickled down her spine, Alina dared to challenge the Countess-Duchess: the woman knew why she was here—or at least had suspicions—but she would not give in easily. But as she continued to hold the Countess-Duchess of Olivares' gaze, knowing for certain the woman had learned of the content of the queens' correspondence, an awful thought occurred to her: the queens themselves were in an embarrassing diplomatic situation. But queens were rarely punished, they used scapegoats—such as a minor baroness from England, daughter of a profligate grandee of no standing: a young woman whose dubious past was about to be made public.

Queen Isabel stood up and said something, and Alina wrenched herself back to the present. "I'm sorry, Your Majesty, I didn't quite catch what you said."

Isabel gave her a warning glare. "I was proposing we take a turn in the gardens as the day is cooling. You will accompany us for supper, will you not, Baroness? We have invited your father to join us. Won't that be pleasant?"

Astonished, Alina suddenly realised it was her own father's loose tongue that had led the Countess-Duchess to this room at this precise moment. Trapped by decorum Alina smiled and said, "That would be delightful, Your Majesty."

As they strolled in the rigidly formal garden with its wide manicured paths, large, right-angled pond and perfectly sculpted shrubs, the queen's party met the king's party coming in the opposite direction. Their respective buffoons entered into an elaborate dumb-show of long-lost lovers, which Alina found embarrassing. Raising her fan to hide her discomfort, she caught the king watching her. She executed a low a curtsey and when she looked up noticed her father some distance behind him.

The Conde de Pamanes came closer and gave the smallest of bows as etiquette demanded, but he could not conceal a very real grin of pleasure spreading from cheek to cheek. Alina responded with a wary smile then gulped in horror as the king gave a nod of amused acknowledgement.

Whether the queen or the Countess-Duchess noticed, Alina could not be sure, but Isabel must have been aware of something, for as the two groups mingled she beckoned to Alina and, strolling slightly away, said, "Tell us more about the court in London, Baroness, where my dear sister resides."

"The court in London?" Alina responded, taking two or three small steps to be nearer the queen. "Yes, erm... As I was saying at the banquet, it moves from palace to palace; sometimes their majesties are in London, sometimes at St James's or Whitehall, or they may be at Hampton Court, or their country palace of Oatlands."

"And the court follows them, as they do here?" Queen Isabel bestowed a knowing half-smile on the Conde de Pamanes.

"Naturally, *Majestad*, when Queen Henrietta Maria travels most officers of the household accompany her, and her personal attendants, of course. Queen Mary, Queen Henrietta Maria that is, is particularly fond of court entertainments," she added then regretted it. Henrietta Maria had an unfortunate reputation as a *comedienne*, taking part in theatricals of which the sober-minded and stricter Protestants thoroughly disapproved, as, Alina thought ironically, the austere Catholic court here probably would. In this she was wrong.

"Entertainments!" Doña Isabel's face lit up. "Tell us about these entertainments. We once loved entertainments here, but then our life became sad with the loss of our little ones..." She sighed and looked at her husband. "Tell us about these English entertainments."

"They are masques, *Majestad*... That is a type of theatrical performed in the palace by—um—members of the court, with dancing."

Joining them, King Felipe met Alina's eye again. "Indeed, we are curious. And what is in these masques?"

Aware the king was studying her in front of the queen's very eyes, Alina became even more nervous. Trying to still her hands, she replied as plainly as she could, "First, there is an ante-masque, whereby the audience see a world in disorder... with vice and sins and humorous events, then there is the masque itself which involves the audience sometimes in—um—dancing. Then there is more acting, and in the end disorder is banished and a better world is created in its place." She finished in a rush, not sure why she should feel guilty or ashamed about relating what after all was the queen's sister's passion.

The Spanish monarchs were silent for a few moments then Isabel touched her husband's arm saying, "Rather different to *your* theatricals, I think."

The king laughed. "They were jolly romps, though. What say we alleviate this summer tedium in the sierra with—not a play—with a masked ball?"

"Yes, why not?" Isabel clapped her hands like her pet dwarf. "Let it be like old times—a ball, but not indoors. Let us dance here in the moonlight."

A ripple of excitement ran along the path. Pairs and small groups separated to chat among themselves. Alina relaxed and waited while the monarchs and their favourites discussed the proposed event, pointing at the artificial lake and around the gardens, where they could set up dance floors and torch-lit booths.

Discussion then focused on whether the ball should have a theme and spectacles, and firework displays, as well as dining and dancing. It was gradually decided that as they were in the sierra, and to some minds 'living among rustics', the ball should have a pastoral and woodland theme and be entirely celebrated *al fresco* here in the gardens. Delighted, the queen laughed out loud like a girl and announced that it would be held in one week's time.

"Seven days?" Alina responded with surprise. "I don't believe such an event can be arranged in one week; it's too much, the servants and cooks..." She lowered her eyes, feeling shock and disapproval around her, and stopped speaking.

"How charming—defending servants," the Countess-Duchess said, coming to stand alongside Alina. "You must understand and appreciate the role of underlings very well, Baroness. Perhaps living in a much smaller household—you do have servants in your English home, I assume?—perhaps having never lived on a grander scale... shall we say,"—she gazed meaningfully at the Conde de Pamanes—"means you are also unfamiliar with quite how rapidly and effectively a properly run palace can produce such events."

Alina looked at her father, who was observing a butterfly on a leaf with studied interest. *How much do these people know about us?* she wondered. *Everything, it would appear.* She tried to smile benignly and refrained from making the rejoinder the barb merited, but the Countess-Duchess was not finished.

"Or is it because your 'travels' have brought you more into contact with the lower orders, slaves even? We were informed you were taken by corsairs and incarcerated in a harem."

Fans flicked excitedly; heads, male and female, came together in urgent whispers: "So this is the woman..."

The Countess-Duchess had achieved her objective, but rather than cowing Alina it put her on her mettle. Standing very straight, she focused on the branch of a delicate cherry tree above the vicious-minded woman's head. "You are misinformed, Countess-Duchess. I was indeed *nearly* captured by Barbary corsairs in Santander, but I was saved by a brave English priest." Alina wondered what Ludo or Marcos would make of that lie. "He kindly accompanied me to safety in England, where—and now I do have to make a confession—I married a British aristocrat *close to the royal family*, Baron Metherall... for love. Perhaps those who have never travelled might think that dangerously exotic or an adventure. I have to admit even I see it as *romantic*."

The Countess-Duchess nodded her head slowly in response, silently declaring an unspoken war. Forced to look away, Alina met the curious and perhaps challenging stare of the king. Giving Alina a look that she chose not to interpret, he turned to his courtiers, saying, "At this point, gentlemen, I believe it may be politic to leave the ladies to their gossip."

As King Felipe's party sauntered away from the queen's, the king suddenly turned back and, addressing everyone in a clear voice, he said, "Let us celebrate the end of the San Cristóbal *fiesta* with fireworks and our masked ball, *eight* days hence."

Then he strode on through the garden, followed by his attendants, sycophants and favourites, including Alina's father.

Before the king turned the corner of the path, however, he looked at Alina once more. This time she could not fail to interpret the meaning, his reputation as a womaniser being what it was. Felipe was intrigued by her story—and would like to know more. Alina grabbed a handful of her rose-coloured, silken skirt: this would add another layer of difficulty to her stay in Spain.

The next hour passed agonisingly slowly. They returned indoors, ostensibly to play cards. Alina lost each hand as she fended off the overly curious and the downright impertinent, all wanting to know personal details about her life in England, and *exactly* how she had arrived there.

When finally she was released, Alina realised she had no companion to escort her home. Marcos had brought her into the palace, but had refused, in the most uncharacteristic and unchivalrous manner, to wait for her. Hitherto, the absence of a respectable dame at her side had not been commented upon, at least not in her hearing, but all eyes were upon her now as she made her farewell obeisance to the queen and retreated to the outer chamber. As the double doors were opened for her by liveried flunkeys, Alina felt the Countess-Duchess's dark eyes boring into her back. Maintaining perfect posture, she exited the room, but a panicky interior voice was screaming, *What does she know? What has she told her husband?*

To Alina's relief, her father was waiting in the third anteroom. "I shall escort you, my dear," he said, but then began to lead her through a maze of apartments and reception salons further into the palace and away from where Alina believed the main staircase to the courtyard to be.

"Is this the long way round to my lodgings?" she asked, half-jokingly but somewhat wary.

"You'll see," he replied, opening a gold-decorated door of blond birch wood. "Someone wants to speak with you before you leave."

There being no flunkeys here, the count held the door open for Alina to pass through then closed it behind her, staying outside.

The room, which was small and intimate like an inner study, was lit only by two low sweet-scented candles.

A tall figure was seated in the shadow. "Baroness Metherall, welcome." It was the king.

Alina took a deep breath and made another low curtsey. "*Majestad.*"

Rising to his feet, the monarch offered her his hand and led her to a chair very close to where he had been sitting. "Come: share my frugal supper with me. Will you take a glass of chilled wine?"

Having no option but to accept, Alina said, "Thank you, Your Majesty."

Felipe went to a sideboard and with his own hands poured her a glass of wine from a cut glass decanter. Alina's heart raced. They were alone. No servants, no favourites. Except perhaps the one outside the door. And he, she was suddenly sure, had only very recently risen to this status. Alina shuddered: the Conde de Pamanes was buying favours with his own daughter.

Arranging her skirts on their awkward frame as best she could, Alina tried to sit with decorum but her head was whirling in a panic of conflicting emotions—because the man now handing her a glass of wine was clearly intending to be her lover, and she wasn't at all sure it would be possible to refuse.

As she sipped the cool wine, Alina closed her eyes and tried to savour the moment. She had reached all that as a lonely, motherless daughter of a penniless grandee she had ever dreamed of and desired. But as she had once told another lover: she was not as she was.

Chapter 22

In the spacious studio of the court artist Diego Velazquez a few days later, Ludo watched the Spanish monarch guide Alina from one half-completed canvas to another, pausing with her to examine preliminary sketches of boots and spurs, hands and eyes, and entire heads—human, canine and equine.

The royal hand on Alina's back moved her towards larger sketches resting against an easel in the far corner of the room. The royal head bent down and whispered words that shouted across the room to all present that he had made another conquest—or was about to. The monarch had a reputation as a womaniser: was said by some to have rare skills and stamina in the bedchamber. Ludo sighed, annoyed at what he was forced to see. Annoyed that it mattered to him.

Alina stooped to pick up a wooden board with a charcoal drawing. As she studied it Felipe bent over her shoulder again, and Ludo felt the undeniable tug of an emotion he was not prepared to name. And yet, was this affair not entirely to be expected? Alina had always craved attention, always paraded her aristocratic demeanour and pedigree, had never attempted to hide her personal ambition. Now she had got what she'd always wanted.

Ludo turned away, suddenly wondering if this was why she was so close to the English royals as well, if her relationship to Henrietta Maria stretched to Charles Stuart. Sour and irritable, he stretched his neck to the right to ease the pain in his left shoulder, trying to dismiss unpleasant thoughts, then wandered through the open space on the top floor above the royal apartments to stop at a big window. Acres of open land stretched as far as the eye could see, then all the way down to the city of Madrid, fifty or so miles away. The scene lifted his humour; it held a sense of freedom. Combined with the fresh morning air it was almost exhilarating—especially after being shut in a stuffy chamber recovering from yet another attempt on his life.

Contemplating the panorama for a few minutes more, Ludo decided the sensation was not so different to being at sea in the aspect of being free of the constraints of civilization... He was interrupted by voices from behind him: the king's slow drawl—a voice that suggested the speaker was almost too lazy to talk— and another, deeper, more resonant voice. He turned back to face the room. Felipe was now holding a swarthy man of middle years by the arm and pointing with his other hand at a half-completed brown horse prancing away from the viewer. The artist, whose jet-black hair and moustache contrasted sharply with his surprisingly clean smock, responded cautiously but firmly. Felipe wasn't going to get his own way, by the sound of it.

Deciding not to listen for fear of being dragged in as adjudicator, Ludo began looking at portraits in various stages of completion, noting how the Habsburg jaw ruined gentle brows above smiling blue eyes; how the present queen was painted into an armament of upholstery; how—and this could be useful —the artist Velázquez had recreated the faces of his sitters to perfection, but had been unable to capture any semblance of equine beauty in the equestrian portraits. Prince Balthasar, for example, a good-looking boy despite his lineage, had been saddled with, literally, various lumps of bay rump and diminutive hooves pawing the air. The 'draft' for the latest portrait—Ludo had no idea of the terminology, but these were evidently practice runs—lost any intimation of forthcoming majesty in its subject as the eye was drawn to the over-fed quarters of a barrel-bellied hack.

Lost in his musing, Ludo failed to see Doña Isabel enter the long studio with a young lady-in-waiting. When he noticed her, she was already at his side.

"Your Majesty," he blustered, "forgive me. I was thinking about the paintings."

"Don Ludovico, what a pleasure. We did not know you were here. You are admiring Don Diego's work."

It was a statement not a question, and indeed, who could not admire the man's work, or that of his apprentices mixing paints and preparing palettes further down the open studio?

"I am, Your Majesty, although..."

"*Although?*" Doña Isabel's pleasant tone with its slight French accent rose questioningly. "You find something at fault?"

"No, indeed, Your Majesty, I was merely lamenting... No, that is not the correct word. To be honest, I was regretting that the young prince, as heir to the throne, could not have been seated on one of my special Arab horses. They are so fine, so exquisitely designed, they would—erm—lend more grandeur to his youthful nobility." Ludo found himself running out of imagination... He could not recall a woman with such dark perceptive eyes, except Leonora in Goa, about whom he chose not to recall anything if he could help it.

"Arab horses, you say? Don't we have such in Spain? We must, for the Moors were here for many generations."

"I cannot say, ma'am. I first encountered them in a country across the other side of the world. They are exquisite."

"And how do they differ, please, from my son's mount here? How are they better?"

"I would not say they are 'better', ma'am, but they are more beautiful. They have large, honest eyes, and a face that is appealing, attractive; they are not large, as our working horses here are large, or broad as is the prince's mount here, but they are immensely strong, and so full of life... Let me tell you a refrain, a proverb, about the Arab horse: *God spoke to the south wind, saying: 'I will create from you a being which will be happiness to the good and misfortune to the bad. Happiness shall be on its forehead, bounty on its back, and joy in the possessor.'"*

The queen stared into Ludo's eyes. A smile formed about her small, full mouth. Ludo had to school himself not to take her hand. To cover his feelings he added, "'*Bounty on its back and joy in the possessor'*—this would be a mount worthy of a future king and emperor."

"If he has an empire over which to rule," murmured the queen quietly.

"Everything you do, *madonna*, is for your son?" Ludo ventured, playing his second card according to his discussion with Henrietta Maria and his subsequent commission.

"Everything."

"Could you not use your son to maintain what is his, ma'am?" Ludo half turned so no one watching them could see what he was saying. "Take the prince with you to the king and let him explain to His Majesty how this country is being wracked by continual wars, how Prince Balthasar Carlos might lose his birthright and suffer because of..." Ludo dropped his voice even lower, "your enemy."

"Use a child as a pawn?" the queen snapped, her voice now sharp with disgust.

Heads turned. Surreptitiously, Ludo moved her on to another painting and they stood as if observing its lines and colours. "Tell me," he said, "why such a simple honest strategy would not influence the king? Surely he must think of the prince's future above all."

"Yes, of course he does, but our son is still under the Countess-Duchess de Olivares' tutelage. For this approach I must wait until he is free of her control."

Ludo recognised the excuse: Isabel was more afraid of the dragon-wife than the gargoyle husband. "Might I remind Your Majesty that in Florence it is said a true Florentine's first waking thought is 'Who can I dupe today?'—I say 'dupe', 'cheat' is too strong and I cannot find a good translation for the Spanish word *engañar*. But my point is that you are of Medici blood, *madonna*. Use your wiles to obtain what you seek."

"My mother is a Medici, and all her life she has done exactly what you have described. And what has she obtained? Exile, ignominy and poverty. I also have proud, noble Habsburg blood, Don Ludovico: I will not be seen to be meddling in His Majesty's affairs."

So you want me to do it, Ludo thought, inclining his head as if accepting Isabel's reasoning. Expecting to be dismissed, he bowed again, ready to leave.

To his astonishment, the queen placed her hand on his arm, saying for anyone to hear, "I would speak of this more—and other matters related to your more recent travels. Attend us this evening after the siesta hour." She then turned and went to her husband's side, saying, "Don Ludovico promises to tell us of his travels this afternoon."

Ludo stayed rooted to the spot, unsure, for a very rare moment in his life, what to do next. Then he gave a mental skip and a jump: the seeds of his release had been sown. Isabel had rejected his logical strategy too quickly; she would be thinking about it for the rest of the day. Thinking about it and realising, consciously or not, that he was not in Spain to murder her enemy. Henrietta Maria had told him to 'get rid of' her sister's enemy and there were various ways that could be achieved without violence.

Excluded from the conversation between the artist and his patrons, angry with Alina and worried for her safety, confused now by an emotional reaction to another woman—one he could never hope to woo—Ludo began to speculate how he could turn the new elements of this Spanish venture to his advantage more rapidly and get away. Time was slipping from under him like the fine, dry sand of an Omani beach.

Walking slowly past the wide windows overlooking the flat Castilian plain, then pausing at one and standing at an angle out of habit, but also to avoid giving his back to the monarchs, Ludo watched the heat haze shimmer over the ochre stubble. Then he moved his line of sight more directly below, to the low, sculpted hedges, right-angled pathways and the large, green-topped pond of the palace gardens. An army of sweating servants were erecting booths and shaping small arbours for the forthcoming ball.

A tear of sweat sneaked between his ear and eye. He wiped it away with the back of his hand and fell once more into an uncomfortable reverie. Gradually, though, his attention was drawn back to Doña Isabel. In his mind's eye he dressed her for the ball in softer, looser fabrics, gave her a background of palms or gently swaying cypress branches, not the austere stone of the Real Sitio and granite sierra that formed the natural back wall of the studio. He touched the pocket over his heart: a ruby worthy of a queen: *Rani Saahasi*—queen of courage. Dare he give it to Doña Isabel? What might he get in return? *Nada, that's what I'd get. This queen is more subtle and far more astute than her younger sister in England. There'll be no flirting here—and the ruby is not for wasting on the possibility of a hazardous dalliance.*

Wiping his brow with a fine lawn handkerchief, Ludo chided himself and came up short on another unpleasant realisation. *No wonder Alina has been so antagonistic; she thinks I am here to eliminate the Count-Duke—physically... Damned if I do, and damned if I don't.*

Chapter 23

The deep orange and red furnishings, the gilding around frames and mirrors, lent the receiving room a hint of hellfire, upon whose coals Ludo knew he was about to tread. A dowdy green parrot in an elaborate wrought-iron cage watched them morosely in silence. Equally morose, Ludo waited for the Queen of Spain to broach the matter he knew she wanted to discuss. Obliged to sit straight, not only because of the very close proximity of the queen but because of the wounds to his shoulder and ribs, he was in no mood for light-hearted remarks, which usually helped him avoid troublesome issues. And to make matters worse, Alina was watching his every move—watching that she might report back to Henrietta Maria, of that Ludo was quite certain.

Isabel flicked a black fan: it was the anniversary of a baby's death. Ludo waited. She flicked it again and a head peered around the door, a large head in what looked like wig of grey candle-curls—close to the floor.

"Not yet, Obdulia!" the queen snapped.

Ludo and Alina exchanged glances, Alina making the slightest of gestures with her head, indicating 'ignore her and get on with it'.

The queen gave a huff of annoyance and turned her dark eyes on Ludo, then away. "Well," she said bluntly, "what are you going to do about it?"

Ludo swallowed: direct to the point—unusual diplomacy, but the odd creature at the door had evidently reminded Isabel there was little time for niceties if they were to speak in private.

"Ah, 'it'—that," he prevaricated. "Yes, well..." Ludo tweaked at a loose thread on the arm of his chair, noting that even the upholstery here was stitched with gold. There had to be a way to take advantage of this mess: if the ugly, humourless Olivares could make himself wealthy and indispensable to the Spanish crown, what might he, Ludo da Portovenere, with all the tricks of Christendom and beyond, not achieve?

"You are aware I want him gone. As fast as possible now," Doña Isabel stated.

"And who might replace him, *Majestad*?" Ludo replied, instantly regretting it: the queen might think he was angling for a role he would hate.

"That matter is already decided: his successor is actively engaged in the... situation. His role is prepared—although naturally he cannot be seen to be involved."

"Naturally," Ludo muttered, realising the 'situation' was as good as out of his hands before he'd even begun. "So all that remains is to 'be rid of' the subject in question?"

"Yes, and I want it done while we are here in the sierra. When we return to Madrid a new regime will be in place." Isabel flicked open her fan then closed it with a snap.

Ludo inclined his head to one side. "And by 'rid of', in this context, you mean..." Here the queen balked. It was the first hopeful sign. "Precisely, Your Majesty. May we consider alternatives? Enforced retirement might serve equally well."

"That is exactly what I have been trying to achieve for years, Don Ludovico. But as we discussed in the studio this morning, time has run out. Action must be taken."

"However, there are still alternatives, are there not?" Ludo waited for a response. The black fan signalled he should continue. "I have studied the situation in some depth since I arrived, *Majestad,* and it seems to me there are two linked options which will achieve the desired result without causing over-much suspicion. Whether they will terminate your problem before your return to Madrid, though, I regret that I cannot promise." Ludo waited again. Again the royal hand indicated that he continue. "The person in question is ailing, ma'am—gout and old age exacerbated by over-zealous physicians, who may or may not be acting with his best interests at heart. I am informed the man is bled on a daily basis. This in itself may be causing the harm he does—leading as it does to light-headedness and fancies." Ludo paused, as if seeking the courage to speak again, then proceeded with exactly what he had planned to say. "Encouraging a physician to insist on bed rest and... er... the need to extract the ill humours causing the gout and other maladies might be the quickest route to a terminal solution. That, combined with an unfortunate—"

He was interrupted by the warning squeak of hinges. A door, visibly but not audibly hidden in a mural, opened and the grey ringlets falling almost to the floor appeared once again some distance below the handle.

"Obdulia!" the queen snapped again. "Not yet! I will call you when we are ready. You are not required while this gentleman is here."

The head and shoulders inched forward until Ludo could make out the diminutive but very well endowed form of the smallest woman he had ever seen. She looked at him and made a mock-angry face. He gave her one of his grins, and the expression became genuine. Did she think he was trying to usurp her role? *Reduced to a court buffoon*, he thought, then remembered it was a useful technique for obtaining truth and evading responsibilities, and winked at her. She slammed the door shut.

"Our apologies, Don Ludovico, pray continue. Your second option is?"

"An unfortunate accident: something incapacitating and requiring a deputy to step in—but not lethal. Something that would encourage the man in question to see retirement as an ideal situation whereby he can recover his health and enjoy his final years."

"And how might this be achieved with a man who moves no more than from one chair to another?"

"Remove the chairs, *Majestad*."

The queen shot him an angry glance worthy of her court dwarf. Ludo responded with one of his twinkling-eyed grins. After a heart-stopping moment Queen Isabel began to laugh a gay, light laugh that transformed her face, returning her to the mischievous, fun-loving girl who had been married by proxy into the austere Spanish Habsburg court before her adolescence —according to the gossip obtained third-hand via Marcos and Kit Windebank. Gambling on that had been a risk, but a risk worth taking.

"Obdulia," Queen Isabel called.

The door opened a fraction; the little woman had been listening, waiting. A fluffy little dog scampered in, launched itself onto the queen's lap and began licking her chalk face paint. Decorum now completely compromised, Isabel said, "You may enter now, Duli, and bring my ladies and Fadrique with you."

The ensuing nonsense cost Ludo his Omani khanjar. Taking it from its half-moon gilded-leather sheath, he kept the court ladies and the queen entertained, demonstrating why it was less a weapon than a mere adornment: quite useless for anything compared to a dagger—useful only for peeling oranges, for example. He then succeeded in making Isabel relax and laugh again by demonstrating how the double-edged, curved—and fortunately blunt—khanjar massacred a citrus fruit, resulting in orange juice up his sleeve and across his lap and "Oh, look, the orange is under your chair, ma'am!"

Queen Isabel let her attendants join in the fun. Her ladies squealed with delight as Ludo played the fool, much to Obdulia's continuing annoyance. Watching with undisguised contempt, she finally retrieved the misshapen fruit and fed it to the dowdy parrot, who had not uttered a squawk since they'd entered.

Throughout the charade, Alina sat taut as a guitar string—an instrument played quietly in the corner by a beardless young man whose appearance was more appropriate to a Constantinople harem than the rigidly governed palace of El Real Sitio. As Ludo left he felt Alina's eyes burning into him.

Why are you angry, carina? Because I won't do as you think I have been ordered? Surely you do not wish to share lodgings with an assassin—or do you?

Attempting to wipe the sticky juice from his wrists outside the royal suite, Ludo was joined by Marcos, who at Ludo's insistence had been waiting for him in the antechamber.

"Hopton sent me," Marcos said. "You're wanted by the Count-Duke de Olivares."

"No, please, not now," Ludo sighed. "I need to rest my aching body. Do you have any idea how difficult it is to sit absolutely straight with bruised kidneys, a stab wound and broken ribs?”

“No.”

“No sympathy from you, then?”

“No, and as you don’t need me with Olivares, I’ll—”

“I most certainly do. Why do you think I’ve been putting up with your fussing for the past week? I need you right by my side, as witness and, if needs be, rescuer, especially if your dubious pal Windebank is within hailing distance.”

“Ludo,”—Marcos was serious—“supposing he sends us both to the dungeon? He must know it was me working with you in Amsterdam.”

Ludo stopped rubbing his hands and put the handkerchief back in his breeches pocket. Voice low, he said, “Do you think you’ve been watched in Plymouth?”

“In Plymouth? No. At least, I’ve never thought I might be. Rogelio only ever tried to attack you, although I—and everybody else—would have gone down with you if that smelly Dutch fluyt hadn’t been so nifty sailing out of Amsterdam.”

“Don’t worry, I’m pretty sure you are safe; nobody’s had a go at you in the last week—only me. Come on, let’s get this over with. Where are we expected?”

“Somewhere behind that door there.” Marcos pointed to a polished, iron-riveted door to his left, very different from the light wood of the doors in the queen’s apartments. The significance of the difference and proximity was not lost on either of them. “He must be important if he’s got rooms on this floor and in this suite as well,” Marcos muttered.

“He’s the king’s *valido*, the *special* favourite, and has been for twenty years. And his wife’s raised all the royal children that have survived so far. One could call them deputy monarchs in a way. Lead on.”

Chapter 24

Olivares' skin was yellow, his short, black hair lank and greasy; a sagging chin overlapping a dirty white collar wobbled as he spoke. Ludo watched the way he moved his limbs as they crossed a cluttered private study, recognising him for a sick man and thinking *she need only be patient and her enemy will be dead or retired within a year—exactly as I suggested.* Uncomfortable and aching from his wounds, Ludo sympathised with the ailing chief minister, recalling what Hopton had said about the physicians bleeding him until he could barely stand.

Sitting by the empty fireplace with a long, lean female hunting dog sprawled at his feet was a man Ludo had seen at the banquet and around the palace, but did not know. They were introduced; Marcos was naturally ignored. Luis Méndez de Haro y Guzmán, Marqués de Carpio, was Olivares' nephew. There was a physical similarity about the heavy jowls. Don Luis made no move to get up and Ludo deliberately raised an eyebrow at the rudeness. A flicker of amusement played around Olivares' fleshy lips as he indicated a chair for Ludo on the other side of his ornate desk.

Waiting until King Felipe's chief minister had taken his, Ludo opened his black silk coat to demonstrate the absence of any weapon then lowered himself carefully into his seat so his own countenance would remain in profile. He didn't want Olivares reading all his expressions. Out of the corner of his eye, he noted Marcos edge along the wall to stand beside a bookcase and within hearing distance.

"You are wondering where I am going to start this time," Olivares said, looking directly at Ludo, "with past successes or present difficulties."

"I was indeed, Count-Duke. My thoughts were precisely along those lines."

In a more private meeting five years ago Ludo had enjoyed the way the Olivares' subtle mind had belittled the financial scandal they were accelerating in Holland while also making adjustments to ensure the desired outcome. "I am pleased you considered our previous liaison a success, Count-Duke," he said. "Not everyone saw it that way. I made a number of enemies, in fact—on your behalf. But shall we omit the small talk and address the current issue?"

"The current issue being?"

"Why I am here this time: His Majesty has no doubt apprised you of our agreement. You want to know now exactly what I proposed and what I can offer."

"In return for?"

Ludo cocked his head to one side. "Two pretty palfreys and an abandoned *cortijo* in the back of beyond..."

"Or a fine new galleon belonging to the Spanish Armada?"

"I already have one, *Excelencia*. It was my reward for the Dutch venture, if you remember? I only took possession of what your Count Azor promised me. I don't see him here, by the way. Is he not in the sierra for the summer?"

"He went to Flanders."

"And fell in a ditch. Oh dear, he will have muddied his fancy cape."

Olivares reached across his desk for a lidded jug of white wine. It was out of his reach, and as Ludo couldn't bear to see an old man flinching with the effort of getting to his feet, he did the honours himself. Pouring what proved to be a very good Rueda, ideal for the weather and time of day, and taking a glass to the silent marquis but not the secretary, Ludo said, "On the other hand, starting with my galleon is probably a good opening."

"You are going to lend it to us, are you?" Olivares sipped his wine, watching Ludo over the rim of the engraved crystal goblet. "We are in serious need of vessels, and of sailing men, come to that."

"Yes, I am, actually, in a manner of speaking. His Majesty will have told you he has commissioned me to return to the East Indies in order that I may find him special precious gems and spices, and extend his trading empire in the process."

"Yes, he has." Olivares drew out the word 'yes'. "But why, I asked, do we need you for that, given we already obtain such goods from the Philippines and New Spain. What is it, or what other services, I asked, can Don Ludovico provide that our other merchants cannot?"

"The short answer is: cloves, cinnamon, diamonds and rubies. The longer answer will be the result of this discussion, will it not?" Ludo ran a plump finger around the fine edge of his glass. "A pretty filigree design, so intricate. It must have been made by a skilled craftsman—an ordinary glass-blower can turn out a decent enough goblet, of course, but the extra *elaboration* is not so easily achieved."

Olivares studied him for a moment. "Elaborate your plan, Don Ludovico."

"First you must give me something to work on, Excellency. It takes more than the profit from spices and precious gems to make a dangerous voyage worthwhile."

"I give you tax-exemption in Portugal," Olivares said, jolting Ludo upright into a serious issue and a twinge of pain. "You are surprised? You planned never to return to Lisbon? I don't blame you. If ever there was a country that never quite gets things right, it's Portugal. Not that it *is* a country—being part of Spain—but you catch my drift."

"Are you asking me to catch the drift of Portugal away from Spain, though?"

"Yes and no: it is for discussion." Olivares sniffed noisily and removed a grubby square of linen from his tunic to blow his nose. The dog lying by the empty grate stirred and woofed in response. Ignoring her, the ageing Chief Minister continued, "Let us discuss Portugal and *England* first. You have been in London; you know Charles Stuart is endeavouring to rule without his vexatious parliament again: I wonder if he is also approaching our neighbours to support him in future religious plans as well?"

"*His* plans or his wife's plans, Excellency?"

"Good, I see you are aware that matters of religion are fundamentally—I use the word advisedly—his French wife's plans. You can trace them back to her mother, Marie de Medici, who, I'm sure you know, is also mother to Queen Isabel." Olivares attempted a rotten-toothed smile. "But this, for now, is by the by. Except that the wife in question is also seeking other support from Spain. Again, a matter for discussion."

Ludo maintained his silence and to his surprise the Chief Minister filled it. He was agitated, but then the content of the queens' letters meant he should be.

"Henrietta's religious views and intentions are well known in England and elsewhere, are they not?" The old man coughed then wiped his face with the disgusting handkerchief.

"I couldn't say, Excellency, I have been away in the East for some time. There were clerics from the Vatican in the chapel at Whitehall, now I come to think about it." Ludo played with the stem of his glass.

"One of them is here now."

"Really?" Ludo did not look up.

A brief silence edged between them. Olivares broke it first.

"Returning to the matter of our Iberian neighbour: we are currently drawing up a treaty between Britain and Spain, to our mutual benefit, but the word Portugal appears nowhere on it."

"We are beating about the bush, Excellency, and if we go on like this we shall either run out of metaphors or get bored. Can we get to the point, please?"

"Your move—another metaphor, but meant appropriately."

Ludo put his glass on Olivares' desk and moved it next to a book, then he took the Count-Duke's glass and placed it north of the book. "My cup is Portugal; yours is England. If Portugal separates from Spain, your Atlantic coastline defences are lost. The French can sail into Portugal and walk across the border to attack you on land all the way from Galicia down to Andalusia, and there is no way you can protect that length of exposed terrain. The English," he tapped a fingernail against Olivares' glass, "can also invade, but—worse, perhaps—they can *support* Portugal and—and this is where I may be of use—they can undermine your East Indies trade and all the shipping coming up from Africa and currently entering Lisbon and Oporto. If, however, you support Henrietta Maria's Catholic cause, and provide funds to help equip an army if it comes to civil war in England, which from what I have seen myself is very likely, then you can prevent England supporting Portugal or threatening your borders elsewhere. And there is the old alliance between the Dutch and Portugal to think of. If Portugal separates from Spain, Lisbon can go back to supplying Amsterdam, and the Dutch can even threaten Spain that way."

"Well-reasoned, and I agree with all you say. But we are overstretched supplying our own army and keeping those pestiferous idiots in Catalonia under control. What do you propose?"

"What I suggested to His Majesty—that being 'over-stretched' you find another source of income."

Olivares blew his nose again. "A summer cold," he whined nasally, "I get them all the time. Age, you know." He returned the crumpled cloth to his old-fashioned doublet, then said, "You also told the king you could influence Murat Reis to desist in attacking Spanish vessels."

"I did. I can."

"A very large claim, Don Ludovico—even for a member of the Doria family, as you also claim you are. Genoa and the House of Doria have provided ships and admirals, and supported Spain in her wars, and financed our armies, but I wasn't aware they had contacts or influence over Berber pirates as well."

Ludo looked away then said quietly, "One of them does— did: a Dori-*a* joined forces, for a time, with a very well-known Berber corsair."

Olivares stared at him and Ludo knew he understood for he then said quietly, "Agostino, Doge of Genoa—his wayward daughter: I heard about it. Well, well, well, and I was wondering about your parentage only this morning..."

It was at that moment Ludo decided to stop playing games. Olivares was sick and physically repellent, but he was far too astute to outwit, and too perceptive not to like. "I tell you what," he said trying to direct the conversation away from further awkward revelations, "I will arrange a cessation of attacks on Spanish vessels coming into Cádiz and Sanlúcar from the East Indies for as long as I am engaged in trade for the royal house of Habsburg in Spain and Flanders."

"And you shall keep your ship thereafter, for as long as you set your Berber friends on Portuguese ships sailing for Lisbon, if or when Portugal reclaims its sovereignty. But why should the Berbers do this for you? They stand to lose a great deal."

"They will not be doing it for me alone. You will naturally have to offer something in exchange."

"Such as?"

"Allowing residents of Salé and Rabat to return to Spain."

Olivares' jaw dropped. Even their silent observers gaped.

"The Moors were expelled from Spain two hundred years ago," Olivares spluttered. "You cannot seriously expect me to allow them re-entry on the off chance a bunch of cut-throat pirates might stop raiding our shipping!"

"Many of the Moors I speak of are Christians, Excellency. They are also artisans, surgeons, members of the liberal arts, leather workers... Spain will benefit from their industry. There are far too many people here who produce nothing—no wonder the country is 'over-stretched'."

Olivares gulped back a goblet of wine, poured himself another then said, "Continue."

"Many residents of Salé, apart from the Christians, are also being persecuted by their co-religionists for not being Sunni. They would be happy to return to Spain and bring their skills with them. Or, no—was it the Shi-ite? I never remember. You know, I can sit at a table with a Jew and a Moor, a Protestant and a Catholic, and when we are hatless for the life of me I can't tell us apart."

There was silence. Marcos shuffled his feet, causing the dog to raise its head again. Don Luis de Haro bent down and ran a soft hand down her back.

Olivares said, "Luis, you are expected in His Majesty's apartments this evening, are you not?"

The nephew got to his feet and with a mere nod of the head, left. The dog watched him go. Reading the anger in his spine, Ludo wondered why Olivares had requested his presence then so obviously dismissed him. The answer was soon to come.

"You are not in league with my nephew, I see," Olivares said as the door closed. "I did wonder."

"He covets your chair, Count-Duke?"

"He covets my power and place by the king, and commands a significant clique, which is why I would discuss this matter without him. Are you in a hurry or can you spare me more of your valuable time?"

"My time is yours, Excellency. But please remind me to mention a particularly annoying aspect of our previous arrangement before I go: a tenacious and wholly despicable priest called Rogelio."

"Ah, yes, Rogelio. I fear he may not be very pleased about our meeting today, or its outcome." Olivares paused then indicated Marcos by the door with sweaty palm.

Ludo said, "Marcos, wait for me outside. Check that any lackeys and messengers out there aren't listening in, will you."

Marcos exited the room with a polite nod. Once they were alone, Olivares lifted the wine jug and poured them each another generous measure, saying, "My nephew will contact you within the next twenty-four hours."

"At your request?"

"No, because he was on the pilgrimage to Santiago with Queen Isabel. He makes suggestions, encourages her dramatic imagination. Perhaps even helps to write her letters..."

"Ah."

"You will accept his offer, prevaricate and keep me informed."

Ludo raised his eyebrows. "I will do all I can and more, sir, *if* you will amend an existing document and provide me with a new charter to trade from Goa. The document I speak of, and I have it in my lodgings, must be amended to excuse a Portuguese widow from the *Carreira da India* taxation and, more importantly, provide her with guaranteed protection from the Inquisition. In return for my tasks related to Portugal and the Berbers—depending on how much you are prepared to offer in that quarter—I'd also like her to be given a certain *cortijo* near Sanlúcar for her home, if it is still available?"

Olivares started to laugh but it turned into a coughing fit. When he was able to speak again without wheezing, he said, "It is a lot to ask in return for a few arrangements relating to trade."

"No, Count-Duke, in return for your life."

There was silence again.

"The wording in the letter to England was, I believe, to 'be rid of' me." Olivares took a sip of wine, savouring its bouquet, extending the moment, watching Ludo's face all the time. "I want an assassination attempt to be linked back to Don Luis and made common knowledge."

"An assassination *attempt*?" Ludo queried, genuinely surprised. "Is that necessary? To 'be rid of'—as I explained to a certain lady here not two hours ago—does not necessarily entail assassination."

"What did you propose, Don Ludo: kidnapping? An unfortunate accident that maims but does no vital harm? A political manoeuvre to push me into retirement? Kidnapping presumes someone will pay the ransom." Olivares gave something resembling a smile.

"Within your means, I would have thought, and when you return safe and sound you have every right to hound your kidnappers to death or throw them in a dungeon and lose the key."

Olivares' smile widened. "And if it were more than a kidnapping, if it were sequestration to lose me forever?"

"I think the king would be so angry he himself would seek out the perpetrators and have them executed at dawn with a rusty sword."

Olivares laughed out loud. "Shall we discuss details?"

"Discuss on, Excellency. As long as it is understood that you and your monarch know *I am not the perpetrator*... but perhaps Her Majesty Queen Isabel believes otherwise."

Olivares winked, drank down more of his wine and began to outline a plan. "It is the *romería* cavalcade for the San Cristóbal celebration the day after tomorrow..."

Ludo sat back and listened, making comments now and again, asking for clarification, and finally trying to persuade the long-serving *valido* that what he was suggesting could prove both dangerous and very painful for an elderly man with crippling gout.

"I have means of dealing with pain—not altogether unpleasant, either," Olivares said. "One of the significant benefits of the East Indies trade, in fact."

"Sticky black opium?"

"Just the merest smidgen... Don Ludovico, I want what happens in this *attempt* to be very public and the San Cristóbal *romería* cavalcade is an ideal opportunity."

Ludo stared hard at the man in front of him, trying to weigh up whether he had been correct in his earlier assumption that Olivares was still very astute or whether the unceasing bleeding meant he was losing his wits. It then occurred to him it made not a scrap of difference as long as Leonora's documents were signed and he kept the *Tulip*.

"Very well, Count-Duke," he said, cautiously. "I will make the necessary arrangements. Can I ask that when you sign the document for my wife in Goa you also sign another excluding me entirely from blame—for what *you* alone have decided upon? Give it to Sir Arthur Hopton for safekeeping, in case the king or anyone else tries to throw me in a dungeon. Duplicate copies to be handed to my secretary, please. I'm sure Kit Windebank will run the errand."

"The widow you speak of is your wife? What is it you require?"

Cheered by Olivares' genuine interest, Ludo explained what had happened in Goa, glossing over the actual marriage arrangement, but making it clear he wanted immunity and protection from the Inquisition for his wife and new business.

Their discussion concluded, Ludo got up to leave, but Olivares said, "Those gems you are peddling... His Majesty says he has authorised payment for a set of uncut diamonds and two dozen large, black pearls."

"Yes, I am to collect payment tomorrow, I hope. I'd prefer Spanish silver—pieces of eight are so useful, and I need to pay tradesmen and craftsmen and other daily costs for my stay here, and also finance my next voyage."

"You *are* definitely planning to return to India then?"

"Yes, that is why I require you to sign the documents of *limpieza de sangre*, sir. I shall be stopping in Salé en route to make arrangements with Murat Reis—depending on what you deicide in that regard. Either way, I hope to leave at the earliest opportunity once your... er... incident at the *romería* has been expedited."

Ludo's tone was positive, although he was not entirely positive he would return to Goa at all. He had been considering asking someone suitable to carry Leonora's documents for him, and to act as a manager or factor on his behalf in Goa when he got there. There was a personal matter requiring attention in Portovenere before he made that decision, however.

Jerking Ludo from his travel plans, Olivares said, "Do you carry precious stones with you today?"

"I do, yes. What did you have in mind?"

"Something special and unusual for my wife: I will pay in coin. I will also hasten your payments tomorrow that you may leave Spain without delay—once, as you say, our 'incident' has been *safely* concluded."

Ludo's right hand strayed to his secret pocket. He was tempted to let the ugly man have the wonderful ruby for his unpleasant wife: he could ask a ludicrous price, which Olivares was well able to pay—in coin—possibly right here. It was tempting. But was the gorgon really the right woman for such a fabulous gem? And, more importantly, would he stay alive without it? For surely it was the ruby that had saved him twice now, not counting ensuring his survival on the perilous voyage to Plymouth—and he was about to put himself in danger's way again doing as Olivares wanted.

Leonora had once told him Indian warriors inserted rubies under their skin to bring victory in battle and protect them from harm...

Decision made, the saving of his own skin a priority, Ludo said, "I do have a few good-sized rubies still. They are unpolished but of very high quality, sufficient for a necklace. If you purchase some diamonds to set them off, that would make a very splendid gift."

Olivares' sallow, wily face transformed into that of a besotted old husband. Ludo remained on his guard, nonetheless, and said, "Might I suggest you also take a ruby for yourself, Excellency? They have protective properties: Indian rajahs and their warriors wear them to protect them from enemies. Worn as a talisman, a ruby, I am reliably informed, protects the wearer against danger and disaster."

Olivares inclined his head and held out his hand, "Do you have them with you?"

Ludo lifted a soft chamois pouch from his breeches pocket and shook the contents onto the Count-Duke's hand, holding back an extra stone for himself in case the bit of theatre Olivares wanted to create for the *romería* turned nasty—or Olivares intended it to turn nasty. *Damned if you do, damned if you don't… and I am giving him a 'very public' reason to jail me forever—or worse.*

Don Luis de Haro, Marqués de Carpio, arrived at Ludo's lodgings within the twenty-four hours. Ludo wasn't surprised the man knew where he was staying, but that he would lower himself to street level boded ill.

José showed the middle-aged, unsmiling nobleman into the shared salon and left the room smirking as Ludo entered. The boy was no doubt amused at the nobleman's moustache, which curled up round his cheeks like a creeping black caterpillar while failing to hide the sour expression beneath. Ludo had heard about Haro's opposition to his uncle. That he was also 'the queen's man' had come as no surprise. How far he was prepared to go to replace his uncle was a matter of daily court speculation, according to Marcos, who had naturally heard it from Kit Windebank.

Courtesies concluded, Haro opened the proceedings in an unexpected manner. "You have displeased Her Majesty the Queen."

Surprised, Ludo said, "I regret that greatly, Marqués. In what way? And in what manner may I amend it?"

"You came here to fulfil a mission for the Queen of England and the Queen of Spain: we cannot believe that you, a mere merchant, can have the temerity to oppose their wishes."

"I do not, Marqués. The business I believe we speak of is in fact underway and will be concluded very soon. Perhaps you can help me?"

Now it was Haro's turn to be surprised. "Oh—how?"

"It is the *romería* for San Cristóbal tomorrow. The confusion and excitement all the horses will provide offers an ideal opportunity. It will be easier than a botched attempt inside the palace with men-at-arms and gentlemen-in-waiting coming to the rescue, or perhaps even preventing the sad—incident."

"You have a point."

"Shall I continue?" Ludo asked, indicating a chair.

After the marquis had left, Ludo called José and Marcos into the salon. "Pack your things," he said. "Be ready to leave in a hurry if necessary. José, admit no one, whatever their excuse. Tell anyone who asks for me that I have been called away on unexpected business. Marcos, stay with Alina—don't let her out of your sight."

"What's going on?" Marcos demanded.

Ludo turned to José, "Go on, get packing!" Then he beckoned Marcos closer. "I have agreed to do something for the Marqués de Haro, who, as you know, acts on behalf of Doña Isabel. I cannot tell you what it is, but if it goes wrong…"

"How does this affect Alina?"

"She brought the message suggesting the action."

Marcos's face went white. "I'll stay with her. Tell her to pack and be ready to come with me—but she'll be missing the masked ball if we leave tomorrow. She won't like that!"

"No, I know. Nevertheless, we must be ready, although I'd prefer not to leave in too obvious a haste if it can be avoided. It will bring suspicion down on us all. No, I want to be battle-ready, as they say, but maintain a passive front for as long as possible and leave without being under suspicion. Are you with me?"

"*With you* as in, 'Do I follow your meaning?', or 'Will I be involved?' Because if it's the latter, forget it."

Ludo did a double take. "Is there something I need to know? Have I offended you in some way?"

"No, not specifically, but I don't want to be involved in a…"

"What? Spit it out."

"Assassination."

"Oh, that. You won't be."

"Will you?"

"*Maria Santissisma*, not if I can help it."

"And if you can't help it?"

"You have become such an old woman, Marcos. Where's my sparky helper from Holland?"

"Gone: I told you, I have a wife at home waiting for me to return in one piece."

Ludo sighed. "Look, it's the *romería* tomorrow. Something will happen during the procession with the saint. All I want to do after that is get away quickly, but not at a gallop. Understand?"

"I think so—but there is going to be trouble and Alina and I are caught up in it, aren't we?"

Ludo shook his head in genuine despair. "What has happened to you? Yes, there may—will be—trouble. But the only person to blame will be the Marqués de Haro—unless I get it horribly wrong."

"What can I do to protect Alina?" Marcos asked quietly.

"Protect her? Oh, keep watch and... You do know she came of her own free will, don't you?"

"Yes."

"Do you also happen to know why?" Ludo's voice dropped to barely a whisper.

"Henrietta's bribed her with promises of—I don't know—greatness."

"Hah, I might have guessed." Ludo shook his head in mild despair. "Just tell her to pack. What she doesn't know won't harm her."

"You hope," Marcus added, acidly. "By the way—what have you asked Kit to do? He says he'll be away all day and it's something for you."

"That boy talks too much."

"But what?"

"Nothing for you to worry about."

Marcos looked at Ludo sceptically and nodded. "It's all right, I don't want to know."

Chapter 25

Alina opened the door to the street, took one look at what was happening outside, and slammed it shut again. A fruit vendor had set up his stall right on the steps of their lodging house and the street had been cordoned off in preparation for the San Cristóbal mounted games of ribbons and rings, meaning the carriage her father had arranged for her would not be able to get anywhere near their door.

"*Fiestas!*" she huffed as she turned and stumped back upstairs. "Stupid peasant *fiestas* for stupid peasants!"

Close to tears, Alina recognised she was in a constant state of tension these days: worried that the Countess-Duchess of Olivares would tell Queen Isabel of her apparent liaison with the king, or worse, that Isabel would accuse her of precisely what she was trying to avoid. It was what Ludo called a 'damned if you do and damned if you don't' situation. Felipe found her assertions that she was modest and faithful to her loving husband amusing, and, unfortunately, a challenge. The whole thing was getting out of control and she was more anxious than ever to terminate her involvement in Isabel and Henrietta's dreadful scheme; desperate to escape the all-seeing gaze of the Countess-Duchess and, above all, desperate to rid herself of the all-consuming doubt that the man not her husband, whom she could not prevent herself from loving, was capable of murder.

The previous evening had been the final straw: trying to convince her father she was not going to let the King of Spain turn her into another of his concubines, despite the benefits that would surely come of it—to the Conde de Pamanes himself —had been a nightmare. Calming her breathing, she returned to their shared sitting room.

Marcos took one look at her hot cheeks and said, "Don't tell me, your carriage can't get to the door." He raised two hands in mock surrender. "I'm surprised your father didn't know this would happen. I thought he attended the court here regularly."

"Maybe not quite as regularly as he would have us believe," Alina said, throwing her wide hat onto one chair and flopping unladylike into another. "He does have a carriage, though, which I didn't expect. His widow must be wealthy to provide for that as well. Unless it's the price she pays to get him out of her house. *That* wouldn't surprise me."

"Wealthy widows must be in vogue."

"Meaning?"

"Meaning," Marcos lowered his voice, although there was no one else in their rooms apart from the silent, ever-miserable, Fanny, "I think our Genoese friend has found one on the other side of the world."

"A widow?"

Marcos grinned and nodded. "I've been detailed to collect documents for a certain Leonora Figaroa something or other in Goa—from the Count-Duke himself. But Ludo won't tell me who she is."

Alina grabbed a fistful of skirt. "Do you think he has actually ma— I mean, could he have...?"

"Got married, be already married, be in love, have a wife, two wives and a dozen children? Yes, to all of them. He told me he'd got two or three children in Liguria himself years ago, but not as in *a family*, if you see what I mean? Don't look surprised: you don't imagine a man like him travels the world without planting a few seeds along the way, do you?"

"You sound exactly like him, saying that," Alina snapped. "Where are you going?"

"To see the festivities and find out what Ludo's up to without me. Would milady like to join me?" Marcos offered his arm then said, "Don't forget your hat or you'll be as brown as a peasant by the time we see the saint. We have to walk, remember."

Holding Marcos's arm with one hand to avoid losing him in the crowd and swatting at the unwary with her fan for getting in their way, Alina was for once grateful for a hat. It was a new acquisition, a wide-brimmed straw affair not dissimilar to one she had worn during her girlhood summers in Santander but far, far more expensive and elegant, and it protected her fair skin from the fierce morning sun very well.

Before they reached the Alameda gardens, though, she was perspiring just as she had done when she had picked greens or scattered corn for the chickens during those interminable girlhood summers. Banishing the memory, Alina turned her attention to the chaos around her. Pedestrians and riders were gathering to follow the effigy of Saint Christopher to the countryside shrine for its blessing. The effigy itself, a large plaster saint with a carved pinewood child Jesus perched on its left arm, was being hoisted onto burly male shoulders. Behind the effigy, equines of all shades and descriptions, from powerful battle-chargers and prancing stallions to humble mules and laden donkeys, were being manoeuvred into rows of three or four abreast, ready to pass the stand where the king and queen were waiting to salute the saint and mark the beginning of the *romería.*

Seated beside and above the monarchs were the royal family and their favourites. There appeared to be no vacant seat for her father, who was not there. *Did he want to attend in his carriage to avoid embarrassment at not being invited to join the royal party?* Alina wondered. Inés, Countess-Duchess of Olivares, was sitting at the end of the royal row next to the Chief Minister, who was perilously near the edge of the open stand. He looked as if he was drunk, and it wasn't even noon. Ludo, who had disappeared before she was up, was nowhere in sight.

As the horses jostled and shoved and their riders attempted to drink wine from goatskin *botas* an order came for them to move forward. The *romería* had begun. Raucous trumpets blasted the air; fire-crackers set nervous mounts up on their hind legs. Alina grabbed Marcos's arm again and tried to pull him away. Meeting strong resistance, she remembered what level of society he came from. This was the sort of popular event he'd probably enjoyed as a boy. The look on his face told her she was right.

Catching her looking at him, Marcos grinned and said, "*Ven!*" and walked into the moving crowd, right under the broad chest of a foam-flecked, black horse, then dangerously close to the shanks of another two, all the time attempting to get to the other side of the procession. Alina swatted her closed fan this way and that, certain they'd either be kicked or trampled, but Marcos knew what he was doing. "If we go round the back of the stands," he explained, "we can get to the end of the Alameda gardens faster and see them get out onto the track to the sierra shrine. Then we'll join the walkers with Saint Christopher."

"I'd prefer to stay further back, behind the horses, not in front or with them, thank you."

"What, and get your pretty slippers covered in dung?"

Alina had no chance to protest further as Marcos tugged her around a donkey pulling a farm cart and into the path of a tassel-decorated mule then under the wooden struts of the stand, heading towards the exit to the gardens. Coming out from under the wooden seats of the royal row, Alina glimpsed a figure she half recognised in another mule cart, this one driven by a farm boy. The figure was Ludo's size and shape but wearing a broad straw hat, countryman's smock and rope-soled shoes. Hurrying to stay at Marcos's side, she gave him not a second thought for she had just noticed the effigy of the saint was being carried by men with bare feet.

Gradually the men shuffled up to the royal stand to receive the priest's and the monarch's blessings, then they manoeuvred the heavy carving into the open and through the small town onto a track through the umbrella pines of the sierra. Following far closer than she liked, Alina stumbled on the rough, stony ground and winced, wondering how the barefoot men with the saint could possibly bear the pain. Distracted, she suddenly became aware of a commotion behind them. Another stallion out of control, no doubt. Marcos grabbed her hand and pulled her to the side of the track then half lifted her up the bank and into the pine trees for safety. A group of country boys carrying bunches of vicious, crackling-dry thistles had joined the procession. Another horse careered out of control, bucking and kicking, lashing its back legs and sending other mounts into a huddle before three, at least, careered off at a gallop. Scenting danger, another followed, then another, and another. Screaming with laughter, the boys rushed back up the procession, looking for new victims.

"What are they doing?" Alina demanded.

"Stuffing thistles under horses' tails. Don't tell me you've never seen that before."

"But that's cruel, awful, *dangerous*. Why doesn't someone —"

Alina's words were whisked away in a cloud of choking dust as a mule cart hurtled past them, scattering pious walkers and knocking San Cristóbal sideways. As the men bearing the saint on their shoulders tried to regain their footing, one of them stumbled, pulling another down with him and sending their entire precious cargo somersaulting over the edge of the track. Alina put her hands to her mouth as the boy-child Jesus was launched from the saint's shoulder to bounce blasphemously down the steep hillside, out of sight and beyond repair.

In appalled fascination Alina turned her attention back to the cart disappearing in the distance. It looked very unstable. "Marcos, look!" she cried, pointing as a nearside wheel worked itself loose, teetered backwards, then rolled unhindered across the path of soft-shoed pedestrians to follow the holy boy-child down the stony hill.

Another mule cart appeared to her right, this time driven by someone Marcos recognised. "I don't believe it," he murmured.

Drawing up beside them, the driver shouted, "Get in!"

Without a word, Marcos lifted Alina by the waist into the back of the cart, an easy task despite her skirts because they were standing at the same level, then jumped in beside her.

"Hold tight!" warned the driver in English and they set off hell-for-leather after the mule now dragging a three-wheeled, broken dray at right angles to the sharp flints of the track.

Marcos scrambled onto the driver's bench. "Can we save them?" he shouted in English.

"Bloody better or we're all in for a nasty ending!"

Alina grabbed the side of the cart, splinters jabbing into her fingers, trying to keep her balance as best she could as their chariot gained on the boy and man in the broken farm cart.

"Someone's fallen out!" Alina screamed as their English driver steered around the well-dressed body of a man in the middle of the track.

Before she could say anything more there was a thunderous drumming of hooves as a tight group of riders including men in royal livery approached behind them.

"Shit! Bloody fucking hell!" their driver cursed, lashing their poor beast into a gallop only to haul it to a stop as they came alongside the broken vehicle, wheel rim to wheel rim, at a curve before a fork in the track.

The Englishman now screamed, "Get in!" again, and waited just long enough for the farmer to abandon his son and climb aboard their cart. Then they were off on another race, this time over the grass and boulders separating the two forks in the track, then full pelt at a gallop beneath low trees and out into the stony sierra.

The farmer they had rescued pulled off his straw hat and passed it to Alina. "Put it on, *carina*—you've lost yours and you'll get sunburnt." It was Ludo.

Alina sat down on the bare boards with a thump, then bounced painfully as they passed over a boulder.

"In the nick of time!" Ludo shouted in English, edging forward to lean over the driver's seat. "Where to? Anywhere?"

Their driver, a dark-haired young man, shouted, "Might as well use the hide-out the old man planned."

"You know about that?" Ludo asked, surprised.

"I'm the one who was supposed to find the old devil."

"Who else knows, apart from you and Hopton?" Ludo demanded.

"Pff, this is Felipe's court in the countryside, apart from the old boy's body-guard, who were all in on it, anyone and everyone could know. A good few would like him to be lost forever, of course, but that was his risk. Stupid idea from the start, but he's been barmy like this for months." The cart lurched over a hidden boulder and he said something that Alina couldn't hear but made Ludo laugh.

Pulling herself up, Alina now leaned towards Ludo. "That poor man... We should go back... help him!" she cried.

Ludo nodded and tapped the driver on the shoulder. "She's right. We ought to go back for him. He could be seriously hurt."

"Don't worry, there'll be plenty there to save him by now," shouted the Englishman. "Apart from his bodyguard, Hopton's watchers will be following for sure. They'll save him—get him back safely. Let them sort it out between them. There's a surgeon and his helpers waiting back at the palace. He prepared for the worst. Not that this was part of it, but accidents do happen. He's doped to the eyeballs anyway. Probably think it was all a dream when he comes round."

As the cart slowed, the mule now at a marginally safer trot, Alina tapped Marcos on the shoulder. "What's going on?" she hissed.

"No idea. Ask him," he said pointing behind at Ludo.

Ludo gave her a one-dimpled grin. "I'll tell you later, promise."

Finally, they slowed to a walk and turned onto a narrow goat track leading up the mountainside; they then took another track along a ridge overlooking the Castilian plain below. Eventually the mule came to a halt, sides heaving, nostrils flaring, at a tumbledown hovel. A goldfinch on a nearby branch trilled a warning into the air and was answered by another. Alina noted an aerial splash of colour, but she was shaking too much and too bruised to appreciate it.

Ludo helped her to the ground then doubled over, holding his arms across his ribs. "*Maria Santissima*, I shouldn't have done that," he gasped, rocking in pain.

Bursting into tears, Alina scrambled for the shade of the hovel.

The Englishman ignored her and said to Ludo, "Get your breath back and we'll get going again. You're not safe from Haro's men yet. He'll pin the blame on you first, if he can, even though you've ruined the so-called abduction."

"I didn't arrange for the wheel to come loose." Ludo was indignant.

"Maybe not, but you could have been a bit more vigilant. Someone tampered with the dray, that's for sure." The Englishman shrugged his shoulders as if to say 'nothing to do with me' and turned to Marcos. "Go back down to the main track, keep out of sight but try to see if we're being followed."

Marcos ran into the jumble of rock roses and brambles littering the mountainside and disappeared.

After checking the mule's traces then turning the beast full circle to face the way they had come, the Englishman said to Ludo, "Do you want to go straight back and mix with the mob? We can stay here inside otherwise, if you like. It's dry and clean —I checked it out when he asked me to find somewhere suitable. We can get back into town as if we've come from the opposite direction later in the day: once the fuss has died down nobody will recognise you dressed like that, with all the chaos going on."

"We should have brought the boy with us," Ludo said.

"You paid him in advance, didn't you? What you are worried about? Hopton will take care of him, get him back to his family all right."

"What if Haro gets to him? His cart's broken—he won't get home without drawing attention now."

"Don't fret, Hopton will see him all right."

"Where is Hopton, anyway?"

"He stayed with the other dignitaries. They were going to follow the saint as well. Don't worry, it was him who arranged for me to have this cart and stay behind you in case anything went wrong. I was to stumble upon the poor, sequestered *valido* by accident, remember. Given my fancy for rural girls in humble places and all that, it was supposedly plausible. A crazy idea, but the planning was sound."

Ludo was quiet for a moment or two, then said, "I'd prefer to stay away for the rest of the day, if that's all right? The crowd will be gasping and gawping, everyone will be talking about it— just what the old devil wanted, in the end." Ludo paused, kicked at a stone with his espadrilles, then said, "You're right, it might be better if we don't go back until after dark. It'll look odd you and I in a farm cart—too many people know you."

"I could take you to some people I know. We can stay there until the evening. The main thing is, I think the old man's all right."

"He was all right when he got *into* my cart," Ludo replied in a lighter tone. "We loaded it with fleeces and sacks of loose wool so he wouldn't get too bruised, and he'd popped a lump of sticky poppy into his morning gruel."

The Englishman took another look at the mule, whose breathing had nearly returned to normal, then climbed aboard the driving seat, saying, "He should have stuck to poison; a day throwing up and it would all have been over with. He could have paid a doctor to bring him back from the brink of death."

Ludo laughed. "He should have consulted you, then. He told me he wanted to be abducted and how else do you get a chief minister and king's *valido*, who can barely walk, out of a palace the size of El Sitio without being shot or thrown in a dungeon by anxious men-at-arms in the process?"

"Yes, but that wheel wasn't part of the plan, was it?"

"No. It wasn't an accident, either," Ludo grunted, climbing painfully onto the running board to sit next to the driver and leaving Alina to get into the back of the cart on her own, ripping her new gown in the process.

This time she arranged herself on the rough planks in such a way as to hold onto the side of the cart but stay sitting upright and more balanced.

As they moved off the Englishman said, "That priest was in Hopton's office yesterday."

"So it could have been his minion who tampered with the wheel, or Don Luis de Haro himself—or Olivares playing his own double game," said Ludo.

"I don't think Olivares would have taken a risk like that; he wasn't meant to get hurt physically, just abducted," the driver replied, chatting away as if they were on a Sunday outing.

"I'm not so sure," Ludo replied more pensively. "Olivares doped himself stupid and he wanted maximum publicity so he could put the finger publicly on his nephew. It's not impossible he arranged for the wheel to come loose."

Marcos was waiting at the junction of the tracks. "Nobody's passed by yet," he said, climbing nimbly over the backboards to sit next to Alina.

Looking over his shoulder, the driver seemed to notice her for the first time. "Have we met?" he asked in Spanish.

Marcos raised a hand. "Ah, no. Alina, may I introduce a friend of mine, Kit Windebank, secretary to the English Ambassador. Kit, this is Doña María de los Ángeles, Baroness Metherall and daughter of the Conde de Pamanes, whom I'm sure you know."

Kit Windebank reached an arm behind him to shake her hand, but Alina narrowed her eyes and glowered: she wanted to slap him.

"*Dio mio*," Ludo said, interrupting them, "my shoulder's opened again. I'm bleeding like water down a drainpipe."

Chapter 26

They stopped twice on a journey that took them along a high ridge with a sheer drop. The first time to check Ludo's shoulder wound, which was bleeding copiously, the second, for Alina to remove another length of petticoat to be used as a bandage. By the time they finally came to a halt at a smithy on the edge of a hamlet, it was well into the afternoon and Ludo was close to fainting.

The farrier came out at their approach and exchanged words with Kit, then helped Ludo out of the cart while Marcos assisted Alina, who was also close to dropping. The mule was taken from its traces and led into a stall; the cart upended against a wall with Marcos and Kit's help, to look as if it hadn't been used. Then all four followed the farrier up a set of outdoor steps to a cramped dwelling above the smithy. A rosy-cheeked housewife raised her hands in surprise and rushed at Kit.

"Have you brought her home?" she yelled, as if Kit were in another province.

"No, *Mami*, I can't even see her, but they promise she will come home to you soon—as long as I go back to England first."

"Bastards," spat the farrier, "taking our daughter, ruining our lives like that. They've no right. What are you here for if she's not with you, and why all the fuss with that cart?"

"Ah, it's like this…" Kit began, edging back from the tirade, evidently regretting his decision to seek shelter in the smithy.

"Brought us more trouble, have you?" continued the farrier, jabbing the air with a forefinger the size of a hammer head. "I don't know why I don't horsewhip you."

"No, Paco, no, leave the boy alone. It's not his fault," the wife shouted. Then, turning to Kit, she asked, "Who's this fine lady, dear? Your mother?"

Alina's jaw dropped. "*Su madre!*"

"Oh, beg pardon, I'm sure," the wife huffed. "You're not English then?"

Before Alina could say another word, a heavy male foot trod none too gently on her summer slippers. "The lady is my wife, *señora*," Ludo explained. "We have been in a carriage accident and this young man has very kindly saved us. I regret I'm bleeding rather a lot. Do you mind if I sit down?"

"*Siéntese, siéntese,*" the woman gushed, noticing the red stain spreading across Ludo's farmer's smock then turning to take a second look at Alina, who was far too well-dressed for a farmer's wife, even for a *fiesta*. "I'll get some water and cloth," she said, nodding knowingly at her husband then disappearing into another room.

The farrier stood arms akimbo and stared from Kit to Marcos to Ludo, then at Alina. Addressing Ludo, he said, "*Carriage* accident, was it? You're not dressed like a gentleman as befits this lady. Had to borrow some clothes, did you?"

"Yes, as a matter of fact, but—if anyone stops by to ask after my health, do you mind saying you haven't seen us?"

"Thought as much," the farrier replied drily.

"Would it be possible, Papá—" Kit began.

"Don't you 'Papá' me, you—you—"

"– for Don *Lorenzo* and his wife to stay here until the evening?" Kit asked affably, ignoring the farrier's anger.

Alina's hands and eyebrows shot up in unison. "Here, why?" she demanded.

Ignoring her tone as well, Kit continued speaking to the farrier, "We think it would be better for Don Lorenzo to rest and give his wound a chance to heal before returning to El Escorial. I'll ride back into town with my friend and return with a better conveyance for him this evening. If that is all right? I'm sure Don Lorenzo will reward you—handsomely."

Alina turned to study the Englishman called Kit, trying to gauge his age, and how he came to be involved with the British ambassador and know a country blacksmith's daughter. Then she stopped worrying; it was none of her business. She really didn't care who anyone was as long as she could wash her face and get a drink of clean water, or wine, or small beer or anything at all, right this moment, because she was going to faint if not.

Sometime later, slightly refreshed from a drink then a wash in cool well water, Alina returned to the kitchen from the farrier's surprisingly clean outdoor wash-house, and paused at the door to listen. Marcos had evidently said something to irritate Ludo, who was saying, "I'll be with her, you fool. I've got a cut in my shoulder and a couple of broken ribs but I'm not dead yet. You and Kit drive back into town, and return the mule. Get me some decent clothes and come back in my carriage. My driver's staying over the livery stable. Make sure you bring Fanny, though, to cover Alina's good name."

Marcos looked up at the open door; meeting Alina's gaze as she entered, he said, "You will leave with your father for the north when we go south, won't you?"

"Why? Are you leaving tomorrow?" Alina asked.

"Possibly. Probably, yes." Marcos looked at Ludo, who gave a Latin shrug then regretted it for it caused him pain.

"Well I can't leave tomorrow," Alina retorted. "I am taking all my new clothes so I'll have to wait until the fiesta is over." She joined them at the table. "With that booth on our doorstep, we can't get anything bigger than a bucket out at present."

"Pay off the vendor, Marcos," Ludo said. "It won't cost much. That reminds me, Marcos, check my *bizalho* boxes that had the jewels in: they're inside my bedroom chimney full of silver. Olivares paid me last night. It was a risk leaving them with José and that soft creature Alina calls a maid, but I gave strict instructions for no one to enter again. If—for any reason I don't get back or I get arrested when I do—make sure you take it all back to Plymouth with you."

"Do you think you *will* be arrested?" Marcos's voice admitted the possibility. "Don't come back in that case. Stay here; I'll bring you all our goods in your carriage and we'll go straight down to Sanlúcar from here."

"That is very tempting,"—Ludo tried to lean back in his chair in his accustomed manner but it was too painful.—"but what do we do about milady here? No, I need to be seen in El Escorial tomorrow, and I can hardly sneak off without making my farewell to people in high places, not after the preference I have been shown." As he said this Ludo looked directly at Alina.

She met his gaze and raised her eyebrows. "Are you trying to tell me something?" she asked.

"Yes, but we can discuss it on our return."

"I look forward to it," Alina countered, trying to still the flutter in her chest. *Had Ludo had been offered a title? What difference would that make to their relationship?*

Lost in future possibilities, Alina came back into the conversation as Ludo was saying ". . . given the next stage of my journey or one of its possible outcomes," and put a hand to her throat. *Was he planning to take her away with him—again? Would she go this time?*

"I thought you were coming south with me," Marcos said.

"We are for part of the way, then I have to go... elsewhere, and I don't need you for that."

Marcos looked at Alina, then shook his head. "I'm not even going to ask."

Ludo grinned. "I wouldn't tell you anyway, but it'll prove to our advantage in Plymouth. Your father-in-law will be pleased at any rate."

Marcos turned to Kit Windebank, who pulled a face and shrugged. "Nothing I know about," he said.

"Besides," Ludo continued, "I particularly need Olivares to know *I* wasn't playing a double game and actually trying to kill him. After all I've gone through to gain his trust and get him to sign my blasted documents for Goa—"

"Goa—where's that?" Alina demanded.

Ludo sighed. "Can we discuss this later as well? Or, better still, never—I need to rest so the bleeding stops."

Kit got to his feet and went to speak to the woman he called Mother.

It wasn't the first time Alina had ever spent a siesta in a hayloft, although she didn't tell anyone that, so she remembered to ask for a blanket to go under her to prevent straw prickles. The farrier's wife was horrified that a 'proper lady' should rest in straw, but the husband had no reservations and showed them to the ladder above the smithy stalls with undisguised amusement.

Lying separately from her improvised and heavily bandaged husband Alina gazed at the sky through a crack in the rafters, intermittently wondering what Ludo was planning to tell her, and not tell her, and if her father would be concerned or curious about her absence.

A voice, distant but from right beside her, said, "You were planning to leave with your father without telling me."

"You were planning to kill a man—without telling me."

"Not true."

"Then why are we hiding in a hayloft?"

"Because I abducted him so no harm would come to him."

"Riddles: why can you never be serious, never be straight?" Alina was getting angry.

"A riddle, but not of my making: the man in question knew —knows—his life is threatened; we used the event today to sink the evil-wisher. Naturally he knows about your pretty queen— both of them, as it happens."

"Are you talking about Olivares? You can't be; he wouldn't be mad enough to... although Doña Isabel says he is quite mad. That's why she's so afraid of his power over her husband and wants him gone."

"Mad? What is 'mad'? Irrational, unpredictable: yes, I'd agree with that. But surely many of the things we do—most, even—can be interpreted as illogical by another. Take my foolish longing for you, milady. Could you not say but a few kind words to me now and again? Why so much hostility? What is past is past—regrettably."

"Is it?" Alina's voice was a whisper. "I don't think it will ever be over for me."

"Do I hear María de los Ángeles, Baroness Metherall speaking? I cannot believe it."

Alina huffed and rolled onto her side. Ludo tried to shift into another position and grunted with pain.

"Does it hurt very much?" Alina asked, contrite.

"Yes—a straight answer."

"Can I do anything to help?"

Ludo slowly lifted himself to lean on an elbow and look at her. "Yes, you can," he said. "Soften to me, Alina. Soften and forgive me. I should not have left you the way I did in Cornwall; I should not have come back expecting you to leave all... all that you had wanted... give it up for an uncertain life with me. I have thought on it greatly, from many angles, and I see I was wrong from start to finish. But the truth is that I love you: have loved you since you bit my hand on a Santander quayside, although I would not accept it then. I have loved you since I found you asleep on a pile of unwashed fleeces in a stinking cargo hold, have loved you since I walked with you in the moonlight in a place neither of us belong—"

"*I* do," Alina interrupted, tears in her voice.

There was a pause then Ludo whispered, "Love me or belong?"

"Both," Alina sighed. "And that is also wrong. A woman may not love two men: she must choose."

Ludo was silent. Eventually he said, "You chose security."

"Was that so wrong? You have met my father; have you any idea what it was like trying to look after him with no money and care for my brothers and a house falling to bits? I used to make bread and feed the hens, for heaven's sake. You cannot imagine what it is like to live such an uncertain life and not yearn for comfort and security."

"I can. But I took the opposite path: I chose uncertainty, I chose not to belong or be tied down—for fear of..." Ludo swallowed whatever he was going to say next.

Alina waited, then said, "Ludo, who are you?"

"I am, I believe, Ludovico Janszoon di Doria, son of Jan Janszoon and Gabriella Doria."

"I've heard those names before."

"No doubt—Jan Janszoon, a Dutchman by birth, also goes by the name of Murat Reis, infamous leader of Berber pirates. Gabriella Doria of the Genoese Doria clan—you may have heard of Andrea Doria, admiral and tactician of the Tunisian Mahdia siege—or the Doria who became indispensable to Spain's shipping in the Middle Sea. My grandfather, Agostino, was Doge of Genoa. A *doge* and a pirate leader—powerful men—and my pretty, flipperty Doria mother caught between them."

"How is that possible?"

"Because my mother, as a young, unmarried woman, was captured by Berber corsairs, just as you nearly were, except when Janszoon discovered who she was he actually tried to protect her, while seeking a vast ransom payment, of course. The messages and payment took their time in arriving; and during this time..."

"He *used* her!"

"Oh, no, nothing like that."

"You mean, they fell in love, and you were conceived: how romantic." Alina's voice was edged with a scorn she did not entirely feel.

Ignoring her, Ludo continued, "My mother was returned to Genoa when the ransom was paid. When the family discovered she was accompanied by a small child they exiled her to a castle overlooking Portovenere, miles from her beloved friends and cousins in the city of Genoa. Apart from missing her pretty companions, she was—is—a well-educated woman. She became *very* resentful. And I was a constant reminder of her fall from grace. It doesn't help that I am apparently very like my grandfather as well, except for the northern eyes and a nicer nose."

"Did you ever meet him?"

"Agostino Doria?" Ludo moved too fast, "No! *Aagh...* He died two years after my mother brought shame on his name. The family acted against her as they believed he would have wanted. Though I sometimes wonder if he would have been more forgiving—being a man of the world. In some respects I can see their dilemma. Genoa is a small city state, my mother committed a sin for which she—we—had to pay."

"Poor woman, I feel sorry for her."

"Do you? I don't know whether that surprises me or not. If it makes you feel better, a man arrived when I was about seven who was prepared to overlook her unfortunate circumstances. A distant cousin from Rome, paid off by my uncles, no doubt... You can imagine the rest."

"Did your real father know? "

"Oh yes. When I was about thirteen or fourteen, my presence in the castle became too embarrassing even for me, so I went to live with him for a while, in as much as being on dry land for a month here and there can be called *living* somewhere."

"And you never went back to Portovenere?"

Alina waited while Ludo plucked a handful of straw and in the dim light then watched it fall like confetti.

"I go back now and again—to Portovenere. I love the place like a... I don't know what I love it like. I still have many friends there. As a boy I ran wild down on the quayside, catching octopus, helping local 'free-traders' with their cargoes. Someone always takes me in and feeds me proper food when I go back. You have never eaten until you have tried seafood pasta in Portovenere." Ludo sighed. "Maybe one day I will live there in my own house overlooking the sea. It would be good—with the right woman at my side."

"But," Alina paused and rephrased what she wanted to say: it was awkward and she wasn't altogether sure about what she was asking herself. "But... how do you come to be who you are now?"

"Neither fish nor fowl? On my own? Because I am illegitimate, obviously, and not welcome among the respectable Doria clan, and because I find no pleasure in the life in Salé. I have no stomach for living like a corsair. I heartily dislike violence, *carina*, or have you never noticed?"

Alina rolled onto her back and stared up at the bright scars of sunlight through the gashes in the roof. "What a pair we are," she sighed.

"What a pair we would make. Alina, stay with me now. I cannot bear to lose you again."

Sitting up, Alina smiled across at the man she'd loved from the moment he saved her from pirates on a Santander quay, then she inched across the itchy straw and snuggled into his side. Ludo tried to put his arm under her shoulders but gasped in pain. "Ssh," she murmured, "let us just lie together warm and close like this."

"And tomorrow? You should leave with your father for the north as soon as you can."

"And miss the spectacle and excitement of the royals playing country-folk and dancing in the dark?—no, I want to be there."

"I'd rather you left; it's for your own safety."

"Nobody is interested in me, Ludo, except the king, and I've kept out of his clutches so far."

"But you should go—"

"Shush..." Alina placed a finger on Ludo's lips. "Don't spoil this moment. Tomorrow will take care of itself." She began to untie the neck-laces of his peasant smock. "Let me see if your wound is closing." Her fingers traced the open scar, still sticky with half-dried blood.

"According to Marcos they stitch men like cushions in Flanders with wounds like this."

"Stitch them? How? No, don't tell me." Alina bent over him and kissed around the puckered red skin, ran her fingers down his throat to the start of his chest hair. "Am I softening to you, do you think?"

"You are, you are," Ludo said, kissing her head, "but beware, I'm not a total invalid, and most definitely not softening."

"Prove it," Alina whispered in his ear.

It was an awkward yet gentle coming together. The slowness of their moves and their laughter at the discomfort told each of them this was a grown-up romance. There was no need for frantic scrambling, no desperate scratching or biting—just a long, joyous, calm acceptance that they belonged with each other, and that this was the start of a new phase in their love and their lives.

Later, after they had dozed a while, Alina asked, "What will your house in Genoa be like?"

"A pretty house painted pink—coral, perhaps—in keeping with the area. It is on a hillside overlooking the sea. There are terraces full of flowers and trellises. On one sits a beautiful Spanish woman combing her golden hair in the morning sun... Would you come? No, let me rephrase this: Please, Alina, come live with me and be my lady in Liguria."

Sitting up again, Alina spread her loosened hair over her shoulders and started picking out bits of straw. Then she laughed out loud with joy and snuggled back into their rustic bed to whisper, "When?" But Ludo had fallen asleep.

Waking much later, stiff and uncomfortable, Alina knew she still had to ask him what had gone wrong with Doña Isabel's mission. Had he caused the desired accident and thus extracted himself from her foolish request? And if he hadn't, what then? How would it affect *her* position at court? Was that what he meant about her leaving? Not that it mattered, because she wasn't going back to England, ever. Thomas could send her son to Genoa; perhaps she could persuade Marcos to collect him. Her thoughts drifted into a vague future of sunshine and eternal romantic love, and she turned and met Ludo's beady, sea-green gaze.

"You are the loveliest woman I have ever met," he said.

"Do you still like my hair—straggly and full of straw?" Alina shook her mane of golden waves a second time and made another start on removing bits of straw. Outside, a wooden bucket thudded to the dry ground. A dog howled—kicked for stealing milk, perhaps.

"We should have accepted the wife's offer of their bed," Ludo said, trying to get up.

"And have them listening to our every word and move? No, wait," Alina put an arm out to hold him back. "I have to ask you some questions."

"Mm—does this sound positive or ominous?" Ludo's mouth twitched.

"Ludo, what you suggested to Doña Isabel—is that what was happening this morning with the cart? Have you succeeded?"

"Succeeded in 'getting rid' of her enemy? Not exactly, although I fear he was hurt a lot more than he had prepared for."

"He was prepared for? You mean you told him! The Count-Duke *knew* you were trying to abduct him and... Actually, what were you trying to do?"

"Abduct him—as *he* wanted. His nephew, Haro of the creeping moustache, is in league with Isabel. I thought you knew that. That's who Isabel was referring to as the person ready to take over: Olivares' own nephew. Families, I tell you... By a convenient coincidence—and this is most strictly only for you to know—Olivares wanted me to help him *pretend* he'd been abducted so he could go back to the palace and accuse Luis de Haro, his nephew. The thing is, the court physician has been bleeding him for his rheumatics and headaches and the like, nearly to death, but he can't accuse the physician of trying to kill him because that will look as if Felipe and Isabel are involved, the doctor also being *their* physician, so he needed something everybody could see and discuss... Are you with me? It's a bit complicated, but that's how Olivares' mind works."

Alina was silent, trying to grasp the fundamentals of what Ludo was saying then she said, "So you weren't trying to assassinate him, or cause him grievous harm?"

"No, of course not."

"But that's what Queen Henrietta Maria asked you to do."

"I know. I mean, she *assumed* I would do it and I let her think that because it was a way of seeing the old devil in a relative position of safety. Being on a mission from the British royal family would, I hoped, give me a degree of security to pursue my own interests. I was in a difficult situation."

"What situation?"

"I acquired a new galleon belonging to the Spanish armada by slightly devious means in Lisbon, and kept it. It is now fundamental to my new enterprise, so I can't risk having it re-possessed, either loaded at sea or empty in dock—especially not loaded at sea."

Alina sighed. "So you thought—what?"

"That this was a way of showing whose side I was on so he would endorse Felipe's involvement—investment, I suppose—in my new East Indies trade. I was doing what he wanted in the hopes he would confirm his involvement in my new enterprise, if you like.”

“But Henrietta Maria and Isabel think you are here to kill the Count-Duke—for them!”

“Yes, he knows that as well, which is why you need to get away. He’s been intercepting their letters for years. Alina, he has spies in every nook and cranny in Christendom—you really must be careful.”

Alina took a deep breath, “And what about these documents you mentioned—for Leonora in Goa?”

Ludo froze, then very slowly kissed her forehead. “Nothing for you to worry about, I promise. I can tell you that on certain religious matters England should now have better, closer relations with the Spanish royals, as requested.”

“You mean England will be turning back to the True Faith?” Alina’s gasped.

“I suppose so. I’m just the messenger.”

“Then you have done a wonderful thing,” she kissed Ludo’s lips. “Thank you.”

“You may not thank me when you see the trouble it is going to cause.”

“Why should it cause trouble? Oh, because the English peasantry won’t like it.”

“There is no English peasantry, Alina; you of all people should know that. The men in your fields aren’t slaves or tithe peasants—they’re day labourers, and don’t you forget it.”

“But I do intend to forget it, and them—all of them! Isn’t that what you were asking me?” A doubt crept around Alina’s heart. Her face flushed hot with fear and foolishness: had she misinterpreted Ludo’s words about their future together? Could she trust him? No! Ludo da Portovenere was never to be taken at his word. “What did you have to mention Crimphele for!” she snapped. Scrambling to her feet she began brushing frantically at her skirt.

Ludo lay back in the straw with an exaggerated sigh. "You are still playing at life, aren't you? Facts have to be faced; choices have to be made. I choose you and take the consequences of that choice, which will mean a very great change for me."

"How? Why?" Alina demanded.

"Because, as I have just been trying to explain, I have been setting up a new business for a merchant fleet sailing to the East and returning with all manner of riches. If we go to Genoa, I will have to change all that, which *I am very happy* to do," Ludo added hastily, "but if we go, we have to go very soon. I can't risk getting caught up in Olivares' machinations again. Not if I have to worry about you as well."

"You will be making sacrifices. I see," Alina said tartly, putting a foot on the first rung of the loft ladder. "Can you manage to get down on your own? Check your bandages when you get into the yard. I'm going to get something to drink."

"What?" Ludo demanded. "What have I done to upset you this time?"

Alina glared at him in the musty, dusty light, then backed down the ladder and opened the heavy door into the yard. *What had he done? Exactly what she hoped he would—then spoiled it all with reality.* Leaving for Genoa with him would be wonderful, but it would prevent her from obtaining the promised position with the Queen of England...

Confused and angry with her indecision, Alina hoisted her skirts as she had done when she was younger and strode purposefully across the yard to drink directly from the water pump.

On the journey back to El Escorial in Ludo's coach, Alina said, "Where is 'elsewhere' and why are we going there?"

Ludo looked at her, frowning. "I don't follow."

"You told Marcos you wouldn't be going all the way south with him because 'we' were only going part of the way then going 'elsewhere'."

"Ah—um, I meant 'we' as in José and I."

"So you don't want me with you?"

"Not for this, no: I have to go to Lisbon. I... we... That is, I agreed to this commission before the events of this afternoon."

Alina went hot then cold. After a long, awkward silence she said, "Castles in the air. That's all it is, isn't it?"

"No—we just need to think things out and decide where you should go while I'm in Lisbon, that's all."

"Men organising my life again..." Alina huffed and lifted the leather curtain to look out into the darkening night. There was a smell of damp straw, the sweet, barley odour that comes to dry land before a downpour. "There'll be a storm before we get back," she said.

Chapter 27

On the morning of the masked ball, Alina attended the queen's rising as she had been invited, and then joined the special coterie of noble ladies for their morning chocolate in a pretty room overlooking the formal gardens. The gardens, which this evening were to become a woodland glade lit with torches and alive with chatter and excitement, were currently crowded with ladders and saw-horses as labourers created temporary booths and bowers out of pine branches and ferns, and joiners put the finishing touches to rustic benches. Alina's spine tingled: this was the life she had dreamed of as a girl coping with genteel poverty and the prospect of being a drudge forever. Her eyes a glittering blue, cheeks aglow with anticipation, she immediately attracted the queen's attention when she joined her favourites at the window.

Rather than participating in their speculations on what might occur this night, with whom and between whom, however, Isabel tapped Alina on the shoulder and said, "My dear, you are positively glowing. Have you something to tell me?"

Alina stared at the queen, then, as it occurred to her how the woman was misinterpreting her appearance, flushed scarlet. She could hardly say she *hadn't* slept with the king, that she wasn't aglow because of him... As she searched for a reply, the queen again misinterpreted her reluctance to answer. Pursing her small mouth in anger, Isabel said brusquely, "Come with us, please? I have a matter of importance to discuss with you."

Alina swallowed a moment of panic: the Countess-Duchess had discovered their conspiracy and she was going to be used as a scapegoat because the queen assumed she'd been bedded by her royal husband. The Count-Duke was going to... She was to be blamed for. . .

A dozen competing, appalling causes and effects raced through Alina's mind as she was led from the pretty royal chamber into a much smaller adjoining office. In the middle of the room was a carved, inlaid table and on it, resting on a square of trimmed red velvet, were three tiny boxes.

The queen sat at her table and tapped each box in turn with her right forefinger. "Treasure, treasure, treasure," she repeated softly.

Back rigid, chin high, ready for what she feared was to come, Alina was taken by surprise at the queen's gentler tone. "Treasure, *Majestad*?"

"Treasure indeed: that is all you need to know. Each of these boxes contains more than the value of your husband's estate, certainly more than your father's estate."

Alina opened her eyes wide with polite curiosity. "And may I know, ma'am, what they contain?"

"No, but you may study the containers, for they are works of art in themselves."

Queen Isabel handed one to Alina. The box was slightly larger than the palm of her hand and made of exquisitely carved reddish wood, soft to the touch and warm. "I do not recognise this wood, ma'am," Alina said.

"Mahogany from New Spain—beautiful, is it not?"

"Indeed: very beautiful." Alina handed it back, terrified she would drop it.

Queen Isabel stood up and studied Alina. "You *are* looking very lovely this morning, something or some*one* has brought colour to your cheeks."

Alina's heart skipped a beat: *She's brought me in here so she won't be observed or overheard.* The queen inclined her head, waiting for Alina to answer.

"It may be my gown, ma'am. I have been told it is the same blue as my eyes."

"Yes, and that is something I have wished to ask you. Your father being the Count of Pamanes you naturally have pure blood, *limpieza de sangre*, but how is it that a Spanish woman, even of noble birth, can have such golden hair and blue eyes?"

"Because we are of the north, ma'am, I believe. Cantabria is very different to this part of Spain, and of course being on the coast, and constantly raided by all manner of pirates, I wouldn't be surprised if we have Viking blood in our... veins." A foolish statement made without thinking. "Although my father and my mother's family both have noble lineages, going back very many generations, naturally."

"Naturally: that would explain it."

Alina's hands disappeared into the blue silk over the uncomfortable frame at her waist as she waited for her expulsion from the palace and public disgrace.

The queen tapped her desk with her forefinger as if deciding what to do, then went to her door and addressed a secretary outside. "Don Fernando, come in. Wrap the boxes as I instructed earlier. Each one is to be carefully protected against damage and the wrapping must be double sealed."

Waiting for the secretary to enter and close the door behind him, Isabel then looked at Alina. "Baroness," she said, emphasising the English title, "I am entrusting you with a very great commission. These boxes are to be taken to my sister Henrietta Maria. You must take care of each as if it were your baby, your dowry, your life! Keep them safe at all times and deliver them *in person* to my dear sister in London. Do you understand?"

Astonished, Alina nodded. "I understand, *Majestad*. I will guard them with my life."

"See that you do. They will be ready for you briefly. In the meantime, let us discuss another matter of particular importance to me, as a wife... Do you follow?"

Alina didn't know whether to nod or shake her head. She was saved by the little woman she now knew as Doña Obdulia, who suddenly popped her head out from under the table, saying "Treasure, treasure, treasure. The queen's treasure is in little boxes and the king's little boxes, too!"

"Duli!" chided Isabel. "Don't be vulgar."

Doña Obdulia clapped her fat, little hands together. "But our baroness hasn't seen the king's little boxes, Queen, not like you."

"Obdulia!" Isabel's voice was sharp. She looked at Alina, attempted a smile, then slapped Obdulia's head very hard. "Get back on your mat, naughty girl," she said, pushing the dwarf back under the table. Addressing Alina, she continued, "Obdulia goes too far, but—and this I *will* give her—she misses little. Perhaps I am mistaken. Perhaps Don Felipe is—how shall I put it?—interested in your rather exotic personal history, that is all."

Alina gulped. "I fear I may have disappointed him, *Majestad*. No, no, no—not disappointed, that is wrong—I mean I may have *displeased* His Majesty in that I am reluctant to discuss the, erm—embarrassing, mortifying experience that *nearly* befell me—but did not happen—with Barbary corsairs.

Forgive me, Ma'am, I do not like to discuss such personal matters."

"Ah, yes, and he would be interested to know precisely those. . . I understand."

"Told you so," said a voice from under the desk. "Can I come out now?"

"Yes, then get out! I don't want to see you again until I retire this night—go!"

Doña Obdulia pulled a face like a reprimanded child then skipped out of the door, turning to wink at Alina before shutting it behind her.

Queen Isabel gave a short, angry sigh, "I don't know why I keep her."

But Alina thought she did. Tiny, overlooked Obdulia was Doña Isabel's unlikely eyes and ears. What the court buffoons didn't know between them wasn't worth knowing.

Isabel confirmed this by saying, "Good, now she's gone I can continue with another matter very close to my heart. I confess it rested much upon your previous response and I do hope you—and Obdulia—have been entirely honest with me, for I will not proceed if it is otherwise."

Alina lowered her eyes. Crossing her fingers hidden in her skirts she said, "I understand, Your Majesty. I am a loyal and faithful wife myself."

Isabel was silent; she then leaned around Alina to check that her secretary was busy wrapping the boxes, and took a sealed letter from a pocket. Holding it towards Alina, she said, "This is a matter of the gravest importance and for now its contents and purpose are very strictly between you and me. You may not speak of it to anyone, not even once it is delivered to my royal sister Henrietta Maria, not even when the proposal I make to her here becomes public."

Alina took the thick letter in her right hand, but the queen retained a corner, reluctant to let go. "It will be safe with me, Your Majesty," Alina said softly.

Isabel bit her lower lip then said. "You do not ask its contents as with the boxes?"

"Should I, Your Majesty?"

"Now I doubt my wisdom. Perhaps knowing something will help you keep it safe, and if—anything happens—then you may deliver a verbal message..."

Alina stayed as still as she could, waiting for the queen to make up her mind. After a few moments Isabel said, "Fernando, leave the room, please. Return when I call, and ensure no one is waiting or listening at my door."

The secretary left the room and Isabel led Alina to the small window. "Sometimes," she said, "we women have to take matters into our own hands, without letting our husbands and, in this case, ministers, know exactly what we are doing. Naturally this must always be in the men's own best interests— why else would we do such a thing?"

Alina nodded, "Why else, ma'am."

Surprisingly, the queen stroked her arm. "I am going to place my trust in you, Baroness, for letters can go astray and pass into the wrong hands. It is my wish—our wish, my sister of England and mine—that our children be betrothed, that England may once again return to Spain as it was in the time of my great, great aunt Catalina of Aragón and then of her daughter Mary. This letter suggests how Henrietta Maria may present to her husband, and thereon his ministers, the betrothal of our son Balthasar Carlos to either the Princess Royal or the Princess Elizabeth. In turn, either the young Prince Charles or his brother James will marry our little Maria Teresa. In this way, my sister and I will not only be responsible for returning

England to the One True Faith but for ensuring its future. It will be our legacy to the world. It will also consolidate the House of Habsburg in England... as our mother wishes."

Alina was lost for words. Isabel stared unseeing out of the window, perhaps envisaging the double matrimonies to be held in Madrid and perhaps again in Westminster or at Whitehall.

"Ma'am, may I ask one thing?" Alina's voice had gone dry with the great responsibility being placed upon her.

"Ask."

"Why must this be a matter only for women, if it is of such great import? Why are your ambassadors not drawing up agreements?"

Isabel turned and gave a wary smile. "Because the men in question here cannot see beyond Flanders and France; and because the men in question in England, and *from* England, are weak—Sir Arthur Hopton excluded, but he is a devious creature and too close to my enemy Olivares to be trusted with anything *I* believe in."

Alina wondered if she dare refuse the task, but immediately knew she didn't want to. This matter unquestionably would raise her to a high position with Henrietta Maria in the English court. She was now in every way a royal emissary, carrying the future of her husband's nation in her hands. Coming down to earth, Alina suddenly wondered how she was going to hide the letter until they departed for London: a pocket was not safe; pockets could be picked, laces snipped with little knives. Obdulia would make a perfect pickpocket if she were in the Countess-Duchess's pay, which was not impossible. The only place for the letter would be down her bodice. *Was this why she had been quizzed about her relationship with the king— because he might discover it in her bosom?* Silly ideas sent her mind spinning: she felt intoxicated.

Queen Isabel, however, returned to her formal, icy manner. Taking a black velvet reticule trimmed with dark violet lace from a drawer, she said, "A gift for you, Baroness, to carry our treasure."

Chapter 28

"There's a box come for you, milady." Fanny struggled sideways through Alina's bedroom door, carrying a shallow, wide wooden box.

Alina, drowsy from a long afternoon siesta, sat up in bed and peered through the curtains. "Who sent it, Fanny?"

"Don't know, milady."

"Didn't you ask?"

"No, milady."

Alina studied the size and shape of her gift. Much wider and flatter than a jewel box, not strong enough to contain gold, certainly not small enough to secrete in her portmanteau with the letter and packages with which she had been entrusted. She got out of bed. "Open it. There's bound to be a card or something to tell us."

There was nothing, only a divine costume for a dryad with a gold and white silken mask on silver ribbons. The fabric of the dress, such as it was, ran through her fingers like liquid. "It must be from Ludo, for the ball," she murmured. "He's the only person I know who would give me..." She let her thoughts drift over the silk and gold-trimmed gauze of the costume then dismissed Fanny with a snap of the fingers. "I will manage on my own," she said. "Come when I call."

Waiting until the maid had left, Alina held the soft fabric to her chin then hastily pulled the silken affair over her shift. The costume fell in soft folds to her calves. Its touch was sensual. Dancing around her chamber, Alina wondered if she dare attend the masked ball in such a flimsy garment.

The gardens were lit with torches and thick candles under glass domes; tables draped in green cloth were laden with bread and chorizo and herby sausages, cheeses and quince *membrillo*; crude ceramic jugs and flagons held red wine, and sugared sangria was ladled from wide bowls bobbing with slices of crisp, green apples. Around the edges of the formal gardens rustic huts and booths with benches and small round tables for diners had been erected. Tree stumps and logs served elsewhere as seats.

Leaning on her father's arm, flanked by Ludo and Marcos, and his friend Kit Windebank, Alina laughed with joy. "I was wrong!" she said. "Look what they can do in one single week."

"Not so difficult with a pastoral theme," said the count, squeezing her arm.

"I'm surprised you like it so much, milady," Marcos added meaningfully, "being surrounded by rustics again."

Alina glowered at him but refused to let the uncharacteristic barb spoil her delight. Ignoring her old friend, she turned to Ludo and took his hand. "Thank you."

He looked slightly bewildered but gave her one of his special grins. Gently releasing himself, he said, "Let me get us some drinks."

Looking around now, Alina noticed she was not the only dryad, but she was, as far as she could see, the only one with a gold and white silken mask on silver ribbons. The court's pastoral and woodland costumes included characters from folk tales and legend, milkmaids and foresters, tree fellers with axes in belts and harvest gatherers with straw hats, men wearing smocks and carrying shepherds' crooks and various men sporting bulls' horns, which she didn't understand.

Her father, not being someone to wear a peasant's smock, had taken a lateral approach and donned a glamorous black mask with the rather too young doublet and hose of a young prince from a medieval tale. Ludo had settled for a buff, calf-leather eye mask and a simple woodcutter's outfit, an olive green jerkin over the loose white shirt he wore in their lodgings. Marcos and his friend had somehow made or acquired wood sprite costumes with devilish goat horns like the English Puck. It was, as the queen had so rightly said, so much fun.

As they sipped strong fruit drinks laced with brandy, a group of musicians set up a lively jig and couples joined hands for a traditional dance Alina did not know. More people joined in, forming groups of six, eight, ten or more. Smaller groups swelled to larger and angled for space. Unwilling to display her lack of corsets so soon in the revels, Alina stayed with her father until he slipped away to join a card game in a royal hovel and she was forced to stay with the two Pucks, who were into their second or third fruit cup and laughing at nonsense of their own fabrication. Ludo had disappeared long since.

A tall forester, also wearing a buff mask and olive green jerkin with wide, white linen sleeves, made his way to her side. The mask covered his eyes, but could not conceal the Habsburg jaw and its wispy beard. Alina sank into a curtsey but was lifted by strong, very pale fingers. Kit Windebank stopped mid-sentence and made a hasty bow then stepped back three paces, grabbing Marcos on the way. To Alina's dismay, they evaporated into the shadows, leaving her alone with the royal forester.

"A fine evening for our entertainments, madam," the forester said.

"Indeed, sire, a beautiful evening," Alina replied.

"And a beautiful dryad to ensure the spirit of the occasion is... amenable? I hope you are more comfortable, less restricted, in this costume."

Alina took a sharp breath, suddenly feeling stark naked. The bones of her *guardainfante* corset and frame, and the absence of a lady's maid to help her re-dress had protected her during three royal encounters. Don Felipe would have her tonight unless she was very careful. "*You* sent me the costume," she said slowly as revellers, drinkers, dancers and servants whirled around her on the garden path.

Even in the poor light she could see blue-grey eyes glittering behind the mask. At a loss as to what to say next, Alina smiled, while frantically glancing around for help. They were surrounded by people, but who could she turn to?

And there he was: another woodsman of similar height but a more robust figure, standing arms akimbo, legs apart, very nearby. Alina sighed with relief.

The sigh was misinterpreted. Before she could take another breath, a pale be-ringed hand pulled her into the shadows.

Ludo stepped forward. "Alina! Where are you? Come and dance," he called ingenuously.

"Here, Don Ludo, I'm just here."

The king reluctantly let her go, whispering, "Later, my lovely Baroness. I will seek you out after the midnight toast and we shall enjoy revels of our own."

"I regret, sire, that cannot be. I must leave at dawn and..."

"Without a fond farewell? No, *milady*, you cannot refuse me this time."

"But sire, I..." Alina's words fell into a gap in the night—the royal woodsman had disappeared.

As the evening wore on, Alina drank sangria with ladies of the court and chatted amiably with the queen in a rustic hut as they ate chicken legs with their fingers then giggled like girls as they cleaned their fingers in scented water. Not wanting to remain on Ludo's arm for the entire evening, for that would also draw unwanted comment, Alina did her best to stay in company, dreading what might happen after the midnight toast. She could not, would not, return to England carrying a royal bastard. She had given the possibility much thought in the past week, for it was not without advantages, but it would oblige her to stay in Spain and that was not to her liking. Especially now she had an understanding with Ludo—that she would travel to Lisbon with him, then leave him there while she took ship back to Plymouth and travelled up to Crimphele to collect her son, and then sail for Genoa.

Suddenly she was seized by panic—she had to go back to London, not Plymouth, because she was entrusted with a letter that might change the course of English history—and three strange little boxes containing treasure. But the real treasure was her son, little Tomás... It was all getting out of control—too, too much. Flopping into a bower, her head a whirling muddle, Alina became aware for the first time since she'd arrived in Spain how much she missed her gentle husband; how much she wanted to be with her little son; how much she just wanted to go home to the rural Tudor fortress of Crimphele.

At midnight servants came into the garden bearing trays with fat bottles of clear *aguardiente* and minute cups, and cream and ochre-coloured ceramic bowls containing hot liquid. Other servants followed with tiny braziers, which they set up on tables. Courtiers and servants then set about making *queimada*, the ancient Celtic drink adapted and modernised to include coffee from New Spain. As the little cups circulated, chatter increased, laughter became louder; cups were re-filled, laughter became raucous; couples took another cup each and disappeared into the bushes and shadows, and once more a tall forester in an olive green waistcoat was at Alina's elbow. Offering her another cup of *queimada*, he stood very close but remained silent. She drank back the delicious hot liquid, enjoying the sensation as it reached her throat then relaxed her limbs. The tall forester took her arm under his, a long, bony arm, by no means that of a real forester, and led her towards the lake. Only half of the lake, which was really a deep water tank serving the palace, was lit—the rest was in shadow. Moving skilfully and silently he led a tipsy and rather weary Alina away from the masked throng to a dark patch of garden. Halting her where they could not be seen, the forester placed two hands on her trembling shoulders—and gave her a mighty shove.

Alina lost her footing and fell backwards into water as icy cold as sierra snow. The gauzy muslin of her dress floated to the surface above her head, but she could not swim and soon it disappeared beneath the black surface. Alina sank down and down. Spluttering and choking, she thrashed her arms, trying to keep them above her head, only to sink down and down further, the fabric of her costume twisting like a water serpent around her, pulling her under—down and down and down into blackness.

Coughing, face down on muddy ground, Alina retched. She retched again and again, and gradually returned to life. A dripping wet Puck leaned over her. "Cough, Alina, cough." It was Marcos. She wanted to cry. After what seemed an hour she finally rolled over. Clasping her soaked, torn costume over her knees, she looked up. A well built woodsman in wide, white sleeves crouched down to speak to her. But her ears were full of the roaring sound of drowning.

She shook her head and stared into his face. "Ludo?" she whispered.

He pulled off his mask. Kit Windebank did the same. Alina glanced around. No one else was near. No one else to witness... what? Her foolishness in drinking too much alcohol and falling in the lake? A monarch pushing a woman into a lake for refusing his attentions...? Or had she stepped backwards and fallen into the water to escape mauling hands?

Frightened, confused and ashamed beyond measure, Alina began to weep. Gently, Ludo lifted her into his arms and took her to a garden seat, where he held her cradled her like a small child. Gradually her breathing returned to normal and she started to feel safe again. "Ludo..." she whispered again.

"Sssh, I'm here. It will soon be over. Quiet now."

A man leant over his shoulder, an old man in normal clothes with white hair and beard. "Take this," he said, removing his jacket and placing it over her diaphanous garment.

Grateful, Alina let them arrange it over her then snuggled against Ludo's chest. "I want to go home," she gulped.

"Not yet. Marcos has gone to get you some clothes. We'll wait until the garden has cleared."

"No, I mean I want to go home. I must leave, because. . . I haven't. . . I wouldn't... The king is very angry. He pushed me..."

"No," Ludo said, kissing her wet hair, "that wasn't Don Felipe."

"I fell in?"

"You were pushed."

"Why? Who... who would do that?"

"Someone I think I know—who hates me." The old man with white hair mumbled something and Ludo said more loudly, "He's sending me a message." The old man swore in English then muttered something else Alina didn't catch. "No, it's me he's after," Ludo replied.

Alina tried to focus. They were speaking in English. She recognised the hair but couldn't find a name. Leaning more closely against Ludo's chest she suddenly remembered his wound and said, "I shouldn't be here. I'm hurting you," and started to cry again.

Ludo kissed the top of her head and rocked her gently in his arms until Marcos arrived with a blanket and an assortment of female garments.

Later, when they were back in their lodgings and Alina was warm and dry in bed, she said to Ludo and Marcos hovering about her chamber, "How did you know?"

"I was keeping an eye out," Ludo said. "I followed."

"Hopton told Kit to watch out for you," Marcos said. "And I was nearby all the time."

"Why?"

Ludo and Marcos exchanged glances and Ludo said lightly, "Think about why you are here and give me a list of reasons in the morning."

"So I *was* pushed."

"Yes." Ludo's voice was low and serious. "I think the forester by the lake was a certain Roman cleric. That's what Hopton was worried about, too. You being the wife of an English baron means he's in some way responsible for you while you are here."

"Rogelio knows we can swim after what happened on the Thames," Marcos said.

"We can, yes, but not milady, apparently. That's what bothers me," Ludo said, exchanging a sharp glance with Marcos. Turning back to Alina, he said, "The good thing is that almost nobody saw what happened so you don't have to go into hiding out of embarrassment. We'll be leaving later now, though. Can we postpone it for a few days while I make enquiries?"

"Postpone what?" Marcos asked.

Ludo shook his head and looked at Alina.

Alina closed her eyes: it was all too much. "I want to go home," she mumbled.

"Ask your father to take you in the morning," Marcos suggested. Ludo said nothing.

As the two men were leaving her room, Alina heard Marcos say quietly, "Why would Rogelio go for Alina?"

"Because he's not in Olivares' pay, but he *is* in the Countess-Duchess's pay... because the Vatican is backing Luis de Haro... because he simply wants to get at me. . . Because, just possibly, Alina has or knows something we don't, or he thinks she's taking messages for Felipe and Isabel back to England against the Vatican's interest. *Yo qué sé!*"

"But that means Alina's not safe anymore."

"She never has been," Ludo whispered sharply. "That's why we came with her in the first place. Or hadn't you worked that out?"

The door closed shut and Alina began to sob into her pillow. A little while later Ludo opened it again. "If you need me for anything send Fanny, or just call."

Alina looked up from her damp pillow. In a voice husky from crying she said, "I need you."

The door closed. Then it opened once more and Ludo sidled in. "Fanny will sleep in my bed tonight and José is condemned to the salon floor," he said. "Move over."

Chapter 29

Two days after the royal garden party, Ludo visited Sir Arthur Hopton's office to pay his respects and say farewell.

"Have you seen the Count-Duke again?" Hopton asked.

"I have just come from his apartments, Sir Arthur. He is recovering well, although still very bruised and shaken." Ludo knew Hopton was angling to know what Olivares had said at their farewell, but held back the information.

Seeing the conversation was going nowhere, Hopton handed Ludo a letter with the unmistakable Stuart seal. "This arrived late last night."

Tracing a finger over the royal red wax impression, Ludo raised an eyebrow and asked, "You know who it is from?"

"Of course I do," the British ambassador replied, "but not the contents—on this occasion."

Ludo cut the seal with Hopton's knife, went to the window and opened the letter.

After reading it through twice, he folded it and placed it in his breeches pocket, saying, "You are to inform the sender that I have received the letter."

"As a good secretary should, hmm," Hopton's voice was dry but had lost some of its animosity.

Ludo returned to his table and drummed his fingers on the thick felt cloth. "I am to go to Portugal. Everyone wants me to go to Portugal!"

Hopton placed a finger over his thin lips and checked the door to his inner office. "Please do not tell me anything more. My position here is difficult enough regarding our Lusitanian neighbours: I would prefer not to know more while we conclude the treaty between England and Spain over Flanders."

Ludo nodded. "Yes, of course. But if Charles wants me to influence the rebellion against Spain in Lisbon—"

"That is enough, sir." Hopton raised a warning hand. "Enough."

Ludo clenched a hand with annoyance. "I understand your position here, Sir Arthur, but do you know, or can you at least give me some intimation as to whether Olivares knows as a fact —rather than speculation—what King Charles wants in Portugal, given that when I spoke with the Chief Minister a few days ago he asked me to do the opposite?"

"Spain cannot afford to lose Portugal, neither financially nor strategically." Hopton's voice was toneless, his expression blank. "Your wound is healing, I hope. It will not trouble you on the journey?"

"Very likely it will, but if that is the only hindrance I encounter I shall be happy. I don't suppose you can tell me whether my arch enemy Father Rogelio will be joining me in Lisbon?"

"It is not impossible. Events in Lisbon and Oporto are also a matter of concern to the Vatican."

"I'll bet they are." Ludo tapped his pocket.

"Perhaps not as you assume, however." Hopton's voice dropped to a whisper and he walked Ludo to the window away from the door. "It is my belief the Vatican would not be disappointed to see Spain lose Portugal. The Pope complains of Habsburg power and the inability to make decisions without their—er—participation."

"Losing territory and reducing their empire... I see. Is this why the Vatican agent Rogelio is here?"

"Ah, him. To that I cannot say. But you have been active in a similar tricky situation in Holland—you know to tread carefully."

Ludo gazed down at a group of horsemen in the courtyard below. After a moment he said, "I see, thank you. He was trying to hinder me there—the Vatican never wanted to undermine the Dutch at all." Hopton inclined his head but refrained from saying anything so Ludo continued, looking now at the door across the office, "As English ambassador here you are in also in a 'tricky' position, Sir Arthur. What do you advise? You cannot be impartial to the Duke of Braganza's claim to the Portuguese throne."

"My job is to deal with events, Don Ludovico, not influence them."

Ludo looked Hopton in the eye. "I have had two separate and opposite commissions foisted upon me, neither of which give me the option of refusal or preference. What are *you* expecting me to do, Excellency?"

"I expect you to feather your nest and go your own way." Hopton returned to his dour, brusque manner, adding, "And now I really must say good day to you, sir. I have pressing matters to which I must attend." Striding rapidly across the office he swung the door open, causing Kit Windebank to almost topple in.

While Ludo made his farewell in the English manner the young man slipped a note into his hand. "Ah, about your secretary here..." Ludo said, causing Kit's eyebrows to shoot up in concern.

"He cannot be spared. Not to travel with you," Hopton replied.

"But might he return to England instead? He could travel with the baroness—when she leaves. She will be going to the West Country and that is his home as well, I believe."

"Christopher Windebank is required here. His father has made that plain to us both. Please do not concern yourself further with his predicament: he got himself into it without any help." Hopton's voice softened, "And he has his uses."

"Oh, indeed he does." Ludo winked at the round-faced young man still standing by the door then looked back at Hopton. "Should I thank *you* for that?"

This time Hopton did smile. "Young people enjoy adventures, and it was good practice for him, helping during the *romería* then with the sad event with the young baroness, and we are all grateful for that."

"But how did you know. . .?" Ludo started to ask.

"That she was at risk?" Hopton narrowed his eyes. "Perhaps I didn't: perhaps it was all a terrible coincidence. Was there anything else, Don Ludovico?"

Ludo raised his new Spanish hat and strode down the corridor bordering the palace offices. As he was going down the wide stone steps to the main entrance he glanced at Kit Windebank's small note. It contained only a name written in a clear schoolboy hand: *María de los Milagros García González.*

Ludo paused on the penultimate step, taking stock of all around him: elegant visitors entering on horseback; royal grooms rushing forward to attend their mounts; ushers leading people this way and that; men-at-arms asleep on their feet; small dogs running in and out among legs. A scene that probably hadn't changed since Philip the Second's time and it would continue thus. His presence or absence would make not a jot of difference. The same applied to Portugal. Two kings asking him to influence events, a pope wanting to influence, or not influence, events to be free of his overlords... but whether Ludovico da Portovenere went to Lisbon or not would probably make not a jot of difference. That being the reality of it, the logical move was to do just sufficient as to secure the *Tulip* and his trading licences—and keep Alina with him. They could then sail to England from Lisbon to collect her son together, and never be apart again.

Still lost in thought, yet knowing he was being watched, Ludo lifted his hat. "Adios," he called and made his way out of the palace.

María de los Milagros García González was waiting at the inner gate to the main palace courtyard, a large woman, not ill dressed and not entirely unattractive, with wild black hair arranged like a cottage loaf, and shoulders like a stevedore. Taller than Alina, broader than Marcos and of servant status: she would do nicely. Taking her arm, for she was expecting him, he escorted her to the main gate.

"So you are Mary of the Miracles," he said. "Let us hope you can work one at least. You know why I need you?"

"I do, sir."

"The English gentleman told you my terms and the generous price I will pay, did he not?"

"He did, *señor*."

"And you have agreed?"

"I have, *señor*."

"Good. Is there anything you wish to know before we go to my lodgings?"

Mary of the Miracles slowly ran the tip of her tongue across her bottom lip.

"No," Ludo said. "And never—" Before he could finish, a horse charged out of the melee in the courtyard, completely out of control, and with a sweat-lathered shoulder knocked Ludo sideways to the ground. Winded, Ludo, tried to roll over, but the gash in his shoulder opened again. He lay back to get his breath —just as the rangy bay horse turned on its haunches, ready to trample him into the hard-baked dust. Ludo caught a glimpse of a vicious, blood-covered spur and wide, iron-shod hooves as the horse wheeled around. Wincing, he tried to get up but was then pushed flat again as María de los Milagros cut in front of the beast to turn him face down. Taking fright at the woman in its path, the bay nag shied, nearly sending its rider out of the saddle. Re-seated, he turned the beast again for another run at Ludo, but the horse, ill-treated, terrified, had had enough. It reared up and this time sent its rider to the ground.

Winded, but with all his senses about him, the man grabbed his hat, struggled to his feet and disappeared into the gathering crowd.

Milagros lifted Ludo to a sitting position. He looked at her and forced a grin. "You'll do," he said.

The inconvenient fruit vendor had finally moved on and, the fiesta being officially over, their street had returned to normal by the time Ludo and Milagros climbed the stairs to the lodgings. Every room was in turmoil and Fanny was in tears. Ludo was tempted to turn straight round and go back out again but he needed to clean up and change his clothes. Alina came into the hall white-faced.

They stared at each other for a moment. "What's the matter?" Ludo asked, for Alina's eyes were red from crying. "No welcome, no smile? I have returned alive from yet another attempt on my life and you don't even notice?"

Alina glared at Milagros.

Sighing, Ludo turned to Milagros. "Stay here a moment, please."

Milagros gave a slight impolite shrug and settled herself on a chair in the hall to wait.

Ludo followed Alina into the shared sitting room, where Marcos, aided by José, was closing a new trunk.

"I'll take this with me, if it's all right?" Marcos said referring to the new clothes Ludo had purchased for his secretary.

"Take it all, take anything you like."

Marcos peered at him, "What happened?"

"The fourth horseman of the Apocalypse or the devil's steed, anyway—tried to flatten me. Actually, now I think about it, there was something familiar—could have been the rider that followed us up from Santander. Whoever it was, it's time to get out of here, and fast."

Marcos looked at Alina, who took a deep breath and nodded.

"What?" demanded Ludo, instantly suspicious.

Keeping his eyes averted, Marcos said, "Can we talk to you?"

"You are talking to me. Talk about what?"

Alina arranged herself on the window seat. Ludo gave his hat to José and told him to make himself scarce. The boy was out of the room in a skip and a hop.

"Well," Ludo said, glancing from one dour face to another, "what's this all about?"

Marcos sat on the corner of his new trunk. "We need to go home, both of us," he said. "We've been talking, and we think you don't really understand our situations."

Ludo sat on a chair at the table. "Go on."

"The fact is, we're married now, both of us." Marcos continued. "I want to see my parents in the south, but I'll only stay a few days then I'll go straight back to Plymouth from Sanlúcar to be with Joanna. And..." Marcos looked at Alina but she shook her head, unable to speak. "And Alina's got an important position with the English queen now and a little boy at Crimphele—and a proper husband."

"A *proper* husband—what's that supposed to mean?"

"No, sorry, I meant..." Marcos bit his lip.

"You mean someone who stays at home and cares for his family and bores her half to death."

"No," Alina said quietly, "that is not true. He doesn't bore me. He is good and kind and clever. And he loves me. I—I—I have to go back, Ludo. I'm sorry, but I have to go back. I'm not free to make my own choices like you. And now I have another commission and..."

Ludo looked away then said, "The one thing I have learned since being here is that you cannot trust anyone: no one has an ounce of integrity. Basically, you can't take anything anyone says at face value because they are all, without exception, playing a double game. Next time—if—I ever return from the East again I'll be bringing a game called 'Snakes and Ladders' for you to play. What?" Ludo demanded, seeing Alina crushing the fabric of her skirts between her fists.

"Ludo, please, let me explain. Come into my room."

Alina led the way through the cluttered salon to her door, opened it and let Ludo enter before her. As she closed it behind her, she said, "Please try to understand. I was telling the truth—but now things have changed. I can't just leave everything I've ever wanted to live in a pink house in a place I've never been."

"I was thinking more along the lines of a palace, *carina*. If I complete the Lisbon venture to my advantage you shall have a palace and a hundred servants, I promise."

Alina shook her head. "You don't understand."

"No. I don't understand. I thought I did, after all those sweet *nothings* in the straw, but I was wrong." Ludo strode across Alina's chamber, flinging his words as accusations then turned and faced Alina square on. "I let you make me look stupid in front of a galley of cutthroat pirates once, madam. It took all my skills to hold them in check until we were out of the Tamar River. I was a fool then and I'm a fool now. I should have let them take you and raid Tamstock the way they wanted. But don't worry, you're *still* safe—from me, at least—because our paths will never cross again, I can assure you of that."

"Ludo, listen to me!" Alina cried. "I'm not free to do as I please, and not just because of Thomas and my child in Cornwall. Queen Isabel has given me a message to take back to England and... other things for Henrietta Maria. It's important; I can't fail them. I can't simply take the message back to England then suddenly leave again for who knows where. And I can't *not* go."

"Two spoilt women dabbling in affairs of state, and now you are three," Ludo scoffed. "Let us hope they reward you accordingly—that's what you're after, isn't it, *milady*?"

"That's not fair!" Alina retorted. "I don't need to curry favour with anyone, I'm already—"

"A lady. Yes, yes, so we've been told on innumerable occasions. Lady or no lady, *milady*, you might lower yourself to learn to swim and save your own life next time, because I fear whatever little messages you're carrying for your darling queens are what got you pushed under. Stay well away from the rail when you cross the Narrow Sea in a ship this time. And keep your eyes open night and day because these little queens have a much bigger opponent. You are so wrapped up with your petty court gossip in Whitehall you don't hear what anyone outside your very exclusive coterie is actually saying. You are going to encounter serious opposition in England. If you ever get there, because Rome has a nasty habit of finding then losing forever inconvenient people running errands counter to its wishes."

Alina's hand shot to her mouth.

"Which is why," Ludo continued, "I have brought you a present, my dear. Not that you deserve one."

Alina frowned. "What?"

"Not 'what'—who. The lady in the entrance hall is called María de los Milagros; she is now officially your lady-in-waiting and bodyguard. Milagros has excellent credentials, a fine character reference, and until recently was the female wrestling champion of a pueblo whose name I forget. *Don't go anywhere without her*. She is to sleep in your chamber—as you prefer to sleep alone now. She is to stay at your side wherever you go as far as England. Once you are *home* safely you will then provide her with sufficient funds to return if she so chooses. I hope the arrangement meets your approval; it is entirely for your safety."

Before Alina could respond, Ludo stormed out of the bedchamber, saying to Marcos, "As Alina will not be travelling with me, please arrange for her to be collected by her father. She'll tell you what I said about her new maid; see that they both do as they've been told."

"Yes, all right," Marcos stammered.

"And not a word to anyone about what madam here is up to, or what I've been saying, especially not to the flamboyant grandee Pamanes. As far as anyone is concerned, Mrs Whatsit here is hurrying home to her loving spouse."

"But..."

"But what?" Ludo huffed with annoyance.

"Ludo..." Marcos started warily.

Ignoring him, Ludo shouted, "José! Bring me my hat, I'm going out again." As the boy arrived, Ludo said, "Pack all my things and turn in early—don't wait up."

"But aren't you coming part of the way south with me?" Marcos interrupted.

"No." Ludo swung round, pulling Marcos into his gaze, and in a lowered voice he said, "Tell Alina to watch out for Hopton while she's travelling, and when she gets back to England as well. He's Olivares' personal friend but he's acting for others in England as well. That was the word we came with, wasn't it, 'personal'? A lot of what has been going here has been *personal*, hasn't it?" Pushing a hand inside his shirt to check for leaking blood, he continued, "Hopton and his clever Kit could be intercepting all manner of correspondence. I suspect he's reading people's letters and sending his own messages back to Charles Stuart—but also I wouldn't be surprised if he's informing English Parliamentarians as well. He's untouchable as an ambassador and it could just as easily have been he who arranged Alina's evening dip—with or without Rogelio—to prevent her going back to England." He fixed Alina, who was now standing at the doorway to her chamber, with a sharp look. "What might you know or be carrying for Henrietta Maria that is not in Protestant England's interest?"

Alina's eyes opened wide. "I..."

"No, don't tell me. I really, really don't want to know. But trust no one, Alina. Not that anyone can trust *you*, of course."

"Trust me! You are the arch deceiver here! You have been working against Henrietta Maria since you arrived. You said you would help her, and what have you been doing? Lining your own pockets, getting promises out of Don Felipe for your precious *personal* business plans. You have used her—and me—to get what *you* wanted." Alina paused.

Ludo met her eye. "Not quite, *madonna*. I have not got what I discovered I wanted—although I shall now be making the most of a very attractive alternative."

Alina's head shot up; fixing her gaze at some point over his head, she said, "Fine! Leave, Don Ludo Nobody; go back to sea, where you belong with your pirates or corsairs—call them what you will, they're all lowlife."

Ludo stared at an Alina he'd known existed and had chosen not to see. "After what you told me in that barn..." he said his voice barely a whisper.

"In a barn, yes: a fitting place, methinks, rolling in the straw like peasants. I wanted to believe you, Ludo, then, but there are other people in this world more deserving of honesty and loyalty than a pirate's bastard who never says a straight word."

Ludo's right hand moved of its own accord; if he had been near enough he would have struck her and slithered straight down the Snake of Rage. As it was, he schooled his anger and tried to ignore the gripping sense of loss and betrayal closing in around him. In a hoarse voice he said, "Right, I think that brings our parting to a timely end so I'll bid you both one last farewell." Raising a dirty, grazed hand, he turned on his heel.

"Ludo, stop, sit down," Marcos said. "You've got blood all over your collar—you've hurt your head—"

"As you predicted—my head on a plate. Not to worry, I've still got my wits. Right, I'm going."

"What do you mean you're going? Where are you going now?"

"To disappear!"

As Ludo marched down the street towards the livery stables where he had lodged his coach and horses he stopped in his tracks. In all the chaos, the danger and personal tragedy of the morning a moment of perfect clarity came into his bruised head. "Idiot!" he said out loud.

I've been trying to get promises out of the wrong people: I should have been focussing on the new man. That's where the future is—in Portugal—and Portuguese Goa. It's time to formulate a new strategy—and disappear.

Chapter 30

The Isle of Ibiza, late September, 1640

The peppery smell told Ludo he was still on Spanish territory, and he regretted coming. The pungent air, the sudden thrilling song of a goldfinch... it reminded him of El Escorial with Alina and the ill-fated *romería* for San Cristóbal.

Pausing to let his heartbeat return to normal from the steep climb up from the harbour, Ludo wiped his brow and studied the scenery. High, brittle bushes of *maquia* scrub sheltered clustered yellow flowers; pale grey stalks smelling of anis crowded around him; white cistus flowers emerged from among dense green leaves. Once over the brow of the hill he would he would see the sea again, the glittering, cleansing sea.

Waiting for his boy José to catch up, Ludo scuffed the remains of dry, ochre-brown straw beside the narrow goat track with his rope-soled shoes, checking for vipers. *Latet anguis in herba*—a snake is lurking in the grass: Virgil's words. He remembered exactly where he'd learnt them, too—another memory he had failed to erase.

Eventually José scrambled to his side carrying their loaded canvas duffle bags, his face a red sun, his brow a fountain of perspiration. Ludo looked at him and smiled: somewhere across the Ligurian Sea he had two sons about this age, and a girl. At least their mothers said they were his—and he'd been young enough at the time to be flattered into paying for them. He provided for them, plus their schooling.

Answering José's unspoken question, Ludo said, "Not much further," and offered him a goatskin *bota* of water. The boy gulped down the warm liquid then handed it back and ran a wrist over his mouth, then a sleeve across his forehead.

"Give me a bag," Ludo said. Slinging it over his right shoulder, where it wouldn't rub against the now healing wound, he strode on, yearning for complete physical exhaustion that he might sleep that night. José fell behind, as before. After a while Ludo turned and called out, "Come on, you're the one in the pink of youth with all the energy, not me."

José ran, gasping for air, to rejoin him, and one behind the other they crossed the top of the hill and joined a wider cart track coming up from another direction.

"How do you know where to come," asked José, marvelling at the way Ludo knew where to turn off in a scrub-filled hillside.

"Because I've been here before, obviously." Ludo stopped. Had he been right to return to the very place where he'd licked his metaphorical wounds before and made the absurd plan to abduct Alina with his corsair friends? Perhaps not, but he needed sound counsel and Friar Caritas, who was mad but also wise, still lived hidden away from the world on this island hillside.

As they strolled along the rough cart track Ludo pointed to his left. "Over there," he said. "You can't see it from the track but there's a small stone house tucked in behind those trees."

A square stone-built dwelling came into view at the end of a narrow track, and a grey mastiff the size and texture of a donkey went berserk at their approach. As the great beast barked and lurched at the end of its chain, an old man, who Ludo was relieved to see still alive, hobbled grumbling from his seat on the front steps to pat it on the head like a palace lapdog. Someone spoke behind him and the old man turned and replied. Ludo caught a glimpse of a peasant woman's traditional black.

The old man, white-haired now and lacking a tonsure, returned to the dog, saying, "Quiet, Lola, quiet. I think I know this gentleman," and peered through the bright, shimmering sunlight at his visitors. The great hound licked his hairy chin then settled into a lying position with a satisfied groan at having done its duty.

"Don Ludo, it is you!" the old man cried, coming down the track with a surprisingly sprightly step. "I never expected to see you again."

"Nor I you, Brother Caritas, but here I am."

"In trouble again, are you?"

"In a manner of speaking."

"Well, you can stay here if the harpy will let you," the elderly friar indicated the peasant woman with a knobbly finger. "I doubt I can be of any more use to you than that."

"Actually, Brother, I think you can. Is there somewhere my boy José can sleep?"

"He can make a bed in the kitchen area; it's spacious enough here. You arranged it, remember."

On the afternoon of his fourth day on the island of Ibiza, having made no trips down to his old haunts along the quayside or in the back streets, no visits to pretty girls in colourful skirts, no drinking or singing or carousing with fishermen and corsairs in any fashion, Ludo was beginning to feel better, both physically and mentally.

Passing the patio area around the well after his siesta, he found Brother Caritas sitting at the outdoor table teaching José, as he'd requested. So far they had established what José did not know of Latin and arithmetic and Castilian grammar. Ludo wanted them to work on the boy's arithmetic and accounting, but the friar had little knowledge of how numbers worked. He was teaching the boy how to write a formal letter, though, which would come in useful one day.

As he approached, José looked up with a beaming smile of amusement at the friar's funny ways and something more. "What are you grinning at?" Ludo asked.

The boy shrugged. "I like it here."

"You can stay if you want to. Take six months with Brother Caritas and do what you can to finish your education—although I'm not so sure you won't end up being the teacher."

The old friar huffed. "I am here, you know."

"Brother Caritas knows everything about natural history," José offered.

"And you have a generous soul, my son," his teacher said, patting the boy's brown arm.

Ludo sat down on a rickety chair and leaned back, taking in their rustic surroundings and sampling the peppery air, which no longer irritated him quite so much.

Brother Caritas studied him then turned to José and with a nod of the head indicated he should get lost. Ludo swallowed a smile: it was evidently time for his confession.

"Right," said the friar, "are you ready to tell me why you are here?"

Ludo drummed his fingers on the stone table then said, "Could you manage to climb up to the cliff with me?"

"I can try. You may have to carry me, like Saint Christopher."

"Funny you should mention him; he's one of the reasons I'm here."

Reaching the edge of the high cliff, Ludo gazed down into the turquoise waters below. "I think I hid *Tulip* here the last time I was seeking refuge…" He let the words drift into the wind with the seagulls circling below. "I should have stayed," he said. *And not gone back for Alina. It won't happen again.*

Brother Caritas selected a warm boulder, lowered himself with some difficulty then struggled to exchange the stone for a softer tussock of grass. A mother lark lifted from her ground-floor nest, cursing them in trills. Further to their right, a kestrel rose into the air, a limp mouse between its claws.

Ludo watched the friar watching the birds then joined him. "Mother Nature is telling us we don't belong here," he said, folding his tall frame onto the boulder the friar had vacated.

"Ah, but we do," the friar replied. "I am writing about that very subject: how Man belongs among Nature and should stop trying to frame it or employ it for material gain. I began not long after I came here. I was reflecting on what had been happening in the Netherlands, how the heretics—Calvinists, Protestants, name them as you will —believe they can find God through objects of possession and material prosperity. It is a fallacy. God is in all we see. It is not for us to adjust His Great Scheme but rather to find solace and joy in that which He gives."

"You have become a mystic, Brother."

"I always was; I am a Franciscan, after all. Aspiring novices with property are obliged to sell all they own before they enter the order, did you not know that? Not my case, as it happens—I was too young to own the clothes on my back. But I have never regretted anything from the material world—except, I confess, I would like extra blankets and a warm rug in winter. Now sit, and listen, and when you can hear your heart and the turn of the wind, begin your tale."

When you can hear your heart and the turn of the wind... Ludo gazed unseeing into the air about him and was brought back to the moment by the friar picking grit from between his filthy toes. The old man then rolled the hem of his rough-spun habit over his legs, exposing swollen arthritic knees to the sun before settling himself back in the grass, the image of man at one with his environment.

No snakes or scorpions here... Ludo waited until he could hear the wind rustle the rock roses and thistles. A donkey brayed in the distance and a dog, the huge mastiff on the chain by the sound of it, had a barking fit, then everything returned to peaceful normal. Ludo closed his eyes and heard the wind gently ruffling the arid terrain again and opened them to see the lark return to her nest.

He began to speak, unburdening himself of all that had happened, his doubts and fears, since he'd been mistaken for a secret courier in Vigo and opened a letter destined for a queen.

Brother Caritas moved to a better position as Ludo left Spain and crossed to Ibiza, then pulled down his habit and arranged it decorously around his ankles like a maiden. "And what would you like me to say?" he asked.

"What you think I ought to do."

"Pff—what I think you *ought* to *do*... You have told me what you doubted you should do, and the consequences, but why were you going to England in the first place?"

"For my new enterprise: I am a merchant, remember."

"Ah, yes. Back to material goods."

"I was bringing spices and gems from the Indies—do they not count as God's bounty? I was only intending to share them among people who lack... pepper, for example. In the East they say cinnamon heals aching joints."

Brother Caritas leaned forward. "Does it? Do you have any with you?"

Ludo grinned. "I will send you a box. There's plenty in a warehouse in Plymouth."

"And you plan to return to England now—to collect your ship and take it back to the Indies, perhaps."

"Yes."

"Then why are you asking me what you should do?"

Ludo looked at the friar. "Because of what I should be doing in Lisbon—and what I think I could do—given the chance."

"I thought you said you were going to England."

"I am, via Lisbon. Or the other way round. I have messages to convey—and other things to do there."

"Oh, for the love of our dear Lord, take back your life, man! Since when did Ludo da Portovenere run errands for anyone?"

"Hardly 'anyone'—we're talking about two monarchs."

"Monarchs, bollocks," huffed the friar, making Ludo laugh. "That's better. That's the first time I've heard anything more than a whine and moan since you got here. Go back to what makes you happy, Ludo. Live your own life on your own terms like you used to. Why let yourself be ordered about? Men and monarchs alike are fickle. Power, real power, belongs only to the Almighty, who can send down lightning to destroy the land or rattle it with earthquakes. Anything else is playing at being top dog."

Ludo looked out to sea. "I knew I should come here first."

Friar Caritas was silent for a while then slowly, very quietly, he said, "Have you asked yourself why two such apparently powerful men, and a chief minister, need to employ a merchant to do their bidding? Hmm? Is that not somewhat suspect? Does that not give you pause?"

"Because I was offering glittering riches in return. I put them in a position where they thought I could increase their wealth."

"I bet you did. Wouldn't be the first time, would it?"

"It has worked before."

"You could sell sand to a camel."

Two lines of ants were passing each other in strict formation a yard from the friar's grubby feet. One line was carrying grass seeds, the other setting off to do their bit for the good of the nest.

"You were playing with the common man in Holland," the friar said, picking up the conversation again. "You've got yourself into palaces now, played for higher stakes, and won by the sound of it. So why is it not enough?"

"It's not that. I've come to the conclusion that I've been agreeing to do things for the wrong people. I'd be better off backing a newcomer—but it carries great risks if I am wrong, or he fails." Ludo picked up a stone and threw it at the two lines of ants. They altered their course in each direction and moved round it, undeterred.

"I hope you're watching," the friar said. "Tell me what you really came here for."

"To hide—and decide what to do next, and where to go after that: back to India or stay in the Mediterranean. And if I do that, what to do about... another personal issue."

"The issue about the man you call your father."

Ludo gasped. "How on earth can you know about that?"

"For someone sharp enough to cut himself, you are exceedingly naive at times. Where am I living, Ludo? Thanks to you, I must admit. Do you think I don't go down to the port and take a drink now and again? Do you think tittle-tattling Doña Juana doesn't come running in with gossip about her charming gentleman visitor after she's picked up a tasty morsel in the market? Who else lives on Ibiza, Ludo? Your fellow pirate friends, that's who. You've been coming here since you were a boy, haven't you? Haven't you! I know exactly what happened in Cornwall when you went back for the girl; I probably know more than you do about that."

Ludo sighed and let his shoulders drop. "I was wrong, I shouldn't have come."

"God sent you here for something, though, didn't he? Shall we move on to your father?"

"Why did you say 'the man you call your father'?"

"I have never had the so-called pleasure of a woman's company, but I have confessed enough females to know not a few men feed children not their own."

"What are you suggesting?"

"I'm suggesting precisely what has always worried you: that you find out who you really are." Brother Caritas pulled the seeds from a stalk of grass then lifted his arm and let them fall onto his lap. "Go to Salé, talk to him. Speak with him and find out the truth once and for all. Then go back to wherever you are going and be at peace with yourself—and stay there."

"And if it sends me back to Genoa—to my Doria family?"

"Would that not be a boon and a blessing?"

"I don't know," Ludo groaned, easing his shoulders.

"No, but you do know that it is this that's at the root of all your troubles."

"Yes."

"Well, then..."

Ludo got to his feet and held out a hand to help the friar get to his, then they wandered back in companionable silence to the square stone dwelling where Ludo had found a safe hiding place for a friar at risk from a Vatican agent's ire. As soon as they neared the house, though, everything changed.

Chapter 31

The woman with whom Brother Caritas lodged came scuttling down the path, the hem of her vast white apron clasped to her throat. "They've come, like you always said they would. The Pope's sent someone to get you!" she gasped.

"The Pope!" Brother Caritas repeated. "What are you inventing now, woman?"

"Cardinal, then: someone important. They've come for you."

Ludo step sideways off the track into the rock roses and tall hawthorn.

"He's important," the woman continued. "Must be—he's got a gold cross the size of a meat cleaver, he has."

Ludo leaned forward and grabbed the friar's hood, ready to yank him out of sight, but the landlady said, "They're talking to the boy. I gave them water. Do you think that was enough, Brother?"

Ignoring her, Brother Caritas turned to Ludo, who was making a rapid plan to extract them all from the situation. Rogelio had followed him all the way to Ibiza—all the way from England, reminding him now and then that he could, and one day probably would, eliminate him. He had come for *him,* not the friar, but he'd make the friar's life hell on earth when they found him. Ludo was tempted to rush the old boy down to the port and get the first boat, but that would leave José in Rogelio's hands.

"The boy," muttered Brother Caritas, whose thoughts were running along the same lines, "get him to Rabbi Rafael in the town... Go to Don Rafael, he's a good friend."

"The rabbi?" Ludo queried. "We're still on Spanish territory—won't that make things worse?"

"No, you'll be safe with the *Chuetas*. They have an underground system designed for saving their own. *La bicha* will never enter a Jew's house, even for you—even if he knew where to look."

Ludo nodded and turned back to the woman. "*Señora*," he said, adopting the tone of a grandee addressing a great lady at court, "I cannot present myself to our visitor in my current attire. *If he asks you* if you have seen me, tell him this: 'the gentleman has gone to his lodging'—understand?"

The woman nodded, her eyes as large as gulls' eggs. If she failed to see the faulty logic—that the port was an hour's hike down the hillside—she didn't mention it.

Ludo then turned back to the friar. "There's no point pretending I'm not here. José will have blabbed it all by now, but say I have returned to the port. Do what you can to get José out of the house and send him to the rabbi if that's best. If possible, come down to the port with Rogelio. I'll get you away from him one way or another down there, where we have allies. How do you fancy sailing with me and becoming a ship's chaplain, by the way?" Ludo regretted the offer the minute the words were out of his mouth, but this was no time to fret about irritating old men with dirty habits. Before he could retract or say more, a more unpleasant thought occurred to him. "Doña Juana, you said 'they'—how many are there?"

"Two with those gun things in their arms. They stayed outside. I think another one went in with him—he's got a shorter gun. We've never had guns up here. Never."

"No need to fear. One cannot expect an important man such as this to travel in remote places without an escort. How did they get up here, do you know?—in a carriage, a cart?"

"The priest was on a donkey."

"How appropriate. Very well, off you go, and if they ask, tell them you've seen me, but, as I said, I cannot present myself in this garb." The woman dithered. "Off you go," Ludo insisted. "Tell them I'll come back as soon as I can, but once you've told them you must go straight to your room and stay there. You live over the stable, don't you?"

"Wouldn't be right for me to sleep in the house, not with him there." The woman pointed at the friar with friendly animosity.

"Good—you go back to your room *and stay there*, all right? Brother Caritas will deal with the important gentleman." He gave the friar a sharp look and disappeared into the dry vegetation.

Pushing through the brambles, slipping on loose stones and the sandy soil, Ludo made his way downhill for a few yards, then looped up around the dwelling until he was looking down on the roof of Doña Juana's low, square house built into the hillside. From here he could all but walk straight onto the roof, but he couldn't see the outdoor table or the well, nor if there were two men with muskets on guard. Staying close to the ground, he edged around to where he could see the track leading down to the town. Lola the mastiff was still pulling on her chain, her coat a good five inches off her frame, all hackles raised.

Parched with thirst and stiff in the limbs, Ludo tried to enter the small house through its single upper room; this being late summer, the shutters were open. Not without difficulty, he pulled himself into the friar's small bedchamber and waited behind the open door. There was no noise and he wondered if they had all fallen asleep, then a chair scraped across the stone floor and a voice speaking in colloquial Roman Italian said, "I've had enough. Get the boy down to the galley, and *don't* lose him on the way. Lock him in my cabin and keep him out on the water. If I don't return by the midnight chimes, shoot him. Mateo, go outside, I want to speak to the friar on my own."

Ludo clenched his fists. *Save the boy, save the old friar? Is there a way to save both?* Whatever he did, it would have to be quick.

The mastiff went berserk again as Rogelio's hired men frog-marched José along the track, barking and barking and straining at her chain. Then, gradually, the barking subsided. Giving José's escort a little longer to get out of musket range, Ludo stayed where he was, his ears tuned to whatever was happening below. The sound of voices speaking in incongruous church Latin curled up the stairs. Ludo poured a cup of water from a jug on a bedside table and drank it, then drank another. Finally, straightening the open neck of his rough cotton blouse, he descended the stone staircase, making no attempt to stay quiet.

They had lit a candle. Brother Caritas was sitting down and appeared to be relaxed and unafraid. The Roman cleric had his long legs wound round each other—a foolish habit, for all Ludo had to do was dislodge the chair from beneath him and the man would fall in a tangle onto the hard floor.

He fell sideways, painfully. Ludo lifted the upturned chair by a leg and set it across his narrow torso, trapping his arms.

The snake hissed, caught in the forked wooden sticks. "Ah, you!" it said.

"You were looking for me, I believe."

The noise of the fall had brought a musketeer into the open doorway. Brother Caritas's chair scraped and the candle was snuffed out. Blackness fell about their shoulders as the man in the doorway aimed his musket this way and that: peering into the dark interior, seeing nothing. Then with a grunt he was suddenly shoved out backwards, his weapon fell from his hands with a crack onto the stone steps. There was a scuffle outdoors, then a gurgling sound, then silence again except for the soft slap of departing sandals on baked earth.

"What's happening?" demanded the Vatican agent. "Manzani, is that you? Giancarlo?"

"It's nobody anymore," Ludo said, wondering if the friar had actually strangled the guard with his cord belt.

Rogelio writhed beneath the chair, his legs swivelling across stone. "*Aiutami!*" he squealed, a thin voice in the thick darkness.

No one came. No one answered. Ludo leaned down on the chair, keeping his eyes wide open to detect any movement in the darkness.

Rogelio stopped wriggling. "They'll come for me," he said. "You won't escape this time. And if you do, the boy dies. Think on that. You like your boys, don't you? Got this one now, José, pretty José; sweeter is he than the one in Amsterdam?"

Ludo shoved a foot down. His soft shoe touched flesh and the man swore in a vocabulary no cleric should know.

"Careful, you're showing your origins, Father," Ludo said, putting more pressure on his foot.

The Roman squirmed from under it. "You won't kill me this way," he hissed.

"I'm not trying to—but I will if you want."

Rogelio grunted and squirmed faster. The musketeer outside finally got to his feet and began poking around for his weapon. A hand grasped Ludo's ankle, he jumped back but too quickly, too sharply and the chair shifted. Rogelio grabbed the seat above his chest with both hands and pushed it away. Ludo leaped out of his reach, dodged the vague bulk of the musketeer and leaped up the stairs just as a large head the size and shape of tumbril became visible in the open doorway.

Doña Juana's mastiff growled; an earth tremor shook the furniture, raising the hair on the back of Ludo's neck. Brother Caritas had let the she-beast off her chain.

"Get *in*, you stupid creature!" the friar's voice came from outside. He was pushing the great dog into the room.

Ludo leaped up the remaining stairs to the room above and shut the door, dropping the latch with a shaking hand. The only person not an enemy as far as the dog was concerned would be the old friar.

A knock came at the door, "It's me," Brother Caritas said as if he'd come on a social visit.

Ludo opened the door a crack, "What's going on?"

"I think Lola's got Rogelio cornered."

"Lola?"

"Lola, the dog." The friar pushed his way into the room. "Nobody'll get out with her loose, and it's too dark for his men to see who or what they're shooting. If they do shoot, there's a good chance they'll hit *la bicha*. Now, what are we going to do about you?"

"It's not me I'm worried about—they've taken José."

"Yes, you'll have to get a move on. I'd come, but I'd only slow you down. You get down after the boy and Lola and I'll try to keep Rogelio here. Come on, you can get out through the window here."

"That's how I got in."

"Obviously. Here,"—the friar began pulling his grey habit over his balding head, "put this on and get down to the port as fast as you can, and save that boy."

"How will wearing this help?" Ludo tried not to gag at the melange of sweat and spilled foodstuffs about to go round his neck. "You haven't got fleas, have you?"

"Probably."

Ludo pushed the disgusting garment back at its wearer. "I'll manage on my own, thanks."

"They'll see your white blouse, but it's your carcass, so suit yourself. Remember where I told you to go?"

"The rabbi, but... I can't leave you here."

"Of course you can. They won't hurt me with Lola loose."

There was a crack of musket fire. "Lola!" the friar yelled, opening the door and rushing back down the stairs.

Arriving in the town—bloody, bruised and totally out of breath—Ludo headed for the nearest tavern. "*Compañeros, amigos!*" he shouted, barging among the tables where he had played dominoes and dice many a time. "Help me, please. They've taken my son. A priest's got him. They say he was conjuring the devil while he was stirring my stew. You know what that means."

The men in the tavern knew what that meant. "Where?" they shouted.

"A Roman priest came in on a galley. Came in yesterday."

"I've seen them." A mixed-race, curly-haired giant rose to his feet, towering over Ludo. "The galley's tied up at the far end of the quay."

"Hurry," Ludo shouted, "they're going to take him—said they were sailing at midnight."

A soberer man said, "They won't leave port in the dark."

"Maybe not," Ludo replied, adding hastily, "but what will those *devils* do to my boy *in the dark*, eh?"

As one, the men barged through the door and followed Ludo down the narrow street, gathering help and lighting torches on their way. By the time they reached the broad quayside the group had grown larger and angrier. Nobody had any time for priests on this island—there were too many pirates and Jews who'd escaped the Spanish mainland not to know the evils of the Catholic Inquisition.

They soon located the galley, but there was no one visible on board. The group hesitated. It was one thing to save a boy, another to step aboard a vessel belonging to the Inquisition. Ludo faltered, and as he did so muskets fired from the galley. A man in the group beside him fell with a scream. Two companions pulled him into the doorway of a harbour cottage; the rest scarpered. Ludo walked towards the galley, waiting for the next shot.

"Don Ludo," came a young voice from behind him, "I'm here."

Without turning round or taking his eyes off the long guns he imagined were resting on the gunwale of the ship, Ludo took a step backwards. Then another, then another, then turned and rushed for a gap in the whitewashed walls.

José was hunkered down in the nook of a wall, sobbing with fear. "They're looking for me," he said. "I got away from them, but they're looking for me."

"Ssh," Ludo warned, holding the boy's scrawny shoulders. "Stay quiet, I'll think of something."

They had little cover and even less chance of making a run for the steep streets leading away from the water. A bright moon was lighting the white walls, and in a white-washed town all cats and fugitives are black—and cast telltale shadows.

A rat ran across José's feet. "Ugh!" he yelled in surprise.

Two men came from opposite directions: one grabbed José so hard and fast his feet left the ground, the other rammed the stock of a modern pistol into Ludo's face, then set about his body with leather boots. A third brute came running from farther off to join in the kicking spree, slamming the stock of an old musket at any open flesh he could find in the process.

It went on for what seemed a lifetime. Until, from somewhere Ludo could not see—for by now his eyes were swollen and closed—a horde of angry women came pelting down the town streets from every direction. Yelling, screaming blue murder and filthy insults in local dialect, Catalan and Castilian, they set on the men who were beating up their beloved Ludo of the one-dimpled grin and generous pockets; the Ludo some had known since he was a boy seeking refuge on Ibiza with a bunch of cutthroat corsairs.

Chapter 32

Ludo woke, battered and bruised beyond recognition, in the rabbi's house. Brother Caritas was sitting by his side. "Don't move," the old man said.

Ludo tried to say "I can't," but no words came; his mouth would not open, nor would his eyes, so he slept once more.

The next time he woke a warm, damp cloth was being passed across his face and there was the smell of fresh orange juice. "Can you drink?" asked another old man.

Ludo tried to speak and regretted it. A scab opened painfully. He wanted to cry and closed his eyes against the light and what he feared had happened, and slept again.

The third time he woke there were flickering shadows from a candle in a draught. Brother Caritas was snoring in a chair. Ludo reached out a hand, "*Aqua,*" he mumbled.

The elderly friar woke with a start and leaned toward his charge. "What is it you want—water?" Setting a leather beaker gently to Ludo's swollen lips, he waited as the patient made two attempts to drink then placed it on the windowsill beside a stub of candle.

"What happened?" Ludo asked.

"You were beaten up. Badly."

"José?"

"They took him to the galley. He put up a struggle, but they got him. They're still looking for you, but they won't find you here."

"No?"

"*Very* unlikely.

"What of José?"

"There's nothing we can do." The friar's face was as grained and grey as his habit. "I tried. I went to the galley, offered myself in his place but Rogelio didn't want me. He won't release the boy." Brother Caritas paused, took a breath, then said, "I tried to get aboard but they laughed at me. I begged for him... I heard him cry out for help. I failed him."

Ludo swallowed and turned his head. "Ransom?"

"Exchange—you're the ransom. I insisted they have me as the hostage instead of the boy, but I'm old and useless, no value to anyone, not even that snake Rogelio."

"Not useless," Ludo wanted to reach out, touch the old man and offer some comfort, but he could barely breathe for the pain in his chest.

"I think he'll be all right, though. I mean, your boy—I'm sure he'll survive. He might even do well out of it, if he's smart. Rogelio doesn't kill for no reason."

"You believe that?"

"No." Brother Caritas's voice was less than a whisper.

"How did you get away—from the house?"

"I went to a place I go to for prayer then I made my way down here. They didn't bother looking for me. They shot Lola." Candlelight pricked at tears in the old man's eyes. "My poor, innocent friend Lola."

"So how did you—"

"Hush now. We can talk in the morning. Think not on the boy if you can. I'm sure he'll be all right."

Ludo took a deep breath: Rogelio was still on the island and looking for him, using the boy's life to bring him out of hiding. *So why hadn't they taken him when they could, when he was too beaten to resist?* Then he remembered the girls. "Women," he muttered. He tried to sit up; he had to get up, confront Rogelio. As he moved, pain scorched through his chest. The infernal dagger wound had opened yet again, and now he had more internal bruising to add to it. He groped across his torso with a hand wrapped in rags. "Did I try to grab a knife?" he asked, but no one answered. With the other hand he explored his aching stomach and chest: more broken ribs. *Later, I'll get up later. . . go to the galley...* He closed his eyes and did not wake or eat or drink for another two days.

When he did wake, the rabbi was with him. Struggling to his feet from the small chair by the bed, he peered into Ludo's face. "Can you see me?" he asked.

Ludo opened his eyes. They were sore but no longer quite so swollen. "Yes."

"Good—we feared for your sight." He put cool fingers on Ludo's eyelids then nodded. "Can you move onto your side? We should look at the wounds on your back and change your bandages." Ludo pushed an elbow under himself and grimaced, then levered himself slowly to a sitting position.

The rabbi nodded again and began to unwind a length of muslin from around Ludo's middle. "Stay like that if you can for a few moments. Let the air get to your skin," he said then went to fetch the friar and clean bandages.

After Ludo had taken some liquid the friar said, "Your boy... There was an incident, an accident perhaps—last night. They say he tried to escape."

"And?"

"We don't know for sure. They say he went over the side of the galley, perhaps to swim to the quay—or perhaps away from it."

"Who says?"

"Some of the crew from the galley were drinking in the town. You don't have to believe it. It's probably a message to flush you out."

Ludo sighed. "I should have gone for him. It's my fault."

"It is not *your* fault," the rabbi said, peering at Ludo's face like a man studying a portrait.

After a while the friar said, "Can the boy swim?"

"Like a fish."

"Maybe it's true, then. He jumped overboard. He'll be all right."

"If he was alive when he went in the water."

"Must have been, if they were keeping him until you appeared. Why else have they stayed out in the bay?"

"They weren't moored? No, they'd be afraid of being boarded." Ludo turned slowly to look at the friar. "But we can board them in the bay. I'll round up some men—why didn't I think of that earlier? We'll ram them." As he tried to get out of the narrow wooden bed there was a knock at the outside door.

The rabbi went to answer it and returned almost immediately.

"News?" asked the friar.

"Not good," the rabbi replied. "Fishermen have been out all day; nobody's found the boy and he hasn't come ashore—yet."

Ludo lay back on his straw-filled pallet. "Would he have tried to get back to Doña Juana's house?"

"She'd have let us know," Brother Caritas said, placing a hand gently on Ludo's shoulder. "This is not your fault. Stay here until you heal then your corsair friends can get you away on a galley. You do not have to face Rogelio to get José now."

"Rogelio is sending me another message." Ludo paused, swallowed hard and said, "He's telling me he can—will—get me on water. First in London; then Alina; now José. He wasn't yet fifteen."

The friar wiped his eyes with a sleeve and looked up at the small glassless window. "I will go back to Rogelio and find out about your boy. Stay here with Rafael. Stay here and let yourself heal."

"No!" Softening his tone, Ludo said, "Thank you, but I must deal with this madman myself. I should have confronted him a month ago, not let this happen. José's blood is on my hands." Seeing blood in his mind's eye, Ludo put his bandaged right hand to his chest. "My shirt," he asked, "what have you done with my shirt?"

"Rafael's girl tried to wash it. It was a waste of time."

"There was something in a pocket—inside the shirt." Ludo's heart skipped a beat.

"Ah, you want the blood stone." Brother Caritas picked up the precious gem from the windowsill where anyone could have reached in and taken it.

"It's not a blood stone," Ludo said, wondering momentarily if the stone was something else that was proving false; if he'd been tricked into believing what he wanted to believe.

"A talisman, is it? Would you not prefer a crucifix?"

Ludo relaxed. "Put it under my arm, please. My left arm."

"By your heart? You getting sentimental or superstitious?" The friar was back to his sarcastic old self.

"Both—neither. Someone told me it would protect me, that's all."

"Ah, well, no point taking more risks." The elderly friar did as asked then patted Ludo's pillow, saying, "Sleep now, you will heal faster."

The rabbi exchanged a look with Brother Caritas and left the room. After a while the friar followed him. Ludo closed his eyes and slept...

... Two women are fussing about his black curly locks. One says he is too old for such hair and he escapes to play with his friends.

José is playing on the wide, low steps to the church. It has a black and white façade like the one his mother took him to in Genoa. They only went once, but he remembers it clearly: the floor inside like the board on which he plays chess with his new father...

... They are playing hide and seek on the wide church steps. José is grinning and running up and down, up and down. He's trying to count to a hundred but forgets his numbers and starts again at random places. Marcos is hiding behind a cart, the only cart. Ludo moves and shoves him into view. Marcos runs to the sea wall and climbs through a gap onto the narrow rocky ledge above the sea; he looks in now from above the water, peeps through the gap, laughing, gripping the smooth stones so as not to fall. The surf is surging and crashing, surging and pouring over the jagged rocks below. Ludo is so excited his stomach hurts. José is coming towards him, he's seen him. Marcos peeps through the gap in the wall again. José runs there, scrambles through the gap and falls, falls, falls onto the rocks below then into the white water of the churning sea... They see his little blue cap bobbing on a wave...

Ludo's eyes open wide. In his waking dream he sees the villagers making a human chain. All the adult men and women link together to bring the boy back to a piece of land that is like an island but is not an island—called Portovenere. He wants to help but they won't let him. They blame him because he's the ringleader; he's the one the boys all follow. He tries to wake up. The rabbi has put something in his drink to make him sleep. He closes his eyes again, drifts back to a jumbled past...

...It isn't José they bring back to the land: it isn't Marcos; it isn't him, although he wishes it were—it is Paulo... Little Paulo Pannini was on the steps running up and down, not José. Little Pannini, not yet ten: the baby of the group, who always wanted to play, but didn't know his numbers. Ludo is too old for games everyone says. Ludo's new father says he should leave...

...Ludo is on a boat with Jan Janszoon, who some call Murat Reis. They do not know where he is going. They do not care. His mother waves from high up in the castle. She loved him when he was little. But he was always in her way.

Two days later Ludo faced Rogelio over a Vatican galley cabin table. "What is it you want?" he demanded. "What is it that I can give you, do for you or not do, that will stop this persecution... and release the boy?"

"Persecution: I know of no persecution. I only know a Doria by-blow is making trouble wherever he goes, and now he has a Jew-woman as a wife?"

"Olivares told you."

"Naturally, although I did hear by other means beforehand."

Ludo squinted painfully at the expressionless priest through sore eyelids. "Who?"

"The church has a long arm and an efficient messenger service: you know that."

Ludo wanted to ask if the message in this instance had travelled directly from Goa in India, but dared not pursue it for fear of alerting the agent to what he didn't need to know. "Did Olivares also tell you how I am helping him?"

"'Helping' in Olivares' world is a dubious concept. We know of your somewhat conflicting roles as—what was it?—'special emissary' for the monarch in England *and* now for Spain as well. Can't be easy..." Rogelio left the phrase unfinished and gave Ludo a look that said 'explain'.

Ludo weighed his options. Rogelio would know what had transpired in Whitehall with Charles Stuart and his Catholic wife, and in El Escorial. Finally he said, "Doing what Spain wants is entirely to the Vatican's favour, as is helping Charles Stuart to return England to the Catholic faith. I do not see my dilemma. Surely this is what the Vatican wants."

"Yes and no. The Pope, like his predecessors has no great wish to see the Habsburgs extend their influence."

"I was warned that might be the case."

"But you ignored it."

"The Vatican has no control over what I do or choose not to do."

"Really?"

Ludo took a deep breath. "Tell me what you want."

"Not what *I* want—but a cardinal in Rome insists you can help us again."

"Help you! After what has happened to my cabin boy? Are you mad?"

"Don Ludovico, you brought that about yourself. I only wanted to talk to you."

Ludo's heart stopped: *could that be true?* "After what happened on the way to El Escorial, and while there, you must see I am a little confused about your attitude toward me, *Padre*."

"Put it down to *my* conflicting orders. As you know, serving two masters can get awkward."

"Tell me," Ludo said, "what is it your cardinal wants this time?"

"Portugal."

"Him as well: I shall die with Portugal stamped on my heart. What does the Vatican want in Portugal?"

"*Sollevazione*: a rising, a mutiny, the Duke of Braganza on the throne."

Ludo forced himself not to smile and blanked his features. "You mean the Vatican wants Portugal to no longer be under Spanish rule? Why?"

"Some people in the Vatican are of the opinion that the Habsburgs have too much territory and too much power, and are misusing it."

"You will be helping the French."

"It will be no bad thing if France breaks through the feeble defences along Spain's Portuguese border and marches in from both east and west."

"Depleting Spain's excessive territory somewhat further," Ludo added. "Except this also means you will be opening Portugal, as a self-governing nation, to better relations with England... Ah, yes, Portugal will be in the Vatican's debt—and England may not be a Protestant country for much longer. I see."

The Roman cleric placed his bony elbows in their tight black sleeves on the narrow table and steepled his fingers. "All roads lead to Lisbon and to London, for the next year at least. You will do it, of course."

"Do what? How can *I* possibly do anything that will make a difference?"

"By *not* doing what Olivares and King Felipe in Spain have requested."

"And if I don't do as you ask: if I do not conduct the business King Charles has requested in Lisbon either—do not even go to Portugal at all—what then?"

"The Inquisition in Goa is currently very active, my friend."

Ludo closed his eyes. When he opened them again the Roman was smiling, his thin lips a harsh streak across cadaverous features. "Tell me," Ludo said.

"You simply do not do as you have been instructed by Olivares to *prevent* the revolt in Portugal: instead, you offer funds to the Duke of Braganza's party."

Ludo raised a black eyebrow. "What funds?"

"They will be provided. Once you have done this for us, you are free to conduct your own business and go your way."

"Back to Goa; where my wife will be waiting for me, *safely*?"

Rogelio opened his hands in a gesture of clarification. "That depends on you."

"And Brother Caritas may remain here—*safely*?"

The Roman now whisked his hands into the air in a Latin gesture. "What difference do men like him make in the world?"

Ludo stared at the unchristian priest. "If we were all a little more like Brother Caritas the world would be a better place. Tell me what I am to do."

"In Lisbon there is a lane between the palace and where the large ships bring in their goods. In this lane there is a tavern known by the sign of the Green Moon. Above the tavern is a dwelling with green shutters. Go there. You will find a chest of

Venetian ducats, Dutch florins, doubloons, other coins, gold and silver. The funds are for Luisa de Guzmán, Duchess of Braganza—who, as you may know, is also sister to the Duke of Medina Sidonia and a relative of our mutual friend, Olivares. It is a small world. First you will need to speak to a contact, a man you may have heard of, Armando Cabrera—he is connected to your wife, I believe."

"He was."

"As I say, it is a small world."

"So you are financing the Duke of Braganza?"

"Don Ludovico, we are supporting both sides; one slightly more than the other, that is all."

"This Spanish woman, Luisa, she'll report straight back to Olivares and..."

"Oh no, she won't do that." Rogelio leered in satisfaction. "Dona Luisa, as she is known to her acquaintances—"

"Of whom you are one?"

"– is a very ambitious woman. The break with Spain is entirely to her advantage: she wants to be a queen."

"And I present a treasure chest as a gift from a humble merchant nobody?"

"Ah, you are playing me along. You have been chosen precisely because every woman *sees* Ludovico da Portovenere—except perhaps, his mother, but we'll leave that for another day. And a new generation on its way already, I'm told."

Now Ludo was genuinely confused. "The House of Doria?"

"Indirectly: if your claims are valid. I was speaking of your wife. She is your wife, isn't she—this Jewess? The priest attested to a legal marriage but one can rarely be sure in such far off places."

Ludo sat back, his mind racing through the implications of a Vatican agent knowing his family background, then faltered on the words 'wife' and 'marriage'. Here was a way out. He could agree to do all Rogelio wanted in Lisbon, which was perfectly in accord with what he had planned to do anyway, and do it all in exchange for an annulment instead of a Vatican certificate of *limpieza de sangre* for Leonora. "Father Rogelio, if I requested a divorce... is that also within your gift?"

"It could be."

Ludo got to his feet, but there was nowhere for him to pace. He sat down again, and because he was not thinking straight— because his body pained him and there was an ache in the region of a left rib named Alina—he tossed an imaginary coin from Rogelio's treasure chest in the air.

It came down on a lovely head of jet black hair on a white pillow in an exotic house far across the seas. He would return. Alina had gone to her husband, Marcos to his wife; Kit Windebank had pledged himself to the daughter of a farrier; even the ugly, conniving Olivares couple had each other. It was time.

"The Gasca family and the Figaroa have been Christian for three generations at least," he said.

"And you, Ludovico—do we consider your taint of Jewish blood?"

"I wasn't aware of it, but of course you know more about me than I do."

"You have gained access to two royal courts using the name of Doria."

"Which just goes to show, doesn't it, how little religion matters to *important* people. Certainly in Genoa we make little of it—as they do in the Royal Spanish court, with its portraitist Velázquez and Chief Minister..."

"Regrettable, but true I'm told. But that should not lull you into security, *Genovese*. When an excuse is needed, blood will out—literally, in many cases. Remember also, if you decide to play me false, that the rack is a pretty device—suitable also for women—with or without their clothes."

Ludo willed himself not to respond to the threat. "What about my cabin boy, José?" he asked.

"You speak to Cabrera, and you take the money where you are directed, by ship if need be. Is that agreed?"

Ludo sighed. "Yes. May I have my boy back now?"

Rogelio gave a slight shrug, "If you want the trouble. We did keep him in case you requested it." The Vatican agent slowly got to his feet and went to the door. An old sea dog was standing outside with a long blade across his left arm. "Take my visitor to the boy," Rogelio said.

José's broken body was rolled in a torn length of canvas. His face, what Ludo could see of it, was distorted, blotched where he had been hit—a clump of hair matted with dried blood. Ignoring screaming pain, Ludo bent down, picked up the dead boy from the polished deck and carried him off the galley. As he stepped onto the quay Rogelio appeared on the foredeck and folded his long arms—the tentacles of Rome.

J. G. Harlond

Part Four

England

Chapter 33

The road to Santander, Spain, September, 1640

Waiting to make his farewell surrounded by trunks and portmanteaux, Marcos studied Milagros the Miracle Wrestler standing opposite him in the small hallway, then became distracted by Alina berating her feeble maid in her chamber.

"What are you snivelling about now?" Alina demanded in English. Fanny mumbled something, to which Alina screamed, "Well sit on it! Oh, move over, I'll do it." Marcos smiled; he'd had a similar problem with his luggage. Something fell to the floor and Alina shouted, "Leave it! I'm never wearing that thing again anyway."

He looked at Milagros and caught her eye. She didn't understand what was being said, but she'd heard her new mistress in full spate and her mouth was twitching with amusement. Marcos schooled his features: it would not do for a merchant such as he to share a joke with a servant. "Where are you from, Milagros?" he asked to divert her attention.

"Becerril de la Sierra."

The name meant nothing to him. "And your family is there?"

"My mother and brothers. My father's dead."

"I'm so sorry—typhus?"

"Tree fell on him."

Marcos bit his upper lip, then said, "He was felling trees?"

"Yes."

"And now you are with the baroness."

"What's a 'baroness'?" Milagros asked.

"A lady of the nobility in England. Less than a countess, I think, but more than..." Marcos struggled; he had little idea about the ascending ranks of aristocracy, despite revelling in his recent status as *un hidalgo* and—as a boy—dreaming of becoming a knight serving the King of Spain. He mentally gave himself a pat on the back for having actually risen to attend the royal court—albeit as a pseudo-secretary, then gave himself another for being sufficiently disillusioned by it all to want to escape the meaningless gossip and frippery and return to a more worthwhile life in England.

At precisely that moment the Conde de Pamanes knocked on the door. Marcos inclined his head, indicating that Milagros should answer it. He had at least learned how to behave as *un hidalgo*.

The stylish Conde de Pamanes sauntered in, bringing with him a waft of various scents. Marcos gave a suitable bow and cast a calculating eye over the count's buff-coloured travelling apparel.

"Is all this for my daughter?" the count said, referring to the assembled luggage.

"Some is mine, the rest belongs to the baroness, and that bag belongs to..." Marcos struggled to find a word to explain Milagros—'bodyguard' seeming too dramatic and 'companion' out of the question—"the baroness's *señora de viaje*," he concluded.

"*Señora de viaje*? Well there's no room for her as well. It'll be a squeeze with just the three of us inside. My man is already riding atop."

Alina appeared from her room carrying another portmanteau and directing Fanny, who was tugging a leather trunk across the marble floor, to mind the doorjamb.

"*Cariño*," began the count, "there's no room for all this in my carriage, and I certainly can't allow two maids to travel with you. I, er—only have one horse."

Alina blinked. "You said you had a carriage."

"Oh, I do, and very pretty it is, too. But—um—small. My dear Pilar of Pamanes—'Pammy', I call her, our pet name, 'Pammy of Pamanes'—she bought it upon our marriage—for our wedding, you see—and it is more comfortable to travel all the leagues from Santander to Madrid under cover. But it is not a stagecoach by any means." The count gave a theatrical twist of a beribboned wrist, indicating the luggage. "Choose one travelling chest, my dear, and have your new servant take the rest to England separately."

"No," Marcos interrupted, "the new travelling companion *must* stay with Doña Alina. She can leave her maid instead."

"I can't leave Fanny here. And she certainly can't travel on her own, she has no Spanish—she'll be useless," huffed Alina, crossly.

Marcos went to the window overlooking the street and looked at a pretty carriage with a leather roof waiting below. It was, as the count insisted, small. He beckoned Alina, who took one look at the conveyance and exploded.

"Hardly a coach and four, is it? I thought you'd married a wealthy widow," she cried.

"So did I," her father answered sheepishly. "Pilar is not as wealthy as I was led to believe, unfortunately, but... but she is a good woman, kind-hearted. She will be so pleased that you are visiting her, so pleased to know her new daughter has married into the English nobility—as was only her due, being the eldest daughter of a grandee, naturally, but well..." The count's voice trailed off.

"Quite." Alina huffed then turned to her new servant. "Milagros, thank you for agreeing to be of assistance, but I shall not be requiring your services."

"Oh, yes, you will!" Marcos intervened hastily. "You are not to go anywhere without Milagros. You promised."

"Don't be ridiculous, Marcos. I can do as I please as long as I get the queen's... those messages back to London. Four of us aren't going to squeeze into that fancy cart."

"You promised you'd keep Milagros, and you know *why* you promised," Marcos added in a lower voice.

Alina looked at him and grabbed a handful of skirt. Noting the action, Marcos took the upper hand. "I shall travel with you. We'll hire a carriage and travel together behind the count."

"But you were going south to see your family," Alina responded.

"Yes, I know, but plans change. Honestly, Alina, I don't want you to travel alone, even with two women and your noble parent."

"Ah, well, now," the Conde de Pamanes said, "if it's not strictly *necessary* for me to return to Santander, well, the court will be returning to Madrid within the next week or two and His Majesty, I know, will miss my presence..."

Alina threw her hands up in the air, "*Maldito sea!* Why are all the men in my life so useless... so... wrong!" she yelled.

"I'm neither of those," Marcos whispered quietly behind her back.

"You don't count," Alina hissed, swinging round so fast that her skirts swished across the marble floor. Fanny burst into tears again. Scowling at her father, she continued, "We shall travel with Marcos, as he suggests, Padre. Thank you for your paternal concern, but I shall not need you now."

Marcos gasped at her offhand, hurtful manner, simultaneously regretting his generosity and remembering what Edward Beale had asked him to do in Sanlúcar while he was supposed to be with his parents. He closed his eyes and waited, hoping the Conde de Pamanes would change his daughter's mind.

The count made no attempt to persuade her to travel with him or even stay with him in Madrid. Whether Alina was also disappointed Marcos could not say, but she was on one of her rampages, that was clear. Narrowing her eyes, she turned on him, hissing, "Did you two plan this?"

"Us two? You mean Ludo and I? How could we?" Marcos replied while wondering if perhaps Ludo had foreseen this outcome as well. Alina's sudden anxiety to get back to the royal court in London had brought their happy reunion to an end, for which Marcos was not entirely sorry. It was even worth the journey back with her to see them separated once and for all.

Milagros rode with the driver on their hastily hired coach, primed to keep an eye out for robbers or anyone who looked too interested in their party. Seated above the closed wooden carriage she reminded Marcos of one of the larger than life women with huge breasts and benign countenances that graced the prows of ships in Plymouth Sound, an Amazon, a siren—a useful woman to have beside you in a fight.

The first stretch of their journey was uneventful, and they reached Burgos without any hindrance. Less than a league out of the busy city, though, the nearside horse cast a shoe. The driver handed Milagros the reins, jumped down and walked back the way they had come to retrieve it. He found it within yards, still thick and shiny from a recent shoeing. Using nails he kept in a box under his seat, he hammered the shoe back on with the horse still in its traces and they continued on their way. The second horse cast a shoe from the same foreleg four hundred yards on.

Alina and Fanny got out of the hot carriage and Milagros once more held the reins while the driver got down to see what was to be done. Marcos climbed out of the carriage and went to speak to him.

"I haven't got enough nails left," the driver said. "Some coincidence."

Marcos lifted the affected horse's foreleg. The hoof was surprisingly sound, no cracked horn or damage. It looked as if there had been a deliberate extraction of nails, leaving just one or two, and the closed edges of the shoe at the toe and the sides of the heel to keep the iron in place. Dropping the hoof, he looked around. The road was deserted, the landscape flat and bare except for a few bent hawthorn trees and a clump of dusty brambles. It was altogether too open and too quiet. He was just about to warn Alina to get back into the carriage and get the pistols Ludo had left him when he saw the *bandoleros*.

They must have sneaked out from among trees, for Milagros had not seen them either. One of them, a short, brown-capped ruffian, grabbed Alina round her neck, bending her backwards, for she was considerably taller than he; the second held a pistol to her head; the third set to business with the portmanteaux and trunks at the back of their vehicle. Marcos stayed where he was under the horse's broad chest and looked up at Milagros, hoping to catch her eye and develop a strategy, but she was staring down at Alina, who was now on her own in front of the gun. Fanny was standing in the road, her hands to her face, crying.

Marcos dithered. With a gun pointed directly at Alina's head what could he possibly do? Even if he drew the man's fire so he used his powder and had to reload, they'd surely have knives as well.

"Stay here with me, *señor*," whispered the driver. "Bit of luck they won't bother with us. Nothing we can do. They're only after the lady's jewels and any coin you've got."

The contents of the first portmanteau flew off the back of the carriage, then the second. A soft shift hovered in the gentle breeze before dropping slowly to the stony road. Ribbons and white lacy nothings floated into the air, then the heavier skirts were tossed overboard.

"*No hay nada*," the *bandolero* called to his mates.

Marcos froze: they weren't common *bandoleros*; they were looking for something specific. Alina was carrying something valuable, and if she was doing that it was for one of her queens. *That's why she's in such a hurry to get back...*

The third man heaved a trunk onto the ground, breaking it open to reveal more skirts and bodices—yards and yards of fashionable pastel silks and satins. "Search her," he shouted, leaping to the ground to stand in front of Alina.

Marcos suddenly visualised a black reticule Alina had brought with her and kept on her lap in the coach. But before he could make a move to save it, there was an almighty yell from above as Milagros launched herself like the angel of death from the high driver's seat onto the man holding the long-barrelled pistol. Flattening him to the ground, she rolled him into a pile of Alina's gowns, trussing him up like a newborn babe.

The man holding Alina started to laugh. Wrenching herself from his grip, Alina locked her hands to make a single fist and swung round to knock him backwards. Taking another locked-hand swing, she sent him rocking backwards again and then again until he fell onto the road, cracking his head on a convenient length of exposed granite. Marcos ran round the horses to jump on the third man's back just as he emerged from the carriage with the bag. Ducking out of Marcos's reach, the robber with the reticule started to run.

By this time, the trussed up robber had unrolled himself and was also making a run for it. Cursing, he limped across the stubble of a harvested cornfield as best he could to catch up with his companion. Once he reached him, they tore open Alina's reticule together and began opening some small packages, tossing the wrappings into the air.

"The queen's treasure!" Alina screamed. "Marcos, get the bag!"

Marcos set off in pursuit, but as he neared the two men they tossed away the empty reticule. Assuming they had got any coin Alina was carrying, he stopped, and breathing heavily due to the unaccustomed exertion he slowly returned to the carriage.

Milagros had jammed the third man into a neck lock. "What d'you want?" she demanded, squeezing until he was blue in the face.

"*Nada!*"

She squeezed again.

"Let me go—for the love of Christ—let me go."

Alina picked up the pistol and aimed it at his head. "Who sent you?"

"Nobody."

Marcos took the gun from Alina and Milagros gave the robber another tight squeeze.

"Nobody," the man gasped. "We—we thought you'd be easy..."

"Easy pickings," supplied Marcos. "But who sent you?"

"Nobody sent us. We don't—aagh—nobody! We work on our own."

Alina studied the robber for a moment then said, "Let him go Milagros—we've got the pistol."

"It ain't loaded—we ain't got no powder left," the robber whined.

Milagros released him, but before he could take two steps she grabbed his right arm and ran it up his back.

"Jesus, missis, have pity on a poor harmless father what must feed his infants."

While this was going on, Alina began gathering the wrappings from around the little wooden boxes, then gave up. "I've got some of the paper wrapping," she said, coming back to speak to Marcos, "but I can't find the boxes. Come and help me look—there were little notes with them too... I think."

"Boxes?" Marcos asked, then realised he might be alerting the robber in Milagros' iron arm lock and directed Alina away from the carriage. "Show me."

As they walked a soft breeze carrying a gentle threat of autumn riffled through the low weeds beneath their feet, sending a crumpled square of paper into the air.

"There's something. Quick!" Alina shouted, lifting her skirts and rushing across the stony stubble. "Got it!" she called. "And here's another one. But where are the boxes? Please God, let me find the boxes."

"Boxes, boxes! What boxes?" asked Marcos. "Jewel boxes—what?"

"Treasure. Three little boxes of treasure. That's what Queen Isabel told me. That's all she told me. I had them with me in the carriage."

"Three jewel boxes?"

"No, I don't think so… I don't know…" Alina's voice drifted into despair.

"Never mind—let's see if we can find them," Marcos said, his heart lurching at the sight of Alina so close to tears.

Like children hunting the thimble, they ran, doubled over, hither and thither, gathering bits of paper, lengths of ribbon, even a round of red wax with the royal seal intact—but finding no small boxes.

"Oh, excellent, a nail!" Marcos called out ironically. "That'll be useful anyway." Then he picked up a slither of wood that looked out of place in the stubble. It was shiny, as if polished. Out of curiosity he studied it for a moment then tucked it into a pocket.

A stronger gust of wind rippled across the stubble and a wisp of blond thistledown spiralled up in a dance among the sharp stones and desiccated sheep droppings. There were no valuable gemstones, no miniatures of royal personages, no… whatever a queen was sending to her sister.

Finally Marcos said, "I know you were probably told to keep it secret, but what are we actually looking for?"

Alina shook her head. "I don't know. There are three tiny, mahogany wood boxes with close fitting lids. They were wrapped and sealed. I don't know what's in them. Doña Isabel just said 'treasure'. Jewels, I suppose. I've got the three notes she wrote, though."

As they stumbled back towards their carriage, Marcos said, "All this is a nuisance, but it could be worse. I don't think those men can have been sent by Hopton or Olivares, or even you-know-who."

Alina paused. "Who is 'you-know-who'?"

"Ludo's arch enemy, and someone you really don't want to underestimate."

"Why would he bother with what I'm carrying to England?"

"Because you are connected to Ludo—"

"I am not!"

"No—perhaps not like that—anymore—but he doesn't know that, and he'd love to get his hands on anything Isabel is sending to England."

"Why?"

"*Yo qué sé!* If I knew that I wouldn't have been masquerading as Ludo's secretary, I'd have been lording it at those banquets with all the other nobles. Actually, that reminds me, I wanted to tell you something about what I'm thinking of doing in England—ask me later. Now, explain about these boxes."

"They're gifts for Henrietta Maria. There's also a very special letter..." Alina edged a corner of cream vellum from her bodice. "But nobody will ever take this from me."

"What's so special about that letter?" Marcos asked suspiciously.

"This is why I have to go back to England."

"So you know what's in the letter, but not in the boxes. And you are not going to tell me what's in the letter."

"No—you'll find out one day, and you will be so proud that you knew the royal messenger who took it to England and—made things happen."

Marcos stopped in his tracks. "You're not joking, are you?"

"Oh no, I'll tell you this, though—you are helping me to influence the future of an entire nation."

"Is any of this to do with Ludo?" Marcos asked quietly.

Alina went pink. "No. It's the opposite."

"The opposite."

"It's why I had to leave him. Why I'm going back to London, not going... wherever he was going. But Marcos, you won't ever tell anyone about that, will you?"

"No," Marcos sighed. "Thomas will never hear of it—from *my* lips, anyway."

Alina gave a grateful smile. "Ludo refused to understand." After a moment or two she said, "The enemy you mentioned—was he the one who pushed me in the lake?"

"Ludo thinks so. That's why he got you Milagros."

Alina lifted her head and stared at the barren scenery. There was a brief silence, then she whispered, "What I'm doing for the queens—it will help Thomas, and Crimphele, too. He will be rewarded greatly, and he won't be able to refuse being made a viscount or marquis now... If I can get back safely."

Marcos took her hand. "I'll stay with you, protect you, don't worry."

Alina kissed him on the cheek like a sister, like a cousin. Marcos sighed again: *would it always be like this between them?*

When they reached the carriage, the driver was hammering a spare nail he'd found into the second horse's hoof. "We'll have to turn back and get a farrier to shoe them properly, but they should be all right until then. We'll never get up over the mountains unless we do, though," he said.

"Ah, I found a nail in the stubble." Marcos took a short twisted length of square-topped iron from his pocket.

"Looks like it's been used," the driver said. "Come out of a loose shoe, I'd say. Stick it in my box over there. 'Any nail in a crisis' is my motto."

"Ma'am, what do I do with this?" Milagros asked, still holding onto the poor father what had got to feed his infants.

"Let him go," Alina said. "Pathetic creature, he won't bother us again." Then she changed her tone, "No! No, don't. Listen to me, *band-o-ler-o*, your *compis* have got my property and I want it back. It's no use to you. Three little boxes—they're worth nothing—except to me. Tell your *compis* to leave them... Leave them... where?" Alina turned to speak to the driver. "Where are we going to now?"

"The nearest smithy, ma'am."

She swung back to speak to the robber. "One of you is to come to the nearest blacksmith from here. You or he brings the boxes intact—if you do I'll reward you with some of the money you weren't able to steal, understand?"

"How much?" asked the robber.

"Depends on what you bring me."

"All right—the nearest smithy—that'll be Paco's by the sign of the White Horse."

"We'll wait until the noonday bells—that's all—that's if you want the reward."

The robber nodded then, groaning with pain from having his arm trapped for so long, ran off like a frightened rabbit.

Marcos watched him go and scanned the area around them for more trouble. Seeing none, he climbed back in the carriage. Alina joined him, sat down and looked at the square of paper they had found in the stubble then handed it to Marcos. "You read it," she said, "I'm afraid to."

Marcos smoothed the small square and read what was on it. "*Madre mía de mi vida*," he murmured, and slowly got out of the carriage and went to the driver's toolbox to retrieve the short length of twisted iron he'd just put there.

"What are you doing?"Alina demanded as he returned.

"Retrieving one of the nails from Christ's Holy Cross."

Marcos passed Alina the note. Written in tiny handwriting it said: *My darling Sister, please accept this very special Relic. Pray over it and it will bring Comfort. Soon your days will be peaceful once more. This is a Nail from our Saviour's HOLY CROSS. Keep it with you at all times.*

Alina gasped. "Is it?"

"It's a nail from a horseshoe, according to the driver."

"But *you* wouldn't know if it was or wasn't?"

Marcos took a deep breath. Alina was angling for a quarrel; she was feeling foolish or in the wrong, or perhaps just frightened, and this was her usual strategy: pass the blame onto someone else, namely him. In an attempt to pacify her, he slipped the slither of polished wood from his pocket and held it out to her. "Probably from the Holy Cross itself," he said.

Alina unfolded a second scrap of paper, then tossed it to the floor, saying, "Yes, it is! It must be." Taking the tiny slither of wood in her right hand, she closed her eyes and held it to her chest. "I hope with all my heart that this is true. For this is treasure indeed: blessed comfort. What more wonderful treasure could there be?"

Marcos opened and closed his mouth, astonished. "You don't believe in all that nonsense about relics, do you? They're just bits of old teeth and mutton bones—and horseshoe nails and splinters."

"You don't know that."

"No, no I don't. But I do know the price of something is what someone is prepared to pay; or in this case, prepared to believe in. Give me that other note."

Alina handed him the second tiny square of paper written by Queen Isabel in El Escorial.

Marcos read it then said, "We've lost some locks of hair. Listen: *My dear sister, I do so congratulate you on the safe delivery of another healthy son. Here is a lock of hair from my darling Balthasar Carlos when he was a newborn himself. It is the blond-white of a true Habsburg infant. May it bind our Boys in eternal friendship, that there be no enmity between them. Marietta, if you have a remedy for the delivery of a healthy babe, send it to me in return, I beg you."*

"Oh, damnation!" blurted out Alina. "Baby hair: where can we get that?"

Marcos shrugged.

"Your wife expecting, isn't she?" Alina asked. "We can use your baby's hair. Will it be fair like yours?"

"I hope so," Marcos grinned. Then he started to laugh. Then he was serious. "Who else apart from Doña Isabel knows about the letter you're carrying? Someone could be following you, and these *bandaleros* may be decoys to put you off your guard. I'd say you're carrying something much more important than the little boxes; something people might like to have or learn about —a foreign king or the Vatican, for example."

"I am, and I'm not stupid—I do know that," Alina huffed. Then, leaning out of the coach, she screamed, "Fanny, have you re-packed those boxes yet?" Turning back, she said, "What foreign king?"

"France, Portugal, they'd both like to know what Spain and England are up to—if they are joining forces. A casual letter, one sister to another, might include all sorts of valuable titbits."

"Portugal's part of Spain."

"Not for much longer, it isn't." Now he leaned out of the coach and called out, "Milagros, help the driver get the boxes strapped up again, will you?"

"Those relics are worth a fortune," Alina muttered, folding the notes and pushing them into a skirt pocket.

"An old nail and a bit of wood?"

"The relics are real, idiot! If they belong to a queen they must be real." Alina lifted her hands in a gesture of desperation, then said, "You're right, we'll have to be more alert from now on. Thank heavens for Milagros."

"Thank heavens," Marcos repeated dourly.

"Cheer up, Marcos, it'll all be over soon." Alina patted his knee.

"No, it won't—we've got to get to Santander and cross the Narrow Sea yet." As he spoke, Marcos conjured a picture of his pretty wife with a tiny infant in her arms. "I can't wait."

The driver turned the carriage back the way they had come and slowly they trundled back towards the city. At some point down the dusty high road, Alina looked at the vacant seat in front of her. "Where's Fanny?" she asked.

Fanny was standing in the middle of the road exactly where they had turned and nobody had noticed her. As they waited for her to catch up, Alina said, "You were going to tell me something earlier. You said to remind you."

"Oh, yes—seems a bit irrelevant now, but I've been thinking about all the fabric that goes into your skirts."

"Have you?" Alina responded dubiously. "Why?"

"You know Ludo's business in Holland is called the 'rich trade'—silks and spices and tea. I'm going to try and join him. Import his Indian cottons and silks, if he'll let me."

"If he ever comes back."

"He will—if he's still alive. But I can get fabrics from other merchants; the British East India Company bring them into Plymouth."

"I thought you were building a wine and spirits business," Alina said, brushing dirt from her skirt.

"I am. I'll do it all and become part of the rich trade as well."

"And get rich in the process."

"That's the plan." Marcos pulled in his legs while a voiceless Fanny climbed into the carriage.

"Why do you want to go to all that trouble?" Alina insisted. "Isn't what you've got enough?"

"Look who's talking," said Marcos, and closed the subject.

After a while Alina said, "So you have acquired something worthwhile from this venture then, if only ambition."

"Huh," laughed Marcos drily, "I've never lacked for that. That's why Ludo took me on in Sanlúcar, did you not know about that?"

"No." Alina closed her eyes, uninterested.

"Actually," Marcos said, half to himself, "one way or another I've acquired quite a lot over the past two months."

"Being here has changed everything for me," Alina sighed, her eyes tight shut, "but I shall need a completely new wardrobe."

As the carriage rolled back onto the cobbled streets of Burgos, Marcos said, "Do you want to stop and see your brothers before we sail?"

"They've all gone. José Luis is in New Spain, Álvaro is there, too, to become an engineer. Even Fernando... he's to be a priest, God save him, and he was such a funny boy."

"Your father suggested you visit his new wife."

"Oh, heavens, Pammy of Pamanes! That would be the last straw. No! Take me home to Crimphele, Marcos. I'm going to enjoy a few days with my own little boy before I return to Whitehall. What I'm carrying is of prime importance, but I need to tell Thomas about it all first. He will have to come to London with me."

"Whatever you wish, milady."

"We'll stop on the way so you can see your wife and new baby, if it's arrived—and get that lock of hair. I'd like to meet them as well, if I may, please?"

Alina's gentle yet positive tone and sudden gentleness made Marcos smile; he gave her hand a friendly squeeze. Leaning back against the hard leather seat he heard a sniffing noise. At first he wondered if Alina had given way to tears after her fright with the pistol, but it was Fanny, as usual.

"What are you crying about now, Fanny?" Alina asked, brushing a length of hair from the girl's face and attempting to be kind. "It's all over. The robbers have gone."

The girl started to howl in earnest. Between sobs she said, "I let them see the boxes."

"Let who see...?" Alina's tone sharpened. "Who, Fanny? Who saw the boxes? You don't speak any Spanish—how did you...?"

"The man was English. He spoke English. The lady wasn't, though. She was very grand. I was frightened."

"My God, they actually came into our rooms. Who were they?"

Marcos raised a hand and said, "What did the Englishman look like, Fanny? Was he old or young?"

"Young, a bit fat."

Fanny's voice wobbled and Marcos gave her a reassuring smile then turned to Alina: "Kit Windebank and Her Grace the Gorgon of Olivares, by the sound of it."

Alina slapped a hand to her mouth in horror, then said, "They'll have taken the real relics. *Dios mío, qué hago ahora?*"

"Not much you can do, apart from never mention it—to anyone—ever."

"But why would Kit be involved? He was your friend."

"Yes. And why was he my friend, I wonder. Kit will do anything to get his wife back."

"His wife?"

"Hopton and Kit's father decided the daughter of a blacksmith wasn't suitable for a young milord destined to be an ambassador so the Countess-Duchess Gorgon had her sent to a convent. Kit doesn't know which one, or where." Alina shook her head in dismay and Marcos said, "No need for you to pretend to be shocked—you think social rank matters."

Alina huffed and leaned across to pat her maid on the knee. "You can stop crying now, Fanny. That's an order."

"They said you'd dismiss me without a reference if you found out, or if I told you," the girl spluttered between sobs.

"Oh, I'm going to, just as soon as we get back to Crimphele. I'm not cruel enough to abandon a girl in a foreign country, though. I know what that is like."

Chapter 34

The voyage to Portugal, October, 1640

Fuelled by anger, Ludo decided to pay lip service to the contradictory tasks for which he had been commissioned and do only that which was in his own, direct interest. 'Take the bull by the horns,' Leonora had said and Brother Caritas had told him to 'take back his life'—so he would. Enough time had been spent trying to heal his physical and emotional wounds; now he was fit and keen to be on his way again.

Standing beside him in the cramped space of the Chueta rabbi's little house, Brother Caritas said, "I doubt we shall meet again, Don Ludo. Go with God and find whatever it is you seek —then find a good woman, settle down, and raise a family to love and be loved by. All this wandering and trying to... whatever it is you are trying to do—it's time to stop."

Ludo smiled for the first time in weeks. "I know, and I shall do what you say, Brother, very soon."

Rabbi Rafael watched them without speaking then lifted the door latch. A strong gust of autumn wind blew the door from his hand and the rabbi nodded as if he had been passed a message. Turning back to Ludo, he said, "In your Bible, in Ecclesiastes, it is said '*The wind goes toward the south, and turns about unto the north; it whirls about continually, and the wind returns again according to his circuits.*' Let the wind take you, my son; let it help you find your place. Then do as this good friar says, settle down and raise a loving family."

"'The wind returns again according to his circuits'—a pretty phrase," Ludo said, unsure how to respond.

The rabbi took Ludo's arm. "The treasure you think you seek may elude you, but there is a deeper treasure, a truth behind the images you have in your mind. That truth, I hope, will lead you back to your origins and give you comfort—if you have the patience and the courage to seek it out."

Ludo met the rabbi's piercing gaze. "And can you tell me what it is I seek behind these images?"

"Belonging. Find out who you are, Don Ludovico, and let that knowledge dictate what you are." The rabbi smiled and patted Ludo's arm. "It is my firm belief you are one of us. Come back to us when your search is over."

Ludo tried to find words to respond to something he had felt —suspected—for many, many years, but his throat was dry. Wordlessly, choking back emotion, he embraced the two men, then lifted his heavy duffle bag and set off down to the harbour.

Walking down the steep, terraced street to the harbour, catching glimpses of a sparkling sea between dazzlingly white walls on this autumn day, Ludo was reminded of the Arab colts on the Omani beach: sons of the wind. He would go back there —if he survived the return voyage—and make an arrangement with the sheik. If such beautiful creatures could live in the Oman, how might they thrive in temperate, green Christendom, or on the west coast of India? Horses in India were a valuable commodity... an interesting proposition. And they would command a healthy price.

The vessel taking him to Lisbon was in the harbour. A salt-laden galleass loaded also with dried fish, she was nevertheless beautiful to a man of the sea.

As this daughter of the wind slid through the waves, Ludo stayed in the prow, legs apart, arms akimbo, watching dolphins leap alongside. With his black hair long and loose now, and dressed in his version of Indian pyjamas, he felt free again. Truly, he belonged at sea.

For the course of the voyage he supped with the upper deck crew and joined their betting games and banter. It was an amusing release from the rigidity of El Escorial and the guilt-ridden remembrance of how he had failed a brave, loyal young boy on Ibiza, and by the time the Tagus estuary came into sight, he was feeling a lot more like his old self.

It was the first time in many years that he'd arrived in Lisbon by sea. The Tagus, wide and unusually calm on a late October day, almost fooled him into believing his mission would go smoothly. He scanned the harbour to see if Toxo had received the message he had sent some weeks before with a Galician trader, and already arrived.

Disembarking as a member of the galleass's crew, he found a room in a damp tavern just outside the Alfama district and remained there all evening, endeavouring to consume a large plate of tuber roots and salted cod, while listening to a woman wailing the longest and saddest song known to Christendom. Despite his opinion, diners clapped in appreciation. When the woman launched into a second caterwaul, Ludo slapped some coins on his greasy table and walked out.

Checking his inner top pocket and the purse tied under his loose pantaloons, he wandered down to the water's edge and called in at another tavern, where drinkers were happier and conversation more likely to lead to what he wanted to know.

Talk was excited, agitated. The Portuguese rebellion against their Spanish overlords had started. Listening to what was being said around him then good-naturedly joining a game of dominoes, Ludo began to feel positive again. Events beyond his control for once were in his favour.

After he had inspected his straw mattress by candlelight, squashed various unwanted bedfellows and covered the bolster with a clean shirt, Ludo lay down in yet another foreign room and closed his eyes. Before he fell asleep he finally decided how he was going to fulfil Rogelio's task for Leonora's sake, then complete his own business regarding the Duke of Braganza—then leave as soon as he could. Olivares' Spanish mission to keep Portugal he would ignore altogether. He had the signed documents from the old man, he'd done what he wanted in El Escorial, and if Portugal was this far ahead with its *sublevação* he could safely—fairly safely—ignore any Spanish threat to his well-being. "*Allora!*" Ludo laughed, raising his hands above his thin blanket. "*A-o diavo i spagnòlli—non si meritavano di meno.*" To hell with the Spanish, they deserve all they get.

He rolled, still uncomfortably, onto his right side and tried to sleep, but his head was abuzz with what was to come: Ludo da Portovenere was going back to Goa with all the security a lovely New Christian wife might ever need, and if all went to plan, a treasure chest full of Vatican money plus the patronage of the new Portuguese king. "*Perfetto!*"

The next morning Ludo set out once more in his grubby shipboard attire to locate the tavern named the Green Moon. Wandering through narrow alleys, he studied the shamble dwellings of dock workers, fishwives and thieves, looking for a sign bearing a green moon and a dwelling above with green shutters.

The tavern was in a wider thoroughfare than Rogelio had described, nearer the palace, where mules pulled cargoes to and from the harbour and better-dressed folk went about their daily business. Leaning against the wall of the dwelling next to the tavern there was a ladder. Someone had been painting the shutters a more nauseous shade of green than those of the neighbouring house and left the ladder conveniently in his way. Ludo moved the ladder one house down then climbed it to look in an open window.

A well dressed man and a very elegant woman were seated on chairs facing each other. Behind them was an older man, evidently of lesser status for he was standing. Beside him on a table was a domed money chest.

Ludo focussed on the woman: her back was erect, her head covered in a veil. Was this Dona Luisa perhaps? Would the Duke of Braganza's wife risk her reputation to visit a house above a tavern? Yes, if she was as ambitious and desperate to be a queen as Rogelio suggested. The man opposite her was speaking earnestly—a wealthy merchant, perhaps. The smaller man behind them had the look of a civil servant, a tidy dog's body—definitely no merchant-venturer or fanatical Portuguese aristocrat. Whoever they were, they were discussing something serious in low voices. Ludo strained to catch something he could understand.

"Hey!" called an indignant house painter from below.

"Hey!" Ludo called back, forming his face into an imbecilic grin as he descended the rungs none too steadily. Once at street level, he grinned stupidly at the painter and dribbled a bit for effect. The painter rattled off something in harbour dialect and Ludo ducked as if expecting a blow, then, half-crouching to disguise his above-average height, he scuttled across the street beneath the straining chest of a pack mule. The mule reminded him of his previous adventure in Lisbon when he'd taken possession of *The Tulip*, and he didn't know whether to laugh or feel angry that he'd been forced into another bit of theatre.

Later, seated in a barber shop, trying to shut out the gentle scrape, scrape of the sharp blade caressing his neck, Ludo wondered what, if anything, his latest move in the physical game of Snakes and Ladders had brought him. Square 76: Knowledge… not much. Square 51: Truth, or was it Reliability…? He closed his eyes and tried to visualise the game board, but he couldn't remember all the squares, just that there were far more snakes than ladders. Then something on the edge of his consciousness reminded him that the evil serpents of Lying and Theft were very close to the virtue of Reliability. . . And damn it to hell, he was going down both of them, because by the time the barber had shaped his straggly black beard into something fashionable for polite society, Ludo had worked out what to do with the Vatican chest of gold coins.

Cleaner, tidier and back in full control, Ludo changed his garb and set out to meet his old friend Toxo, captain of *La Magdalena,* in a harbour tavern. After a convivial hour discussing winds and voyages, and planning their next two sailings, Ludo then made his way to his wife's ex-brother-in-law and agent in the Casa da Índia.

Armando Cabrera was the civil servant he'd seen in the house of the green shutters: a fortuitous ladder.

"Ludovico da Portovenere, I have been waiting for you," Cabrera said, making no attempt to greet him further in either the Spanish or Portuguese manner.

Ludo took his measure: he was one of those paltry, grey men it didn't do to upset. They conversed in Spanish on civil terms, Ludo playing his relaxed, open-faced merchant role, listening acutely to every unspoken word. Then he set out the document Olivares had given him making the firm of Gasca Figaroa his and free from the restrictions of Lisbon's Casa da Índia. The document proclaiming Leonora's *limpieza de sangre* he kept rolled.

The small official instantly became angry. "This document is unnecessary. Whether you are the titular head of the firm or not, while you trade in Lisbon I am your agent and import duties are mandatory."

Ludo cocked his head to one side and gave his genial, one-dimpled grin. "Don Armando, I trade under the Genoese flag, in ports of my own choosing, and as a merchant from the state of Genoa, with connections to the Spanish crown, I have been made exempt from your taxes." Cabrera opened his mouth to speak but Ludo raised a hand. "That is not to say I shall be depriving Lisbon of income from the East Indies. I do, in fact, have a proposal that could benefit Portugal greatly, should you care to listen, always remembering that the profits and benefits we merchants create can be shared under the appropriate arrangements."

Cabrera was already lost, but he made a valiant attempt to save face by saying rapidly, "Portugal has a monopoly over trade from Goa."

"You had better tell the Dutch and English, then, because I see their ships in Indian harbours all the time. You have heard of the Dutch East India Company, the VOC? And the British East Company? Ah, I also have this document, a licence to trade directly with the British royal household. It was signed by the King of England himself—there is his signature." Ludo rolled out a third document, bearing a royal seal, and waited to see what effect this information would have on a Portuguese actively conspiring to wrest his country from Spanish dominion, and by extension, not interested in falling foul of potential English investors or buyers.

Cabrera smoothed his neat, grey beard, rubbed a manicured hand down his thick, brown breeches, patted his chest pensively, then finally said, "I understand—you retain your independence while supplying the English."

"The English and others. You might be interested to know, Don Armando, I am also supporting—financially backing—*a particularly valid* cause here in Portugal."

Cabrera's eyebrows shot up. "This is not what I was told last week—" To cover whatever he was about to reveal, Cabrera made a business of rolling the documents on his desk and handing them back to Ludo. Then he said quietly in a phrasing that suggested he had learned his words by rote, "I wonder Don Ludo, if you could help us in a small task of transporting goods from Lisbon to Oporto by sea."

As this concurred with Rogelio's demands in Ibiza, Ludo said, "Willingly. My carrack is in the bay. What exactly will I be transporting: pepper from the East—or wine, or other domestic produce?"

"Various commodities: some spices, crates of tea and other goods of similar value." Cabrera indicated a wooden chest in the corner of his office, not the domed coffer Ludo had seen in the house of the green shutters, but the iron clasps and substantial lock spoke of similar contents. "There are seven more chests at a warehouse in the harbour. We need a reliable, *trustworthy* person to arrange for their delivery in Oporto. Given my position here, I cannot be seen to be, er—cooperating with revolutionaries, hence we—I—require an independent shipowner to deliver the goods."

"Revolutionaries!" Ludo repeated in mock horror.

"Hush, hush," replied Cabrera waving his hands up and down in panic.

"Ah, I understand: a government official cannot be seen to be supporting such a cause, not if there is any chance the revolt might fail." Ludo watched Cabrera wince and regretted putting him on the defensive, but it was too late now, so he continued, "And these chests, I assume we need to keep them out of sight."

Cabrera winced again. "Yes, of course."

Ludo gave him a knowing look, inclining his head. "What you are trying to achieve is a laudable enterprise, Don Armando, which, as I said, I do wholeheartedly support." He gave a dramatic sigh. "Did I mention that I obtained the documents for my wife and my new firm from the Count-Duke de Olivares himself *while I was a guest* at the court of Don Felipe in Madrid... It is in disarray—the court, and all who pertain. What more can I say but that you are taking a wise path separating yourselves...? However, you would be well advised not to make me regret my allegiance. Who was it that informed you of what you were to inform me last week, by the way?"

Cabrera stared at him, trying to unravel the question then said, "A representative of... a man who had also been in Spain. The chests contain funds to pay supporters. It is imperative they reach Oporto intact as soon as possible to pay followers in the north."

Ludo wondered why Leonora had been so concerned about Armando Cabrera, then how this ordinary little man had become involved in a national rebellion. Then he shrugged it away: he didn't care. Inclining his head again, he said, "Pray, continue—what exactly do you desire of me?"

"The chests to go to an address in Oporto. They will be concealed in a cargo of oriental goods—fabrics, China tea, indigo dye, spices, that sort of thing. Failure to deliver them, I have been instructed to say, will regrettably call into question your wife's *limpieza de sangre*. I'm instructed to warn you that the Inquisition is now very active in Goa... They are aware of your marriage, but your wife's family history is not affected by it, naturally—nor by what you have been telling me here. That is, I don't think the documents you have shown me will influence them, *if your enterprise for us goes awry*."

"Them?" Ludo asked, although he already knew the answer.

"The Inquisition in Goa."

Ludo tucked the document for Leonora into his doublet, saying, "Ah, *them*. Yes, I have been warned—by a Vatican agent, as it happens." Cabrera vacillated, unsure how to respond. "Tell me what I need to know," Ludo continued, "and I'll go directly to the port to arrange for your special cargo to be loaded—to ensure the enterprise does not go 'awry'. Will someone inform you personally once the delivery has been made?"

"They will." Cabrera pulled a sheet of paper from a drawer and handed it to Ludo, who glanced at an address and a ship's manifest. "And the Green Moon? The house with the green shutters? I was told to go there to collect the goods."

"Ah, no, that has changed; there is now more than one... erm... Please arrange for your crew to collect what needs to be delivered from the warehouse stated there,"—Cabrera indicated the piece of paper. "Tomorrow, if you are ready."

"The day after tomorrow," Ludo said. "I have matters to deal with regarding my ship. In the meantime, can you make arrangements for me to meet the Duke of Braganza?"

"The Duke himself? No, sir! He is away on his estate, hunting, I believe. It is the Duchess who is here. You could possibly speak to her. She is in fact the dynamic force behind our movement."

Ludo tapped the fingers of his right hand on Cabrera's desk. He had no objection to 'dynamic' women—on the contrary, he was attracted to them... Alina, Leonora... his own mother fell into the category, but when it came to political and fiscal matters it was the men's names—not their wives'—that went on documents; the men, not their wives, who made final decisions. Suddenly he was sick of it all: the documents and complications, the conniving and conspiracies. Looking away, he said, "Actually, thank you very much but it won't be necessary for me to see either the Duke of Braganza, or his duchess." Then he turned back. "Was there anything else you were informed to inform me of, or may I go and arrange the loading of my carrack?"

"That's all for now, Don Ludovico. Except, a personal matter, which I feel obliged to communicate for my late brother's sake." Cabrera's voice had dropped to a whisper.

Ludo waited. The small man took a deep breath then straightened up and said, "Your marriage to Dona Leonora—it has put her at risk."

"I can't see how: I married her precisely to protect her, and her late father's business."

"Then you would do well to return to Goa at the earliest opportunity. From what I was told last week..." Stepping around his desk, Cabrera opened his door.

Ludo stayed where he was, waiting for Cabrera to finish what he was saying. When nothing was forthcoming, he said, "Are you threatening Dona Leonora in my absence? She told me you would."

"Me? Not me, Don Ludovico. And I'm sure if you fulfil this commission as directed neither you—nor she—has anything to fear. Nevertheless, I was advised to warn you. Oh, and yes, I must offer felicitations on the safe delivery of your son."

Ludo schooled his features. "Your intelligencers are more rapid than mine in this respect, Don Armando."

"A healthy boy to inherit your fine business, I am told. If he and his mother survive the climate and rigours of living in Portuguese Roman Catholic Goa, of course."

Chapter 35

Toxo was waiting in the low-ceilinged tavern where he and Ludo had first met: where sharp white wine seared teeth and greasy bacon congealed on trenchers, but where tavern-keeper and drinkers alike were silent when questioned. Ludo ducked into the interior then waited for his eyes to adjust to the gloom. Bandy-legged Toxo was leaning against a pillar smoking an American clay pipe, watching a game of cards and the door as well. He nodded to Ludo and moved to an empty bench.

"We've got an interesting little cargo job," Ludo said.

"*Interesting* meaning it'll make us some money or do we have to run under Dutch guns again?"

"Nothing like that, but once we've completed the job we'll need to stay out of these waters for a good while."

"Not sure about that. Javi and me've got a livin' to make, remember."

"I know, and I have a strong alternative for you." Ludo waited for two cups to be filled by a wench with a jug. "In the meantime, and with that in mind, it would be better to change the carrack's name and flag. A neat refit and a bit of disguise should serve, all right. I was thinking of putting her under the English Union flag—you can sail her in and out of Vigo under that, and besides, you'll be carrying cargo for a firm in Plymouth."

"Will we?" Toxo murmured doubtfully. "I thought you said *Magdalena* was ours now—me and Javi."

Ludo hadn't expected this. "Yes and no. I meant she was yours *for the use of*—but listen to what I propose then decide. I can offer you a lucrative business transporting cargo for a Spaniard in England after we're finished this task. You won't lose by it."

"You talking about losing money or losing ourselves? I'm not interested in your adventures risking life and limb, not anymore. I've taken to being at home, see. Being back with the wife, seeing the little ones growing up..."

Ludo drank some wine. "Right," he said. "I'll go back to what I promised: you can keep the *Magdalena* for your use when I don't need her. But I need her now. It's a simple job of loading a cargo here in Lisbon and taking it to Oporto, then sailing to Plymouth. After you leave me and some cargo there the *Magdalena*'s yours once again—'for the use of' and under your Spanish flag."

Toxo grunted a grudging assent then asked, "What's to be loaded?"

Once Cabrera's mixed cargo of suspiciously heavy wicker baskets, wooden crates and watertight bales was stowed in the *Magdalena*'s empty holds, Toxo and Javi took her out of the Tagus on a freshening wind. Once out of the estuary, they joined Ludo below deck and began opening the cargo.

First they opened a crate of peppers, then a crate containing lacquer. Neither contained what Ludo was seeking. A heavy wooden crate labelled 'dyestuffs', however, contained sawdust and the domed coffer from the house of the green shutters. It was securely locked.

Javi examined the mechanism and went back to his cabin for his collection of bodkins—useful for repairing sails and thick clothing, and picking locks. Eventually the right implement was found and the coffer opened, revealing exactly what Ludo had been expecting, or at least hoping for: a fortune in mixed coins. "Put that coffer over there," he said, pointing to a pile of tarpaulin.

"You going to keep it?" Toxo asked.

"I am."

"All of it?"

"All of it."

Toxo sniffed. "Wouldn't it be safer to just take *some* of the money and put the coffer back where we found it?"

"That would be deceitful," Ludo said, moving to another crate.

Toxo opened a mouth of blackened teeth and roared with laughter. Javi grinned and set about locking the coffer, which proved impossible.

"Not to worry," Ludo said. "We'll use this one first. I'll keep it in my cabin, though. No point leaving it in temptation's way."

Inside a suspiciously heavy tea crate, also containing sawdust, they found a smaller wooden coffer full to the brim with bright new pieces of eight.

"*Esto vale un Potosí,*" muttered Toxo, rifling his hand through the silver coins. "*Reales de a ocho...* A man could live well for the rest of his days on this."

"And spend it anywhere from the Levant to Goa to Amsterdam: I know of no single place that won't accept Spanish pieces of eight," Ludo added, closing the lid and debating whether to keep it or not; debating whether to do as Toxo suggested and take only a portion. But he'd be hounded for a percentage as fast and far as the money box itself. "Put it under the tarpaulins with the other one," he said. "We'll unload it in Plymouth."

Slowly, they located eight more of the smaller coffers and took four; leaving the remaining four in their camouflaged, protective bales and baskets.

Laying the tarpaulin over their loot, Ludo said, "The first one for *Tulip*'s voyage back to Goa, then one for you and one for Javi, one for Marcos, to pay him for his troubles, one for my wife and child."

Toxo exchanged a look with Javi, then nodded and wordlessly set about organising the containers back as they were in the hold. Speaking to Ludo without looking at him, Toxo said, "So—why are you doing this exactly? I mean, you don't have to tell us, but as we're involved we'll catch it just the same if *they* catch us—just so we know what we're being nabbed for?"

Ludo stood as straight as the low-ceilinged deck would permit and studied the wiry, no-nonsense Galician. "I was told to deliver it all to an address in Oporto."

"Yes," said Toxo, keeping his eyes averted, "and you're not going to. I worked that bit out for meself."

"That's all we're doing, more or less. Hopefully the recipients don't know exactly what's in the cargo, but even if they do—we'll be out of reach. Don't ask me who we're doing it for, because it won't do you any good knowing that. Let's just say Ludo da Portovenere is more than a delivery boy. It's something of a parting gesture—to show I can, and I am not afraid, and that I don't take orders from people I don't respect."

"Riddles," Toxo grunted.

Before they climbed back onto the open deck Toxo had another go. "So why not keep *all* the boxes? Might as well be hung for a sheep as a lamb."

"No, in this I am following the lead of the eminent Vatican cleric who arranged the nonsense: keeping one foot in each camp and fulfilling conflicting orders at the same time. I'll let some go to help the new Portugal, but not all of it. I promised a certain statesman in Madrid to impede the rebellion as best I could. By keeping those coffers for us I am fulfilling that part of my orders—on my terms, you see."

"No, I don't see, but don't try to explain. Javi and me don't need to know nothing about clerics and statesmen."

Without consulting Ludo, the brothers-in-law climbed back up on deck. As Ludo joined them in the open air, Toxo said, "Right, so we deliver the cargo to a warehouse in Oporto—then what?" He sniffed and looked over the gunwale. "Weather's changing; we're in for a squall tonight, then proper autumn storms'll be setting in—remember what happened when we sailed this coast this time last year."

"That was how it all began," Ludo muttered. "If I hadn't opened that letter José would still be alive."

Toxo and his ever-silent brother-in-law exchanged glances again. "Your cabin boy? What happened?" Toxo asked.

Ludo nodded. "It's a long story, long and complicated."

"It would be," Toxo grunted. Then, seeing Ludo's distress, he said, "Tell us what's after Oporto—what's next?"

"We sail for Plymouth. I introduce you to a merchant there, Marcos Alonso, who needs cargo moving between the Mediterranean and Plymouth and maybe the Thames estuary. You can decide if you want the work or not. But you'll keep this old tub if you do, and you can sail in and out of Vigo, as long as she's got another name."

"We don't speak English."

"Marcos Alonso is Spanish—it's his import business."

Toxo sniffed. "Javi can decide with me later. What you going to do?"

"I pay a man I know for rounding up my cargo to take back to India—wool, pots and pans, that sort of thing, and I take *Tulip* back to Goa."

"Back to your wife and child?" asked Toxo quietly.

"Via the Barbary Coast, yes."

"You're never stopping in Salé again! Jesus, Ludo, you never do things the easy way, do you?"

"Is there an easy way back to Goa? I was told only one in three ships ever make it there and back again—or was that outward bound only?"

Toxo pulled a face. "*We* wouldn't go back—but *under the circumstances* I s'pose you've got to. Wife and kiddy, did you say?"

"Yes, I've got to go, and as fast as possible, after this," Ludo replied, ignoring Toxo's fishing. "I need to get back before them —"

"Them?"

"Various others, but one in particular—or his agents, anyway. I thought you didn't want to know."

"Oh, sorry I asked," Toxo grunted.

"Come on, more sail, and get us in and out of Oporto, then round Finisterre as fast as you can—I've never wanted to be in English waters so much in my life." Ludo suddenly turned back to Toxo. "That barrel of indigo, keep it back. I'm going to have *Tulip*'s sails dyed midnight blue."

"Blue now, like us. I always wondered why they were wine red."

"It was a fancy I had, for the colour of a dress a woman was wearing when I found her—saved her, as it happens, from the slave market. You should change back to white when you change *Magdalena*'s name. Just in case they're following me."

"Who?" Toxo insisted.

"Interested parties—your *Santa Inquisición* among them."

Javi crossed himself rapidly. Toxo rolled his eyes. "Now he tells us."

Leaving them, Ludo collected his spyglass and made his way to the poop deck to see who or what was following in their wake. As he leaned over the railing, catching the Atlantic spray but keeping his spyglass under his arm, out of harm's way, he calculated how long it would take for whoever was receiving the coffers to realise what had been taken. Two days, if they knew exactly what had been sent; longer, if not. Either way, the *Magdalena* needed to get to Plymouth as fast as she could.

Chapter 36

Plymouth, England, late October, 1640

As she entered the house where Marcos lived with his wife's family, Alina was assaulted by various smells: turnips cooking in the kitchen; cats—the smell of cat was everywhere; and, as they ascended the stairs to the living rooms and chambers, there was the distinct sweet odour of breast milk and a baby's napkins. By the time she reached the new mother's bedchamber she was gagging into a handkerchief. Nobody noticed. All eyes, all attention was focussed on the baby in a pretty wicker crib.

Marcos pulled down the soft blankets and gazed at his new daughter. Alina tutted; the child's wispy hair was the right texture, but it was dark brown. "I suppose we could use the hair of a puppy, or a baby goat," she said, thinking aloud but unfortunately in English.

Joanna's eyes rounded in horror. Obviously fearing witchcraft, she said, "A goat? Whatever for?"

"It's all right, my dear," Marcos said. "I believe the baroness wants to make a special poppet for our little girl."

Alina turned and gave Marcos a weak smile of appreciation for quick thinking then made an effort to coo over the crib to make up for her *faux pas*. Moving to speak to Joanna in the vast, over-ornate tester bed, she managed to make meaningless conversation about babies before leaving the young parents alone together for the first time in months.

Mrs Beale, who had been hovering at the chamber door, led her through to the family living room and offered her refreshments, but she begged to be allowed outdoors. "I have a fancy to see the other new houses in your street—this has become such an elegant part of the city now... And the harbour, I do so love a harbour," she added grasping at any excuse to get out of the cat piss and baby pee-smelling, house. "My maid is in the kitchen. She will accompany me; I shall be quite safe."

"Well, if you're sure..." Mrs Beale looked suitably shocked, but a baroness was a baroness, and Alina was soon out of doors, with Fanny tagging behind.

Leaning against some new railings, gazing out across the busy water scene at pinnaces and gigs ferrying men and cargo to and from merchant vessels in the sound, Alina wondered where Ludo might be. *One of the ships out there could be the Tulip,* she thought, then dismissed it because she had no wish to see the *Tulip* or her owner and fall back into her personal sea of despair. She had turned Ludo against her forever, there was no point remembering their happy moments together.

Except Ludo was here, she could feel it. He was nearby, busy organising his vessel and cargo, conning cut-rate terms out of some unsuspecting tradesman or, more likely, conning the virtue out of some unsuspecting maiden. Ludo didn't pay for whores, that she knew. She tried to conjure lurid images of Ludo as a depraved monster, and failed. As much as she tried to hate him, she couldn't. *Perhaps... perhaps if I could see him one more time—explain why I cannot be with him, make him understand... perhaps then he will at least... What? What is*

*there for us? I should go home to Crimphele and forget him—
again.*

Turning back to the Beales' tall, wood-framed house, Alina quickened her step, anxious to get Marcos away from his wife and on the road to Crimphele as he had promised when they had paid off the female giant Milagros in Santander.

"Home to Crimphele," she repeated aloud, grabbing Fanny by the neck. "Come on, we've a good way to go yet, and then I have a very special journey to London!"

Within two hours they were in one of Edward Beale's carriages crossing the Tamar on the horse ferry in driving rain. Winter was setting in early and by the time they turned into the lane leading up to the Tudor fortress called Crimphele it was well into the night and Alina was chilled to the bone.

As the horses clattered into the courtyard the rain stopped and a pale moon briefly lit the soft beige stone of the old house before a cloud swallowed it. A motley pack of dogs and hounds surged out from their resting places, barking at the horses and running round and round the carriage in excitement. Some subsided as Marcos got out of the coach, recognising his scent, but then they went into a frenzy of tail wagging and whining as he helped Alina to alight. Fanny stayed inside, evidently afraid of dogs as well.

Alina leaned back in and pulled Fanny out like a rag doll from a toy box. "You can go now," she said with a wave of the hand. "Come back in two days. I will instruct the steward to pay your wages and possibly give you a reference, depending on how I feel. Now go."

Fanny pulled her single bag from the carriage and scuttled towards the servants' quarters over the stables.

Marcos watched her. "Poor child, she was out of her depth."

"Which is why she'll be no use to me in my new role with the queen," Alina countered.

In the carriage lamplight Alina saw Marcos raise an eyebrow but ignored it. He made no other comment on the matter, only saying, "It's seems quieter than when I worked here." But as he spoke a squeal of pleasure burst from a small boy covered in straw coming out of the stables.

"Mama!"

Hurrying after him came the boy's father carrying something white. He stopped in his tracks then dashed over to Marcos and deposited a fat puppy in his hands.

Alina gathered her son in her arms and lifted him in the air, then together with the child fell into her husband's open arms. When she finally remembered Marcos was with her, she took her husband by the hand to greet him properly, the child clinging to her neck on her other arm.

"Marcos has brought me safely home, Thomas."

"Our good, faithful Marcos," Thomas said, clapping the bigger man on the back. "Thank you, thank you a thousand times. We are a happy family once more. Ah, yes, you've got the puppy... What are we going to call her, Tommy?"

"'Milky', because she's all white like milk," the child replied.

"Hmm, not really an appropriate name for a sheep dog—she will have to work for her living, you know. Perhaps we should wait another week or two and see what she's going to be like before we choose a name," Thomas said diplomatically, eyeing Alina with a warm smile.

Suddenly remembering who Marcos was, the child flung out his chubby arms shouting, "Marcos! Marcos!"

Alina passed him to Marcos then remembered it was nearly midnight. "Thomas, is anything wrong? What are you doing up at this time of night with the little one?"

"Ask him—he wouldn't sleep, said the puppies were going to die of cold or some such nonsense."

"And you went along with it? Let him drag you out of bed?"

"Yes. I'll explain later. Come, we should go indoors." Thomas began to walk towards the main door and Alina followed. Marcos, back into his old Crimphele steward role, was giving the driver instructions on where to stable the horses and where he could sleep for the night.

As Thomas opened the door and stood back to allow Alina entry, he said, "Tommy will be more settled now you're home at last."

Alina halted: this was not part of her plans. But then, entering the old great hall she had a distinct and grateful sense of coming home. She hadn't been sure it was the right thing to do; she had been tempted to make her way directly to London, but she was glad she was here—and that was a good thing.

Marcos—holding the child, and the child holding the puppy—joined her by the fireplace, its embers still pink and warm enough to encourage the dogs from outside to settle here instead of the stables as they used to do before she first arrived.

Alina put a hand on Marcos's arm. "This is what it will be like for you now; a wife and a lovely daughter. You have a home and family, and a whole new business in England, too. Isn't that wonderful? And a fluffy, white puppy; look at all those wispy tail hairs."

"Habsburg breeding, obviously," Marcos grinned. "How much do we snip off?"

Alina laughed and kissed his cheek. "Thank you for bringing me home," she said. Then, gathering her son into her arms and sniffing his soft hair, she whispered, "You smell of stables and straw," and tried to banish an unwanted memory.

Next morning, lying warm and relaxed in bed, Alina defied Marcos's advice about staying silent on the matter of the Queen of Spain's little boxes and told her husband all about it. "I need you to help me put them back together again, so it looks like they haven't been touched," she said and began explaining how ignorant *bandoleros* had scratched the wood. "We can wrap them in the vellum you keep for your journals, but how do we forge new seals?"

Thomas, who had remained silent throughout her tale, said, "I'll do my best, but I don't think we ought to even try to make new seals."

"No, it will look suspicious," Alina replied, "as if I have been peeking." Snuggling her head into Thomas's shoulder, she then said slowly, "You will come with me, won't you, back to Whitehall to deliver them?"

"If that is what you want, although I have been trying to avoid my duties for Tommy's sake. Of late Prince Charles has become more interested in my natural history journals and has begun investigations of his own, which I have tried to encourage that he may work independently. But it is better that we stay here, Alina. These are difficult times; we are not as safe as we were..."

Alina wasn't listening, wrapped up as she was in her own parcel of future royal favours. "There is something else, Thomas, something of very great importance. I have a special letter from Isabel of Spain for her sister." She pulled from under her pillow the crumpled letter that had travelled in her bodice.

"It's a bit wrinkled for a royal message," Thomas laughed, not taking her seriously.

"I know, but I've had to keep it hidden in my clothes for weeks. I sleep with it under my pillow. You can't imagine the treachery, the intrigues that go on in Don Felipe's court. It's awful; you cannot trust a single person. They are all playing double games, saying one thing, doing another."

"That's precisely why I prefer to be here rather than in London—or Oxford, now. That's become a hot pot of intrigue as well. Can you not send the letter by courier, now you're England? I really think we should stay here."

Seeing how reluctant her husband was to return to London, Alina sat up, letting her golden hair fall over her shoulders. Brushing it out of her face, she said, "Thomas, this letter... it is very important. I mean, it will *change* the future of England. It's vital that I put it into Henrietta Maria's hands, and I'd like you to be with me when I do it."

Thomas regarded her seriously. "Why?"

"Because it will change your future, too. The queen has already promised me I shall be made a lady-of-the-bedchamber, but for sure you will receive great benefits and *promotion* as well."

"I very much doubt that. London is in turmoil. Known Catholics are being targeted openly in the street. There are rumours that Charles's chief advisor, Strafford, is going to be sent to the Tower—or worse. If that happens, all Catholics are at risk—and receiving 'benefits' from the queen will not be to our advantage, believe me."

"But Strafford is a royal favourite. Who can send him to the Tower of London? He's more important than anyone after King Charles."

"Parliament can."

"But they are common men—what gives them the right or the power to do that?"

"Common*ers*," Thomas corrected her, pushing open the bed curtains, "and Members of Parliament elected by the British people. That gives them the right and the power to make decisions, and act against those they see as traitors."

"Traitors! How can Strafford be a traitor when he has been loyal to the king all his life?"

"That is his downfall. The queen has gone too far, and ordinary people have had enough. All these years she's been conspiring to make England a Catholic country again... it's already caused a religious war with Scotland. We need to be very careful, Alina," Thomas said, getting out of the bed and walking barefoot to the washbasin.

"But I *must* get this letter and the gifts to Henrietta Maria." Alina sat up and pushed the covers off her. Noticing how cold the room was, she asked, "Why doesn't the maid build up your fire at night anymore?"

"See, we need the mistress of the house here, not in London," Thomas replied, splashing water over his face and grabbing a linen towel. "Is it *really* that important, a letter from one sister to another?"

"Yes! And don't underestimate these sisters; they could manage their kingdoms better than their useless royal husbands, given the chance. Isabel would bring peace to Spain and—with what is in this letter—Henrietta Maria will resolve the stupid religious problem in this damp, grey country of yours!" Alina slumped back on the pillow and gave a great huff of annoyance.

"You are angry at me, but I am only telling you the situation you have returned to."

Alina repented her mood; it was unfair to be angry with Thomas.

Coming back to the bedside, Thomas said, "What bothers me, Alina, is that if you are named a lady-of-the-bedchamber you cannot be here with Tommy and me—ever, or at least almost never."

Alina wanted to cry: that which had made her so positive, so willing to rush back to England had turned sour. "I think, knowing the relevance of the letter, Her Majesty will ask for you to be made a viscount."

"A viscount? Pff! And that is what you want?"

"I did, but you have made me wonder now. If I give her the letter and ask her to release me, would that please you more? Thomas, I don't want to make you unhappy." She put her arms out to him and he sat on the side of the high mattress.

"And how will you persuade her to release you," he asked, "now that you are so important in her scheming?" He smiled, but his tone was deadly serious.

"It's more than mere scheming!" Alina turned and stared at the window. Sunlight showed where the leaded panes needed cleaning. The housekeeping had slipped in her long absence. She really ought to be at Crimphele.

Running rapidly through her choices, that weren't choices, only mere options—a matter of choosing the lesser evil—Alina murmured, "I could tell her I was pregnant, that it is a difficult pregnancy and I need to be here—she won't want a fat, ugly woman gracing her chamber. I've seen her turn away pregnant ladies-in-waiting before, even when she's the size of a house herself."

"So we go to London, you deliver the letter and the little boxes, and we return here—together."

"If that is what you wish, yes."

"It is to keep you safe, Alina. You are Spanish and too many people know that."

Alina shrugged. "If you say so."

"Well, if that is the case," Thomas said, pulling back the covers and climbing back into bed, "we should make your little deception a definite possibility."

Cocooned by closed curtains in the late-morning comfort of the act of love, Alina studied the mousy brown hair of her husband's head as he ran his lips over her breasts, marvelling at their roundness. He made a gentle nip and Alina jumped. It hurt. "Sorry," he muttered and moved down over her stomach to nuzzle between her legs. Involuntarily, Alina's mind wandered back to her still aching breast. "Oh," she gasped. Thomas, interpreting the words otherwise, pushed his tongue deeper. Alina ran a hand over her breasts and belly, and remembered her reaction to the smells in Mrs Beale's house; at how her moods switched from anger to tearfulness in the space of seconds; how she had blamed her missed courses on the events of the royal masquerade and the long journey. Closing her eyes, she knew there was no deception in her plan to be released by the queen: she was already pregnant. But now her husband was inside her, kissing her cheeks, her lips, her ears. He loved her; she loved him. It would be all right.

Chapter 37

By the time Alina was dressed and downstairs the men had already taken their breakfast and Marcos was in the courtyard saying goodbye to Thomas, anxious to get back to his own family. As Marcos was giving little Tommy a hug, a rider trotted into the courtyard.

"Letter for the Baron Metherall," he declared, jumping from his sweating horse.

Thomas took the letter, saying, "Thank you. Please leave your horse in the stable and take some refreshment before you go."

Marcos went to Thomas's side. "If it is urgent I can take the reply to Plymouth and send it by mail from there."

Thomas opened the seal and unfolded the letter. Taking a quick look, he said, "We'd better go inside," and led the way back into the great hall. The message was brief and to the point, and from his sister's husband, writing from Truro.

The King has summoned Parliament. Francis Windebank is accused of sympathising in another popish plot and likely to be taken. Strafford is said to be for the Tower, if not the block. Puritans and the Commons are looking for excuses to accuse more. Brother, take GREAT CARE.

"Francis Windebank is Kit's father," Marcos told Alina. Then explained to Thomas, "We met him in Spain."

"Is that why Kit's in Spain?" Alina asked. "Oh, but that is good—he and Hopton were on our side after all. Why didn't they tell us?"

"On your side?" Thomas demanded. "Who is talking of sides? There will be no taking of sides here until—and only if—I am forced to raise a trained band."

Alina looked at him. "I don't understand, what is happening?"

"I've been trying to tell you, people like us are being targeted. The new Parliament is taking the Puritan path and those of us who have been at court and favoured by the queen will suffer for it." Thomas said gravely. "The king and Henrietta Maria have made too many enemies."

"But why are they warning *you*, Thomas?" Alina demanded. "You're not even in London—you are just what they call a country squire."

"Rather more than that, my dear. I am also he who, if you remember, was called to serve the queen in Oxford when Tommy was born; who has translated a Latin text taken from a Catholic monastery for her; who has been tutoring the king's sons and—this is what I fear—was called upon four years ago to join a special 'Catholic court' by Lord Rundell. This is why I don't want you to go back to London. Send your blasted letter and gifts with a courier. Use the man who's just arrived, for heaven's sake."

"I can't. I promised I would put them in the queen's hands myself. I promised the Queen of Spain—how can I go against that?"

Marcos looked at Thomas, then back at Alina. "She is a foreigner," Marcos said. "Surely they can't accuse her of anything if she's a foreigner."

"Exactly—well thought, Marcos—I am Spanish!" Alina cried, slapping her hands together and startling the dogs that had sneaked around them. "I'm a foreigner, so they can't touch me without causing a diplomatic problem with Spain. I shall take the packages and letters to London as I have been asked and nobody can prevent that. I am an emissary from Spain."

"For heaven's sake, Alina, that is enough! This is not Spain and Spain has never been popular here. They tried to invade us in the days of Queen Bess, remember."

"That was in the last century. How can it affect me? How can ordinary men, *commoners* as you call them, have such power, anyway? The king is mad to let it happen."

"Therein lies the problem, my dear, but King Charles has had to call Parliament to get funds and this parliament cares nothing about diplomatic relations with Spain." Turning from Alina to Marcos, Thomas continued, "Can you wait while I pack my bags? I will take these blasted Spanish treasures to London myself. I am involved in no plot that I know of, although I wouldn't be surprised if Rundell has my name to a list without me knowing about it. I should be safe enough." Looking at Alina again, he said, "If I am able, I'll be back here for Christmas."

"Thomas, no! It was *I* who was commissioned." Alina straightened her back, preparing for a verbal fight. "Queen Isabel gave me the commission, not you."

"But you are indisposed, my dear. You contracted a fever on your return to England and must not travel in winter weather. Besides," he added knowingly, "you are with child, are you not?"

Alina gave an inward gasp: had he guessed? His voice was determined, deeper and more certain than Alina had ever heard. The small boy now in Marcos's arms began to wail. Alina took him into her arms and hugged him. Holding her child, she was forced to take stock of what Thomas was trying to tell her. That, and her condition. She decided to give in. Leaning towards Thomas, she kissed his cheek. She was going to lose a prestigious position in the court, but she had a fine new husband in its place.

And a quiet voice in her head said: *You won't be free to return to court until after your lying-in anyway.* That same voice reminded her that another night with her husband would be providential. Letting her shoulders relax, she looked at Thomas and smiled her special honeyed smile.

Putting down her small son, Alina said, "Go and check the puppies, *cielo*, and mama will come and see them in a moment or two." The child ran off on his strong little legs and Alina felt a tug of love go with him. Then she turned to Marcos. "Could you bear to be away from your Joanna one more night, *please*? You will be with her for the rest of your life now, but I may not see Thomas again for at least a month—or longer. Besides, we must equip him properly if he is to attend court. He can't go in his country clothes, can he?"

Marcos nodded. "I suppose so."

"Excellent—you are the kindest man I know, after Thomas, of course. You had better warn Mr and Mrs Beale when you get back. They are Catholics, too, are they not?"

"Mr Beale saw the way the wind was turning before I left for Spain; good Anglicans they are now."

"And you?" Alina asked.

Marcos shrugged. "I was educated by monks, but honestly it makes no difference to me. I bend my knee in a Protestant church of a Sunday as we're instructed, although my mother would flay me for it: needs must when the devil drives, as the English say.”

“Indeed, they do,” Thomas sighed. “Right, I must go up to my study, write a reply for my brother-in-law in Truro, then I must pack. One day I ought to hire a proper manservant.” Marcos stepped back, hands in the air. “No,” Thomas laughed, “you have risen too high for that status now. Thank you for waiting for me, though.”

Marcos grinned then said, “But we leave tomorrow, first thing in the morning, all right?”

“Agreed.” Thomas gave a small salute and strode into the house.

Marcos walked over to the Beales’ carriage driver and explained what was happening.

Alina, who had been half listening to the two men’s conversation, muttered ‘needs must when the devil drives’ to herself. *And where is the devil now? Has he sailed for India already? Is there the tiniest possibility he might come to Crimphele...* “No! And I don’t want him to,” she said aloud.

“*Qué pasa?*” Marcos asked, coming back to her side and slipping back into their mother tongue.

“*Nada.* I was just thinking that this wasn’t the outcome I envisaged, but it will do for now.”

Marcos turned towards the stable. “Shall we inspect the puppies?”

Alina followed him, lost in thought. She had risen high, she knew the secrets of two queens, had been desired by the most powerful king in Christendom... Once her baby was born she could start again, return to Whitehall and remind the queen who it was that had brought the letter arranging the next royal matrimony and the alliance of two nations a thousand miles across land and sea.

As if picking up her thoughts, Marcos said, "You don't seem too disappointed."

"I have achieved too much to be entirely disappointed. I have achieved preference, been favoured by queens with their trust—that is prestige, Marcos, although I didn't imagine I'd climb so high only to come back to being a country wife lost in the middle of nowhere." She gave a brief sigh. "Events aren't going according to plan, that is true, and between you and me I've returned with rather more than I expected..." Marcos eyed her suspiciously and, seeing she was about to fall into a foolish revelation, Alina added quickly, "Thomas will be raised to a viscount or even a marquis one day—sooner or later. Then I can return to London and start again from a better position."

"You never give up, do you?" Marcos was only half joking.

"Why should I? I was born to be a great lady—you know that." Alina tried to lighten her tone, but she meant what she was saying.

"Oh, I know that," Marcos replied, "to my cost." After an awkward silence he said, "Ludo told me about a game with snakes and ladders. The ladders take you up to the top of the board through virtues and integrity, but snakes named 'lust', 'vanity', 'greed' and other vices pull you down so you have to start all over again."

"Lust and vanity, heaven protect us! He should sell it to the Puritans; he'd make a fortune," Alina snapped and pushed ahead into the gloom of the warm stables so Marcos should not see her face.

Chapter 38

Plymouth, November, 1640

Ludo drank in the sharp odour of a cold sea, felt the chill air on the back of his neck and clamped his old black leather hat down tightly as a freezing wind buffeted him from behind. "Pushing me away, are you?" he laughed.

Captain Guthrie looked up, "Sorry, sir, I missed that."

"Thinking aloud, Guthrie, but it'll be good to be back at sea."

"We're in for a difficult few weeks; sailing down to Africa in December will be tough on the crew."

"I'm paying them well enough for it. I was surprised how many signed back on, though. You have done well with that, Guthrie. And this time we have a full complement—well done for that as well. There'll be a bonus for you if we all arrive in Goa in one piece."

"Your pay and conditions beat the Royal Navy's hands down, sir. There's press gangs doing the rounds every week in this part of the world, and not a few have signed on as the lesser of two evils, so we'll likely lose a few in the Canaries, if we put in there."

"We won't be. We're putting in to the Moroccan coast—Salé. If they want, they can jump ship to turn Turk and join the Barbary Rovers." Ludo watched Guthrie's already pale face blench. "As I was saying, I'm truly glad to have you running my ship again." Ludo clapped his captain on the back, nearly sending him over the edge of the quay. "Right, into the pinnace and let's get aboard once and for all."

As they were rowed out to the now-laden galleon called the *Tulip*, where the crew were ready and waiting to raise her new indigo sails, Ludo took a last look at England. He would return, one day, if he survived the voyage, for his licence to trade from King Charles came with an obligation, but it wouldn't be for a very long time.

A brisk nor' westerly sent them flying toward the self-declared city state of Salé. Captain Guthrie set the crew on alert, every able hand armed from *Tulip*'s new and comprehensive stock of modern weapons and old-fashioned cutlasses, including the ones they had acquired off Zanzibar on their previous voyage. The crew were given strict instructions to fire only to repel boarders. Excited by the prospect of action, various lads—some holding muskets longer than their arms that they evidently had no idea how to fire—set themselves nervously along the gunwales; Older deckhands wielding short swords and pirate cutlasses arranged themselves around the masts—even up the masts. Midshipmen, quarter deck officers and the captain himself pushed new pistols purchased in England into their belts and strode about looking this way and that. If corsairs dared to board the *Tulip* they'd have a fight on their hands.

Ludo didn't believe it would happen. He said as much a dozen times, but Guthrie, and many of the crew knew about corsairs; how they ran in and raided villages from waiting galleasses, how they rammed vessels at sea with their specially prepared prows and threw grappling hooks so they could swarm over gunwales like marauding apes. When Ludo realised the depth of their hatred he gave up trying to calm their fears. If Murat Reis had died from the wounds he'd acquired escaping the Knights of Malta, Ludo had lost his protector, and the tall Spanish-built galleon would make a valuable prize.

As soon as they dropped anchor, Ludo called for volunteers to accompany him to the souk so they could load the pinnace with fresh fruit and vegetables. Two cabin boys eager for life and two young midshipmen anxious to show their worth were ferried into the port on the west bank of the Bou Regreg estuary.

As the pinnace reached the quay and moored beside a corsair galleass, Ludo looked about him, trying to guess the mood of the place, identify if there had been changes. The human cargo being unloaded from the galleass caught his eye. The corsairs must have sailed far north, for the captured men were tall and strong, red-bearded and burly in their sheepskin jerkins, un-cowed by their conditions or what was to come. The girls, of whom there were many, clasped woollen shawls around their shoulders; most were white-blonde and well built; they'd fetch a good price in the slave market. Many, Ludo knew, would go inland to the sultan, although some of the stronger males would spend the rest of their lives at the oars. It had never bothered him before, except when he had saved Alina—but that was different.

As he climbed onto the quay, three or four fair-skinned mothers carrying babies and a few heavily pregnant women were jostled into a group and led away, not unkindly, by a mixed gang of mulattos.

"Are they for the market as well?" Ludo asked, suddenly wanting to pay their price and set them free.

A black sub-Saharan team-leader pulled a face and ignored him; a northerner turned Turk—a Fleming, perhaps—answered him. "The babes will be taken, but they'll not suffer. Some of the women may be ransomed and get home."

"Without their babies?"

"Little ones are taken to be raised by the sultan. It's not such a bad fate; some rise high."

The team-leader was eager to move on and Ludo let them go.

"Do they all go for slaves?" a Devonshire boy asked, staring after them.

"Most, yes, not all. Look, here is the souk."

They passed through a tall entrance and the lads all went quiet: here was a market such as they had never seen before. Ludo led them through a labyrinth of carts and ground level displays on mats offering everything from ochre-coloured cumin, red- and blue-coloured cups, brass candlesticks, carrots and beetroot, geometric-patterned jugs and leather-thong sandals. He stopped at a stall whose odour brought the boys to a halt. The tang of bright oranges, the musty fragrance of fig cakes flavoured with anis, the sharpness of fresh lemons beside succulent, sweet raisins, plump as thumbs and begging to be eaten. More than one hand sneaked out and snatched a delicacy.

"Later," Ludo laughed. "Let me buy them first, then you can have your share, but leave enough for your companions or I'll tell them what you took before they even clapped eyes on the goods."

Ludo purchased fruit and sacks of vegetables, trays of sweet almond cakes and pastries, and told the lads to take their hired laden donkey train down to the quay and load *Tulip's* pinnace as best they could on their own, to avoid losses—and be sure to return the donkeys to their owner or there'd be trouble. Slapping one of the Devonshire lads on the back, he said, "There you are; a feast for growing youths, and extra rations to sweeten the next stage of the voyage, because we might not see land for fifty days or more, and a happy Christmas for all the Christians aboard."

Wandering away from the food market into the narrow aisles of the souk, wilfully delaying what he feared to find, Ludo paused to talk with perfume vendors, ascertaining their sources of musk and the prices currently being paid to Turkish suppliers, taking his time to discuss the virtues of obtaining solidified musk over the liquid form and securing a few orders for both. He dawdled on through the goldsmith's alley, recalling the hours he had spent as a boy studying how brooches, necklaces and bangles were made and sold; then on to the fabric section, reaching out to touch bright taffetas and vibrant silks, and, as before, ascertaining prices and suppliers. Eventually there was little alternative but to pass through the inland gate and make his way up a steep lane of white-washed, blue-doored alleys then on up the lower part of the open hillside crowded with low-hung orange trees, bowers of late-flowering jasmine, white stephanotis and violet bougainvilleas. Everything was alive with colour, birds sang and his heart lifted. Then he reached the house of Murat Reis.

As he strolled into the outdoor patio, he paused and looked down on the sea, noting that Guthrie had taken the *Tulip* further out, but she was at anchor and at peace.

It came to him now that when he spoke of having a proper home this house was what he had in mind: a modest villa on a terraced hillside overlooking the water. The garden was crowded with unkempt rose bushes, not so very different to a place he had once visited in Cornwall. Not that that was something he chose to recall—and it didn't fit at all with what he was here to do. Setting fancy and nostalgia aside, Ludo straightened his shoulders and continued with controlled calm around the trickling central fountain to the main door.

It was opened not by a servant but by a round-faced, middle-aged *housfrau* he had never met before. She spoke to him in Dutch. "Yes?"

"I'm here to see Murat Reis." No one had ever blocked his entry before.

"Through here," the woman said, leading him into a wide room he knew well.

A strange odour hung in the air, the warm, throaty smell of old hashish overlaid with lavender or roses. An elderly, ailing, grey-faced, grey-haired Dutchman in a long woollen robe was sprawled awkwardly on a thick Turkey carpet and a pile of sheepskins. His upper body was half on, half off an over-sized cushion, as if someone had lifted him and dumped him down without thought for his comfort. That impression was incorrect, for the *housfrau* immediately set about manoeuvring the cushion and adding a crimson-tasselled pillow under his shoulders then tucking a woollen rug around his legs.

Noting Ludo's silent presence, the old man said, "So, you're here as well. Vultures landing before I'm even dead. I told her she was wasting her time if she'd come for her inheritance." He shifted his backside and feebly tossed a small cushion at the woman's retreating figure. "Here Lysbeth, you can have that..." His voice failed and he started to cough. Eventually, he managed to splutter, "You all think I've got treasure chests— buried loot... Fools."

Ludo sat down cross-legged beside him and waited. After a while, the old man said, "You're Ludo."

"I am—" Ludo bit off the word 'father', though he wanted to speak it dearly.

The Dutchman, Jan Janszoon, who had terrorised the Canaries and the Middle Sea, who had raided villages as far to the east as the Levant and up into the North Sea as far as Iceland for decades as Murat Reis, looked up and gave him a grin. "I'm going, boy, but I'm not gone yet. What've have you come for?"

"To see you. I heard about Malta. Your escape is the talk of the seven seas."

"Is it?" the old man beamed. "That makes me feel better. But it's done for me. Those knights, that dungeon—it's done for me. I'll never sail again."

Lysbeth, Janszoon's daughter by his first Dutch wife, Ludo now recalled, returned with a brass tray of sweetened orange juice. Among the bright fabrics and blue-painted walls of the high-ceilinged room she looked out of place, but the room itself was as chill and damp as the Ijsselmeer in December.

"Is there not a brazier you can bring from another room?" he asked. "There used to be braziers in winter, when I lived here."

Lysbeth glared at him with undisguised dislike. "I'll get another sheepskin," she said and left.

Ludo turned back to the old man. He had fallen asleep.

After a few minutes the woman returned with a fluffy sheepskin and placed it tenderly over her father's chest.

The old man woke. "You can say it in my hearing," he said tetchily. "Tell him, Lysbeth, I'll have no secrets here. The Knights of Malta have finished me. I'll not sail again, unless they give me a Viking funeral. I'm an old man dying and that's that."

"Not so old," Ludo countered. "Lysbeth here will bring you back to strength. Once winter is over, you'll be back on board—"

"I won't and you know it."

Ludo turned away and looked through the glazed window at the fountain in the patio, still trickling and glittering as if it were a summer's day. "You need a fire in here," he said, "like you have in Dutch houses."

"We sit round the brazier, when he can get up. I never thought to be so cold in Africa," Lysbeth answered and left the room.

After another short silence, Janszoon said, "Why are you here, Ludo?"

"I told you, to see you. I came earlier in the year, before you were back. Before Lysbeth came, I suppose. I'm going back to India now."

"Are you? There's a voyage I've never made."

"Come with me," Ludo said, and meant it. "The climate in Goa will bring you back to—"

"Life?"

"I was going to say 'health'."

"No, I've had enough. I'm going nowhere now except to my eternal rest."

Ludo rubbed his chin, smoothed back his hair, then, finding no neat way to open the conversation that would lead to the answers he needed, he stated baldly, "I've been thinking a lot about Portovenere. How you used to put in to see us, and how I used to sail with you as a boy, then when we went to live down by the souk... father."

Janszoon twisted his head, the veins of his neck like the cords of a turkey-bird strangled for the pot. "I'm not your father, Ludo."

Ludo clenched a fist; something inside him rose and fell and made him feel empty.

"Lysbeth is flesh of my flesh—look at her. My sons in Holland, they are flesh of my flesh, but you, my boy..."—he paused to cough into a silk handkerchief—"you were never mine, although damn it to hell I wish you were. You were the best of them: the quickest tongue, the best on a boat... but, no, you are not flesh of my flesh."

After a while Ludo said, "Tell me how I came to be here, Murat. Tell me all, please."

The elderly pirate leader sat up and drank some of his orange juice; a little colour came to his cheeks. "I do believe I've been dying of boredom," he chuckled, bringing on another coughing fit. "Got any brandy with you?"

"No." Ludo pushed the pillows up behind him and adjusted the sheepskins over his lap. "Better?"

"Stop treating me like an old woman," the old man snarled.

"Who, me or you? I'm no old woman," Ludo countered, causing Janszoon to smile. "Tell me, please."

Jan Janszoon who'd become Murat Reis rested his head against the fat, red satin pillow. "Your mother should have told you."

"Yes, well... She never has."

"Give me some more of that orange juice."

Ludo handed him the cup and let him drink, then Janszoon took a deep breath, wiped his mouth on his sleeve and started his tale.

"Right then, Gabriella... She was brought into the harbour after a raid. I wasn't with them, I just happened to be on the quay when she was brought off the ship. Fate, boy, never underestimate troublesome fate. So there she is, all fine figure and 'how dare you even look at me, you low-born dog'; black hair she had, masses of black hair all flying in the wind, and white, white skin and those eyes—your eyes. My, but I was taken, smitten from the first glance like a loon with a lady; the Doge of Genoa's daughter, a princess of the House of Doria, and the tastiest ransom you could dream of. What fools we men are." He paused and coughed. Ludo held the cup for him to drink but he waved it away. "I wasn't Murat Reis then, though, just plain Jan Janszoon, but I could usually get what I wanted, so I told them this woman, who's a real lady, is for me until she's paid for. She's not for the market or for slave work—except for me: I'm taking her. And I did. Took her to the house I lived in then, three rooms over a cloth merchant's in the souk, it was, you remember. She shut herself in a room, lodged something under the handle, though there wasn't a chair to sit on, and stayed there for two whole days. No food, no water, and where she peed is anybody's guess. So I got an old woman to move in and I went off on a raid—leaving a guard, of course, so as no one would take her—or worse. When I got back she was helping the old woman make bread. I never touched her until well after you were born, and then because she wanted me to."

Ludo smiled. "She told me once, I think, but I may have invented it, that I was born at sea."

"Damned near. She loved the water, came with me on quieter expeditions..."

"And night raids?"

"Night raids sometimes—she loved them. Loved the 'adventure', she called it. Sometimes she'd come with us in the daytime as well. Only nearby, though, round the Canaries. We were coming back from there the night you were born. We had the hell of it getting her back here in time. Ibn Rachid brought you into the world down on the quay."

Ludo pondered the character of the mother he was learning about. The woman who could persuade cutthroat pirates to let her on a ship and sail with them while she was with child bore no resemblance to the sad, often silent woman who would fly into a rage at the least thing when they lived in the castle above

Portovenere. Her family had tamed her in exile, and destroyed her spirit. Was that why she had been so eager for him to leave her, to let him sail with a Barbary corsair? Lost in unhappy thoughts, Ludo realised Murat Reis was speaking again.

"We lived like husband and wife—as you might remember, though you were only little—long after her ransom was paid. She wouldn't go back. Didn't want to go back to her old life, but then you got to be old enough to learn your letters and were for the *madrasa*, and she wouldn't have that. So I sailed her back to Genoa myself. Broke my heart."

Ludo waited to be sure Murat had finished then he said, "She had a husband in Genoa before she came here?"

"Erm, I'm not so sure about that. She never mentioned a husband, and she wasn't eager to get back, I can tell you. No wedding ring, though she'd got a nice few sparklers—which I never took. Soon as she got back they sent her to Portovenere in disgrace. Mind you, soon as she got word to me we found a way to be together, and that old castle suited us nicely. I could get into the harbour easily and there were no questions asked by locals. A pirate and the Doge's daughter—how the tongues clacked, but never to our faces, and never, I don't think, in a bad way. Locals were proud, in a way: you know how they are there. We saw each other regularly for a few years until they found that excuse of a man to be her husband and he got suspicious and had her watched."

"Agostino, same name as my grandfather," Ludo said. "He was a second cousin, or a poor relation, anyway. He took her on as damaged goods and never let her forget it. Payment by my grandfather or uncles for some bit of politicking, I think."

"I expect that was the way of it."

"But..." Ludo gathered words together, trying to frame questions for the answers he needed, "why did they send me away to live with you, or sail with you when I was older?"

"*They* didn't. I took you. Gabriella and I set up a raid and I took you. I heard later Agostino sent a message to say he'd pay no ransom, not that there was one."

"You took me, I wasn't sent away?"

"No."

"Why?"

"To save you."

"That raid—was to get me?" Ludo closed his eyes, remembering the day he'd been rounded up by Murat Reis on the quay in Portovenere. He had let the other boys go... *His mother hadn't sent him away—she had wanted him to go—to get away.*

The one question that he didn't need to ask was what Murat had saved him from: his Doria uncles, and the convenient stepfather... a dry, thin, bitter man, humourless with no soul... like Rogelio. The physical similarity struck him so hard he put a hand to his stomach as if landed a blow. "Agostino, my stepfather—he wasn't actually my real father, was he?"

"No! Not him. All whiskers and no breeches, that one."

"So... who was my real father, then, Murat?"

"Ask your mother. She's still alive—her sort live to be a hundred. Agostino's dead, or disposed of just as like. Go back to Portovenere and ask her."

"I used to call in to see her—sometimes. Secretly." Ludo rubbed his chin again, trying to find a name or face that fitted the man he now wanted to find, but nothing came. "I can't go back now, though, I'm going back to India," he said. "I have a wife and child of my own to see first."

"Ah, you've been caught at last, have you? Well, enjoy it boy, it's more important than any raid, or any bit of treasure you can steal or sell. Those sweet moments with my girls, your mother and that lovely creature in Málaga, that's what I remembered most in that Maltese dungeon. A woman's caress, a baby's first smile..." he shifted and started to cough, and Ludo stroked his back like a child.

"We should get him to his bed." Lysbeth's voice came from the open archway behind them. She had been listening.

Together, they gently raised the broken man then Ludo carried him to his big European bed. Lysbeth tucked his thin frame under white linen sheets and woollen blankets and Ludo sat down on the other side of the bed. As Lysbeth left the room a bony hand reached out to him.

"Closer," Murat hissed. Ludo leaned towards him. "There is treasure, boy. I left it for your mother, hoped she use it to get away—but she never did."

"In Portovenere?"

"Across the bay—Tellaro. Take mules up with you... abandoned village above the harbour. Go on up... two cottages— ruins. Two loads. New World silver and—"

"He should rest now," Lysbeth said, standing arms akimbo in the doorway.

Ludo tucked the old man's cold hand under the covers then leaned over and kissed his papery brow. "Rest now," he repeated, then in a whisper added, "Thank you, father."

The meeting with Murat Reis and their farewell, for it would be their last, kept Ludo in his cabin with a bottle of Spanish brandy until the *Tulip* was past the Cape Verde islands and heading out for Brazil to catch the trade winds. He kept to himself, pacing the top deck or dozing in his cabin until one morning a fear grasped him by the throat. He'd been calculating days since the incident with the coffers in Oporto; how long they had taken to get to England; how long he and Marcos and Mr Beale had taken to load the ship; how long he'd spent checking the holds; ensuring each member of crew knew what he was going to, despite Guthrie's fair warnings when they signed, because the last thing he wanted was a mutiny on board. When he added the two days spent in Salé he suddenly realised that before the *Tulip* could reach India Rogelio's church network could get a message overland from Aleppo to the Gulf of Oman and then to Goa, or by sea on the very same voyage he was making.

His time with Murat Reis had turned the old Ludo inside out. Not that he wasn't already half way there with losing Alina again, then what had happened to his boy José. Murat's words rang in his ears day and night—as he tried to sleep, as he stared out into the wild winter ocean: *a woman's caress, a baby's first smile...* He had been expecting some sort of reprisal for his duplicity when they sailed out of Oporto, he'd waited for the expected blow: a cannon shot like in Lisbon; damaged sheets and cut ratlines; an apparent act of God that could not be put down to a Vatican agent's extensive network or assassins—but it hadn't come. *Was that because Rogelio was targeting Leonora? That was his style.*

Every day now Ludo paced the decks, blaming himself, cursing his foolishness for playing games with a man who lacked any form of humour; for not going to see the Duchess of Braganza as ordered, for tweaking Cabrera's pathetic beard. But the deed was done—or not done—and the money from the coffers he and Toxo had taken all given away or spent, except for the domed coffer in his cabin, which would pay the captain and crew their promised bonuses for reaching Goa in one piece, and the money he'd kept back for Leonora.

All he could do was get to Goa as fast as possible, and hope it was before the Inquisition there got their instructions. He berated Guthrie for their tardiness, queried the distance they needed to sail west to catch the winds to round the Cape of Good Hope. Any little thing that might cause delay, he was on it, and yet he knew they would have to put in to land again soon, that the crew needed a respite and the ship needed scouring and re-victualling before it could cross the Indian Ocean.

As the ship rose and fell he paced the decks, the collar of his new English pea coat pulled up under his ears, his beard white with spray. Taking this route—the route the great Portuguese adventurer Vasco de Gama had first risked—they sailed out into the Atlantic to avoid the doldrums in the Gulf of Guinea, and when they were just six hundred miles off Brazil a blessed south-westerly turning wind filled *Tulip's* indigo sails and blew them back towards southern Africa, and his new Indian home.

Erratic waves gave way to vast climbing walls of ocean crashing down like the venom of hellish serpents. "Cape rollers," shouted Captain Guthrie, gripping the slippery rail as he followed in Ludo's wake along the foredeck.

Then the cold water of the South Atlantic met the warm air of Africa and they sailed into what old mariners called the Sea of Fogs and others, the Cape of Good Hope.

Good hope was all Ludo could call on as his crew fought every enemy the sea could throw at them until one morning, during a brief period of calm, a voice called from the crow's nest "Land ho!" and stormy petrels flew in battle formation across their bow. Alongside, leviathans breached, sending the spray of their magic geysers into the warming air until the ship turned landward.

They had nearly made it to a safe haven. *But for how short a time?* Ludo wondered. *Dare I let them enjoy it?*

Chapter 39

As Guthrie's crew brought the *Tulip* under the British Union flag into what they were calling Table Bay for the flat-topped mountain that towered above, Ludo took his place on the foredeck with his Dutch spyglass to study the vessels at anchor. He counted ten, six Dutch, four English; no Portuguese. It did not calm his fears: Rogelio's agents could be aboard any of them.

As bumboats set off from the shore laden with fresh fruit and delicacies mariners would be willing to pay extortionate prices for, Captain Guthrie joined him. "Your orders, sir."

"And my congratulations, Guthrie. You'll get us to Goa in one piece, I have no doubt of that."

"We can only hope so, sir, but there's the eastern fever coast before us yet, and the pirates of Zanzibar—they nearly had us on the voyage out, don't forget."

"But we were ready for them, as we shall be again. Now, we need to re-victual, correct?"

"A good clean up, too; the bow and hull are foul."

"There's not much time for that, but we should give turns of day-release shore leave, I think. No overnighters, though. Arrange mixed-rank teams to go ashore, but tell them to leave their savings aboard or the whores in those drinking huts will fleece them. A week—can you manage what needs to be done in seven days?"

Guthrie gulped. "It'll not be a thorough job, and a foul hull slows our sailing. It may not be to your advantage, sir. I know you are in haste, but—"

"No buts. A bonus to the crew if we are seaworthy again in one week's time, and if not there'll be no shore leave again before Goa."

"We risk losing crew here, sir—they'll not like it."

"Here? In that godforsaken makeshift camp over there? If this is what they prefer, they can stay. I don't like it, but it has to be. If they go, we'll sign on Hottentots. Arrange a pinnace for me as soon as you can, please—I'll go ashore with the first round. Oh, and nobody is to come aboard: no whores, and no priests! Understand?"

Guthrie's head shot up at the vehemence of his owner's voice. "I'll advise all officers, sir."

"No whores, no priests—nobody without my permission."

"And the bumboat boys? They're already here."

"Nobody!" Ludo shouted, turning on his heel.

An hour later, after hiding his portfolio of trading licences and Leonora's certificate of *limpieza de sangre* safely in a bale of English woollen undergarments in the main hold, Ludo joined the first round of mariners going ashore. Dressed in his rough, travel-stained Indian pyjamas, even some of the crew didn't recognise him.

The boat pulled up on a sandy beach and, leaving the crew to enjoy their jolly, Ludo crunched on his own over splendid shells and sharp stones in Moroccan sandals. Anxious yet reluctant, he made his way to a drinking hut to listen in to gossip and catch up with voyagers' news.

The hut was seething with whores. They often proved a better source of information than barkeepers but the type of men he sought were less likely to enjoy their favours so he moved on to an eating house and risked a trencher of root vegetables and a fearsomely tough, nameless meat. He was in luck; a young priest was at a table.

"May I join you, father?" he said in Mediterranean dockside argot.

"*Por supuesto*," the priest replied in accented Spanish. He was Galician. As they chewed through their dubious meal, the young man explained he was setting up a mission on the Cape; that he was tolerated, generally, by the Dutch, and he was offering—through the comfort of prayer and the confession box—spiritual guidance and moral support for the travails of those who set to sea. A modest man with a strong streak of determination, Ludo thought, beginning to admire him until he started to ask questions.

"And you, *señor*, you are a mariner by your appearance, or are you a passenger?"

Ludo vacillated a moment too long. "Passenger, but I can also crew when necessary."

"Travelling to the East to find your fortune—or to your family, perhaps?"

"A would-be merchant, padre, looking for a future, that's all."

The young priest took a spoonful of the milksop that had arrived for dessert. "Wholesome but tasteless," he said laying down his wooden spoon. "We could do with some of that nutmeg here. You're sailing on to Calcutta, Batavia or Malacca, perhaps."

"The spice islands: I'm not sure of their names."

"I'm told Goa is the place to buy the best spices without the risks of the China Seas."

"Is it? That is interesting," Ludo was genuinely pleased to hear it. But then his doubts started again.

"You have no family in Goa?" the priest inquired.

"Me, no—I'm from Genoa..." and then he cursed himself for a fool—a callow, double-blinded cretin. Genoa! Trying to climb out of his own trap he did his best to discover if any priests were sailing for the East, or anyone related to Vatican matters. The young Galician assured him there were not, to the best of his knowledge, and the Portuguese weren't likely to put into the bay with Dutch ships at anchor while Spain was still fighting in the Netherlands.

"I count my blessings every night I return to my bed, then again in the morning, that the Dutchmen have left me alive for another day," he said.

Ludo laughed. He liked him, but that didn't mean he was to be trusted. As he swung a leg over the bench to leave, the priest got to his feet. "Forgive me, *señor*," he said, extending his soft hand. "I am Padre Bernabé, and you are...?"

"Beppo Pannini. *Encantado, adios.*"

Ludo waited outside for the priest to leave and return to wherever he lived or prayed. He proved easy to follow, going directly to a small, dung-walled chapel—regrettably too small for Ludo to enter unnoticed. Whether the young man was writing a note in there or hearing the confession of a waiting sinner he did not know, and it was pointless—and also suspicious-looking—for him to hang around the only silent place in the noisy, beer-swilling encampment.

By the end of the day, Ludo was at odds with himself and the world in general. Weary of watching grown men full of drink behave like idiot children and heartily sick of fending off poxy whores, he made for the beach, where humans were copulating like turtles in the sand and grassy tussocks. Gratefully, he returned to the *Tulip* and the sanctuary of his cabin.

Once aboard he stopped to speak to no one and went straight to the hold to retrieve his portfolio of precious documents, praying it was still in place. It was and he cursed himself again for a fool. He wouldn't go ashore again. If Padre Bernabé told anyone he was from Genoa he was as good as drowned, and his documents with him. Taking advantage of the fresh water still being brought aboard, Ludo ordered his new cabin boy—whom he had taken care not to befriend—to get a bucketful and set to scrubbing himself clean of stink and sweat.

On the eighth day after their arrival, the *Tulip* set sail for the next stage of her perilous voyage. She was accompanied by schools of dolphins leaping alongside and lifting everyone's spirits. Once out of the bay but still in peaceful waters, Ludo set up a barefoot balancing game along the bow rail and created games where old hands challenged young tars to swing through the rigging and climb masts, or race from poop to prow carrying a sack of turnips. It was fun and it was useful; teaching even clumsy cabin boys how to shift through the shrouds up and out of harm's way if they were ever boarded. Ludo took advantage of the convivial atmosphere to get older hands to show the younger crew how to handle the ship's guns properly. Gunners took turns showing anyone who was interested how to manoeuvre, strip and clean the heavy guns; how to weigh out and fill a silk powder bag, and how to lay them out safely ready for use. Volunteers from all over the vessel formed teams to move the guns back into place, to load them with shot and pretend to light the fuses. Up on deck, officers showed galley boys how to fit flints, load and ram home a lead ball in the new English muskets... Lascars and old tars watched in amusement while they silently honed their cutlasses and long gutting knives with whetstones.

By the time the fun was over, Ludo had his ship well prepared for the Zanzibar coast. Ready also for any Dutch man-o-war that might ignore their English colours, or Portuguese merchant vessels that might fire on them for any damned reason, or, more likely, for when the dhow-boys set on them again.

As it was, they were left in peace with not another vessel in sight as far as the Mozambique Channel, although the seas and winds tested all their other skills. One evening an exhausted Guthrie joined Ludo in his cabin.

"I've come to ask about Zanzibar," he said. "You haven't said whether you want to put in or not."

"Can we stay out and catch the winds faster up the coast?"

"It'll take us a month yet to get into the Arabian Sea. We could do with fresh water as well for that stage."

Ludo pushed his long hair off his face then leaned back in his chair in his accustomed manner. "Bear with me, Guthrie—I'm thinking aloud now, so wait and give me your opinion when I'm done. Before I start, will you take a glass of sack, brandy?"

"Brandy, thank you."

As Ludo poured the golden liquid from a thick bottle he watched Guthrie watching him. "I've worried you," he said.

"You have, sir, I'll be honest. You're not... as you were when we sailed from Goa, before."

"No, that I am not. But you are, and I'm doubly grateful for that."

Guthrie coloured at the compliment and sipped his brandy. A modest, serious man not given to repartee, he stayed silent and waited for Ludo to say his piece.

"Well, here are my thoughts: on the one hand I would like to put in to Zanzibar to buy and sell. We have a hold full of hardware that'll fetch decent prices and make cooks and housewives a good deal happier. In turn, I need to purchase some good quality pearls, which I can get there, and other trinkets. So putting in for water and fresh food is a possibility. But, I sincerely fear we will be held back in some way if we do, that something will prevent us sailing on as early as we can..." He caught Guthrie's surprised expression. "I have good reason to believe someone with a lot of long range contacts will either try to steal documents I have in this cabin—or detain me so he or they can get to Goa first. Or perhaps try to prevent me arriving at all."

Guthrie's eyes widened. "I had no idea. So you'd prefer to sail on, perhaps put in to Pemba Island or a lesser known port."

"We could, but then we risk being boarded or raided."

"And if we push on for a month and put in to Salalah again?"

"No. I will return there one day—I have an idea for a new business with those fine horses—but not yet. Besides, we have to hurry to catch the north-easterlies."

Guthrie put down his tumbler and said, "The northeast monsoon blows from October to March, and the southwest monsoon blows from April to September. I'm quoting my first sailing master, and I've been worried since the day we left Plymouth that we'd arrive in the Arabian Sea on a turning wind. Sir, in my opinion we need to push on as fast we can or we'll have to tack against an opposing wind for weeks on end. A short stop in Pemba for water, or Mombasa, and we sail on."

"Excellent, agreed!" Ludo raised the brandy bottle. "A toast to a speedy but safe arrival." Then he laughed, "I wonder what the old natives of Goa will make of our pots and pans and the Birmingham hammerheads and nails?"

After Guthrie left, Ludo stepped out on deck and wandered around the poop rail. There was thunder in the air. Lightning flashed above, illuminating tilting triangles of white dhow sail far below on the black sea: predators out at night looking to catch their prey unawares. A thunderstorm was perfect cover. Ludo whistled up the night watch. "Ready to repel boarders," he said, and returned to his cabin for his pistol and ammunition, excitement rippling through him again.

"I was trained by Murat Reis," he called over the rail in Arabic. "You'll not board us—but you can try!" Checking the ruby in the secret pocket of his shirt under the stab wound, now healed, he then cried out in the Genoese dialect they used in Portovenere, "*Dio mio,* but I love the sea! It's in my blood—from Doria admirals and *Genovese* who defeated the Turk. Try your best, but you'll not take the *Tulip!*"

Chapter 40

Goa, India, late spring, 1641

The *Tulip* sailed into the wide bay of the Portuguese colony of Goa on a late spring wind and the entire vessel gave a sigh of relief. Ludo would swear later he heard the exhausted sea-pummelled timbers groan and relax. Taking his spyglass with him, he crossed the foredeck to scan the bay and mark out what other ships lay at anchor. Two Portuguesers were in, and an English vessel was busy getting ready to sail on for the Bay of Bengal. He trained the telescope back over each Portugueser: they were both quiet, the crews ashore. Swinging round to port, he scanned the shoreline, the fort and the housetops beyond. The settlement had grown in the time he'd been gone. There were signs of activity in the fort and it occurred to him that *Tulip* was with cannon-range. What a drastic irony that they could get this far then be blown to firewood.

It was evening before Ludo was ready to go ashore. As he prepared to climb down to the pinnace, he said, "Leave my cabin as it is. Leave the cargo untouched but put a double guard on it night and day. I'll be back on the morrow to deal with it, and with the master of the quarterdeck and his crew."

While Guthrie and his mariners set the ship to rights, Ludo was rowed ashore. Clutched to his chest was a Portuguese *bizalho* that had once been full of diamonds and rubies and was now crammed with a folded parchment signed by the King of England. A tube of rolled documents signed by the Chief Minister of the Spanish Empire and a licence given by King Felipe to also exploit the wealth of India for the Spanish crown was clutched under his left arm. Leonora's document was safely tucked into his waistcoat. That the Spanish Empire possibly no longer included Portugal, that a rebellion there might have taken place successfully, mattered not. He had a licence to trade and a document that would save Leonora from the Inquisition—if he was in time.

It was a strange homecoming, for he felt a like a stranger knocking at the door to his wife's painted house. The houseboy opened the door a mere crack, as it was evening and dark, and he had to explain who he was, for the boy had no recollection of his face.

He was led to the main living room. The only light came from the open shuttered windows, yet there was a sense of the room being alive, of human warmth and gentle breathing. A voice said quietly, "We are here."

His eyes now adjusted to the gloom, Ludo made out a shape on a high-backed chair. He moved towards her.

"Ssh," Leonora whispered, "he's just fallen asleep."

Ludo put down the box and documents and went to her.

In Leonora's arms lay a round, sleeping child, thumb in mouth but breathing gently, rhythmically.

"You can take him in your arms," she said, looking up and catching Ludo's expression in the moonlight. "I doubt he'll wake now even if we make a noise."

Ludo took the living bundle into his arms and felt a rush of pain that was not physical, yet was—a sensation he had never,

ever experienced: of warmth and joy and something else he could not name but had to be a special form of love.

"Come," said Leonora, getting up from her chair.

Ludo followed her up the stairs to a bedchamber. The muslin curtains at the window shivered with the draught from the opening door.

"Over here," Leonora whispered and Ludo followed her to place the boy in a crib. As he put him down the boy took his thumb from his mouth and gave a huge yawn and then a sigh; and Ludo thought his heart would burst within him.

Leonora pulled the cotton covers over the baby's sturdy little legs and stroked his head, then she said, "Come and see your daughter."

Ludo paused, took a gasp of breath as a stab of doubt punched his ribs.

"Over here," whispered Leonora from across the room.

A woman, the ayah, was sitting by another crib. In the crib lay a bundle of covers and a dark-haired, deeply sleeping child. Ludo touched her body with a hand and knew this child was his as well. "Twins," he said.

"Your twins, husband. I was told you were dead." Leonora was crying.

Ludo turned from the child and took Leonora in his arms. "Whoever told you that was wrong. I am here, and I belong with you." And he held her lovely head to his chest and let tears run down his sea-chapped face.

This novel is a work of fiction based on recorded events in the period leading up to the English Civil War and Portugal's separation from Spain. In Britain, Queen Henrietta Maria (known as Queen Mary in England) was actively trying to influence her husband to return the United Kingdom to the Roman Catholic faith. In Spain, King Felipe relied far too greatly on his *valido*, Olivares, and this was a cause of many problems. Henrietta Maria's older sister, Elisabeth of France, suffered at the hands of the Countess-Duchess de Olivares in numerous ways.

Sir Arthur Hopton and Kit Windebank were in Madrid with the Spanish court. Kit was known at the time as 'a perfect Spaniard', and the story about his 'low-born' wife is based on what was happening when this novel is set.

Ludo's involvement in the spice trade in Goa is fictitious, but all details pertaining to imports, exports and tariffs, and Lisbon's Casa da Índia are based on research. Many details can be found in a fascinating work of non-fiction, *Portuguese Trade in the Asia under the Habsburgs, 1580-1640* by James C. Boyajian (Johns Hopkins University Press, 2008).

I would like to thank all the people who have taken the time to write up their research for use as free information on the

Internet; your websites are too numerous to mention but I am indebted.

In all, this novel took me two years to write, I hope you have enjoyed it. You can read about what happens to Ludo, Alina and Marcos during the English Civil War in the final part of *The Chosen Man* trilogy, *Force of Circumstance,* when Ludo becomes Queen Henrietta Maria's chosen man once more—this time to raise money for Charles Stuart by selling the Crown Jewels.

J. G. Harlond, Málaga, Spain

A Turning Wind © J.G Harlond

About The Author
J.G. Harlond

Originally from the south west of England, J.G Harlond (Jane) studied and worked in various different countries before finally settling down with her husband, a retired Spanish naval captain, in rural Andalucía, Spain. Despite being 'rubbish' at history at school because she wanted to turn everything into a story, she survived the History element of her B.A. and went on to get an M.A. in Social and Political Thought. Her historical fiction, set in the 17th century and the first half of the 20th century, features many of the places Jane has visited—along with flawed rogues, wicked crimes, and the more serious issues of being an outsider. Apart from fiction, Jane also writes school text books under her married name. Her favourite reading is along the Dorothy Dunnett lines: well-researched stories with compelling plots and complex characters.

If You Enjoyed This Book

Please write a review.
This is important to the author and helps to get the word out to others
Visit

PENMORE PRESS
www.penmorepress.com

All Penmore Press books are available directly through our website, amazon.com, Barnes and Noble and Nook,, Apple iTunes, Kobo books and via leading bookshops across the United States, Canada, the UK, Australia and Europe.

The Chosen Man

by

J. G Harlond

From the bulb of a rare flower bloom ambition and scandal

Rome, 1635: As Flanders braces for another long year of war, a Spanish count presents the Vatican with a means of disrupting the Dutch rebels' booming economy. His plan is brilliant. They just need the right man to implement it.

They choose Ludovico da Portovenere, a charismatic spice and silk merchant. Intrigued by the Vatican's proposal—and hungry for profit—Ludo sets off for Amsterdam to sow greed and venture capitalism for a disastrous harvest, hampered by a timid English priest sent from Rome, accompanied by a quick-witted young admirer he will use as a spy, and bothered by the memory of the beautiful young lady he refused to take with him.

Set in a world of international politics and domestic intrigue, *The Chosen Man* spins an engrossing tale about the Dutch financial scandal known as tulip mania—and how decisions made in high places can have terrible repercussions on innocent lives.

PENMORE PRESS
www.penmorepress.com

Local Resistance

by

Jane Harlond

WWII in England, Cornwall smugglers, Intelligence agents, detective story, locals and war in the UK, German navy operations on the coast of the UK. Murder thriller. Espionage.

On a stormy night in March 1941, Maisie Rose Hawkins leaves her drunk husband, Stan, out in the rain—and he disappears. Detective Sergeant Bob Robbins and young PC Laurie Oliver are called out to investigate and discover that Stan's small fishing boat is gone, the rope sawn through. As Bob searches for answers, it becomes apparent that in this small Cornish village where everyone knows everything about everybody, nobody quite knows the truth.

Beneath the surface of village life, a fierce battle is being waged against wartime deprivations. Shopkeepers quietly evade rationing restrictions. Food inspector Archibald Bantry, charged with enforcing those restrictions, dies in a suspicious car crash. Various leads connect a sea cave full of smuggled black-market goods to the missing Stan Hawkins. And what seems like the work of local malcontents becomes more complex and dangerous when Bob stumbles on the truth in a disused copper mine, where a much deadlier affair is underway.

"Uncanny happenings and warm characterization. . . . The realities of wartime life in this novel combine with a lovely sense of place to create a distinctly Cornish mixture of secluded charm and the unsettlingly mysterious." —Robert Wilton, prize-winning author of the Comptrollerate-General historical thrillers.

PENMORE PRESS
www.penmorepress.com

Historical fiction and nonfiction
Paperback available for order on line
and as Ebook with all major distributers

The Empress Emerald

BY

Jane Harlond

Stolen: A child, a priceless jewel, and an identity

Abandoned as a child in a Bombay orphanage, Leo Kazan's life takes an unanticipated turn when he becomes the protégé of Sir Lionel Pinecoffin, the city's District Political Officer in Bombay. Under Pinecoffin's tutelage, the boy, adept at learning languages and theft, is trained as a spy and becomes immersed in international espionage, revolutionary politics, and diamond smuggling. In 1918, during a visit to London, he has a brief but memorable affair with a young English woman Davina Dymond in London before leaving for Russia.

Separated, their lives take different turns. As he matures Leo begins to question his family history, seeking to uncover the truth about his parents. A pregnant Davina is married off and exiled to Spain, where she gives birth to Leo's daughter. They are fated to meet again in Gibraltar in 1936, their love rekindled. But a new war plunges Europe into crisis, the Spanish Civil War tearing them apart, leaving, Leo and Davina in a fight to reclaim their lives and their love amid the violent storms of war.

PENMORE PRESS
www.penmorepress.com

Fortune's Whelp
by
Benerson Little

Privateer, Swordsman, and Rake:

Set in the 17th century during the heyday of privateering and the decline of buccaneering, *Fortune's Whelp* is a brash, swords-out sea-going adventure. Scotsman Edward MacNaughton, a former privateer captain, twice accused and acquitted of piracy and currently seeking a commission, is ensnared in the intrigue associated with the attempt to assassinate King William III in 1696. Who plots to kill the king, who will rise in rebellion—and which of three women in his life, the dangerous smuggler, the wealthy widow with a dark past, or the former lover seeking independence—might kill to further political ends? Variously wooing and defying Fortune, Captain MacNaughton approaches life in the same way he wields a sword or commands a fighting ship: with the heart of a lion and the craft of a fox.

PENMORE PRESS
www.penmorepress.com